THE UNBELIEVABLE Scars

E. ALAN ROBERTS

WESTBOW
PRESS®
A DIVISION OF THOMAS NELSON
& ZONDERVAN

WestBow Press books may be ordered through booksellers or by contacting:

WestBow Press
A Division of Thomas Nelson & Zondervan
1663 Liberty Drive
Bloomington, IN 47403
www.westbowpress.com
1 (866) 928-1240

ISBN: 978-1-9736-3843-8 (sc)
ISBN: 978-1-9736-3844-5 (hc)
ISBN: 978-1-9736-3842-1 (e)

Library of Congress Control Number: 2018910474

Print information available on the last page.

WestBow Press rev. date: 09/14/2018

AUTHOR

E. Alan Roberts was born into a devout Christian family. He was ordained into the British Methodist Ministry in 1956

Alan's ministry with his late wife, Doris, was in Nigeria and Kenya, also in England and Canada. Their children and grand-children reside in Canada, England and China.

After over half a century of active ministry he is now retired and living in Ontario.

He is enjoying creative writing, and is continuing preaching some Sundays in the Retirement Home where he lives with his new wife, Margaret.

``The Courage of Innocence``, his first novel was published by Xlibris (2013),

For any information or comments.
alanroberts@fastmail.com

THE STORY

The story is set in England. Twins were born to a couple who had been waiting for many years. There were complications at birth; there were twins who were joined.

Surgery was performed to separate the boy and girl. The girl was given up for adoption.

The story records the early development of the two babies and eventual entry to University. They do not know of each other's existence. They met at the IVF meeting and also at a weekend conference for IVF leaders.

Both Adrian and Mary followed business studies at University; as well as their academic studies we see them in other activities at the University.

After graduation they work in different locations in Business Offices.

Adrian senses that God is leading him to set up his own business. He decides that it will be based on Scriptural ethics.

Three people from the university course join him, including Mary. Cupid has already fired some arrows at Mary and Adrian.

There is an engagement. The minister when discussing the wedding suggests that a medical examination is appropriate. The doctor advises some blood work.

The DNA results cause some major questions for the doctor. He calls them in only to find that they did not know about the major scars on each other. He insisted that they bare only that part and see each other for the first time.

The doctor informed them that their parents, the Minister and a retired doctor are in the other room to help him find the answer to his big question. He informs them that they are to show the scars again for the people in the next room. They were reluctant but he insists.

One of the doctor's difficulties was that the two people have different birthdates, yet the DNA suggests something different. Adrian's parents confirm his date of birth. Mary's father said it was the one used to register. There was a big but. But the date was the one when we received Mary from the Hospital, the day she became ours.

The retired doctor was asked to report on the birth he attended. He described the pregnancy and the scan revealed twins, and then the unexpected sight on the c-section. The twins were joined, but not with any major organs.

The doctor asked Adrian and Mary to prepare to show each other their scars. There was a gasp of shock from all those in the room. He indicated that his intention was not to be sensational, he wanted some proof.

The retired doctor was asked to comment upon the scars. He indicated that they were the ones he made when separating the twin babies.

Mary asked him to come and put them back together again for a few moments; which he did.

The minister announced there would be no wedding for siblings.

Future plans were re-arranged

ABBREVIATIONS USED

C.U.	=	Christian Union
I.V.F	=	Inter Varsity Fellowship
		(also known as - Inter Varsity Christian Fellowship)
U. K.	=	United Kingdom
C.E.O	=	Chief Executive Officer
B.D.	=	Bachelor of Divinity
D.D.	=	Doctor of Divinity
K.B.C.S.	=	Karism Business Consulting Services.
		Later renamed - Karisma Business Consulting Services

CHAPTER 1

Howard and Dawn Syston had been married for more than seven years. The biggest disappointment for them was that she had not become pregnant. They had come to terms with barrenness and in their prayers was asking God to guide them regarding the possibility of going to a sperm bank for treatment or adopting a child. They had received papers regarding adoption from two agencies. Their attention was towards one located near Bath. It was a mutual decision to wait a couple of months. When asked why they had chosen two months, they answered that they had no idea why.

A letter arrived. It gave them a date to go to the orphanage to talk about adoptions as well as for an interview. That afternoon, Dawn had a doctor's appointment. The doctor wanted to do some blood tests. Just before she was due to leave a nurse entered with some results. She had a big smile on her face but did not say a word.

The doctor did not have to read too much before he placed the report down on his desk. He took her hands, looked deep into her eyes, and asked if she was prepared for some important news.

"If it's bad, I don't want to know!" she said, wondering why he was holding her hands.

"No" he said, "It is not bad news. This is the happy occasion I like to have in my office. What would make you really happy?"

"Something impossible probably!"

"Take in a deep breath, and close your eyes", he said calmly. And then with a wonderful smile, he said "Dawn, you are pregnant".

"I'm what! She exclaimed with eyes wide open and her hands pulling away from the doctor's.

The nurse was jubilant. The doctor was beside himself with pleasure.

Dawn was so elated she thought she might have to be scraped off the ceiling.

"I'm what?"

"You are having a baby."

"Then we don't have to consider further the concept of adoption!"

"Certainly not! In another seven months you should be holding your own baby".

Dawn allowed herself to fall towards the doctor as the tears swelled up and flowed down her cheeks. The nurse offered a tissue, but one was not enough.

It was a few moments before she gained control of herself and said, "When do I tell Howard? What do I tell him?"

"There is a phone in reception you can use, but no doubt you would like it to be more private".

"No. I can't share this tremendous thrill on the phone; it has to be personal"."It'll take some time to digest after we come back down to earth!"

Within a few minutes she was ready to leave the doctor's office and head for home.

It felt like Howard was being deliberately late. Yet when he arrived his first comment was that he was three minutes earlier than usual. Dawn beckoned to him to come and sit for a few minutes. He was about to decline and then saw that she was serious about something. As he was sitting down he mentioned that he could wait awhile before going upstairs for a shower.

He sat down on the settee. She moved closer to him. He was about to register surprise that his wife was cuddling up close before they had eaten.

She fell all over him with excitement. "I was at the doctor this afternoon for a usual checkup. He did some blood tests. Then he said he had something very important go tell me".

"And what can be that important? Howard asked.

"Are you ready for a surprise?"

"I guess I ought to be because you seem so anxious to startle me with something outrageous!"

"Darling" said Dawn. She took ages to continue. "I should call you Daddy".

"You'll call me what! Stop joking, honey".

"Sweetheart, I am about to become a mummy."

"Are you telling me that the doctor has told you that you are pregnant?"

"Precisely…"

"Good gracious! What am I to say? I can't believe it" he stated as his hands caressed her tummy.

They were lost in tears of happiness as they held each other and stroked each other. Howard could not stop tapping his wife's tummy as the smiles got bigger and broader.

Time didn't mean anything to them just then. Their evening meal could be late. It didn't matter. Eating times seemed so mundane.

From time to time one or the other would ask the rhetorical question "Is this for real?"

Eventually they took a break to eat something even though they were not very hungry. The shock of being pregnant had taken away some of their appetite.

The first few days were spent getting used to the idea of a baby. This happy couple began thinking ahead. "What names shall we use, if it is a girl or if it is a boy?" Howard joked', and then he said, "And what if it is one of each?"

"We can't paint the spare room until we know whether we can use blue or pink paint!" said Dawn.

As the weeks passed, it was not long before they were not just counting the weeks but also actual days. At the beginning, seven months seemed an eternity. As the weeks passed they realized the time would be chosen by God for when their baby was born.

What a birthday it would be!

CHAPTER 2

It had been about five months since the doctor had announced that Dawn was pregnant. She had attended clinics regularly. The doctor was happy with the progress.

This was the day for her regular doctor's appointment. After all the usual questions and the taking of her temperature and blood pressure the doctor asked Dawn to go for an x-ray. "It's nothing serious. Just a regular procedure at this stage of your pregnancy".

As it was a morning appointment she was to go directly to the x-ray lab.

On the requisition the doctor had requested that Dawn bring back the results for an afternoon appointment.

She didn't mind. It just meant she would miss her after -lunch rest.

The report was laid on the doctor's desk by the nurse stayed to chat with Dawn until the doctor arrived. He took his time reading the report; in fact it seemed as if he read it at least twice.

"Congratulations, Dawn. You are increasing your family."

"What do you mean, Doctor?"

"You have two babies growing in your tummy".

"I have what? Where did they come from?"

"I was beginning to wonder because of your weight gain. It appears that they are both healthy. I will be monitoring you carefully over the next few weeks. This is not something to worry about I do want you to have your usual exercise but make time for more rest."

"I'll make sure of that. I have been planning to care for one baby, but now I have some major rethinking. I'll be okay. I'm not sure what Howard will say, but he is looking forward to having a son. I told him there is no guarantee, due to the fact that it's fifty-fifty for daughters!"

"We must make sure we stroke them, or rather you stroke her, or I stroke him, and they will be healthy".

"You ought not to be walking home. I'll call for a taxi".

"Thank you, Doctor".

Howard took the news extremely well. In fact he was quite excited. He giggled all the way through the evening meal.

"A girl for you and a boy for me".

"You have two arms so the good God equipped you to hold two babies. Two boys for me. Two girls for you. We have no idea what they will be".

Howard leaned over towards Dawn he wrapped his arms around her and whispered, "God knew you were going to have two babies that is why He gave you two breasts!"

"What a ridiculous thing to say. May God forgive you! But it does sound logical". Dawn then burst out laughing. The laughing was almost uncontrollable for the next fifteen to twenty minutes.

They had settled down to be serious. Pink or blue was talked about again for room color. They shared so many names that they gave up and referred to them as A and B.

The following days became hectic. Singles had to be changed to doubles. As for colors, they decided to go for yellows and greens that were looked upon as non-gender specific.

The biggest item for them was contacting family members and in-laws to announce the double pregnancy. There were various responses. Some said, "Poor old you!" Others seemed quite excited. The sympathy and happiness vacillated.

Dawn knew she was getting heavier and thought that it might be too much. She decided to talk about it on her next visit to the doctor.

The doctor did not say too much while Dawn was in the office.

It was about a month later when the doctor called his nurse into his office and they entered into a deep discussion about the double pregnancy. The doctor mentioned to the nurse that he would like a scan -not an ordinary x-ray. The nurse queried his reasoning. The doctor did not commit himself. His only statement was that he wanted to know.

The next day he talked with the radiologist and expressed some of his concerns. It was agreed that a scan should be done as soon as possible.

The doctor phoned Dawn and mentioned that she should come to the imaging section of the hospital the next day at ten thirty.

"Why?" he heard her ask.

"I just want to do a precautionary check. I want to see what is going on inside there. No reason for worry. You are in very good health".

The next day, Dawn arrived at the hospital a little anxious because she as wondering why this was necessary. She was made comfortable. The technician did the scan, and then Dawn was instructed to stay in the waiting room. She had the feeling that the waiting was going on too long.

It was over a half hour later the radiologist came to talk with her and asked her to stay because he called her doctor to view the scan. Dawn expressed her concern. There is very little I can tell you at the moment, But I'll use the cliché 'don't worry'. I know it's always easier to say than to actually do it.

A lunch tray was brought for Dawn. She had actually phoned Howard to see if he could come and have lunch with her. They had both just finished their sandwich when both doctors arrived.

They all went into the office. There was a large sheet on the radiologist's desk. And report papers alongside it.

Their doctor asked that they relax as much as possible. "There is nothing major wrong but there is something unusual." That got eyes and ears lifted up, because unusual is not always something not to worry about. The full interpretation of 'unusual' was not given. The doctors were perhaps a little more concerned than with normal twins. This probably indicated they were anticipating further .investigation.

The radiologist starts to explain the results of the scan. "You have two healthy babies, a boy and a girl".

It was Howard who said, "But".

"This is highly unusual. You will not be able to deliver them by the natural birth method. We will need to do a c-section for your safety and the safety of the babies.

Dawn just had to interrupt and ask, "Why?"

"They are joined. You have Siamese twins!"

Dawn could not control herself, she shrieked and fell into the waiting arms of Howard. Her expletives were getting louder and louder; "No! No! NO! NO!"

The doctor called the nurse to bring a drink for her.

They were a long time recovering from the shock. The doctor and his nurse were being very helpful and comforting. The radiologist was explaining the situation more carefully to Howard.

"How dangerous is this operation?" Howard asked the doctor.

"It is no more dangerous than other c-sections, except the babies will be in an incubator for some time. We will be informing the specialists and so in consultation with them a decision will be made as to when the necessary surgery will be performed".

Because of the shock it was decided that Dawn should be admitted for bed rest and careful daily monitoring.

Howard wanted to know when this would take place. "We are not sure at this time. After consulting with the specialists and for them to be familiar with the scan, then a date will be fixed".

When the specialists meet there will be deep discussion about the twins. They cannot be Siamese because there is a boy and a girl. Yet they are joined!

It was a meeting of the top pediatrician surgeons. The Boss was there, he only attends when things are important or when there is something unusual. He was attending this meeting because of the unusual pregnancy. They were not Siamese Twins, because they were different genders.

They are not twins from the same egg. They are two separate eggs. Then how are they joined?

"This is what we need to ascertain." The Boss was about to be totally engrossed with this case. "What do we know about the history of the mother?"

"She appeared to be a normal first-pregnancy woman".

"Was there any trauma during the early stages of the pregnancy?"

"She did mention having a fall. She was on a cross-country run and fell at a style in one field. It was decided to call for a doctor and ambulance".

"Why?"

"They thought she had damaged her hip. It was bruised so no treatment was suggested".

"If there was nothing more traumatic, then we must look carefully at that fall".

"What do we know?"

"There were two babies. Not identical in the same sack."

"Is it possible that the fall did something like throwing the two together? That could not have caused them to join?"

"Something was mentioned that she lost some water at the time of the fall".

The Boss is geared up for some outlandish explanation. "If the waters broke, and if she had been protecting herself when sitting and lying down by being in the same position, which may have placed the two close to each other. This is a wild suggestion, I know, but come up with a better one, quickly?"

There was not one hint at another cause. But each one around the table could not grasp the reality of what the 'Boss' had suggested.

The meeting ended when the Boss announced that perhaps no one will ever know how the two got themselves joined together at the buttocks.

"Good day, gentlemen!"

CHAPTER 3

Stretford Royal Infirmary was gaining a great reputation for caring. The pediatric department had attracted the top pediatricians. It was a busy hospital.

Dawn had lost count as to how many different so-called specialists had talked with her and examined her. Her comment to each one was "When?"

Howard was with her as much and as often as possible. But it was very boring for Dawn. Her constant prayer was related to how much longer. Her Pastor had brought some books for her to read – they certainly helped to pass the time away.

Her doctor was in for a quick visit when he was doing his rounds. She asked for him to sit for a couple of minutes. She was desperate for some information. "When do they open me up?"

"In just a few days now. An adjacent theatre is being prepared to care for the babies. One nurse with specialized training for premature births has been allocated to you. She will be in later today to see you. Don't have any concerns regarding her; she is the best for many miles around".

"What will really happen?"

"A usual c-section incision will be made though it will be larger. The babies will be taken out and placed in an incubator in the next room".

"Will I be able to see them?"

"Not straight away. They will be examined and washed".

"When will they be separated?"

Not for a few days. The surgeons are already meeting to discuss the delicate procedure".

"Will it be dangerous for either of them?"

"No, they are not sharing any organ or vital tissue. It should be a straight forward procedure".

"But can I see them before they are separated?"

"That will be a decision taken together with Howard and your parents. The doctors may consider it okay for you. But they will be careful not to let it cause you shock or stress".

With a broad smile on her face she leaned closer to the doctor and said, "Well, can I see a picture of them in my uterus?"

"I'll see if that can be arranged!" With that comment he indicated that he had other patients see.

Howard had brought a sandwich with him so they could have lunch together. A nurse followed him into the room. It was the specialist nurse the doctor had mentioned. After she introduced herself and mentioned briefly what her role would be, she mentioned to Dawn about her desire to see a picture.

Howard had a big question on his face.

Dawn put him at ease. "I wanted to see my babies and the end of that discussion was a request to see them in my uterus". "Is that a possibility, nurse?"

"Yes". I'll arrange a wheelchair for you and then your husband can follow us".

It was wonderful. It felt like the beginning of a marvelous adventure. The two soon-to be parents were astonished to start with; that developed into awe and wonder. The amazement of modern technology astounded them as they gazed at the contents of that womb.

They had no idea how long the nurse allowed them to be absorbed by the pictures. There was a sudden down to earth statement from the nurse. "Come, it's time to get you back to your room".

Howard stayed longer than usual perhaps being engrossed by what they had seen. Then there was a more sober note to their conversation when they contemplated the birth of their twins.

They still had a number of days, which seemed like weeks, before the doctors would schedule the required surgery. It became a time of restless waiting. Dawn's comments were always "Why not today?" She nodded before the nurse could give the usual answer.

The longer they waited the more concerned Howard became. Dawn didn't say much. Both were becoming very anxious. It was the unknown factor they found hard to deal with. They had seen the twins in the uterus but it would be more traumatic to actually give birth to them. It was then they could see them in real life, and possibility be allowed to touch them. Neither husband nor wife dared to think about the surgery to separate the twins.

When Howard was leaving his comment was "See you tomorrow sweetheart – or you might be three of you by then!"

"Good night darling. You might even be a daddy by this time tomorrow!"

Surgery was scheduled for early morning. The surgeon had mentioned to Dawn that he wanted to have quality time for the delivery, and then added they would need even better quality time afterwards for the specialists to examine in order to know where and how to separate the twins. They had consulted together and had made tentative plans but they knew it would be different when the babies had been born.

Howard was told he could be at the hospital to spend time being close to Dawn. He would not be allowed in the theatre during the actual c-section. Actually he did not want to see what was being cut to get the babies out. His imagination was very wild, so he dreaded the possibility of seeing it in reality.

He arrived at the hospital and went straight to the ward. Dawn was dressed in white. He wanted to crack a joke that it was not their wedding day. Dawn smiled and whispered, "Where is your tuxedo?" "Oh, by the way, the Hospital Chaplain came in earlier. Our Pastor knew him and had phoned for him to come pray with me before the surgery. He and our Pastor were together on a one year course at a Bible School especially for those going on into University Education. He said it was a course geared to preparation against false religious cults and religions. According to him it was a wonderful help to maintain a solid faith. He said he will call in again to see me and hoped that it would be a time when you were visiting. I found it a precious few minutes while he was praying. I am surrounded by the loving arms of a God who truly cares for me. Sweetheart, my fears are gone".

"That's wonderful", Howard leaned over and gave his wife a kiss. "Perhaps while I am waiting he may come by. I really would like to meet him".

"Next time you see our Pastor you can mention how helpful he was to me".

They spent about fifteen minutes just holding hands and anticipating. The nurse came in and asked if they were both feeling alright. Dawn nodded. Howard forced a smile and said, "about as well as I thought I should be!" "Not much longer", she said, "the orderly will be here with the gurney shortly". She may have had time to take in two breaths when the wheels came through the doorway.

Howard stood up thinking he ought to leave. The nurse asked him if he wanted to follow down the corridor, He nodded that he would like that. Then she mentioned that he would not be allowed to go any further. "You can go back to the waiting room until after the surgery. I'll come for you when Dawn is back in her room".

It seemed like a long walk. They turned many corners. The door Dawn went through closed behind her. He made his way to the waiting room and called at the coffee stand for a large mug of black coffee to tide him over. He did not know for how long. The nurse would not estimate but said that he might like to find something for his early lunch.

Howard settled down in one corner of the room where he thought he would be on his own to wallow in all the disturbing thoughts vying for consideration in an overly busy mind. After about two minutes he became aware of a couple taking seats in that same corner. He glanced up and acknowledged them. They nodded; it was the fellow that asked Howard if he would be waiting very long. He indicated that he did not know how long he would be waiting.

This started a conversation that helped Howard move away from some of his troubling thoughts. The man's wife joined in the conversation. They wanted to know about Howard's wife. He did not tell them about a complicated set of twins. He did mention that whereas they had been expecting one now they had been informed to prepare themselves for twins.

"How do you feel about that? The man's wife said.

"I'm not sure whether I am excited or in fear of what is ahead?" They all smiled at that.

Howard then found he was becoming interested in the couple so he thought it might be time to know each other by name. He told them his name. Then the man answered, "My name is Clarence Kettleby and this is Betty my wife".

Dawn was not in the prep room many minutes before the surgeon came and gave her his last instructions. She was then wheeled into the operating room. It was quite startling for Dawn because it was the first time she had been into hospital for surgery. The surgeon noticed her looking around.

"There is a lot of equipment in here. I must add that it will not all be used for you. Some of it is there just in case we need some specialized procedure. We are not anticipating that this morning".

Dawn was sure he smiled after that but there was no telling because of the mask covering most of his face.

The anesthetist she had met a couple of days earlier placed monitors and cables and needles and wires all around her with the comment, "These will make sure you have a good sleep. But I must warn you, snoring is not allowed!"

He injected some fluid and within seconds Dawn was fully asleep.

The surgeon made the first incision and the team was fully alert to the step by step procedure for the c-section operation.

The surgeons had performed many c-section births. This was their first for Siamese twins. Everything was routine until it came to the time to lift the twins. Then they were challenged regarding the cords. That did not prove to be extra difficult.

They were able to lift the twins slightly. Making sure there was nothing else attached they lifted them and placed them in the incubator. A nurse immediately began to clean them and the doctor made sure they could breathe easily.

The surgeon let out a 'eureka' and his team were laughing and rejoicing. No one in that room had ever seen Siamese twins. It was a first for all of them. They were elated at the sight of two babies joined together enjoying a little more freedom inside the incubator. One of the surgeons pointed out to the team that often Siamese babies are sharing an organ. That becomes a major and delicate operation. These babies are not sharing any major part of each other. He indicated that most Siamese twins are of the same sex. He shared also that he wondered how they became joined together. The specialists are going to enjoy debating this case.

The surgeon and assisting doctors were convinced that all was well with their patients, and called it a day.

Dawn was taken to the recovery room and the babies into a special incubator anti-room.

It was an interesting time. The more they talked the more interested this couple was on finding out more information about Dawn and her babies. Howard asked quite a pointed question. "Are you pregnant and is that why you are here?"

Betty responded quite quickly, "No. I am not pregnant. We have tried but there is nothing happening". Howard mentioned that he was sorry to hear that, because he knew of others who could not have children, but most of them received the happiness of adopting a baby.

Clarence mentioned that they were looking seriously at adopting. "One of the reasons for our visit to this hospital today is to make enquiries about adopting and what would be the procedures to follow.

Betty said, "We are not sure what the next stage will be for us but we believe God will direct us".

Howard responded quite positively. "We are always dependent upon God giving wisdom and direction in our lives".

There seemed to be a new boost to the growing friendship as they realized their dependence upon God and His daily provision for their needs. Going along His way was a dominant step of faith for both couples.

A nurse came along and mentioned to Howard that the operation was over and his wife was in recovery. "When …?" asked Howard. The nurse knew what was coming and interrupted him by saying the doctor would come and tell him a little later on.

"That was a relief, brother", stated Clarence.

"Yes, it certainly is", replied Howard.

"A great relief for your wife," responded Betty.

Howard's comment was that it would be quite a load off her mind and another part of her anatomy also.

The conversation seemed to take a pause. All three were deep in thought about Dawn having delivered her twins.

Betty was thinking what it would have been like for her to receive such news. She shrugged her shoulders. That gesture was noted by the two men but neither of them made any comment. She was actually crying inside because of the inability of being in such a happy state.

Clarence asked Howard if they had chosen any names yet. Howard indicated that they had been waiting and they had not chosen either a boy's name or a girl's name.

"You've got a big job ahead. The names you give them they will have to live with".

"Names are important," replied Howard, "I think that often the name gives some direction to the development of the child's character".

"I suppose you are looking ahead and wondering what they will be eventually"

"Yes, Clarence. It will be very interesting just thinking about what they will become"

"I know I would be very proud of them no matter what they become".

"I'll be happy if they choose to go in God's direction and live for Him."

"With parents like you the Lord will guide them into His way".

"Our prayers will always be for them to grow to be like Jesus".

"We would say "Amen!" to that alongside yours".

Betty was feeling left out of the conversation and being a typical female she wanted to add her "Amen" as well. "I'm looking forward to meeting Dawn and sharing with her our prayers and hopes for health and happiness for both of you and the babies".

"I don't think there will be a chance for you to meet her today. But some other time that would be great" Howard stated.

They didn't have many more minutes to chat as the doctor came in and told Howard to go with him to see his wife.

Howard bade farewell to his two new friends. They said they would see him again someday. "It might even be soon!" smiled Betty, "and your dear wife also".

15

CHAPTER 4

It was a long corridor with frequent left and right turns. The doctor was assuring Howard that the surgery went well and that his wife was good though feeling a little groggy and sore.

"Do I see the babies as well as Dawn?"

"Not today. They are being examined and procedures are being followed for their special care until they can be separated".

"Are they healthy?"

"Yes, they are as well as can be expected after living in such close proximity while they were developing. It will take time for them to adjust to living outside the womb. We will give them ample time to adjust to that before they are separated".

"When will that be?"

"No date has been fixed. The staff allocated to the care of preemies will be meeting in a couple of days from now".

"What will it be like?"

"We can only speculate. They have moved together. They are breathing together. They only know each other by the parts they can see and touch. It must be a strange sort of world for them".

"Will it be major surgery for them when being separated?"

"Fortunately they are not joined at any organ. I do not know for sure but my guess is that we may not be required to go too deep." He seemed to be thinking of what else he could share with Howard.

"But surgery is surgery. And surgery being what it is we will only know the answer to some of our questions when they are actually performing the separating".

They had arrived at the room. The doctor went in first, looked around and asked a couple of questions, then turned round and brought Howard into the room. There was a large grin on Dawns' face. Howard's eyes sparkled as he walked closer to Dawn. They kissed and Howard wanted to give her a big squeeze. "No", said Dawn, "please, only a gentle hug!"

They were happy with each other. The doctor was about to leave them and commented that he would return later and answer questions and give important instructions. "Just enjoy yourselves for the next little while". And with that he left them.

It was a private room so there were no other patients. They both commented on how well that was for their own privacy. He went to sit on the bed until Dawn expressed concern that the weight might cause pressure on where it hurts already.

He found a chair and slid it over close to the side of the bed. He was then able not just to see her but to feel her and touch her. After a while she congratulated him on being so tender and gentle. That caused a massive smile with the appropriate hug and kiss.

They had enjoyed the time together but Dawn expressed the need to relax and sleep a little. Howard sat back in his chair. Dawn relaxed and was soon dozing. They were like that when the doctor returned to tell them it was time up.

Howard kissed her and she roused to return the kiss. He said he would come back for a visit in the evening. At the doorway he turned to wave and throws a kiss. Then he was gone.

Dawn let out a large gasp of air. The doctor noticed it and went over to her. "It's alright, doctor, I am just catching my breath now that I have three people to care for".

Dawn was relaxing. Amid the pain from the incision she was happy that her babies were alive and well. "What a relief to have them taken out!" she whispered out loud.

She was soon asleep. The nurse was in and out frequently to check her readings and to make sure she was comfortable, "The sleep is good for her", she thought.

Howard arrived at visiting hours. Dawn had been expecting him but realized the visiting hours may be holding him up.

He bounced through the doorway with a large smile on his face. "How are you my queen?"

"Since when have I been a queen?"

"Well, certainly since this morning!"

"What's so different about this morning that you now classify me as royalty?" There was a broad grin on her face, "You have permission to kiss the queen", and she saluted him. He returned the salute while standing at attention. He giggled as he bent down. It was a lingering kiss that they both thoroughly enjoyed.

"How are you, my sweetheart? Still having pain, and somewhat uncomfortable?"

"That's a good description".

"I know there is nothing I can do. Men cannot do much for a wife in your state. But I can make believe that I am helping. Is there any way you can encourage me?"

"That's a load of rubbish. You are being an excellent man; your help is highly appreciated. Keep it up!"

They bantered on like that for quite a while, until the nurse came in.

"Are you two arguing already?" she said with a broad grin spreading from one side of her face to the other.

Howard's reply was, "If it is an argument, then we are both winning!"

"I'm pleased to hear that. What would you like?"

Before she could finish her sentence Dawn jumped in with a question she had asked a number of times.

"No, my dear. You can't go home for the night".

"Who said anything about going home?"

"Dawn, my dear, most mothers want to go home".

"Yes, and they want to take their babies home with them".

"The doctors are not sure how long you should remain in hospital. But you can guarantee at least four or five days".

"And nights?" asked Howard.

"The most important reason to stay in is to make sure you are fully recovered from the trauma of surgery. And also you will need to get acquainted with your babies.

"That is what I was about to ask before you butted in with a totally different subject".

There were smiles all around.

Dawn asked if she could be serious for one moment. The nurse gave a knowing nod; she was expecting the question.

"When?"

There was a male echo, "When?"

The nurse turned to Howard, "There will be a special visiting hour for you tomorrow morning?"

"I think I can make it"

His wife added, "You will make it!"

"Nine thirty tomorrow morning"

"What is so special about that hour of tomorrow?" asked Howard.

"I cannot say. I am under orders to repeat what I have been told. I am only doing my duty. Can you both be here on time?"

"I can" said Howard enthusiastically. But I am not sure whether my wife will wake up that early!"

"I won't be on duty that early but I'll make she another nurse will get her washed and hair brushed and face painted in time to welcome you".

"Now for the disappointing announcement. Visiting hours are now over!"

"That is so kind and magnanimous of you", said Howard sarcastically.

"With that sort of remark, I think you are likely to be escorted off the premises pretty quickly" commented Dawn.

"I'll give you a couple of minutes to say your goodnights".

Howard walked on to the ward the chimes from a clock in the lounge announced that it was thirty minutes after the hour. It could be no other hour than nine. He turned his head around the doorway to make sure his wife was decent only to be met with her hair very tidy and a couple of painted lips to assist her morning welcoming smile. Within a matter of seconds the lipstick was a smear!

Howard was cleaning up the evidence from his lips as the nurse walked in and made some appropriate comment about lipstick often gets into or on the wrong places.

"So what is so important about nine thirty, Nurse?" queried Dawn.

Howard looked at the nurse for the answer. "We are going to meet the doctor.

"Is he coming here or are we being summoned to his office?" asked Dawn.

"The latter".

"Is she expected to walk to wherever the office is located?"

"No, a super hospital chariot will be summoned. In fact it has already been summoned because I took it for granted that you would both be ready by the appointed time".

She had not finished that last sentence before an orderly arrived through the doorway pushing the hospital chariot. It looked like the one she had used on previous occasions.

So this is the visiting promised yesterday, thought Dawn.

It didn't take them long to negotiate a few corners and corridors before the sign on the door indicated it was the doctor they were to meet.

He was sat upright in his office chair and welcomed them quite cheerfully.

"I suppose you want me to tell you why I asked for you to come early this morning. I won't hold you in suspense that is why I did not invite you to sit. We are going off immediately".

Howard was standing near the nurse and whispered if she knew what was happening. Her shrug indicated that she had no idea or was unwilling to say.

The doctor was up and walking towards the door. He half turned to make sure the others were following him.

"Why is he so secretive?" Dawn ask Howard. "He might be taking us to the execution chamber!" was Howard comment.

The comment was heard by the doctor. He must have very good hearing because Howard didn't speak any louder than a good whisper.

"The execution room is not vacant at this hour. Only very urgent emergencies are taken in before ten thirty. So, rest assured we will be in a more interesting venue".

The doctor slowed down just after going round the next corner. The large doors opened and we were invited inside.

Dawn's eyes almost popped out of her head. Now she knew that her desires were soon to be met. She saw almost nothing except cots with either blue or pink blankets covering them.

"Which one? Which ones?" asked Dawn.

"Not in this room we are going into a specialist room"

"To see ..." Dawn was interrupted by the doctor with an affirmative smile and nod.

We walked on and went through a door into a room with all sorts of machines and wires and tubes and monitors.

The doctor stopped and took hold of the wheelchair himself and guided it over to one side. Then stopped near to an incubator. Dawn hadn't seen one so close.

The nurse saw Dawn's reaction and said that these were ones for twins.

"You know that your twins were joined so be prepared for a shock at seeing two babies lying very close together. These are your twins".

There were moments of dead silence as Dawn and Howard looked at the tiny babies in the incubator. They had no difficulty seeing where they were joined. They were wrapped in awe as they looked at two tiny bodies with all the wires and tubes.

"You have wanted to see your babies. Now here they are. This was the best time of the day to bring you here because quite soon there will be a lot of activity and we would be in the way". The doctor was assuring the parents that everything was going well. He added, "I do not know when the surgery to separate will take place. The specialists are still considering the possible procedures".

It was a fascinating time. The doctor was very helpful in answering questions.

Dawn asked if she could just touch them perhaps with one finger, "Not this time" replied the doctor," but next time we'll give you gloves and allow you to just touch them".

It was two days later Dawn and Howard received a message to be ready early the next morning. They were together in her room waiting for the nurse. She was followed by the orderly and the wheelchair. At the doctor's office there was no waiting he stepped out and took them along to the nursery. They had their coats and masks and then given gloves. They proceeded gingerly to the incubator. The doctor opens a small inspection door just wide enough for a hand. Dawn did what the doctor instructed. It was a thrill to be touching her babies. She couldn't get a complete feeling through the gloves but she was thrilled just being able to make contact with them. She gave them both a gentle pat and told them that she loved them. She made way for Howard to put his hand inside. He couldn't express his joy at feeling the little hands of his twin babies.

That was a wonderful day for the new Mum and Dad. A day they would talk about many times. A day that would be impossible to forget.

They were taken back to Dawn's room and Howard kissed her good bye and set off for work. He mentioned at the door he would be back for visiting in the evening.

Whenever the nurse came into her room Dawn was ready with a comment about the tiny hands and the finger nails of the babies. In fact she spent nearly the whole day recalling her thoughts and emotions of those few minutes earlier in the day when sitting beside the incubator and seeing and touching her twin babies.

It seemed an exceptionally long day at work for Howard. He was so delighted to rush off for visiting hours. He arrived in her room to see his wife giggling as a response to something she had been thinking. They giggled together and recalled those precious moments early in the day.

About a half hour after visiting commenced there was a tap on the door and in walked a couple of visitors. It was a surprise for Dawn because she had never met them. Howard jumped up to welcome them and to introduce his wife to them. It was Clarence and Betty Kettleby. Howard had mentioned the time in the waiting room when he met them.

Dawn was pleased to meet them. They pulled up a couple of chairs and sat nearer to the bed. Their conversation was quite general for fifteen or sixteen minutes. Then Dawn burst out with the news that had controlled most of her thinking throughout the day. "We saw our twins this morning. More than that we were able to touch them in their incubator, even though we had gloves on it was still a thrill to be touching our babies".

Betty's comment was that she tried hard to think what that would be like. "I'll never know" she sighed.

There were lots of comments from Howard and Dawn regarding the little hands and tiny fingers and neat looking nails. Howard commented, "The little girl has a snub for a nose". Dawn commented, "And so does the baby boy!"

Howard then asked the visitors if they had any further information about the prospects of an adoption. They had not received any further news. Clarence then indicated that this was their reason for visiting this weekend. They had an appointment to see someone the next morning, so were hoping for something tangible to consider.

Betty said, "We have been waiting for such a long time, I sincerely hope that tomorrow there is something serious to think about".

Dawn's reaction was she also wanted them to receive some kind of hope. "It would be wonderful for you to have a child to love, and be loved by".

They spent a little time praying together. As the visitors were leaving Howard mentioned that they would continue to pray for God to make a way for them to be blessed with a child.

Dawn said to Betty, "The Lord will have some answer to our prayers for you. We'll look forward to hearing about it as it unfolds".

They didn't have long together before it was announced that visiting hours were over. So it was their usual ritual, a kiss and a wave, and a prayer for God to take care of them both during the night.

CHAPTER 5

It was almost visiting time on Saturday evening. An agitating group had gathered and welcomed the comment that it is now time to release you to rush your ways to family and friends.

Howard arrived, his usual joyful self. He burst into the room asking how his extra special wife was doing this evening. There was a pause in his jovial comments. He became quite anxious when he noticed evidence of Dawn have been crying.

"What is it sweetheart?"

"I can't …"

"Let me draw up a chair near to you and then please tell me".

It'll hurt you. It'll continue to hurt me. It'll hurt our babies. It'll hurt our families. "Darling, it hurts!" And with that she burst into almost uncontrollable tears.

Howard was about to call the nurse but was saved the trouble because she walked in at that precise moment.

Howard asked the nurse, "What is this all about? What is hurting?"

"She has been like this on and off all morning. She has not been telling us any details. Is it related to something you two have been discussing?

"Not likely", answered Howard, "We have not had any controversial moments between each other for quite a few weeks".

The nurse speaks to Dawn, "Can you tell us, or can you tell your husband what is hurting?"

Dawn almost whispers, "No … not just yet …"

"Shall I insist that your husband come back later when you have had a time to relax and settle?"

"No! I want him to stay. We'll be alright on our own. Thanks nurse".

The nurse left with a whisper to Howard that if she was needed she'd be available during visiting hours.

They spent a few minutes in silence. They just touched and hugged each other,

"Sweetheart, I don't think there are many more tears that can come out today. What I must say is likely to cause a lot of hurt. But I am convinced that God is telling me that I must tell you".

Howards was urging her to take it steady and not be in a hurry to talk about it.

"Don't hinder me, sweetheart. You have got to hear it. I must tell you. Please hug me tight so that I can have the courage to tell you".

Howard got himself into a comfortable position but close enough to hold her tight.

"I am not very strong", continued Dawn. "I have been worrying about how I am going to cope. I intend to be a good mother".

Howard nodded approval.

"I cannot tackle the big responsibility of caring for a husband and two babies. I don't know where I would get the energy and skill for such a mammoth task".

Howards was about to interrupt.

"No, my sweetheart. Please hear me out. Here is the shock, please don't let it hurt you".

She paused to take in some deep breaths. Then she continued, "I have been thinking about how to cope with two babies. I think we should offer one for adoption! Please don't be angry, and squeezed him tighter.

"How can I be angry with my dear wife? Of course I am not angry. I would like to discuss with you the difficulties of looking after two babies. And, yes, I am willing to talk about adoption, if we believe that it is the way God would want us to go".

They were silent; they both looked deep into each other's eyes. They were trying to ascertain just how serious they were in regard to this major decision.

Howard was full of questions rolling over and over. Dawn was aware of his turmoil. Howard was concerned at a new insight into his wife and he struggled to recognize that sit would not make any difference in regard to their love for each other.

After a few more minutes Dawn asked, "Is it going to be possible for you to forgive me. No, what I want to say, will you be ready to talk about all this with me?"

"The answer to both of those questions is an irreversible 'yes'."

With that they lessened the tension on their hold of each other and relaxed into a loving embrace that began to calm them both, especially after the shock Howard had received. The thought was still being chased around as to whether this was the Dawn he had married. This was certainly something he had never anticipated. But he made sure it was pushed to the back of his mind for the rest of visiting hours. He'd have time to himself later to analyze the pros and cons.

"We will both pray about this and we will spend some prime time talking about it", Howard said.

That pleased Dawn. She gave a gentle squeeze of 'thank you' for that assurance.

"Yes. The first thing is to be absolutely convinced of this being the right action for us in our current situation". Dawn thought that that was like her husband leading one of his classes at the church.

Dawn stated, "By having just one baby then all the love that would have to be shared with two could be concentrated on one. I love them both. I will love either one of them with all the love God gives me. I do not want anything bad to happen to the other one. I want them both to grow up to love Jesus and serve Him faithfully. They are very precious. And we will see just how precious after they have separated them. That is when we will see them as two individuals. Both of them belonging to us. Both of them are flesh of our flesh".

Howard remarked, "I have no doubt about your love or mine for both and for each of the twins. In one sense it is hard to conceive of twins living apart. But in this case they are together and are having surgery to separate them. They will always be twins. It's just that they will not have the fun and frustration of living with each other. Boy, we are faced with a major decision".

"Yes, sweetheart, and whatever we may say it will be a painful decision to let one of the children be adopted by someone else to bring up and train and guide".

"Did the doctor talked to you before you came in?"

"No. Was he supposed to?"

"Oh dear. That is the main item of news, and I have taken up all this time talking about my weakness. Sweetheart, the doctor informed me just before lunch that surgery happened yesterday evening. Our twins are separated".

"That's wonderful. Do we see them this evening?"

"I don't think so because there is a lot still to be done".

"But that is wonderful news. I am happy. … happy for you . … happy for me … happy for them. I will let our parents know as soon as I get home this evening".

Howard arrived home in a daze. Off came his jacket and his tie followed and thrown into the nearest chair. He kicked his shoes off. Actually he had no idea where they landed; in fact he couldn't care less where they went. In sock covered feet he went to the kitchen and activated the coffee maker. He already knew that he would be heading for a long night.

The coffee tasted good. It was helping him. But he wasn't sure what it was helping. He had grabbed a large pad of paper and a couple of pens, one of which had to be red, it was always a must, and if he ever had two pens one had to be red. He had no idea why he was being fussy; He just had never felt like this ever in his whole life. He knew that he would definitely require space for at least two columns of notes or suggestions.

He reflected on the way Dawn had faced him up with a totally new concept of fatherhood and marital adaptabilities. He went into the hospital being the proud father of twins. He came out of the hospital with the wild prospect of being the father of just one of his twins. "No matter what happens or who has one of the twins I will still be the father even if I never see him or her again. That is the predicament I'm in". And so his thoughts began. He realized that a long list could be in front of him if the thoughts continued as they started.

"What about Dawn? Has my wife changed? I still love her, that hasn't changed. But I must try to grasp what has made her change regarding caring for one instead of two of her babies. I think she is strong enough to cope with them both. She is bound to have enough milk. Supplements are easily obtainable at the store if need be. She has a comfortable lap upon which two babies could be very much at ease while receiving an abundance of love poured over them.

"What am I to write on the list? Do I write about my disappointment? Perhaps not, because the crux of the matter is Dawn's attitude towards the babies. She appeared to be fully convinced that's why she said it would hurt me, and hurt her, and hurt the babies, and hurt the families".

"Oh! That is the reminder. I must phone my parents and her parents this evening. But when? Before I get any of my thoughts in some sort of order? Or a little later so that I can be ready to answer some opinionated and embarrassing questions. One of the questions my parents will ask is how do I feel? I don't! I'm dull! I'm numb! I must be an idiot because I cannot think straight at the moment".

"What do I feel? My feelings are a little numb right now. I cannot yet come to terms with choosing just one baby. Would I prefer the boy, someone to be like his dad? Of perhaps the girl to be honoured as a little princess? I do not know how I feel!

"Is Dawn thinking about future economics relating to the size and demands of our family? If we continue with both twins I see no barriers to comfort and adequate care. Expenses would increase because it would be an extra two of everything. That would be compensated for by the smiles and accolades of family and friends when seeing twins looking like twins".

"Has Dawn received some information about their medical condition that has not been shared with me? Kids are bound to pick up the coughs and colds and childhood diseases. If they take after mother and or father they will have quite a strong constitution. Fear of future medical conditions ought not to come into the equation. It won't in mine anyway".

"I'm not getting very far with my lists. What categories should I be looking for? I don't think I am in the right frame of mind to list things in order to make a judgment later. I'll have another coffee!"

Adrian reached over to the phone and dialed the number for his parents. There was the usual hello. Then he mentioned that the twins had been separated. There were many expressions of joy.

He phoned Dawn's parents and there was a similar happy reaction.

Alongside his next mug of coffee he leaned over and chose some soothing background music to cover up the echoes of his thoughts. He was not a very happy man.

"How could she make such a suggestion? Especially because we have had such little time to look at all its implications? Perhaps I'll be better after a good sleep. I doubt if any sleep will be good tonight. Then again, perhaps Dawn will have changed her mind about this by visiting time tomorrow.

"Oh! The complication of trying to decide what a wife will say when you have no idea how she is thinking about the issue. If I am honest with myself I want her to tell me the moment I walk into her room tomorrow that she apologizes for the suggestions she made and of course we will continue with twins as twins".

He struggled on for over an hour and then realized that he wasn't achieving any direction; little was making any sense. It was time for bed.

As expected, Howard did not receive any restful sleep. Having tossed backwards and forwards most of the night he was up earlier than usual and, to his surprise, speaking kindly to the coffee machine. Being up earlier than usual meant that he set could off for work much earlier. Because he was early for work it contributed to a slow start to an uneventful morning.

It was a long boring work day. It just seemed to be endless. In one sense he was desperate to see Dawn and yet quite fearful as to what would develop in their conversation dating back to the previous evening.

He lingered over his lunch break with the hope that it would eat up some of the afternoon time. It didn't.

It was time to find a suitable place for an evening meal. He intended not to go home and prepare anything for himself. By staying around in town that was another contributing factor to the day going very slow. He wasn't really hungry so he made do with an enhanced burger and fries. It was greasy!

It wasn't quite time for visiting to start but he made his way to the hospital slowly, yet deliberately. He knew it was to be a crucial time in his relationship with his wife, but more especially with their twins.

He was walking with little enthusiasm along the corridor. He became aware of someone walking with him. He turned to see who it was.

"Good evening, Howard" said the nurse.

"Are you likely to tell me what happened yesterday? Did you know what my wife was going to talk about? What is your opinion? Why do we have to face mountainous problems when we are hoping to settle down to a typical family life? Why? What?" Howard was just unloading a stack of questions.

"Steady on, sir". The nurse had absolutely no ideas what he was rambling on about. "What am I suppose to know?"

"You were not in on the slam Dawn threw at me during visiting hours last evening?

"No. You both were talking. Dawn looked as if she had been crying. But that is not unusual in these circumstances".

"Sorry, nurse. You obviously do not know what happened. I do not want to burden you with it. In one sense it is no concern of yours. Yet it might be later on. I can't go into details now. But I would like you to be aware of Dawn's changing attitudes. Post-partum stress, you might want to call it! Thanks for listening. That's it! It's post-partum whatever. Now I've to learn how to cope with that in order to deal with the suggestion she threw out yesterday".

"I go this way. I'll see you later". The nurse went off to report to the nursing station.

Howard continued slowly down the corridor towards Dawn's room. He was not sure how to great her. He told himself to put a smile on his face. Then he told himself not to be a hypocrite. At least he was able to abolish a frown that had been on his forehead all evening.

He was at the door. He had not consciously paused before entering any other time. He glanced around in case anyone had seen him hesitate to enter. There was no one coming down that way at that moment.

He knocked and walked in. Dawn was waiting for him. She didn't give him chance to say hello.

"Hello, Honey. The orderly will be here in about five minutes. We will meet the doctor and we are soon to see our son and our daughter as individuals, no longer joined together".

"That's the best news I have heard all day. I am so happy the surgery was a success".

He made his way to the bedside and gave Dawn a hug and a kiss. That surprised him because he had not anticipated such intimacy after all the turmoil of the night. He felt good and began to be at ease for the time being.

The wheelchair arrived; Dawn stepped out of bed into it. They were on their way to see their babies. The doctor was near the nursery and took them inside. They walked passed different cribs and incubators to a tiny room. Inside were two small units, one with a blue bow the other with a pink bow.

"Here they are. Two perfect babies. The only difference between them and the other babies out there is that each has a scar. No need to be concerned about it. It is not in a prominent place. Normal clothes will cover it".

Dawn went towards the blue ribbon. Howard had already moved towards the pink ribbon. Both stood and looked. The doctor broke the spell by suggesting that they should put their hands in and feeling the flesh of their babies. It was a thrill they would both remember for the rest of their lives. They were at long last not touching the Siamese babies. Here was a separate girl. And here was a separate boy. They changed places so that they could touch their other baby. Both parents had enormous smiles stretching across their faces. "It was a joyful occasion", thought the doctor. Actually the doctor did not know how serious the conversation between this father and mother was to be later that evening when they were on their own. Howard had a wave of fear flood into his mind which he was able to counteract before it had any disturbing effect.

"Have you any questions?" asked the doctor. They both mumbled a negative reply without thinking what they were indicating. They would have many questions, but none were surfacing at that precise moment.

The new mother and the new father just stood and looked at two tiny little babies with tubes and leads. A casual visitor might have thought that they were mesmerized. In one sense they were. Strangely neither of them was thinking about a possible adoption of one of the babies lying in front of them.

The spell was broken when the doctor suggested that they should now leave before any other visitors came to that unit. The orderly was kind to move the wheelchair out slowly, so giving Dawn a longer chance at seeing her babies.

As they walked the corridors there was a natural conversation about what they had seen. They were indeed quite happy. Howard shared with Dawn, "One question that he can answer, or rather he can tell us where they were joined and what happened in separating them. I'd like to know more about the scars. How obvious will it be?"

Dawn answered with similar sentiments especially relating to the scars.

As they approached Dawn's room the nurse was coming towards them. They had a face beaming with smiles. The nurse commented, "I can tell where you have been. You both look so elated and happy".

"I think we are", said Dawn.

"We were just wondering if the doctor can inform us about the surgery, what does it look like now, and are the scars going to be very evident?" added Howard.

"I'll sound him out for you next time I am with him". With that the nurse went on her way.

Almost as soon as they were in the room there was a noticeable change of emotions. Dawn propped herself up on the bed. Howard made himself comfortable in the bed-side chair. Neither spoke.

Both of them where chasing thoughts around in their heads. But neither one of them voiced any concern. There was an important contact between them that assured them of each other's interest and love. The silence was not embarrassing. Both of them realized the weight of each other's thoughts.

Just before the end of visiting hours they both made genuine comments about seeing their babies. Howard stressed the importance of the doctor informing them of the extent of the surgery. Dawn expressed hope that they would both have a better night's rest.

At the door Howard turned and threw his usual kiss, Dawn gave him the usual wave.

CHAPTER 6

Immediately Howard had made his exit from her room Dawn's face dropped and she was soon in tears.

It took quite awhile for her to compose herself to decide what had made that sudden change in her emotions. It was the clash of joy and fear. It had been a high for her to actually touch the babies. But the crash came when she started to think about the shock she had given her husband regarding looking at the option of adoption. She couldn't make up her mind which thought to go with. That made her all the more uncomfortable. She had never anticipated anything quite like this at all throughout the pregnancy.

Was she right to have expressed her thoughts about an adoption? That question bothered her. The longer she lingered over it the more her conscience began to get into the argument. She had to do something about that or she would not get very much rest during the night.

She tried to change her mind – or rather change the activity in her mind. That meant changing the subject. She was pleased about such a prospect; she would go back to the thrill of touching her babies.

That was much more compatible. She re-lived that feeling of the first touch. The first touch had been through the glove and was very impersonal. The second touch was through a glove but somehow the glove was more kind and allowed her fingers to hold on to the toes and hands. How beautiful! How wonderful that such a tiny creature was so perfectly formed!

She spent a long time pondering that. The nurse came in and suggested that it was perhaps 'lights out' time.

"Okay", she thought, "I'll try to sleep and hope for some pleasant dreams".

Howard hadn't rushed home. There was nothing at home to give the impetus to hurry. He noted that he was not has distraught as the previous night. His coat and tie came off as he entered and were thrown onto the same chair. His shoes were kicked into a similar place as the night before. The coffee pot was alerted and ready for use; this was usual, in fact the coffee pot ought to have programmed itself to switch on and off at particular times.

With a mug of coffee and some pleasant back-ground music, he was soon comfortable in his reclining chair.

It wasn't many seconds before his thoughts turned to the same problem. "What am I going to think about Dawn's suggestion of giving up one of the twins for adoption?"

The uppermost thought that would not allow any other idea room for expression was the life-changing concept of part of the present family being given away for someone else to raise up. "That is not natural", he convinced himself.

The hour passed just juggling that one major thought. He did pause at that time to tell himself that if God convinced him that adoption was right, then he would give more serious thought to it. The next step was quite logical but during this mental and emotional upheaval he admitted that he had not been too logical. If he wanted God to give him guidance then he should start asking God for such help.

The next twenty minutes Howard spent praying for guidance and asking God to give direction to his thinking and to help his emotions to settle down. He also included in his prayer his thanks for the safe arrival of the babies; and also for the great pleasure of being able to touch them.

He decided against a further mug of coffee. Instead he turned on a TV news programme. After being bored with bad news he concluded that a half an hour of that was enough for one evening. He picked up his bible and read for the next half hour before going off to bed.

The one utmost desire was that he would have a more peaceful night. The big thing in its favour was that he had not had such a traumatic time with all kinds of possibilities seeking prominence in his thinking processing. As he undressed he was convinced that a better night was ahead.

Clarence and Betty were having a positive and pleasant evening. There was still no definitive statement from the hospital about adoption, but somehow there was a confident atmosphere that was giving them a strong hope.

They had spent numerous hours praying for God's guidance in this whole procedure. Their prayers seemed to be the same. It was always the same 'wait' answer. This evening their conversation was dominated with the whole idea of prayer. They knew that it was absolutely the right thing to do. They were facing a major decision so God had to be involved in it.

Betty appeared to be the leader of their prayer adventure. Clarence was a great affirmer. They made a good couple. They were both fully convinced that God would bring them a child to love and cherish.

"There was a TV preacher talking about faith the other evening", commented Clarence. "I wish I had listened more carefully".

"He made a lot of sense", added Betty.

"He quoted from some new translation of the Bible. "I had never heard of this version before".

"Can you remember which passage he was reading?" asked Betty.

"I think it was James. 'A faith without works is dead'".

"What appeared to be the new thought?"

"A faith that does nothing will achieve nothing".

"That's quite something. Is it saying something to us?"

"It's quite a statement. I have never heard our Pastor bring that thought out when he has been preaching on faith. Sweetheart it is saying something to us. We have faith. That is why we pray".

"Do you know, my darling that is probably challenging us to look at how our faith is involved in our praying for a baby." Betty was intrigued with the thought. But she knew that Clarence was a deep thinking person and that this would be something of a concern for him.

After a few moments of deep thought, Clarence asked the question, "If faith is to be a dominant factor in our walk with Jesus then should we be asking the question 'why?' Are we convinced that God has assured us that there will be a baby for us? Then, if so, how is our prayer request to have a new format?"

"We have been presenting our request to the Lord" added Betty, "We have told Him. But have we ever asked what He wants for us? I think we might have in the early days".

"What has He told us?" asked Clarence. "I think that preacher mentioned something about the need to obey what God says before we can expect a clear sense of direction from the Lord".

That became a major part of the heart searching for the rest of the evening. It didn't take too long before they both realized that they were about to enter a completely new venture in their faith walk with the Lord Jesus.

It was time for bed. They hoped for sleep. It would be sometime before they would stop the thinking process regarding the relations between their faith and their prayers.

Howard was awake at his usual time. He went through his morning chores without having to think about what to do next. It felt a good beginning to a new day. He gave a short 'thank you' prayer for a good night of sleep.

He was having a great day at work. He made the comment to himself more than once that he was achieving something today.

During his morning coffee break, he sat in a quiet corner; the comment to himself was that he had a wonderful talk to his coffee mug. One thing had become clear he must talk to someone soon about this adoption business.

He phoned the Pastor. It didn't ring more than a couple of times and the Pastor came on with a cheery 'good-morning'.

It's Howard here, Paul. This is just a quickie at the end of my coffee break. Can we meet for lunch today?'

"Certainly, Howard, where do you suggest?"

"I don't want a noisy quick food place; rather a quiet spot somewhere".

"There is a nice little restaurant around the corner from your work place".

"I have passed it scores of times but never ventured in".

"So, how about being there at mid-day?

The time was set. It was very close for Howard, no more than three minutes walk from his building.

Dawn awoke without a thick cloud of doubts swamping every thought. She felt good. When the nurse came in the first thing Dawn mentioned was that God had given her a good night's sleep.

"What's on the agenda today?" she asked the nurse.

"Routine!" was the smiling response.

"Am I scheduled to make another intricate inspection of my babies sometime today?"

"I think it might become a regular part of your daily exercise".

"I suppose that on one of these days you will be sitting me down for a lecture on what to do or what not to do in caring for twins".

"It's surprising you should raise that subject. It is one of the things on my list for the next two days".

"Because it appears as if I am in a good mood today, how about the first lesson sometime this morning".

"I'll make the arrangements".

"That sounds ominous!"

"It will not be too painful, I assure you".

"Will you come here into my room?"

"No. I'll take you into a Lecture Room; there I'll have access to charts and models".

"I'm looking forward to my first lesson!"

It was routine. In fact Dawn thought that most of what the nurse stressed was nothing more than good common sense.

Then Dawn paused. "I will need careful guidance when it comes to their dressings".

"That is something you will not have to deal with while you and the babies are still in the hospital. The nurse on duty will be fully responsible for that. You will not be allowed to change any dressings".

"But I can watch?"

"That depends on the nurse. Put it this way, it might be arranged but it will be entirely up to the nurse".

It was lunch time when the nurse deposited Dawn back to her room.

Her comment as she was leaving, "Have a nice restful afternoon, Dawn".

Dawn anticipated a physically lazy afternoon. The mental part would no doubt be active.

Howard and the Pastor arrived at the same time. There were few customers so it was easy to find a place where they could talk freely.

The waitress came with the menus. Her comment was in connection with the day's special soup and sandwich. They did not look into the menu. Both of them decided on the soup and sandwich.

"Well, Howard what is so urgent? I perhaps should not have said that. But it was so unusual for you to phone for an appointment. That almost sounds like going to the dentist!"

"I assure you it is not a dentist appointment but it could be as painful if not worse".

"Now, I am all ears".

"First and foremost you are a devoted friend. It is a long and complicated story.

Let me be as brief as possible. Dawn dropped a bomb-shell a few days ago. She thought that one of the twins should be given up for adoption. That floored me. My mind has been churning in circles whether it is her losing interest in the babies, or whether she considers her physical strength being incapable, or whether it is a mere financial concern. I cannot ascertain where she is coming from".

"Was it just a suggestion or do you think she was genuinely sincere?"

"After all kinds of mixed emotions and churned up thoughts I do think she might be sincere".

"How do you see my role?"

"As my Pastor, I'm looking for some spiritual input to the equation".

"I know you are both capable of dealing with mixed emotions. I would consider this to be a major concern for you both. Does the Lord want you to have two babies to cherish and guide; or just one? If just one, which one? Is it a Christian thing to consider? Is this what the Lord has for you both? It's obvious I am having a lot of questions that you may already have considered".

"That's alright. God's voice is one of many being heard these days. We want to hear Him loud and clear".

"First, there is nothing sinfully wrong about giving a child up for adoption. For one thing it can be the answer to another couple's prayers. But is this what He wants in your case. Should I be talking with Dawn also about this?"

"Yes. At some stage in the early future you will need to understand her mind about it."

'Howard, tell me clearly, what do you want?"

"I'm not sure".

"When will you be sure?"

"I'm not …" After a pause he started slowly to say that he was coming round to accepting the idea of taking care of just one of the twins.

"You see, you are likely to be giving yourself your own answers".

"That may be so, but are they necessarily God's will?"

"God will let you know. That sounds very much like a cliché. It is. But He will".

"Yes. I know but how will He tell me?"

"Through some of your deep thoughts".

"You, the Pastor, will He not tell you what to tell me?"

"He speaks clearly through the Scriptures".

"I am looking to you to hear the right Scriptures".

"Are you are aware of Him speaking to you through the Word?"

"Yes. But my searching for the right word is not too satisfactory".

"Howard. To be extremely serious, He does have a word for you. Only you and or Dawn are going to hear it. There is a text or passage through which you will hear plainly God's direction to take".

"Will He not tell you where we are able to find His special word?"

"That does happen sometimes. In this case you are both mature in your faith and walk with Jesus, He will direct your eyes to the exact passage in which you will find His will.".

They continued talking for awhile longer then Howard realized that his lunch break was over. He thanked Paul for coming and for his help and support.

Paul indicated that he would continue to pray for clear guidance.

They left the restaurant together and went their separate ways to tackle the duties of the afternoon.

CHAPTER 7

Howard had much to think about that afternoon. He was happy that it didn't keep him from his work. But by the time it came around to the tea break he had made up his mind to phone someone at the Hospital.

He dialed the hospital number and then asked to be put through to someone who deals with adoptions. There was a pleasant voice asking if she could be of help. Howard had been hoping it might be a male he would be taking with. However the voice sounded encouraging so he condensed his situation into about three sentences. She wanted to know where the baby for adoption was located. He mentioned that he or she was already in the hospital.

"At the moment I do not want to disclose my name. Would it be possible to see you or another counselor later this afternoon, before visiting hours commence".

She was quite helpful. "An appointment can be made for five fifteen. I leave at six so that would give you time to eat somewhere before visiting begin".

"Thank you. Oh by way I do not know you name and which room to come to".

"That's alright, I do not know your name either. Come to room 424".

"Thank you. See you later".

Howard was able to settle down for the rest of the afternoon. The fact that he had booked to talk to someone had helped him surmount part of his problem. He finished work at five o'clock and had time to pick up a coffee on his way to the hospital.

Room 424 was not difficult to find. There were a lot of offices along that corridor. The names of the occupants were staggering. He walked slower because he was trying to determine the nationality of people with those foreign sounding names.

He had little difficulty when he saw the name on room 424. Dr. Margaret Porter-Brown. There shouldn't be much difficulty understanding each other with an English sounding name.

He knocked and entered. There was a desk in the entrance. He read the notice for him to press the button twice for the counselor. That wasn't hard. She was obviously waiting because within a matter of seconds she came through the door to welcome him. She was petite, tastefully dressed, and a gorgeous smile. Howard was at ease immediately.

"Come in, sir." Howard followed her into the office. It had all the usual trimmings of an office, but to one side were two large easy chairs. Howard went to sit near the desk but she invited him to the other side into one of the large chairs. His immediate thought that such a comfortable situation might so easily lead to sleep.

"I would like you to relax. That does not mean sleep after a busy day at work!" The smile was captivating. He was at ease. More so than at his first reaction when his counselor turned out to be female. He had thought that perhaps his problem might be better understood by a male.

"My opening question is basically what can I do for you? Yet there is one answer I really should have before we commence. What is your name, or what name will you be using with me?"

"Howard. That is my name. My concern is how to proceed and deal with the complications of adoption".

"Were you adopted?"

"No. No. I am being faced with the prospects of one of my children being placed for adoption".

"I do not want the details as to whom. We'll keep the conversation on a possibility level".

"That is appreciated. My wife and I were expecting a baby. Then came the big news there were two babies on the way".

Dr. Brown had difficulty controlling a knowing smile. Howard did not detect it.

"Both of them are in the nursery. My wife shattered my peace by suggesting that we should place one for adoption. The thought had never occurred to me. It felt totally wrong. My thoughts and emotions went on to a merry-go-round. And I was the one about to get thrown off. I have had many restless moments and sleepless nights. But I'm now at the place where I think I am ready take the issue further".

"Let me honest with you. I think I know who you are and the babies concerned. Even so let's leave the identity to one side for now. Is there any way you want me to help you with this major decision? You really must be at complete peace about the rightness of this procedure. I will of course be speaking with your wife about it, not because you have spoken to me. But the nurse feels that I should have a word with her. I will not mention that you have been to see me".

"It will be a major decision when it comes to which baby we keep and witch one goes to someone else. There is a boy and a girl. I would like the girl, but I have a feeling me wife would like the boy. She would like the girl to be dressed like a princess. I would like the boy to enjoy sports and outdoor activities".

"Who will win?"

"That has not been part of the sharing so far. But I think we should decide quite soon. Perhaps on my next visit, which will be later this evening, I ought to raise the question. Please tell me what I must do now?"

"You are right to come to a conclusion as to whether it will be the boy or the girl.

Howard, how much of your decision will be to please your wife?"

"Until today, I think most of it would be in the direction of her choice".

"Are you happy about that? What do you, Howard, think?"

"We have been praying about this whole issue, and I am convinced that God has been helping me with my searching for all the right answers. I do now think that He has revealed to me that we should place one for adoption. But whether the girl or boy, I'm still not quite sure".

"Can you honestly tell me that, independent of what your wife wants, that you yourself have no doubts about going further along the adoption route?

That is so important. I would have guided you into a different decision if you were still wanting only what your wife has said".

"So, doctor, what is next for me?"

"When you are mutually satisfied, then I will meet with you both and take all the details related to a legal adoption. Nothing along those lines will be tackled at this time".

"I'll be seeing Dawn in a short time. Wish me well. Thank you for listening to me".

"You are very welcome. I look forward to working with you in the not too distant future".

That same afternoon Clarence and Betty had spent time seriously going over the pros and cons of their desire to adopt a baby. They had been quite specific in their prayers and it was Clarence that indicated God was leading them in His direction.

"Then", said Betty, "A phone call to the hospital is due, asking for an appointment as soon as possible. What are you doing?"

"I've just picked up the phone".

"What for?"

"Because I thought it was time that we phoned the hospital to get on their list of adoptive parents".

"That's quick".

"I had thought of doing this before you got around suggesting it?

"Hello. I want to speak to the right person regarding adoptions. Yes. I can hold on …

Yes. Hello, my name is Clarence. When will it be possible to see a counsellor about becoming adoptive parents?"

"We have no babies up for adoption".

"Right, so can we have an appointment to file personal details and be placed on the waiting list?"

"When are you next coming near to the hospital?'

"This coming weekend. Perhaps some time on Friday afternoon?"

"What is your name?"

"Clarence and Betty Kettleby. We live in Mansfield"

"That is booked, Mr. Kettleby. Your appointment is at three thirty this coming Friday afternoon".

"Thank you". He replaced the receiver.

"I feel as if we are a big step forward on the right road. The convenience of an appointment so soon. And this alongside the conformation we have received that God is revealing his will and pointing us in the direction He wants us to move into", said Betty.

Clarence added, "I've a wonderful feeling. Everything is progressing smoothly. Praise the Lord".

After he left room 424 Howard did not go out for a meal, He walked towards the cafeteria to read the menu. It wasn't too exciting. However he considered a soup and something would suffice.

He didn't really enjoy it. But at least he had been resting. He had a strange thought. He couldn't remember taking flowers to Dawn for some time. "It's too late to go out to a flower shop", he thought. Then he remembered passing a gift shop in the entrance hall of the hospital.

There was time, so off he went to see. There was one part that sold flowers. He went up to the girl. She looked tired and not very interested in him. He mentioned that he was a serious customer. She muttered something incoherent.

"What kind of roses do you have?"

"Just those on that display", she pointed to the centre of the little shop.

"I would like two red roses, one pink rose and one blue rose".

"You want what?"

"The red ones are for my wife, the other two colours for my twins".

"You must be joking!"

"Not really. I am just trying to be colour co-ordinated".

"I somehow don't think you will be successful".

They had stepped nearer to the display. Howard pointed out two nicely formed red buds. The girl lifted out a pink one. Alas, there were no blue ones.

"What colour can you suggest for a blue one".

"Are you playing games with me. I'm too tired to bother with games like this".

"I assure you, my dear, that this is not a game it is a serious quest. What colour for the forth rose?"

She lifted different ones but none were remotely close to the colour he wanted.

He noticed one that was a pale mauve. "Do you think I could make do with that one", he asked.

"It'll make four, anyway!"

She wrapped them in some fancy tissue paper. He paid for them. Then he commenced walking the corridors up to Dawn's room.

Dawn was dressed and sitting in the bed-side chair.

She showed so much pleasure when Howard walked in. It was only a fraction of a moment before she spotted the flowers.

"That's a beautiful gesture, sweetheart!"

"It is more than a gesture, it is presented to you with all my love".

"I'll ask the nurse to find a vase for them. They are so nice. I love the selection of colours".

"I could not find a blue one".

"I'm not surprised. If you do find one it was grown as a special order and fed with a blue dye. I'll imagine this one to be blue".

"It was the closest colour they had".

Howard remarked how wonderful it was to see his wife fully dressed and sitting out.

"Yes. I have been feeling so good all day. God is being good to me. I've more energy and enthusiasms today than I have had for a long time".

"I too am feeling the best I've been for a number of weeks. I am convinced it is because God is answering some prayers. Mine and yours. But others have been praying. The pastor told me that we have a lot of friends at the church praying for us".

"Is he telling us what to do?"

"Yes. I think He has made it clear what we are to do".

"How can you say that after all the negative comments of the last few days?"

"Darling, God has given me a new peace. He is taking us into his plan for our family. I have finished telling Him what I want and giving him a list of my complaints".

"It sounds as if you have just been born again!" she laughed.

"In some ways I probably have!"

There was a pause in their conversation. But they were not ignoring one another. Howard had pushed his chair closer. Their hands were wrapped in each other. They were kissing lovingly but not too passionately.

Howard gave Dawn a mighty squeeze. She jumped. "We have a decision to make".

"What? When? Now?"

"There is no better time than the present".

"I've heard that cliché many times".

"I'm serious. One of our twins will be offered for adoption. But right now we must be convinced as to which one God wants us to keep for ourselves".

Howard, darling, I'm ecstatic. I'm almost delirious – that is, deliriously happy." I was feeling awful that I had probably destroyed our happy relationship with my suggestion. I prayed hard that it would not affect our compatibility. Now, I'm praising the Lord for the way He has been leading you. I am fully convinced that someone else will have the joy of nurturing one of our twins. But which one?"

"A girl to be my little princess a boy for you to train to be like his dad. Or perhaps the other way around a girl to be your little princess and a boy to be my fellow sportsman".

"I thought we were thinking of the one we are giving away!"

"We are. This is called the process of elimination. The one we don't want is the one someone else will have the pleasure of parenting".

"How are we going to decided, Sweetheart?' Dawn was more serious than Howard now.

"If we leave it until the next time we see them it could easily be impossible. We'll want them both. Do you have any preference that is surfacing? I think there is a choice getting much attention deep down inside me. The more I pray about the choice, the more I find myself thinking of one of them".

Dawn's response was similar. "I have a strong feeling in one direction. It is not that I have less love for the other one, but God is directing my thinking to just one".

"How then do we share our choices? It might be hard to voice them because we may be choosing a different one".

"Then take two pieces of paper and a pen. You go over into that corner and I'll stay here", suggested Dawn. "We will record our choice and fold up the paper. Leave them on the table and when the nurse comes in ask her to shuffle them around and then open them for us".

"An ingenious idea! How long are we likely to wait until the nurse reveals our desires?"

There was a knock on the door with the answer, "Not long. I'm here now. What have I to reveal for you?"

"We are not quite ready. We have to write something on these papers and fold them, then you shuffle them around so you have no idea who wrote what".

They took their papers and wrote. Neither took many seconds. They were convinced of their choice.

The nurse collected each piece of paper and shuffled them around on the table.

Howard remarked, "If you go on that vigorously then the writing will be rubbed off!"

"Okay. I'll unfold them and lay them flat. You are not to peak".

The nurse had a big smile. She hadn't been told what the ballot was for. She took one paper in each hand and told Howard to move closer to Dawn. I do not know which piece of paper belongs to whom. This one in my left hand, and this one in my right hand - they agree with each other".

Howard and Dawn let out one loud "Praise the Lord!"

"Don't you want to know the choice you agreed upon?" asked the nurse. "Or am I permitted to ask what this is all about?"

"Yes!"

As Dawn has just said, "Yes! to both questions".

"So? How long can I be kept in suspense?"

"We are agreeing on one major item that will have almost eternal consequences on our lives especially as a family. Whatever is on those pieces of paper is our choice".

"Choice for what?"

"Sorry we have not filled you in. We have been thinking through a possible adoption of one of our twins. The choice on those papers is the twin we will keep, the other is to be placed up for adoption. That is where we are at – sorry it is so brief, but you'll be earning more in the coming days", answered Dawn.

"Oh!" shouted Howard. "Put us at ease. Is it a boy or a girl, on those papers?"

"It is a boy!" pronounced the nurse. "Have you chosen a name yet?"

"I suppose the simple answer to that is a negative. There are some names hanging around on an unwritten list somewhere. We have left it until now. We can give him a name very soon. For one, I want to know who he is?"

"Perhaps we can give him his name when we go to see him next".

It was a happy time. The nurse did her chores and left the happy couple still giggling with glee about their choice.

They both had a good night and their dreams were exceptionally happy ones. There were some moments when they were awake and that time was spent thinking through a list of possible names for their son.

CHAPTER 8

The birth of the twins should have been registered earlier. This did not get done due to the fact that names had not been chosen. This then is the next top of the list item to be done.

Howard arrived with four sheets of paper, two for each of them. One a list of boys names, the other a list of girls names. Over the past few weeks Dawn and he had thrown out possible names. He knew there would be difficulty agreeing on one so he opted for a ballot. He had each list duplicated; and now for the exercise. He also arrived with two red pens and two black pens.

"We will each separately go down these lists. We will place a red check mark against our first choice for a boy and then on the reverse side our first choice for a girl. We will place a black check mark against no more than three other names that we like. Oh yes, I don't think we need the assistance of the nurse this time!"

"Quite ingenious my dear. Who has the casting vote if there is a tie?"

"No ties allowed! I narrowed down the field by limiting our choices to twelve. By the way, permission is granted to us to add one extra name, if we so desire, at the bottom of the list which will be in red".

They both spent time reading and re-reading the lists of names. Howard had the advantage of having compiled the lists in the first place. Even so he was quite sincere in praying over each name on the list.

There was no time limit for this important procedure. Both had used the red pen. They spent time going over the names, turning over the paper and going over the other names. They apparently had greater difficulty with the alternative names than with their first choice. However they checked off what they considered good names. It was interesting that both of them added an extra name to the list in bright red letters.

When they came together to look at the list, they were not surprised that most of the black marks did not match. But both expressed amazement that their red marks did match. Then they looked at the added names. That was interesting because each one had added the name of their partner.

Dawn's comment was that pointed to an agreed second name for their daughter and their son.

Howard expressed his joy and surprise that they had both chosen the same name for the girl and also for the boy.

Adrian was the name they had chosen for their son. Adriana could be the name for their daughter.

They laughed and made numerous comments about the name for their son. It flowed nicely and appropriately. "Adrian Syston"; they kept repeating in different contexts.

When the nurse walked in they both announced at the same time, "We've chosen their names!"

"So," asked the nurse, "what do I call him and what do I call her?"

Both answered in unison, "Adrian and Adriana".

"That's easy to remember. I can visualize them playing and shouting 'Adi' at each other".

Dawn and Howard smiled at such a thought. Dawn looked at Howard with an unspoken question.

"We would like you to know" said Howard, "they are not likely to be playing with each other".

"We have signed the papers for Adriana's adoption" added Dawn.

The nurse was not overly surprised. "I'll make sure the names are recorded on the identity labels in the nursery".

Dawn had received permission to go out with Howard for a time that afternoon. They bought some announcement cards to send to family and friends. They could not resist going into the 'Baby's Own' store. They took one glance at the pink section but kept walking into the blue section. They had previously decided that their son would wear other colours and not just blue. Even so, the first little outfit they bought was in blue.

They called in at their favourite 'watering hole' for a coffee.

Dawn was thrilled with the freedom of being away from the four walls of her hospital room.

They were busy musing over what their friends will be saying, especially if they have already heard about the twins.

Howard was quite firm as he stressed the assurance that the right emphasis will be given to all queries.

On their return to the ward they were met along the corridor by the nurse. She was looking for them. She showed interest in where they had been and what they had bought.

"Come with me" she said, "I want you to see the new identity labels on the incubators".

How wonderful to see the names in print, and to actually be able to speak to them by name.

It was important that their parents be informed of the names of their grandchildren. So, instead of waiting until he returned home, Howard suggested they phone from the hospital room.

Dawn wondered about the best time to inform their parents of the adoption decision.

"Perhaps we could drop a hint when we tell them of the names", thought Howard.

The two phone calls were made. There was great delight from the grandparents. It did not seem the right time to mention the adoption. Howard thought it best to talk with them in person about such a traumatic decision.

They did not have long to wait because independent of each other both sets of parents had decided to make a hospital visit that evening. They would not have a better time.

The grandparents arrived at the same time quite near to the beginning of visiting hours. They first of all wanted to go see the babies. The nurse was asked to accompany them.

They were thrilled at seeing their baby grandchildren.

On their return to Dawn's room, they were spilling over with the excitement of see such tiny babies. There was a lot of chatter between parents and grandparents.

Dawn broke into the conversation. "We have something to share with you. It will not only be a surprise but a shock".

Howard had already made sure that extra chairs were available for all to sit down.

Dawn looked to Howard for him to continue.

"After considerable thought and prayer, as well as discussions with the pastor and a counselor here, only one of the babies will be coming home with us".

They were shocked but eager to hear the rest.

"Adrian will come home with us. We are placing Adriana up for adoption".

There were various moans, but they were waiting for the reason behind such a massive decision.

Dawn volunteered, "It would have been an insurmountable situation. I could not have given justice to it. I feel inadequate and too weak to cope with such a large increase in the family to care for".

"Of course you are strong enough", said her mother. His mother nodded approval of such a comment.

The two fathers had got up and walked to a corner of the room whispering their comments to each other. Neither of them was showing or expressing pleasure at the shock they had received.

Dawn was trying her hardest to help the two grandmothers understand where she was coming from. She knew it would be difficult, but this was proving impossible.

Every encouraging and positive comment they made was shattered when Dawn stressed her condition. She was not allowing herself to be persuaded. It had taken such hard emotional turmoil to arrive at their decision; she could not face having to battle with all the various options.

For the grandparents it had been an up and down visit. Emotions were exploding at both ends of the scale. When it came to the end of visiting time no happiness was shown. Abject dismay was obvious. It had not been the pleasure they'd anticipated earlier in the day.

Almost as soon as their parents left the room, Dawn was in tears. The upset was so great that Howard was wiping his cheeks. Their immense happiness had not been shared by the grandparents. They wrapped themselves around each other so confirming their love and acceptance. Adrian, their son, would leave the hospital with his mother and they would be the family unit they believed God wanted them to be.

It was the beginning of the last weekend Dawn was expecting to remain in Hospital. Being Saturday it brought a joyful feeling because it meant Howard would be visiting in the afternoon as well as evening.

Howard had only been in the room with Dawn for about ten minutes when there was a knock on the door. In walked Clarence and Betty.

"It's good to see you again, friends" said Howard.

Dawn also expressed her pleasure, "It'll be so nice to have a visit. I was only thinking this morning that this will most probably be my last weekend in Hospital".

"Will the twins be able to leave at the same time", asked Betty.

"That decision hasn't been taken as yet", Howard added.

The conversation continued in a general way.

Dawn opened the topic of names. "We have given each twin a name; we had been thinking a long time. But Howard printed lists of names and duplicated it. We both sat down with a pen and paper and marked our choices. The red check mark was to be ones first choice. The result was that the red mark on each paper was against the same names. Our son is named Adrian and our daughter is Adriana".

There was a lot of interesting comments about the name choices. Both Betty and Clarence liked the names that had been chosen. They thought that somehow the names were appropriate. They expressed interest to know how they developed and where the Lord would lead them.

Betty said there was something very important they wanted to share.

"We are all ears", replied Dawn.

"We came for the weekend. In fact we came up a day earlier than usual".

Clarence interjected, "We had an appointment for yesterday afternoon".

Howard said that he didn't want to be kept in limbo, "Where was your appointment?"

"Here, right here in the hospital"

"Now you've given me bigger ears. I was going to ask if it was exciting. I won't ask that because I can tell it was been a helpful time for you".

"It has been very helpful", said Betty,. "We met with a counselor in regard to placing our names on the registry as potential adoptive parents".

"That's wonderful! Absolutely wonderful! Isn't God wonderful the way he guides?"

"Our prayers changed direction a week or so ago. Instead of listing our desires; we asked for a revelation of what God wanted to say to us. Then God gave us some thoughts to pray through. We had calm and a peace that he was working things out for us. Hence a phone call requesting an interview yesterday".

"Isn't that just perfect", rejoiced Dawn.

"Where you given any idea as to how long you might have to wait?" asked Howard.

"We were informed that no babies are available for adoption at the moment", answered Clarence.

The afternoon disappeared so quickly. The Kettleby's got up to leave.

"Will you be returning to Mansfield tonight?"

"No we thought we would stay the night and return probably tomorrow afternoon: replied Clarence.

"Then you could come back for a visit again this evening?" added Howard.

"We could. But that will be too much for you".

"No. We might have some other things to share with you. We'll look forward to another visit later".

Howard didn't leave; instead he and Dawn went down to the cafeteria for their meal. Dawn commented on how great it was eating away from her bed. Howard commented on the quality of the meal as to how tasty it was considering it was hospital food. They had enjoyed it

They took a stroll via the shop on their way back to the room. They surprised themselves, because they looked inside and did not buy anything.

Visiting time was starting. The doors had been opened and there was quite a rush as people wanted as long a visit as possible.

The comments they made when they got into her room were in connection with the Kettleby's visit. Dawn said that she would like to share their news relating to the choice of their son, and that the little girl was being placed up for adoption.

Howard wondered if it might be too soon. They decided to play it by ear on how the conversation went. If the opportunity arose then they would just mention that they were in the early stages of decision making.

"And of course", said Howard, "It'll be a prayer request for them to be asking God for His blessing upon decisions being made".

The timing was perfect. They would share a little of their major story. There was a knock and in they walked. Lots of smiles!

Betty had a bunch of flowers for Dawn. "It's so special for us to hear about your babies and a delight to see the way the Lord is developing our friendship".

They chatted about every subject under the sun; or so it felt.

"Can we ask a request of you two, please?" asked Howard.

"Why, Certainly" replied Clarence.

"We are at the stage of a major family disturbing decision".

"We know how painful that can be. In fact some members of the family are hardly speaking to us because they were upset about some things we decided upon".

"Well our problem is with our parents. They do not like what we are hoping to do. They were in to visit us yesterday and they were not happy when they left. If the truth be known they probably expressed their anger to each other before leaving the hospital" said Dawn.

"That must have been some earth-shaking news?"

"Yes. It was indeed" Howard said.

There was a pause for a few seconds. It became obvious that Howard and Dawn were being cautious in what they shared.

"Please be assured of our confidentiality", emphasized Clarence.

"I know we can trust you with that" said Howard.

"It is about the babies", stressed Dawn.

"Are they sick or having complications?" asked Betty.

"No. They are both developing well. The doctors are very happy with their progress."

"This is what we want you to pray about. We want to make sure that we are in the centre of God's plan for our lives. He has placed us into a family. It is His doing. And we want Him to give direction at every turn so that we'll bring pleasure and honour to Hm. And we want both babies to grow up in the knowledge and love of God".

Dawn broke the spell. "This is our prayer request. We want what is totally right and part of God's will for us"?

"It is certainly a major topic for prayer. But our God is big enough to do anything, He will give clear directions to you".

CHAPTER 9

"This is the day!' announced the nurse as she entered Dawn's room.

Dawn already had a grin spreading across her cheeks.

"It isn't just a matter of getting you dressed and the case packed. There are forms to be signed. There are dates to see the doctor for regular check-ups. There are instructions as to what to do and especially things not to do". "Do I go to the office for that?"

"No. Various people are scheduled to see you this morning. And then when your husband comes to collect you he will have to counter-sign them".

"Do I get the privilege of dressing Adrian?"

"Somehow I don't think so. You have given the clothes for him to wear, so the nurse in the nursery will be doing that so that he is ready to be picked up my his Mum."

"Do I get to say good bye to Adriana?"

"I think the doctor will be arranging that for you".

"The more I think about it the more difficult it will be. I know that I have not had much motherly love contact with her, but even so it will be a matter of leaving part of me behind".

It was as the nurse said. There were the adoption papers to authorize. Then there were discharge instructions to read, query if needed, and sign. Another nurse came with a list of dates for follow-up examinations both for her and also her son.

She was pleased when lunch time arrived. She presumed that no more papers would require her attention. Instructions for Howard had been given to her. The nurse would take him to the relevant offices to sign his approval and permission.

Howard took permission to be away from work that afternoon in order to pick up his wife from the hospital and take her and their son home. He knew it would not take the whole of the afternoon, but he wanted to help get her settled and help her sort things out.

He was later arriving at the hospital. His last item of business took longer than anticipated.

When he arrived Dawn was dressed and sat in the chair waiting patiently for him. After their usual greetings and kisses Dawn mentioned that the nurse would be taking him to sign some papers. "No" she added, "It is not painful. I've already been through the procedure and I came out unscathed".

"That certainly will be a pleasure".

"Yes, but wait until you get to one page. You may not consider that to be too pleasurable," she laughed.

She hadn't time to warn him of all that was likely to happen. The nurse did not even knock. "I saw you arrive so you must not sit down. I am under instructions to take you immediately before your wife can distract you. So, 'good by', Dawn. Howard, come with me – yes, right now!"

Dawn wasn't left on her own for very long. All the papers were ready for Howard's signature. He asked quite a few questions in regard to the instruction for caring for the baby. He was also asking about how to care for his wife, both physically and emotionally. He seemed to have received some helpful suggestions from the nurse.

When they got back to the room, Dawn mentioned that she had received a message that the doctor would take them to see the babies. They would have a chance to say goodbye to Adriana. She was told that the nurse will carry our baby to the car and make sure he is securally fastened in the baby car seat.

"Is there anything else that needs packing?" asked Howard.

The nurse answered. "I have searched every nook and cranny and even packed a couple of pure bred hospital spiders. Take exceptional care when unpacking!"

The orderly arrived to pick up the bags.

The doctor had sent a message for them to meet him in his office and then they would proceed to pick up the baby.

It was a strange feeling when they saw the two babies. One was dressed in his blue outfit. The other was still in a hospital gown. Dawn, followed by Howard, reached in and as they touched the hand of their daughter they said their 'good byes'. Dawn could not keep the tears from flowing. Howard gave her a reassuring hug. Before he withdrew his hand he prayed for God to protect Adriana and guide her.

They turned to leave and the doctor said that it would be best for them if they did not ask to visit Adriana. "This is your good bye to her".

As they walked the corridors to the Hospital exit there were mixed emotions. Sadness at leaving their daughter, and joy at being able to take their son home.

Howard had parked near to the door so they did not have far to walk before reaching the car. The nurse was expert in fixing car seats, so she soon had Adrian in safely, and she said her farewell.

The mixed emotions continued during the drive from the hospital. As they turned the corner into their street it was joy that took over.

Both sets of grandparents had arrived at the house to give a welcome home. As she saw them, Dawn was so pleased that there had been no permanent break with them. They gave a genuine welcome to them. Both grandmothers were almost fighting over who could pick up Adrian first.

The table was set. There had been some hectic activity in the kitchen prior to their arrival. The refreshments were almost like the first course of a feast. It was a joyful time.

Dawn's mother offered to carry Adrian to his bed. Howard's mother volunteered to tuck him in.

The parents didn't stay much longer because they realized that the couple wanted to get settled.

As they picked up clothes and baskets to leave, they were thanked profusely. It was genuine. They really were happy for the love and welcome on arriving home.

For the whole evening there were expressions of love and joy and amazement and appreciation and wonder. There was a big 'Thank You' to God for his involvement and help.

There was a moment of sadness when they went into the baby's room. They both were aware of only one bed and their thoughts went back to the hospital and seeing little Adriana. She is waiting. But waiting for what? A little more was required before she would be classed as healthy and ready to go into the nursery proper. There was absolutely no idea how long a wait it would be before an adoption would be finalized.

Tears were wiped away.

They had a long hug as they placed a hand on Adrian and asked for God's blessing to be upon him. "He belongs to you God", said Howard. Dawn added, "And you will give clear directions for his future. And as we give him to you so we ask for guidance as to how to nurture and raise him as your child".

It was a goodnight for them. They cuddled. They rejoiced. They fell asleep in each other's arms as they enjoyed their closeness and intimacy

They awoke the next morning. Howard commented on having a good night's sleep. Dawn informed him that he was so sound asleep he did not hear Adrian calling for his dad four times during the night.

This was the beginning of their new life. Alongside certain chores to be performed daily there was the responsibility of training their son. The training would have a physical as well as mental input. Both parents had already accepted the emotional and spiritual influence as having priority in the development of the family relationship. Adrian would know early in his life the reality of God. He would also learn the importance of God and the Bible for his parents.

For the first two months there would be check-ups with the doctor at the hospital. Adrian's development was to be monitored carefully in those early stages. The doctor would be keeping an eye on the baby's mother. Those early months were of paramount importance for satisfactory bonding. In those first few months when with the doctor his second question was, "And how is the mother doing?"

It was a learning experience for Dawn and Howard, but they had decided that their parenting was going to be as close to perfect as possible. Very soon they realized the hardness of their God-given task, but remained undaunted.

It was almost a week after Adrian and his mother had been discharged from the hospital when Clarence and Betty received a letter from the hospital counselor regarding their application to adopt a baby.

They were over-joyed. There was no assurance or promise offered, but would they make an appointment for a consultation within the next six days. That could be arranged easily. They certainly would not try to co-ordinate a visit with the Syston's at the same time.

Clarence made the phone call and had no difficulty obtaining an appointment for later in the week.

The days dragged. Betty was sure some days lasted twice as long as they should. Clarence would tell her to get on and do something constructive or creative. She was apparently spending most of her awake moments thinking about a baby.

"You'll have plenty of time to think through all the rules and regulations after we have been to see the counselor".

"But, I must prepare myself for the ordeal of a question and answer time".

"Don't let us spend too much energy on what we might be challenged with, but more on making sure we are in the right receptive mood for God to direct the outcome of this up-coming consultation".

"You know full well that I agree with that, but … Yes, there is a realistic 'but', I am finding it terribly hard to wait!"

Later that afternoon Clarence came into the lounge to chat with Betty. She was sitting in her favourite chair with a magazine. When he got closer to her he laughed and said, "You can't be thinking of decorating a baby's room right now. We have not yet been promised a baby. I can't understand why you are filling your mind with suggestions for furniture and toys. We'll have plenty of time for some of those practical matters when the prospects turn into reality".

It was hard to calm the excitement when Clarence and Betty were entering the hospital for the interview with the consultant. This was a day they thought would never come. There had been so many negative responses for their desire to adopt. Now right in front of them was going to be a step into the future they had only dreamed about.

They knocked and entered the room. A couple of chairs were available. They decided to sit because they had no idea if they would be asked to wait. They had no sooner sat down when the receptionist told them to go through to the consulting room.

It was a room with comfortable chairs, not arranged around a table but in the corner of the room. The desk and office part was on the other side. They were invited to sit in one of the large chairs. They were comfortable.

Betty made such a comment to Clarence. He had a big smile for his response.

The young lady - well she was younger than the Kettleby's - was slim and quite professional. There was no superiority but a genuine attitude that placed them at ease.

There was a general conversation about the Kettleby's. The consultant wanted to know something of their history relating to their marriage and hopes for a family. Both Betty and Clarence found it non-embarrassing to talk about some of the intimate details.

The consultant expressed her pleasure and surprise at the ease of their telling something of the pain of barrenness and the need for patience while waiting for the possible availability of adopting a baby.

It was made quite clear that no promises could be made. From time to time babies are placed up for adoption.

"There are other couples on the waiting list. But we do try to make a suitable match for each baby. Together with this interview we will study the answers on your application form. We are making sure we understand the emotional and educational standard of each couple; we also take into account the background of the birth mother, and father if he is known. I want you to know that decisions are not made lightly. Quite a number of hours may be spent making sure we can make a good match." The consultant also went on to tell them more about the waiting period.

"I know you cannot give us any date. But is it likely to be soon or is the probability likely to stretch into years?" asked Betty.

Clarence was about to say something, but the consultant interrupted.

"I do not want to appear rude", she said, "but let me assure you of one thing. Your application has been accepted and the process has commenced".

There was a large sigh from Clarence. Instead of making his comment he just closed his eyes and said, "thank you". In fact he repeated himself four or five times. This brought a pleasurable grin from the consultant. Betty added her Cheshire-cat smile.

"I know you will find it difficult to wait." said the consultant, "But I can promise you that you will hear from me or this office as soon as we have anything to share with you." With that she indicated the interview was over.

She shook hands with Betty and Clarence and wished them a safe journey home.

Adrian with his mother were making the second of their regular visits to the hospital. The doctor was pleased with the progress.

"The scar tissue is healing very well", he said.

Dawn had made a comment as to whether her son would have any difficulties later in life from such a large scar. The doctor assured her that he would be living a normal healthy life with no handicaps or disadvantages.

"He has a strong body, I'm sure he'll be a sportsman".

"Then he will have to play soccer", Dawn commented, "Because his Dad says so!"

"If he does, then let me know because I will want to see him running and scoring".

Dawn just giggled her way through her report about the visit to the doctor. Howard wasn't really interested in some of the mundane medical comments. Dawn paused. Howard thought it unusual at that phase of her telling about the visit. His thought was expressed by the look on his face.

"Well, you will have to know one day".

"What will I need to know one day?" asked Howard.

"The doctor seems convinced that he will make a good soccer player".

"That perfects your report for today!"

They spent quite a long time allowing their imaginations to run wild. Dawn was thinking of other sports. Howard's mind went to rugby. Dawn wondered about golf.

"No", thought Howard, "Hopefully he is more masculine than some of the spooky golf players!"

They fully agreed that he would be an excellent soccer player. Perhaps good enough to become a professional. But both parents hoped he would become more successful in a profession or in business.

It was two weeks later on their next visit to the hospital when the doctor mentioned that someone else from the hospital would be with them shortly.

The Medical check-ups were satisfactory. The mother was coping well.

Dawn wondered who would be coming to see them. The doctor would not give any hint.

There was a knock on his door. In walked the adoption consultant.

Not many seconds were used up with niceties and the usual banter about baby getting bigger and the weather improving.

"Dawn", said the consultant, "There is a decision that you and your husband must make, and make soon".

"How difficult will it be?"

"Not very" interjected the doctor.

"There is a possible family that might be interested in adopting your daughter", smiled the consultant.

"That's excellent news" replied Dawn.

The consultant looked at the doctor then continued speaking to Dawn.

"It will mean that very soon information about the Siamese-twin birth will be discussed. They will need to know the details; they will not be told your identity. But we want you and your husband to know that this information will be shared with a couple this coming weekend".

"Howard will be delighted" mentioned Dawn. Then she looked straight at the doctor, "Will they need to be told that her Siamese brother will become a world renowned soccer player!"

The consultant looked at the doctor for some input. "Yes. It's right. On their last visit I noted that the baby had an excellent physique that indicated he would become a sportsman".

The doctor will be brought in to see them. They will want to know the details regarding the large scar. They need to know that somewhere out in the world there is the other half of that pregnancy."

Dawn assured them they would have no difficulty about such information being shared with the prospective adoptive parents.

"No names. No identities. Though they might ask about the name you gave her. They will decide whether to keep that name or change it to one of their choice. You will not likely be informed of any new name to be registered".

"Our main concern will be that it be a good home and sound relationship between the husband and wife, and if possible that they be serious church going folk."

"We cannot guarantee all that, but we can assure you that the relationship between the mother and the father and other relatives will be looked into", assured the consultant.

"I wonder what they will be like", asked Howard.

Her reply, "We may never know".

CHAPTER 10

This was the day that Betty and Clarence thought would never come. They were arriving at the hospital and soon would be in the consultants' office. The letter summoned them to come at a set time on that particular day. They were arriving on time.

They were not kept waiting.

The counselor came straight to the point. "You look excited. As indeed I expected you would. You had been informed of your acceptance as adoptive parents. I want to tell you that your search for a baby is almost over".

"It's what?" exclaimed Betty.

"Alright, honey" said Clarence as he reached over to grasp her hand.

"There is a baby girl", the counselor continued, "We'll go in to some details later. My first question is will you be happy to receive a baby girl?"

There was an affirmative sound from both of them with the normal nods and ringing of hands.

I know that you will be eager to see the baby. But first of all the doctor has some important information to share with you. He will be here in a moment.

"Is there something the matter with the baby? Betty asked.

'No. She is a perfect happy little girl".

"Then what has the doctor to tell us?"

"It's best that he tells the story from the beginning".

They sat in silence for a full two minutes that seemed like hours before the doctor arrived.

There was a typical apology for being a few minutes late.

"You have been informed that a baby girl is available for adoption. I gather you are happy about a girl. It was a traumatic birth. The mother was hospitalized before the birth. The reason being that she was having twins. Yes, yours, or rather the baby in question is a twin." He paused because it seemed as if Betty wanted to ask a question. After thinking for a few moments she indicated that the question could be asked later.

"I think you should brace yourselves for a shock. We had to perform a c-section in order for the twins to be born. Now there was something unusual about this pregnancy. They were joined; certain procedures had to be performed. We had a large incubator into which the twins were placed. They were examined by the specialists and both were perfectly formed and healthy. One major thing in our favour was that they were not joined at any major organ. So when it became time to separate them it was mainly a cutting of the flesh and then dealing with the incisions. The healing process was perfect, though each baby had a large scar".

"Is it a big scar? Will it be seen easily by everybody?" asked Betty.

"I can understand your questions and your concern. The answer is that it is not a small scar. It is on part of the body not normal seen by other people unless bathing or swimming. The scar is on the buttock. It will easily be covered by normal size underpants. A bikini would expose it".

"Does that mean there is a similar scar on the other baby also?" asked Clarence.

"That's true. The scar has healed quite well. Dressings are being changed every day. You will receive instructions on how to give adequate care. Now, I suppose you are eager to see this beautiful little girl"?

Clarence and Betty in unison made it abundantly clear that they hope nothing would hinder them. The uppermost desire in their minds at that moment was to see the baby that could be theirs.

The four of them walked at quite a brisk pace down the corridor to the nursery. The nurse in charge had been warned that prospective adoptive parents would be coming to see the baby.

They stood by the cot and gazed.

Betty asked if she touch her. The nurse lifted the baby and placed it in her arms.

Howard with a smile across his face could not keep a tear back, as he nodded approval his hand reached to touch the baby's hand.

It was a wonderful feeling; far more thrilling than they expected. Their minds were jumping ahead as to how long they must wait until they could take her home. But they had not as yet stated that they were attracted to the baby girl.

The doctor asked if they had any questions, then indicated that perhaps they should see the scar. He asked the nurse to remove the cloth. He turned the baby on to her tummy and exposed the scar.

It was quite big. They didn't like it. The doctor was aware of their reaction and urged them to not spend too much time thinking about the mark but more about the person. It will be less severe as the years pass.

The nurse covered the baby and Clarence had a chance to hold her. He was afraid he might drop her. He was handling her like a precious china doll. The counselor was delighted at the way the baby was quite relaxed in his arms.

Have you any questions?' she asked.

Their response was yes and no, but a no seemed okay at this stage.

The baby was placed back in the cot and they were about to leave. Betty caught sight of a label on the cot with a name on it. "Is that her name?' she asked.

The counselor replied by stating it was the name the parents gave when the babies were being registered. You can keep the name if you wish. Most of the new parents want to choose the names themselves. That's alright because the names you choose will be entered on the form when the baby is registered with you.

Back in the office was a paper to sign. That the prospective father and mother have seen the baby and are immediately attracted to her and are genuinely agreed to love and care for her. "When the magistrate signs these papers in your presence he will tell you that this baby girl is as much yours as if she had been born to you", they were told.

"Yes, there is no doubt, we are excited and willingly desire to be the loving parents of this lovely baby girl" said Clarence. Betty agreed almost word for word with her husband.

"I'll leave you to talk privately for a few minutes". And with that the counselor left her office.

Betty and Clarence were almost incoherent with their comments expressing their deep joy.

Then Betty became serious. Clarence wondered what had happened.

"There is something familiar with that baby" she said."It is as if I have seen her before or heard about her from someone".

"It is unlikely that you have seen her before:" replied Clarence.

"But there is a real feeling that we have heard about this baby".

The counselor returned and noted that they looked very serious about something. "Is something giving you concern about adopting this baby?'

"No", said Betty, "we were just mentioning that we think we have heard about this baby before".

"Is that giving you second thoughts about adopting"?

"Oh, No", was Clarence's response. "We ... I, still want her to be ours".

They finished off the paper work and were told they would receive further instruction soon by mail.

It was an exciting return journey for Clarence and Betty.

They agreed that now was the time to start thinking of decorating the baby's room.

There would be important announcements and letters to write to family members and friends who had been praying for them to be favoured with a baby.

And so the conversation continued regarding the things needing to be done.

They were within a few miles of home.

"It is going to be a wonderful experience entering our home knowing that soon we will be taking in a baby girl. Oh, by the way, you mentioned seeing a name label on the cot. Can you remember what name?" asked Clarence.

Betty hesitated; she knew it was not a familiar name. It took some time as she went through a list of names in her mind.

They were not talking with each other. Both were trying to think of a name.

It was as they turned into the road leading to their home Dawn suddenly shouted, "It was Adriana!"

"We have some serious thinking ahead of us trying to decide on a name that is suitable for a gorgeous princess, as indeed she will be the daughter of the King".

They turned into their drive. They were home.

Dawn mentioned as they were having breakfast that this was the day she and Adrian were scheduled to visit the doctor at the hospital.

"What time is the appointment?' asked Howard.

It's not until the afternoon, I think it is two thirty or it might even be three thirty" smiled Dawn.

"If it's three thirty then I am free this afternoon. I would like to come with you".

"That will be wonderful. I'm sure the doctor will ask how the young daddy is doing".

Just before leaving for work he asked Dawn to verify the appointment time."It's three thirty, honey".

"That was nice, it is ages since you used that term of endearment!"

Howard was at the hospital ten minutes before the time of the appointment. He made his way to the doctor's office. Dawn with the baby was there a couple of minutes before him. They were together in the waiting room for about ten minutes before being called into the doctor's room. He was pleased to see Howard.

"You don't look any older", he said to him.

"I ought", replied Howard, "I could be classed as a sleep deprived father!"

"That is the farthest from the truth I've heard from you today" insisted Dawn, "You sleep right through; in fact you have slept right through every night since we took our baby home!"

"How did you manage such a spectacular fete?" The doctor wanted the formula to pass on to his many sleep deprived fathers.

The doctor went through the routine examination of the baby. He had a wonderful smile when he affirmed to the young parents that the baby was doing just fine.

He had the usual for Dawn, "Are you alright?"

Then he turned to Howard and asked a similar question. Howard was about to respond with the same answer as his wife. The doctor interrupted him,

"Is it possible that you could be the first young father to speak the truth?"

Howard had his innocent look with a natural grin waiting to stretch further across his cheeks. "Some of the lessons have been hard", he replied seriously, "Nobody warned me about dirty clothes requiring to be changed. My nose always turns in the opposite direction".

There were various questions and answers thrown back and forth.

The doctor stood, indicating the appointment was over.

"Oh", he said, "you are to see your counselor before you leave".

They left his office and walked down the next corridor to see the counselor. They knocked on the door. There was a friendly shout inviting them to enter.

There were seats at the desk so they sat down and looked with a large question on each of their faces.

"Nothing serious. At least not serious enough for a frown".

They relaxed. The baby was enjoying a sleep in his mother's arms.

"I need to inform you that there is a couple seriously interested in adopting your daughter".

"Wonderful", Dawn and Howard said in chorus.

"I don't suppose we get to know any names or places," commented Dawn.

"I cannot give you personal information like that. But I will share with you one interesting observation. When they looked at the baby there was tremendous joy on the faces. They will make wonderful parents".

"When will they take her home?" asked Howard.

"No date has been fixed. Probably in the not too distant future".

"Is there anything you can tell us about the couple", asked Dawn. "It is only natural that I would like to know who is going to be caring for my baby".

"The woman took a good look at the name label. She seemed interested in the name you had given her".

"We liked the name, Adriana, because it fitted very well with her brothers' name, Adrian".

"She seemed to think that she had seen or heard about that baby".

"That's strange", commented Howard.

"Do you think she had seen or heard about her?" asked Dawn.

"There is no telling. She may have been so deeply attracted to her that she thought she had already met her".

"Would it have made any difference if she had known about her or seen her before?" queried Dawn.

"Not as far we are concerned. Our policy is to not give out personal information about the birth mother".

"Will it cause any difficulty for the new mother if she does happen to have seen the baby before, or if she has heard about her? Is there any way she would have heard about the Siamese twins that were separated at this hospital"? asked Howard.

"That is a possibility. The news of such a birth and the necessary surgery is something that was not kept a secret. In fact that is perhaps how she thought she had heard about her. In fact it is quite likely because they have visited the hospital fairly frequently over the past few months in connection with their adoption procedure. Rest assured no personal details have been given or will be given them. But they have seen the scar so they are aware of the surgery to separate the babies".

As long as they are kind and loving with my baby, that is my main concern", Dawn said so proudly.

They left the hospital; to return home. Neither of them spoke very much. They kept looking at Adrian in his car sea, and were congratulating themselves on being the proud parents of such a handsome baby boy.

They had not been home very long; long enough to get the baby settled in his cot. Howard and Dawn were sat on the sofa having a cuddle. Suddenly they released their hold on each other. Both started speaking at precisely the same moment.

"I'll be loving and generous. I will allow you to go first!"

"That is very magnanimous of you honey. Being true to my name, it just dawned on me who the adoptive parents might be".

"I was about to tell you the same thing".

"Is it possible?' asked Dawn.

"Anything is possible, sweetheart".

"Then you must be thinking of the same couple I'm thinking of".

"That too is a possibility. Actually we are very similar!"

"Then next time I take Adrian for a check-up I'll make an appointment to see that counselor again. I will ask an outright question, no ifs or buts. I will ask if the surname of the new parents might happen to be, Kettleby".

"Wouldn't that be something if it is?'

"I'll be so pleased for them. And actually I will be happy for them", said Dawn.

"There is no doubt in my mind they will be loving and godly parents".

It was just over two weeks when Dawn and Adrian went for the next doctor's appointment. It was the same questions and the same examination procedure. It was also the same comment afterwards that the baby is doing just fine.

'Had you thought of circumcision for your son?" the doctor asked.

"We have not given too much thought because we decide that we would leave our son whole. The answer is no to circumcision" responded Dawn.

"You may not have heard yet, your daughter is being adopted, the adoptive parents have been given a date to pick up their baby".

"That's wonderful. How soon will it be?"

"I think it is the end of next week".

"Will I get a chance to say my good-bye to her?"

"I am sure something can be arranged. But it will be advisable for it to be a short visit. I'll let your counselor fix the time for you. Perhaps your husband may want to join you at that time".

"I hope so. I would like him to be with me".

CHAPTER 11

The weekend was coming up quickly. Dawn and Howard were patiently waiting to hear from the hospital. They had been promised an opportunity to say their farewells to Adriana. It was now just a matter of receiving the phone call telling the time for their visit.

The call came later that morning giving them their appointment time for the next afternoon. Howard hoped it would be later afternoon giving him chance to leave the office at a suitable time. The Counselor on the phone told them to be at her office by four thirty p.m. That was just right for Howard. They had no difficulty.

Howard arrived at the same time as Dawn and the baby. Dawn said she had brought Adrian because he should also say 'goodbye' to his sister.

The counselor walked them down the familiar corridor and into the room. The duty nurse was expecting them and had placed a pink dress on Adriana. They both looked lovingly with tears trickling down their cheeks. The Nurse offered to hold Adrian while Dawn and Howard held their baby girl. No one said anything about it being the last time; they knew it without being reminded.

Dawn lifted Adriana and gave her a long lingering kiss and whispered a prayer for God to protect and direct her life. She passed her to Howard. A tear still trickled down his cheek. He kissed her, and then decided the kiss wasn't long enough or big enough for such a lovely little girl. Dawn had to remind him that she was his wife not Adriana. They had a good laugh.

Just before handing her back to Dawn he told the others he wanted to pray. They did not object. His prayer was quite simple and yet direct. He was handing their daughter over to God to care for and guide. He also mentioned for God to bless and give guidance to the new parents of the little baby. Even the counselor and the nurse said "Amen" at the end.

Dawn placed the baby back into the arms of the nurse. They turned and left. They had said their "goodbye" to their little daughter.

As they walked along the corridor Dawn asked if she could ask a question of the counselor. "What is it that you want to know?"

"Is the new mother of my baby girl a Mrs. Kettleby?"

"Sorry my dear, I am not allowed to give you any details regarding the adoptive parents".

"I knew that would be your answer", was Howard's response.

Two days later the Kettleby's arrived with a carry cot and other clothes. At the counselor's office it was the time to confirm the details on the papers that had already been signed. The main thing the counselor required was conformation of the full legal name they were giving the baby.

"We like the name the birth mother gave but we do not want it to be used. Yes, we confirm that her legal name is, 'Mary Elizabeth Kettleby'. Clarence spoke, Betty nodded.

"That's the full name on the documents, so off we go", said the counselor.

As they stood by the bed and watched the nurse lift the baby girl, tears were running down their cheeks. The baby was handed to Betty. Within a matter of seconds she had to wipe another tear from her eyes. Clarence also brushed aside a tear as he placed his hands on the baby.

With one glance at the counselor, she nodded and said, "Yes. She is yours". Betty was so excited. "I thought the day would never come when I would hold my own baby. And now it has arrived. How do you feel, Daddy?"

Clarence found it difficult to speak. His new emotions were almost choking him. He did manage to whisper, "I feel absolutely wonderful, Mummy."

The nurse asked if the clothes she was wearing were suitable or would you like her to wear ones that you've brought with you?" "I would like to see her in these. Our own daughter in clothes specially bought for her". "It'll only take a couple of minute or so. Would you like to dress her after I have removed these"? "Yes. Just imagine, I am about to dress by little daughter by myself!"

Clarence was waiting. He had taken the camera out of his pocket. So the first sight of mother with daughter was caught on film, as they walked out of the nurse's office.

Betty said she wanted to carry her to the car and then place her in the carry cot. It was not a long procession. Yet both Mother and Father of Mary Elizabeth felt like royalty even there were no large crowds around to shout and wave. There inner emotions were still having an effect on the tear ducts.

The carry cot was firmly secured to the seat buckles and then they were off to their home. It was a happy journey. Giggles and laughs. Far too often one or other turned around to see their baby. Each time there was a loving comment reflecting their pleasure.

"This is a wonderful birth day" commented Betty."This the day our daughter was born to us".

The past few days had been spent preparing a room especially for their daughter. Naturally there was a predominance of the colour pink. But Clarence had made sure there were, a few places with a colour difference. From time to time on their journey one or the other would make a comment about the room specially prepared. Clarence even wondered if Mary Elizabeth might make a quick comment as to whether she liked the colours or otherwise. Betty suggested that they would have to wait some more months before they would hear their daughter's opinion.

As they turned the corner towards their home there was the surprise. Quite a number of cars were parked alongside the driveway and the road. Someone had been busy blowing up balloons. There were flags and bunting. It was a festal scene. Relatives had arrived immediately after Clarence and Betty had left. They had brought prepared food – they had no idea how many would come and want something to eat. The sight in the kitchen and on the dining room table indicated they were expecting quite a crowd.

It was a celebratory welcome home. There was a banner over the front door welcoming Mary Elizabeth. Grandparents rushed to the car with the hope of the privilege of carrying the baby into the house. To the surprise of everybody, Clarence called out quite loudly that he was the father and would be taking full responsibilities for her care and attention therefore he would take full responsibility in making sure that the baby girl did not get damaged in transit from car to the inside of the house. That caused a loud cheer. Eventually everyone was inside which included many of the neighbours.

Betty took Mary Elizabeth out of the carry cot and made her presentable and introduced her to all the people present. That took a long time because almost everyone wanted to hold her to make sure she was real.

The friends of the Kettleby's were so surprised at the joy being expressed on their faces. Everyone knew they had been waiting a long time for a baby. There had been many disappointments. False hope contributed to their frustration. But oh the mighty difference now they were real parents.

After a couple of days Clarence said to Betty that he had something very serious do discuss. "It is in connection with security. I want the future of our daughter to be safe from anyone who might want to challenge her origin. I am recommending that we change our surname".

"You are what?" responded Betty.

"For one thing I do not want Mary's birth patents searching for us and looking for their baby girl".

"I don't want them looking for us either".

"That's why I am advocating changing our name".

"Have you any suggestions?"

How about Stapleford?"

"Couldn't you have thought of a more classical name like, Buckingham?"

"Let's toss a coin. Head for Stapelford and tail for Buckingham".

"Okay. I spin the coin".

It landed with the head facing up.

"So. Stapleford it will be. I'll contact a friend who can help us with this. It is going to be important to do it as soon as possible. The other shock associated with this is a possible move".

"Why? Yes, or course, all the people around here will find it difficult to use our new name, I can see that. I still want to live in Mansfield. Let's go look around on the south side of the town, off the Nottingham Road".

"That's an excellent idea. "We'll go for a drive tomorrow".

Betty hung her head to one side. Howard was expecting a negative comment.

"I am concerned", she said, "As to what our parents and relatives will say".

"For sure they will not like it. They will probably never understand our reasoning".

And they didn't. They were considered absolutely crazy. The doctor must prescribe some strong medication to counteract such ridiculous ideas they stated as firmly as possible. The new parents did not want to remember the things mentioned by their parents and other family members and close friends.

The right legal person was found to deal with the name change; and it also meant changing the details relating to the adoption papers ready for the magistrate to legalize the adoption. He was able to see them later that week and took all the details. He hoped that it would not take too long. Actually he had no idea how long it would take.

They found a suitable home on a crescent off the Nottingham Road. The owners wanted a quick sale, so they accepted a reasonable price that was offered by Clarence and Betty. A moving-in day was decided; it was dependent upon the quick sale of their own house. They noticed a church nearby that had a great notice board announcing activities.

The next month was filled up with sorting, packing, throwing out, giving away, or things for the Thrift Shop.

It was an exciting day when they had to meet the Magistrate. Their legal friend informed them there was nothing to fear and that procedure would proceed favourably.

"You name has been legally changed," said the Magistrate, "You will no longer be known by the name of Kettleby, but Stapleford."

There were smiles all around.

"Then," he continued, "The adoption has been legalized. You daughter is just as if she had been born to you. Mr. and Mrs. Stapleford, this is your daughter Mary Elizabeth Stapleford".

Betty was convinced that she should soon visit the Registration office and change Mary's name on their records.

The days passed into weeks. Sometimes it seemed as if time went very slowly. On other occasions the time sped by so quickly. The parents were adjusting to the new regime. The baby was having, what the new parents thought were growing pains. In actual fact it was their parental duties and responsibilities that were suffering the growing pains.

They received excellent advice from both sets of grandparents. After all, they were speaking from past experiences. Words of wisdom were received and both father and mother benefited from the caring comments. They were still taking a moment to pause and reflect upon the fact that they were actually parents of the baby girl.

They knew there would be many decisions to make. It was great when they could shelve one by saying there will be time to deal with that one later. Both the mother and the father had day dreams as to what they would like their daughter to become. Then one or the other would bounce back to earth with the reality. Perhaps it was the baby daughter crying for a little attention.

She was a good baby, with a beautiful temperament. No sparks of anger. They commented many times how patient she was, especially when being introduced to something new.

Then came the big day. She took her first step. It was from her mother's knee towards the chair where her doll was resting. Daddy wanted her to bring the doll to him. She looked and thought, then looked again and decided that the doll was too heavy for her to carry to her father. But she wobbled her way towards his chair.

"She's growing up!" expressed her dad. "She's taking after me" said her mother, "I started to walk earlier than many other children my age".

Right from the first Sunday, Mary Elizabeth went to Sunday School with her parents. She was soon the 'doll' of the babies 'class'. When they changed to their new Church the same thing continued.

When it came to preparing for the Christmas programme there was no long debate as to which baby would be chosen to lie in the manger. She looked so sweet and innocent in the rough cradle. Just once there was a little whimper; that caused a smile on the ladies in the congregation.

Betty and Clarence went through all the traumas of children's sicknesses. Each one as it began was thought to be a dreaded disease, how relieved they were when the doctor or the nurse informed them that is was just a kid's sickness.

For one birthday Mary Elizabeth was given a tricycle. She didn't take long to master it. I think the parents and neighbours were pleased that no police patrol came down their street. The tricycle appeared to be breaking the speed limit. It was on one such occasion when she got to the end of the street and tried to turn the corner. She turned too quickly and the tricycle turned over. She ended up on the side of the road crying. Someone was soon there to lift her up. There was some concern when blood was seen from a few places. It was only natural that the rough road would cause some scratches. The bruises came out a couple of days later. The accident slowed her down. Mum and Dad were pleased about that.

As her confidence returned so her speed increased. Out came the rules and regulations for her. She must not bike down the street on the road. She must slow down at corners. Her parents tried to instill into her that she ought get off and walk around the corners. It was a new idea. It was a strange idea. It only worked about three times. Then she realized that it slowed her down too much so she remained on the bike and deliberately pedaled slower around any corner.

Betty and Clarence spent many an hour thinking about what to do or plan for their daughter's future. They had talked about school. The natural choice eventually would be Mansfield Girl's High School. The best in the county. But that was quite a few years ahead.

They did agree to make enquiries regarding the kindergarten at a nearby school. They liked what they saw so enrolled their daughter. Her time there indicated that she would be a bright scholar at least that is what her teachers told the parents. The pleasure given to the parents was that she really liked going to school, lied Betty.

CHAPTER 12

The elation that Adrian had brought to Howard and Dawn did not seem to subside. They had spent many hours planning the bedroom. Dawn made sure that everything was coordinated. Their choices were mutual. And when Adrian arrived he had a smile on his face. At least that is what his Dad said. His clothes were coordinated with the colour scheme of his bedroom.

There was a point of dissent that sparked serious discussion. They were in a Baby Shop looking at pictures one day. The supply of pictures that would bring a "wow" response seemed endless. Howard had a moment of wisdom. Dawn wasn't sure to call it that. But he maintained that it was the wisest moment that day.

Howard asked the question. That in itself was showing a wise approach. He walked over to a different part of the shop where there were more pictures. But these were not all of babies.

He was fascinated by one group that depicted children of various ages. There was a baby one, followed by an infant one. Then followed a series of pictures going through different stage groupings. He liked them. His comment to Dawn was that their son would not remain a baby for very long. He thought the stimulation of a boy doing something different at a different age would help him in his future choices of activity.

This proved to be an excellent choice. Because while he was still an infant he was looking at a picture of a boy playing baseball. Howard went into his room one day and saw him standing in front of the mirror waving his arms as if throwing a ball. Something similar happened a few days later when Dawn went into his room.

Both mother and father agreed that the choice of pictures was inspirational.

Adrian had not been home from the hospital very long before his parents realized that he was trying to take control. It was a difficult exercise for Dawn and Howard; they did not want to frustrate his development. But Howard insisted that it would not be in the best interest to either parent's future unless some discipline could be introduced. It was hard to start with because they appeared to be quite negative. Dawn admitted she did not want to hurt the baby's feelings though she knew something must be done otherwise it would be a negative reflection on their love for their child. Love means discipline.

That was a phrase they had heard when attending a conference of parenting organized by their church. Both mother and father agreed that love was to dominate any decision made on behalf of their son. When they said,"no", it was usually followed by a hug and a kiss, and the introduction of a positive alternative.

Adrian's time in Kindergarten or as it was known in his day an 'infant school' did not show any particular interest in any one subject. His comment to his parents on one occasion was "they are just little kids".

He didn't say much about the teachers except that there were two he really liked more than the others. "And why was that"? Thought his parents. They did not place any pressure on him to do things they knew he did not like. They found areas that were of interest to him instead.

Towards the end of his last year at that school he would occasionally comment about what it would be like in the bigger school. Infant school for him wasn't school it was where time was used up playing with other kids. But it was a beginning for him in choosing play mates. Friends became important for him even at that early age. He was so happy that he and two or three of his friends would be going to the same school.

Dawn and Howard found it interesting that his close friends were not all boys. He made a comment about it one day, 'Most of the girls are wimps, I don't know what it means, but they are wimps!

The girls who were part of his friendship circle were not tom-boys. They were girl girls. They all were able to relate to each other and take part in their discussions and in their games.

It was an important day for Adrian when his mother took him to the junior school. There were a bunch of new kids all with a parent or grandparent. They all had to register. Then they were told which classroom to go to.

His first day at the new school was an orientation. Getting to the areas where it was possible to go, and those places where entrance was forbidden. It wasn't long before such a forbidden place had an attraction. Curiosity took control. When he thought no one was looking he opened the door. He had quite a shock. That was exaggerated when he left other kids close to him also wanting to know what was inside. It happened to be one of the teachers' rooms. He had chosen the moment when the ladies were changing from their outdoor clothes. He was marched off to the head mistress for scolding. He never went to that room again.

He hoped that no report would be sent to his parents; what would they say? What would they do? No report was sent; and the incident was not reported on at a parent-teacher meeting.

Adrian settled quite easily into his new school. It was not a new building both his mother and his father had attended that school.

The picture on his bedroom wall that was drawing his attention was of a boy playing soccer. Soccer became his main leisure activity. Whenever possible he enjoyed watching a professional soccer game on the television. He was particularly fascinated by those who were wingers. Their speed and dribbling skills were not only a pleasure to watch but something to emulate.

He would turn his bedroom into a soccer stadium. He would dribble the ball, then look to the left and then to the right and wave his hand to the people in the crowd. He would hear their enthusiastic shouts as he dribbled across the bedroom floor.

Each class at school had a team. He was chosen and asked about what position he would like. He had made it his position because he was learning how to dribble and cross the ball into the goal area. The coach soon recognized the skill he was developing and showed him how to do various moves. Then the coach was amazed because when he crossed the ball when near the corner he would kick it with his right foot, but if he had to back up the field a little then he would centre it with his left foot.

These skills were noted by other teachers. It wasn't very long before he was asked to join the group for special practice sessions. The school team would be chosen from that group.

It was not a surprise to anyone that Adrian was chosen. Every class had heard about him. And the coach for the school team had watched him often. He became the hero of the school on many occasions. He himself did not score very many goals but he made it possible for those players in the centre had a good chance to shoot and score.

CHAPTER 13

Betty and Clarence wondered just when the new and exciting events might come to an end. Adriana, or Mary Elizabeth, did so well in the early years of school. Her teacher would be filled with superlatives each year. She was progressing marvelously through the various subjects.

The last comment was that Mary Elizabeth should continue in the dancing classes because she is so nimble on her feet and has quite a rewarding sense of balance. Then the teachers added, "You should consider finding a qualified music teacher for her".

Neither Betty nor Clarence had thought of their daughter as being musical. It was the teacher that said what a wonderful voice she had. It needs to be developed by a professional instructor.

Clarence asked, "How many parents do you tell the same thing?"

Her reply was that this time it's the truth!

They had an interesting conversation with the teacher. They were so delighted that their daughter seemed to be progressing at every level.

"But, does she like singing", Betty asked. She knew the answer because every few steps from one room to another could not be navigated without some song streaming from her lips.

That even they had an interesting time speculating as to what their daughter would become. A professional dancer. An opera singer. Or an academic.

Clarence made a typical fatherly comment, "Whichever it is it'll be expensive!".

Mary Elizabeth was comfortably settled at the Mansfield High School for Girls. The parents could not have chosen a better school for their talented daughter. Each year the teachers would indicate that their daughter was in the best school. This one is highly suitable to her skills and abilities.

There was one day when her mother picked her up from school. She was crying, or had been crying. When her mother asked the cause for the tears, she just shrugged her shoulders and said that some other girls had been laughing at her.

They did not say more. But when they arrived home Betty took her daughter and they sat on the sofa where they could sit close to each other.

"Tell me sweetheart. What were the other girls saying to you?"

"It was after our PT class and we were in the shower. One of girls starting laughing and looking at me, then another one poked me and also started to laugh."

"What were they laughing at, sweetheart?"

"They said it looked as if someone had started to do a tattoo on my bottom. Why would they think that, mummy?"

"Cuddle up closer. It is not a tattoo. It is a scar. We'll go in the bathroom shortly and I will describe it to you, in fact we'll get a mirror so you can see it for yourself".

"But why is there a scar there. Did I fall or have an accident?"

"Let's go in to the bathroom".

They went together hand in hand. Take some of your clothes off, especially your panties and lift up your dress,

"I can't see anything", she said trying to twist around.

Her mother produced a mirror and carefully but slowly turned the mirror until the scar was visible in the large bathroom mirror.

"What's that?" she said. "When did that happen?"

The mother sat on the bathroom stool and took her daughter on to her knee. This was one of those times that she had dreaded would come. "How am I going to answer her?" she thought.

"When you were very tiny, in fact you were only a few days old; a very little tiny baby. The doctor informed us that they had to perform a special operation. It was northing very serious he suggested. But it left a scar that was larger than they had hoped.

"What can I do about it?"

"There is nothing that could be done, while you were still quite tiny, they tried later it but gave up because it didn't work. The doctor told your father and me that it would become less obvious as you grew older".

"How much older?"

"The doctor did not go into such details; he just assured us that you would be alright. The scar is nothing to worry about. What you can say to the others in the shower next time is that while you were a very small baby you had to have surgery. Hence the scar."

"Do you think that will stop them making fun …?"

"If not then we must ask the teachers to give a more satisfying answer".

Mary Elizabeth had just finished dressing again when her father arrived. He was his usual self. His first call was to find out where his little daughter was hiding. She wasn't hiding. She appeared at the bathroom door just as her father started up the stairs.

"Oh. Have you been cleaning yourself up so that you look more sweet and gorgeous?"

"Daddy, I don't have to wash my face just to make me look sweet and gorgeous! Aren't I like that all the time?"

"Not when you are asleep and having a nasty dream!"

"Well, then, when I am normal?"

"Yes, my sweaty pie." And with that she jumped up into his open arms and had her usually hugs and kisses.

Her cheeks were a little damp. "Have you been crying, sweaty?"

"No. I mean, yes".

Betty came out of her room and rescued the situation. "We have been having an important conversation".

"Was it so important that it made her cry?"

"No. She had been crying and that initiated the talk I had to give her". Clarence had a large question on his face.

Betty smiled at him and mentioned that the scar had been brought to their daughter's attention in the shower after the PT class. Some girls wanted to know what it was; others teased her that it was a funny tattoo. So, I have just finished explaining the scar as the doctor informed us.

She seemed satisfied. A couple of days later there was another PT class. She was a little hesitant in taking off her clothes. The teacher noticed her but said nothing. She watched carefully. When Mary Elizabeth entered the showers some of the girls were ready to tease her about the funny thing on her bum. The teacher heard her say that it is a scar from surgery when she was a very tiny baby.

Later the teacher asked her for more details. "My mother just told me that the doctor had to perform surgery soon after I was born, and that he was disappointed that the scar was larger than he anticipated".

"Were the girls bullying you?"

"I don't think so", she replied. "Because today I was able to tell them what it was; but I could not answer all their questions".

"I'll see if I can answer some of their question in the next class we have together".

The various positive comments made by their daughter's teachers gave Betty and Clarence a lot to think about.

Those comments made the parents feel so proud. And they thanked God for allowing them to have her in their family. And alongside the thankfulness was the petition that they would be worthy parents, and that they would be given wisdom for every decision that came their way.

It was no surprise to them that she came home one day shaking with excitement; she had been cast as the leading role in the school drama that year.

So, what is the drama, asked her mother. "The Importance of Being Earnest", was her reply. "Aren't there two leading ladies in that play", stated her father. "Yes, daddy, but I'm the one who gets to kiss the real Earnest!"

"And why is that so important", retorted Clarence, with a large twinkle in his eye.

She named the boy. His name had been mentioned in connection with quite a few of her extracurricular activities.

He turned to Betty and said, "Is it time for you to give your daughter a little talk on how to be a young woman in the presence of cute boys".

Mary Elizabeth was probably the best liked girl in the school. As an aside comment, there were times when new students would ask about her as to who she was and why she was so popular. It was almost a standard reply, "Oh, she's our girl with a scar on her bum!" It wasn't just her skills and talents but her open and honest personality that caught the attention of other students and the staff.

The school prided itself with its record of netball trophies. The coach made sure that from her second year in the school that she would be his first choice for the school team.

That coach had one rival teacher. That was the coach for the soccer team. The two coaches made sure that their teams were not playing on the same day; otherwise there would be a riot as to which team claimed her services.

There was one other activity that attracted Mary Elizabeth's attention. That was one specific item on the Volunteers list. A group of volunteers from the school went to the local hospital once a week and volunteered on the children's ward. She always had a sad or traumatic story to tell her parents. Some evening it was as if there was no other topic for discussion.

Betty expressed some concern to Clarence as to the object of the volunteer duties.

Mary Elizabeth's comment was that she was being careful as to how involved she was being with some of the kids requiring a lot of attention.

"I do want to continue because those kids need me. I don't mean that I am indispensable to them. They respond in a very appreciative way. It's as if they know I am trying to understand their plight. I am sure that Jesus wants me to do this".

After a few moments silence she then informed her parents."I do not want to be a nurse. I would not be comfortable having to deal with all the smelly duties that children give to nurses".

There was a sigh of relief from Betty and Clarence. They did not want another possible area of training and work for their daughter. But if that was her main desire then they would have done everything possible to help her in that direction.

As that day for the performance got closer so did the hospital visits become less. A few times she came home after a rehearsal totally exhausted. She seemed on the point of quitting. But after a cup of tea and a rest she was fired up and was soon her usual self.

It was the day of the performance. Betty and Clarence where about to find out about 'The Importance Of Being Earnest'. They had obtained tickets early so they had excellent seats. It was a full house. The demands for tickets had been so good it was decided to have two nights.

There were laughs, in the right place of course. And pregnant silences as the two girls faced the two boys. Most of the audience didn't know which boy would end up with which girl. It was an attractive foursome. The inter-relationships were superb.

Clarence and Betty shuddered a few times when one of the boys got very close to their daughter. His arm was around her waist. He pushed his shoulder close to hers. Everyone in the audience presumed he was asking for a kiss. He was pushed away. The inter-play of characters was wonderful. These four had practiced seriously for a long time. They had mastered their individual parts, and of course knew the parts of the other three.

And Mary Elizabeth got her man. She got the real Earnest. She was seen trying to evade a little blush.

There was a standing ovation and a few curtain calls at the end of a successful presentation of a fascinating drama.

Even in the midst of all the interesting and exciting activities there were times for concentrated study. Some of the subjects appeared quite easy for Mary Elizabeth, but there were one of two that demanded more of her time. She had a good mental approach to her studies. She didn't shelve the ones that were not too, interesting. She didn't shun the ones she had to spend energy and time grappling with. Her work ethic was wonderful. The teachers encouraged her because they saw a tremendous future ahead of her academically.

CHAPTER 14

Adrian progressed through Kindergarten and Infant School with no problems. None were anticipated because he was always ready to go to school. In fact the first sign of impatience was the month leading up to his 'going to school'.

Dawn and Howard were stretched in finding things to occupy their son until he was old enough to go to kindergarten.

He enjoyed being with the other kids, but he seemed a little irritated some days when he came home. His mother asked a few questions. Eventually he said that he thought he was bored with the lessons.

At the next parent/teacher session, Dawn spoke up. "Adrian seems bored some days. Any ideas?"

"He seems to understand the lesson even before I have finished speaking the first sentence", she smiled. Both Mother and Father had to laugh.

The teacher indicated that it was nothing to be concerned about because she would give him a few things to do as 'homework'.

"Surely not, at his age!, was the comment from Howard.

"No, it will not be a heavy load but a few simple things for him to search out and find for me".

Adrian just could not wait for the time to go to the other school.

His teachers had similar thing to say about him automatically being ahead even before the lessons had finished.

"He'll be an academic", one teacher said.

It was the sports Master who informed his parents of his prowess on the soccer field. "He plays well at Rugby, but I think he prefers Soccer".

Soccer was Howard's game at school so he asked what position his son played best in.

"He is an excellent centre-half. If he had any preference I think he would choose to play left-wing".

Adrian was in the school soccer team for most of his time at that school.

He arrived home one day not as joyful as his usual self. Mother, of course, had to ask why no smiles. Eventually he asked, "How much longer do I have to stay with the infants, at least many of them appear as such, at that school?"

It wasn't very long before that that his parents had received a letter to say that he had been accepted in to the Manchester Boys Grammar School. That was a prestigious school. His acceptance was not based on his success on the soccer field.

"Academically we think he is above average for his age; he'll do well at our school". It was another teacher who was standing by heard this and apologized for interrupting. "And we need him in our soccer team!" There was a good laugh from the teachers and also his parents.

So, even Howard and Dawn were patiently waiting for the transfer to the big school. It was a wonderful day when Adrian arrived home celebrating that he had just finished school. "Well, at least that one!"

He enjoyed the summer vacation as he had previous summers. Swimming seemed to be the top pastime. But he enjoyed other summer activities also.

He was a good swimmer. In competitions he usually did quite well. Diving he liked but his feet always made too big a splash.

That summer he was asked to join a small team to train in emergency rescue procedures. His parents thought that he was too young for such responsibility. On speaking to the swimming instructor he informed them that Adrian would only be used for the smaller children.

It was a good summer. Adrian enjoyed his duties as Guard, he always took them seriously. He was totally alert, especially when smaller children seemed to be around with no adult supervision. It was one day when he was making such a comment to himself when he heard a shout. It was not a typical kid shouting. This was more serious. He stood tall on his elevated position and saw a lot of splashing not too far away but it appeared to be coming from a child not tall enough for the deep water.

He was down from the sand in one jump and sprinting to the edge of the water. No one seemed to be helping the child, even though many were looking in his direction and wondering why he was making such a lot of noise. Adrian knew. He was a strong swimmer and reached the boy quickly but not before he had stopped splashing and was under the water.

The water was clear so he had no difficulty seeing the child and went under quickly and brought him to the surface. He started spluttering. That was a good sign. Adrian grabbed him with one arm and swam back to the shore. Other people had gathered to watch. He was able to stretch the boy on the sand and as he coughed, some fluid came up. It was not long before the boy stopped coughing and gave Adrian a big smile. The smile went to the full extent of his mouth. He jumped up off the sand and gave his rescuer a big hug.

A few moments later a man and woman came running up. They shouted at the boy and threatened him with a beating for causing so much trouble. "You might have drowned", the mother said. "But he didn't" added the father.

They were walking away with their son when someone in the crowd shouted after them. "Are you not going to say 'thank you' to the young man who rescued your son?"

"Oh, it probably was not necessary; our son often makes a lot of splashing when he comes here".

"It was necessary", someone added "Your son was already under the water and out of his depth. He was drowning".

"So?" grunted the father.

"Yes, so", another spectator added, "You would probably be pleased if your son had drowned. You ungrateful son of a b …!'

Adrian stepped up. Walked towards the parents and said, "It was my turn to be on guard duty and nothing pleases me more than to see your son alive and kicking. Keep an eye on him. I may not be around next time".

Both the mother and father turned and scowled at Adrian. But there were no signs of gratitude for what Adrian had done. The crowd gave a tremendously loud cheer. Adrian walked back to his post followed by some appreciative supporters.

CHAPTER 15

It seems as if a whole bunch of boys from a nearby boys' school were constantly looking at the girls from Mansfield High. A lot of dates were booked and relationships broken. But there was one girl that no fellow had been able to have a date with. Mary Elizabeth Stapleford was not really interested in boyfriends so would always politely say "No" to requests for a date.

The local boys decided to set up a gamble as to who would have a first date with Mary Elizabeth. Week after week their heads nodded negatively. But they wouldn't give up.

Trevor, one of the boys from that group was in the same youth group as Mary Elizabeth at their church. So they knew each other and often sat chatting with a couple of other couples. One evening the leader announced an upcoming Youth Rally in Nottingham, and asked if any thought they might like to attend. Two hands went up from different sides of the room. Mary Elizabeth was one, the other was Trevor. The leader called both of them after the meeting to see how serious they were about going to Nottingham. Mary Elizabeth mentioned that she wound need to get her parents to take her. Trevor mentioned that he would be driving and she could travel with him if her parents agreed.

There were still three days before the youth Rally. Mary Elizabeth was becoming more interested in what the talks would be about. Trevor could hardly contain himself because he classed this as being a date with the allusive girl from Mansfield High.

Trevor picked her up from home and her parents made some suitable comments to them both and prayed that they would have an inspiring time. It was a well attended Rally.

Youth from various places around the city were there. The singing groups were wonderful. The talks were interesting, lively and informative. They both indicated that it had been an enjoyable evening.

On the way home Trevor slowed down and turned off the main road for about forty yards and stopped. Mary Elizabeth was wondering 'why?' Trevor mentioned that he wanted a short rest from driving and wanted to have a nice talk with her. His talking with her very soon led into him pushing closer to her and drawing her close to him for a hug and a kiss. She was surprised. It felt something of what she thought was a genuine interest. After four or five kisses he reached over and commenced undoing buttons of her coat. "Why?" she thought. He seemed a little uncomfortable but continued moving his hand around her dress and began to lift it up. She moved away from him and asked what he was doing. "This is what happens when couples go on a date", he said. With that his hand went where she knew it ought not to go. She immediately grasped the handle of the door, opened it and said emphatically, "If others do that, I do not", indicating her disgust.

She was out of the car and ran back to the main road and started walking towards home, which she knew was quite a few miles away. Her hair was a mess and she was crying as she walked along. She dreaded Trevor coming after her in the car.

The car that came up behind her was not Trevor's. It slowed down and passed by, then stopped in front of her. It was a Policy Car. "What are you doing out here alone?" a police officer asked her. She could not give him a rational answer because the tears came on stronger. The two officers spoke to each other and recognized that this girl was in distress of some sort. "Has someone abused you, young lady?". She gave a negative nod. "We want to help you". Just then Trevor's car passed and he hooted his horn, then he was very embarrassed when he realized he was passing a Police Car.

"Do you know who that was?" She nodded positively, and commenced shaking. One of the officers had been on the phone to someone and they decided to ask her to get into the car and they would take her home.

The car stopped outside the house and her father saw it and quickly went to the door. As he opened it, his daughter was being helped out of the car. The two Policemen went into the house with her and mentioned what had happened and why they had brought her home. They had to write up a report. Mary Elizabeth was settling down and no more tears, her mother was comforting her as they sat together on the settee.

The police did not stay very long but as they left they did tell May Elizabeth that if she wanted to make a charge about anything then she must contact them as soon as possible.

Her parents wanted to know the whole story. She told them. But when it came to the point where the car slowed down and turned off the road, she hesitated. Both parents had a big question on the faces. She then described about the hug and the kisses which she did not enjoy all that much. Then after a pause mentioned how Trevor played with her buttons and dress. "Do you know what he said", she asked her parents. He said, "This is what they all do when on a date!" It was then I quickly got out of the car telling him it was something that was not going to happen there.

Her mother got something for her to eat and drink, then after a time of prayer was tucked up in bed. The next morning she was alright though still in a little shock as to what happened in the car. Her father left no stone unturned until he informed the group leader at the Church what had happened on the way home from the Youth Rally.

She was to pluck up courage to go to school. She was sure that rumours will have circulated about the in-car incident. It was a pleasant surprise there was not one word mentioned about it; in fact no one asked her about the Youth Rally. She was soon settled into her usual routine and her happy disposition returned.

It was Youth Group night, and Mary Elizabeth was somewhat concerned and reluctant about going. Her father asked her about her hesitation. All she would say, "In the car". He took her hands and gave her a big hug and at the same time said, "If you do not go, then Satan won". "Satan did not win", was her retort, "And he is not going to win".

"See you later", she shouted to her mother and father. Off she went to the Church building. She did pause for a moment at the door but then was encouraged by an inward voice, "You are here, go right in, everything will be fine". She went in and her friends were the same as usual. No scandalous innuendoes about the car incident.

There were some genuine questions about the Rally, but none at all about the journey there and back. After the general socializing time they went into a formal setting for the usual talk. She glanced around; there was no sign of Trevor. It was not her intention to keep looking for him, so she was careful when glancing around to make sure she was looking for someone else. Trevor did not show up to the Youth Group, in fact he was not seen again at any of the meetings at the Church.

There was the usual pressure facing all the students as they entered the last two years of school. Mary Elizabeth was wondering if she should give up some of her extracurricular activities. If so, then she couldn't decide; so she made no decision because she enjoyed them all and they did not take up too much of her time. At least that was the way she saw it.

Music was part of the curriculum, so they included her piano and singing. She thought that perhaps dancing could be put to one side for a year or two. That was until her instructor suspected she might be leading up to saying it to her. "You are a natural", she said. Her comments to other instructors and teachers were that she was the best the school had had in over a decade. "You can handle it alright", was her comment. Drama would be coming up. One of the teachers had written a new work especially for the school. He actually wrote one part with Mary Elizabeth in mind. When there seemed a little hesitation from her the teacher smiled and with the comment said, "It was written just for you!" "You can't be serious", was her reply. His chuckle and wagging head told her he was serious. Then there was soccer. "At least it is not for the whole year", she thought. The coach took her thoughts much further by stating that the team could not win without her. "No one is that indispensable", was her critical reply. He assured her that it was her goals that placed the school as one of the top schools for many miles around.

She was faced with the serious decision. Her inward deliberations were bombarded with the beliefs and desires of teachers, coaches and other players. She could not drop anything. There was a serious short prayer for God to give her the extra energy and wisdom.

It was the beginning of the month when the annual dance performance would be scheduled. The Instructor informed the dance troupe that there would be two extra sessions for the following couple of weeks in preparation for the performance. That brought a sigh from the dancers; they were already over-taxed, according to their parents. But they all took in deep breaths and assured the Instructor that they would be at their best by the end of the month.

It was the second week of the extra sessions. The rehearsal was going well. Mary Elizabeth had a wonderful partner, a strong young man a few inches taller than her. He was an excellent lifter and dancer. The dance was nearing its climax when the man caught his foot on something on the stage and tripped. It was when she was at the highest point of the lift. She went crashing down to the floor. The only movements she made were with the pain from her ankle. The Instructor came quickly and did not think there was a fracture, but she could not stand on that leg.

That was the end of that session. The Instructor mentioned to Mary Elizabeth that he would be taking her to the hospital for an x-ray. The secretary in the office would be phoning her mother. There was a wheel chair available so she was wheeled to his car, and off they went. He drove directly to the emergency entrance. A wheelchair was available so he pushed her to triage. They had to wait for a doctor who immediately sent her for x-rays. It was a long wait after the x-rays until the doctor came again. On reading the results he had pleasure in informing her that there was no fracture but a very serious sprain. "Do no more dancing, young lady. Oh, and by the way I understand you are a star soccer player; there will be no more soccer this year for you". She wanted to say 'thank you' but it did not sound genuine. She did express gratitude just to be polite.

Her mother had arrived and waited with her and the Instructor. He was dismayed at the terrible news of no more dancing for his star performer.

The young man who tripped and dropped her was not injured, but when he heard the news he was devastated and took all the blame. The caretaker at the school examined the stage floor and found one board that was not fitting tightly. That must have put the dancer off his steps. Even so that young man could not get over the fact that Mary Elizabeth would not be dancing with him again.

They used the wheelchair to go to the car park; her mother's car was suitable for her so the Instructor lifted her into the car. He said that he would be in touch with the family to express his concern and the disappointment the school would be experiencing without Mary Elizabeth performing.

After a couple of weeks with no walking she was able to use a walker to go back to classes. It was only natural that she was surrounded by her friends and especially the dance troupe. She told them that she fully intended to be at the performance and was interested to know who would be taking her part. It was one of her very best friends, so she was happy.

Her accident didn't just affect the dancing but also the drama. The writer had written a part especially for Mary Elizabeth, which she now was not able to take because it involved quite a bit of walking around the stage. Not to be deterred, he did some re-writing. There was a slight change to her character but nothing major, he had her seated for the whole show. He was pleased because she was quite excited about the character she was to be. It also meant she had few new lines to learn. The other actors had to redirect their movements in order for the development of the story to make sense. .

The soccer coach was almost in tears when he heard about the accident. His top scoring forward was not available for the inter-schools competition. She stated quite emphatically that she would not miss one of the matches and would be on the sideline shouting and waving the school flag.

There was an announcement in Church one Sunday morning regarding the visit of a special speaker who would be giving inspirational talks over one weekend. Mary Elizabeth asked her parents about the visitor. They remember a previous visit he made to their Church about five years or so earlier.

"What was he like and what did he talk about?" she asked her parents.

"We did not go to all the sessions but the ones we remember seemed very good" her mother answered. "I hope he will publish a list of his topics because I am not going to have the time to go to all his sessions".

"The last time he came he did have a list of his subjects. There was an inset in the Sunday Bulletin", her father said.

It was two weeks later, during the last term of school, when the list of topics was inserted into the Bulletin. Mary Elizabeth appeared to be interested in most of them, but she had already decided that she might only be able to attend a couple of them. One was on the Saturday evening and was primarily for teenagers.

"Does God really expect us to be holy?"

"I think I'll go to that one because I cannot see God demanding holiness in everything, so it will be interesting to find out what he has to say?" That was a thought she did not express to anyone but was the challenge to her prayer preparation for the Saturday evening session for the teens.

The speaker was a cute looking pastor probably in his early thirties. His attitude enabled the kids to relax because it was anticipated that he might be touching on some personal and intimate ideas. He made it very clear at the beginning of his speech, after a very good joke; that he hoped the topics would not come as a shock.

"Why did he say that?" thought most of the teenagers present. He must have expected a question like that because he immediately stated very firmly that he was sure not very many church leaders talk so openly and pointedly as he was going to do.

The young people were not embarrassed like some of the older members would have been. But they were surprised when he got down to specific details. He made sure that the kids were listening mainly because they did not expect a pastor to be saying such intimate things.

He was stressing the ways in which relationships begin. He made his audience aware that he knew what goes on between a fellow and a girl. He was quite descriptive regarding the kissing and the petting. There were a lot of chuckles around the room, most from those who were being challenged by the details he was describing.

He then moved from behind the desk and sat on the corner of the table. He was relaxed. The audience was waiting for him to go on with the development of relationships. But he came up with some crazy joke that received more of a negative response that a positive one. That did not faze him, he probably expected it. But it brought an ease into the atmosphere.

"Now what do you do when your mind is racing ahead and the voice of the world is telling you to go ahead with your desires because everyone else is doing it." He paused. Some of the young peopled gave an embarrassing shuffle.

"At that point how many of you stop and ask God for guidance regarding any next step?" He followed that with a pause. The silence was speaking quite loudly to some of the kids present.

"God has already given His answer to you. There ought not to be any dilemma regarding his answer. Neither should there be any doubt regarding the future possibilities of your petting".

He had convincing answers to the question he himself raised. His audience was indeed deep in thought, some quite positively and others very negatively.

"Our Heavenly Father has made it very clear that the intimacies of love making are to be reserved for the honeymoon. There is to be no sexual intercourse before marriage challenge to each one of you is along those lines. Are you willing to remain pure until you are able to express yourself more intimately with your husband or with your wife?

"Each one of you has answered that challenge. I am not about to embarrass you by asking for an open response in front of everyone else. But during the silence of a moment's prayer time I want you to tell God about your promise or even your unwillingness. You see, my friends, God wants you to be holy, in everything".

There followed a period of silence and then the speaker closed with a suitable prayer that would help those making important promises.

There was quite a lot of interesting chatter between friends as they left the meeting.

"We didn't expect to hear anything like that in our church". "That's too hard – it is ridiculous". "After all, my friend would say that they are doing what comes naturally." "Nobody expects to be like that in these enlightened times." "It is something we should give serious thought to". "It would be good if everyone in that meeting made it a point of prayer". "It's not for us!"

There were those who later that evening in their personal devotion made the promise to remain pure until marriage. Mary Elizabeth had tears running down her cheeks. They were tears of happiness at the decision she intended to keep.

In her final year she was sorry that the dancing was out for her. But she practiced with the soccer players. The coach had indicated that she would not be able to carry on as a forward. Her swiftness and skills with the ball would be missed. There was no way she could have been fast enough to measure up to her personal standard. The coach suggested that perhaps she would be helpful in midfield. So she practiced with that position in mind.

It came time for the first match against one of the rival schools. The opponents were surprised at a new player up front as a forward. They were even more surprised when they saw her midfield. It didn't take them long to find out the reason. She was much slower even though her passing was accurate and challenging. Each time she shot the ball ahead for the centre forward she saw herself chasing it. The forward was not as fast as she used to be. The opposition defense players were soon surrounding her and she lost possession many times. She put her tiredness down to frustration and not the loss of her energy.

At half time she had a word with the coach to say how frustrated she was, but also that her ankle was giving her some pain. "I don't think I can go out for the second half", she said almost with tears in her eyes. The coach reluctantly agreed. He did not want her to go out and seriously injure her healing ankle. She was a verbal encourager during the second half. The result was a draw; every supporter agreed that they should have won; indeed they would have won if their skillful centre forward had not been injured.

The term ended with speeches and presentations. No one was surprised that Mary Elizabeth received accolades for her scholastic abilities and also her sport activities and other extra-curricular activities. One of the teachers mentioned her Christian character and personal devotion to God that had been evidenced throughout her time at the school. It was a great year for her.

CHAPTER 16

There were many imaginative situations as Adrian anticipated going to the big school the following term. His parents were delighted that their son would be going to the prestigious Manchester Boys Grammar School. Howard had a little concern regarding finance because it would be quite costly for that School. Dawn said that she knew there would be no need to worry, because God would take care of the necessary expenses if that is where He wanted their son attending.

A couple of weeks later, Howard arrived home from work. He was almost out of breath, if such is possible driving a car. He went through the usual 'welcome home' procedures. But Dawn wondered why the elation, and was about to ask him when their son came barging in for the usual 'Hello' plus whatever he thought up to show how pleased he was to see his dad.

Dawn said, "Well, what is it?" "What is what?" Howard replied, with a great grin on his face. "Perhaps we should all sit down". That sounded as if it would not be good news.

Wife and son were all ears. "I have some excellent good news but it will be followed by something that may not go down quite so well". "Tell us the good news, Daddy".

"I have received a promotion …" "That's great", was the interruption; it was a chorus from wife and son. "I will be elevated to another office at the beginning of next month". Dawn and Adrian were so pleased for Howard. The small talk centred on the future prospects for quite a number of minutes. Then Howard said, "But there is more". The chatter stopped.

Adrian was interested to know what more was involved. Dawn was anxious because she noted that Howard's smile had faded a little. ""What is it, Darling?" she asked. "It will necessitate a move." "Won't you be able to commute like other people?"

"Not really, that would be very inconvenient". "Where will we move to?" enquired Adrian. With a smile and hug for Adrian he looked directly at Dawn and with a positive nod which she thought indicated a pleasure about the move, "To Manchester." "That's absolutely wonderful, Daddy, because that's where I'll be going to school".

"Is it a certainty that we move to Manchester?" asked Dawn. "Yes, because my promotion takes me to a new office where I'll be heading-up a new project." "When do we start thinking about such a move?" "Fairly soon. Because we ought to be settled in before the beginning of Adrian's first term". "That doesn't give us much time to sort out and pack, never mind looking for a new house. Where in Manchester do you think we should live?" "There are some very nice houses in Chorlton-cum-hardy". "That's a funny name for my new address", was Adrian's retort. "At least we will not be living in the busy down town area. It is quite easy to get into the city from there and I don't think it will be too difficult to get to the School".

"We need to contact an agent quite quickly to get this house on the market and someone looking out for a suitable place for us to move into", was Dawn's practical advice. She was already thinking ahead about the tremendous upheaval this was going to bring. They had felt firmly established in a nice house and pleasant location. "There will be something nice to go to, I'm sure" she thought.

Their regular routine changed dramatically. Dawn organized one place for things not needed, which indicated if it was for the garbage or the second-hand shop.

That weekend they drove into Manchester. They saw the place where Howard would be working. They drove around to see the School. Then drove over to Chorlton and explored the residential areas. They liked what they saw. They passed by some interesting looking churches with informative Notice Boards outside.

It was a challenging time. But they were confident that God would see them through it.

Howard and Dawn had spoken to a house-agent, a price had been agreed and the listing published. The agent suggested that two or three 'open houses' would attract buyers. So dates were set. This meant the house had to be tidy on those days. "How on earth do we sort and pack and keep the house tidy all at the same time", mused Dawn.

Adrian was fired up for a great change. He had thrown out many of the things he had grown out of, but also those things that reminded him of being in a junior school. He wouldn't need those in the Grammar School.

Howard was being challenged closing up his local office and deciding what was essential to take with him to the new office.

They heard from an agent in Manchester to say that he had three houses he wanted to show them in Chorlton-cum-Hardy. Howard made a phone call and it was decided that they would go to see them on Saturday. The agent wanted them on the Sunday, but Howard said that such would not fit in their plans or their regular church attendance.

All three were excited when Saturday morning dawned. There were the regular chores to be done, and then they were on their way to Chorlton (they had already decided that they would drop the other two words when talking about where they might be living). It was not a very long drive, but Adrian let it be known that it was taking too long! That sentiment of impatience could have been applied to three occupants in the car.

The Agent was waiting for them. They transferred into his car and off they went. His comments while driving were centred on the prices which he considered to be reasonable for the greater Manchester area. They were within the range that Howard had suggested; two of them had two bedrooms and the other was a three bedroom. Howard mused on that one as perhaps being suitable for an office.

CHAPTER

Excitement was growing by the day for Adrian. He wasn't sure whether the new house or the new school was uppermost for his excitement. Both were important steps for him to be taking.

Dawn and Howard were at the stage when the move was not an easy step to be taking. They had chosen the three-bedroom and a family conference had decided who would have the other two rooms. The master suite was not an option the occupants for that room had been securely decided.

It was the other two rooms. Howard had given the choice to Adrian. One had the window looking out to the streets at the front. The other was at the back. Adrian spent quite a time making such a major decision. When he mentioned that to his parents they had a good laugh as they acknowledged their son making such a 'major' decision.

He came to the conclusion that it would be less of a distraction if he had the back room. That was his choice. He sarcastically commented, "It's nearer to the bathroom!"

One morning Adrian awoke and he did not seem as cheerful as usual. He had been dreaming, even though he could not remember the details the dreams had left an impression. He didn't feel so happy because making this move was not such a happy occasion after all. The 'new' ahead was definitely a situation to be enjoyed. But what was hitting him now was that he would be leaving everything that was familiar. He did not welcome the moment when he would be saying farewell to his friends. He had so many really good friends living within a few streets. He was missing them now even before actually leaving the area.

Howard and Dawn were having mixed emotions about the move. They too were not looking forward to leaving their friends, yet at the same time loomed the prospects of something quite new. It would be an adventure.

Friends didn't help because most of them said, "We don't know what we will do without you". Some people know how to cheer people up when they needed encouragement. Adrian's friends insisted that they would come and visit him some Saturday.

The "FOR SALE" sign had been up for a couple of weeks. One viewing couple indicated that it was just the house they were looking for. They put in an offer there and then. After a little adjusting to the price it was mutually agreed and the papers signed accordingly.

The day for moving had arrived. The Removal Van arrived quite early and the men were ready to start moving things out. They never did enjoy their usual breakfast. There was too much activity, especially when it was time to remove the furniture from the downstairs rooms.

It must have been about mid-day when they closed up the van and said they would see us in Chorlton. A few minutes later, with personal things already in the car, there was a tear of sadness. Howard said a prayer for blessing and safety in the travelling and moving, and also a blessing for the new owners that they would find the presence of the Lord in that house as they made it their home.

Quite a lot of the neighbours were outside waving. The windows of the car were open so greetings and good wishes could be shouted easily. Then, with no more people at the roadside to cheer, the car picked up speed and headed for Manchester.

It was about the middle of the afternoon when the Van arrived in Chorlton. Howard and Dawn had been placing some items they had brought with them into suitable places. The men brought out the sheets to place around the floors. Fortunately there had been no rain so on a nice clear and dry day the moving of furniture was comparatively easy. Adrian made sure the men knew which room to take his things.

It was good that Dawn and Howard had made a tentative plan of where the furniture might be placed. The rooms were beginning to look quite nice. Even though they had given careful thought about the layout of the rooms they were now convinced that changes would be necessary. But the main purpose was to find space for everything and to see how comfortable they could be.

The men were pleased when the last item had been brought into the house. Papers needed signing, and then the van left. Adrian was aware of neighbours peeping to see the new people coming into their street. Just after the van left one neighboring couple came over to give them a welcome. It wasn't long before the neighbor from the other side did the same thing. When, to their surprise, a lady from across the street came over with a large tray; she had made a dinner for the three of them. What a wonderful welcome to their new home.

The next few days were spent moving some of the furniture and unpacking. They had been able to make up the beds for the first night. Adrian was not too helpful as far as stuff for the other rooms; he was having problems deciding where his things should be placed. He spent a whole morning moving things into different places. Eventually his Dad came up to find out what he was doing and what was taking him so long. ""It's just these things", he said as his finger moved all round the room. "How are you doing downstairs? Am I required to help in any way?" he asked. His father thought that things were going, but slower than he had hoped. "As far as you helping, if you show your face, your mother will have a job for you. Are you coming down soon?" With a big chuckle, Adrian said he would be down shortly.

On Sunday morning Dawn announced that there would be no shuffling of furniture or unpacking that day. This is the Lord's Day and we have Sunday off from our chores. Howard had been making enquiries about churches in the area before they moved. He was given the name of one a friend thought might be a good Bible-based fellowship.

Howard mentioned that it would be four or five minutes to drive to the church but he wanted to go and see what it was like. Adrian indicated that he wanted to find out if there was an active and interesting youth programme.

Monday was the beginning day for both Howard and Adrian. On his way to work Howard drove to the School, parked and went into the reception with Adrian. They had previously had a tour of the facilities, but this was registration day. It was not overly formal, a resume of the rules and regulations which became more a scanning than a reading for most new boys; and signatures for the student and for the guardian. There was a farewell from his Father with an unspoken prayer for him, and then

Howard left to go on to his office further in the city. Fortunately, because he was the leader of this new venture, he was not tied firmly into set hours to start or finish. It was a case of meeting his new colleagues and having an orientation session as to their immediate duties in getting the venture set up and working.

Adrian was directed to the classroom that would be his for the first year. The room was like most others and to his amazement his teacher was a woman. During the break the boys could talk of nothing else but why a woman as their teacher. Some bright spark, he had an older brother in the school, answered their queries. "She is teaching us because she is the best teacher they could find that would help the first year fellows to adjust to the Grammar School". She had special qualifications, though no one was sure what that included; but her personality was wonderful she was genuine and caring; the boys settled easily and quickly.

The first year was going to be a very general one as far as subjects were concerned. But the teacher informed them that by the end of the year they would be venturing into the general academic subjects. During the first afternoon other teachers came into the class to introduce themselves and their specialized subjects and interests. The Sports Master was one of them. He had no sooner mentioned his name than he informed the whole class that he had been doing some homework and there were some students that he had written down for specific sports. There was an amazing silence in the class because each boy was wondering whether his name had been written down for something. "I have not as yet written all your names down, only the ones that were highly recommended from your previous schools", he informed them. Many of the boys were eager to hear if their names were already on a list.

The bright spark that had an older brother in the school, stood and asked, Permission to ask a question. The Sports Master gave him permission. "Sir, can you tell us some of those names, please?" "I could, but I won't, because I want to meet each one first and then tell him what I have in mind". Another teacher mentioned the extra-curricular activities. "There is a choir and a drama group. Both groups are in need of new blood". The next speaker was a part-time teacher. He mentioned that he might be classified as the Spiritual Director. "One afternoon a week after classes we have a study and fellowship time for any Christian students that would like to join".

The visiting teachers were thanked for their presentations by the lady teacher. She stated that the Notice Board down the corridor towards the Hall would have information about the times and days for the various activities.

When the class was dismissed Adrian made his way to the main entrance. He was wondering how he would be getting home. His Father had not given him any ideas. He was almost at the bottom of the steps when he saw a familiar person. It was his mother. There was a sweep of annoyance when he asked himself, "Has she come to make sure I get home safely?" She wasn't standing alone, there were other mothers standing with her.

Adrian went up to her and before any greetings just stated. "You didn't have to embarrass me as if I am still in kindergarten". His mother was shocked and made sure that if any other mother heard him say that they would also hear her answer. "Your Father phoned to say that he did not tell you how to get home by yourself. This is just the first and once only time, as there is no car available I, we, will have to travel by bus. I will take you to the right bus stop and inform you of the number that will take us home. Then from today on, if there is no one with a car picking you up you will know which bus to get to take you home". The lady standing next to her was laughing and said to her. "That's right, my dear, you tell him. I'll be telling my son the very same when he reaches me".

Adrian wanted to apologize for how rude he had been to his mother. But the conversation was about the school and what sort of day it had been. "Mother, my teacher is a woman!" Adrian stressed. I thought I had left them behind in kindergarten. But we were informed that she is specialized in her subject. It appears she knows how to transform us from grubby juniors into the Halls of Grammar School academia.

It was about twenty minutes ride in the bus. Then about three minutes walk home from the bus stop. It was nice to be home, so off came the uniform and on went the casuals.

When Howard came home, he had just enough time to visit the bathroom and wash his hands before being called to the table. It was wonderful to have a full meal together. His father asked similar questions to his mother. His comments were encouraging. Dawn and Adrian wanted to know how Howard's first day had been. "Will you have some skilled people helping you?" asked Adrian. Dawn wanted to know how many people would be employed to work with him.

"Will you be the boss Daddy?"

"Yes, I suppose I will".

"Will you be a good boss?

'"I am not sure how we'll assess whether anyone is good at the beginning; but I'll be able to sort them out as we progress".

Both father and son were interjecting items associated with the newness of their first day. So ended the first day at High School, and the beginning of the new business venture.

CHAPTER 18

The first year at Manchester Boys High School turned out to be an introduction to the new subjects they would be facing. No longer would it be simple or intermediate material but the teacher's lesson material was basically the introduction. Adrian realized the importance of home work which was filling-in what the teacher had started.

Adrian found that he had adequate time to fit in some of the extra-curricular things. The drama and choir gave him the opportunity to launch into developing a new area of expression, especially the drama.

He went to the mid-week meeting for Christians. There were not many attending. He did not expect to see a great crowd anyway. Everyone was friendly and full of questions regarding where you came from and what church you attend. He was looking forward to those times. This would most probably be the group where he would be making friendships.

The first year sports did not give any sense of major concern. The coach was determined that sport was not going to interfere with the academic studies. In fact one of the statements he stressed quite early in the team meetings that if marks were being affected then the sport involvement would be less and in a serious case might be curtailed altogether.

The school teams are fighting for the school reputation – that meant he would be unhappy with failures.

Adrian's reputation as a soccer player had been passed on to the coach. His was a name already on his list. "How versatile are you in regard to the positions you play", he asked Adrian.

"I suppose defense is where I have played most".

"How about up forward?"

"Yes. I would like to score goals, but I intend to be part of the team".

"Have you ever played in mid-field?"

"No, but I have wondered if that would give me more opportunities to develop skills than being a full back all the time".

"Adrian, I want to start you in mid-field. Let me tell you why, your previous soccer master indicated to me that he saw potential for more forward play and not just defense, one reason he gave was that you have good speed and still maintain control of the ball".

"Rest assured I am not going to cast you into stone as a one only position player. Are you willing to adapt to different positions until we know your best position for the team?"

"Yes, sir. I want to be a team person".

'Oh, by the way you will not be playing very much rugby this first year. It just seems that our school does not thrust talented boys into the rough battle immediately".

"That's okay with me. I like rugby, but to be honest, I prefer soccer".

During the first term the coach had Adrian alternate between full back and mid-field. He was beginning to like the mid-field. He found it gave him more freedom of movement than being in defense. He was able to fall back and help the defense sometimes, but there were other times he found a new area of moving upfront and being an extra forward. The coach noticed this but did not mention it at the beginning. In fact it was the last term of soccer when he spoke to Adrian about it.

"You are a natural for mid-field, Adrian. I have watched you carefully as you flowed as a full member of the team. You know when the defense is in extra need. You are aware of opportunities for an extra forward. Next season I think you will find me placing you in a mid-field position for most games".

"I have been enjoying the liberty of movement from defense to attack, but at the same time realizing the importance of a strong holding position in mid-field is essential for success".

"We are going to work closely together in your years here. I like you attitude to the game. There are not many players who work for the whole team, they guard jealously the one position they consider to be their own".

One of the big differences that Adrian found was moving into different class rooms for different subjects. He soon realized the importance of this. Some rooms were equipped specifically for the subjects. He was enjoying the challenge of having to think about some of the new subjects.

Homework became a serious part of this school. There were times when it could be classed as hard work, not homework. He became a diligent scholar, Right from the beginning there was the strong determination to learn; to master the subjects. The end of term exams showed the results of his great retention of details, as well as his ability to write what was recalled from his expanding memory.

As is natural for most boys there were some subjects he was not too enamored with, but he excelled in the ones that grasped his attention and imagination. School for Adrian was not boring. There was always something new to learn. He realized this during the first year at the Grammar school and it set him well for the years of study ahead.

He found the Christian Meeting helpful. It was giving an added spiritual impact to the teaching being received from the church services and youth group. He noticed a couple of boys from the church attending the midi-week Christian Meeting. They were not too friendly; certainly not the ones with whom he thought could become close buddies. They were a mutual encouragement whenever they met.

In the dining room and at recess times he found some of the boys very embarrassing and vulgar. It was obvious that friendships were being formed and he was concerned to have the friends who were also seeking the pleasure of the Lord their God.

It was not long into the first term that clicks were being formed. They were mainly interest groups, though there were a couple of bully-type gangs. As he anticipated, Adrian found his was not a large group but a small group of keen Christian young men. Their leader was a concerned and caring example of leadership; he was also a forward-looking individual who expressed clearly his desires to find new ventures of service for the Lord, and new methods of gleaning precious truths from their Bible readings.

After the second year at the Grammar School Adrian was truly in the rut of expectancy but he often commented to his parents that there was little difference between the years after the immediate initiation year.

There was one very interesting conversation one evening after their meal together. It was towards the end of his Third Form year. He didn't want to get stuck into his homework immediately. He had other things on his mind.

"Are you going to be busy this evening?" he asked his parents. Their response was to ascertain why the question.

"I would like to discuss with you the future?"

"You should talk to the Pastor he knows more about prophecy than I do", responded his father.

"No, Dad. I mean my future?

"Where do you want to go? His mother asked.

"It's about what subjects to major in. I am wondering what to study when I go to university".

"It's a bit early for that", probed his mother.

"I don't think so, because I hear other boys talking about what they intend becoming after leaving school".

"Have you anything in mind. What would you like to study? What type of work interests you? His father appeared full of questions, but at the same time pushing his son's thoughts forward.

"At the moment I don't seem to have any major interest in the professions. I was wondering if business studies would be a basic area for future study".

"Does that mean you might be looking at the possibility of doing something similar to your father?" asked his mother.

"Not entirely, but Dad, is it a safe field to start off with?"

"It would give you a base for the various fields under the umbrella of business studies".

"You mean, he will want to work with you to start with?" she asked his father.

"It depends upon his specialty. It appears as if he has not got to that stage as yet".

"Yes, there might be a chance to gain some experience, but I don't like the idea of his staying in my shadow. He has the potential to pioneer his own work place".

Adrian liked that comment. "Dad, I can see the advantage of working with you for a short time in order to get to know what the business world is all about. But at the moment I am not sure what area to specialize in".

"There's plenty of time for that. We would need to find the university that gives the best course".

"At this early stage my hopes would be the University of Manchester it might have the ideal course, I am not sure. I am not sure as to whether they offer a business degree. I need copies of courses offered by other universities that will help me zero in on what is available and what interests me. Oh yes, It will be not only what pleases me, I want to go ahead in the Lord's direction and for him to guide to the right course and the right university".

""That is excellent, son. Rest assured your mother's and my prayers are already settling into that area of concern. We want for you what God wants:.

"He has a future for you and a work for you to do. So day by day we will be praying alongside your prayers to that end?'

Adrian was fascinated with the choice of dramas and music being chosen for their annual concerts. One day during his Fourth Form year the drama master asked Adrian if he would be interested in a musical drama. His answer was a delighted affirmation. But Adrian stood still and looked direct into the face of the master, as much as to say, "Why ask me?"

"I have one piece in mind that requires a tuneful soloist as well as a powerful actor. The character fits you perfectly, and my friend who leads the choir states quite emphatically that there is only one male in the choir who could fit the part.

"I hope, for your sake that he'll be able to spend the time working on both parts", said Adrian.

"Well, I am looking for one who is diligent in all his studies? Actually Adrian this is why I am having this conversation with you. Are you willing to consider it? I'll give you a copy of the script, for you to look over at your leisure. How about it, young man?"

That was not a very professional or academically phrased last question.

He had no sooner spoken it and realized how awful it must have sounded coming from a master of such a prestigious High School.

With a large grin on his face, Adrian agreed to look at the script and added, "It sounds like a wonderful challenge".

At the end of the next choir practice a script was handed to Adrian. Others in the choir wondered what it was all about. No words were spoken. The master just gave a purposeful nod, and Adrian tucked it in with his other books.

He had a lot of homework that night so he didn't have time to look at the script. The following night was easier and so he spent quite a time going through the dramatic part and then the music part. It was going to be a lot of hard work, especially because he did not consider himself as possessing a soloist's voice.

At the next rehearsal Adrian gave a nod to the master and no words were shared, the nod gave the master the answer he was hoping for. He also realized that it was going to mean more time and energy being applied to the upcoming concert that year.

It was a challenge to master two parts, but as he thought himself into the character it became more natural to sing some parts rather than speak them.

The concert was a resounding success. The applause was remarkable. A voice from the back shouted for an encore that had never been heard in a serious musical drama. The cast did not give a positive response to the voice from the back of the hall. In the back room later nearly everyone was asking the same question as to who wanted an encore. A couple thought they recognized the voice. But no name was attached to the unusual request.

As the years passed it seemed as if the soccer opposition grew stronger. Perhaps the visiting coaches were being more specific when they visited Manchester Boys` High. The skills and reputation of some of the players were widely known and appreciated. This meant that Adrian was facing players who had been through strict practice as to how to deal with him. Unfortunately for the opposition, the coach for Manchester High had been doing his homework also. The coach had also new ideas for his key players that he wanted to experiment with. He knew that as far as Adrian was concerned just give him a few thoughts and his own imagination would take over the development of new moves.

Perhaps the strongest team they had to face was from Manchester Tech. The fellows were tall and muscular. A rough time was always expected when playing them. Not just rough in regard to the clash of skills, but in regard to the heavy tackling. They were noted for dangerous tackles. The coach warned his team to endeavour to keep away from a certain numbered shirt. Such was not always possible. Adrian had to change some of his moves in order to avoid that particular player.

The game ended in a draw. Both teams had played well. It was an entertaining game. After the final whistle the players were congratulating each other and also the members of the opposing team. Before leaving the pitch to enter the changing rooms two men dressed in business suits were noticed mingling with the players from both teams. No one seemed to know who they were. They were intending to meet up with Adrian and just as they stepped near to him the coach came alongside.

"Adrian, these two men have been watching you particularly this afternoon. They want to speak with you. Will you have a few minutes?"

"Yes. Any idea what they want?"

"Yes. I think I know, but we'll let them talk about it."

The coach was waiting for Adrian and together they went into a small room where two men were waiting. They introduced themselves by name. The names did not stir any memories. As they continued to talk it became obvious that they were scouts for some professional soccer club.

Adrian became a little nervous. His coach noticed it and indicated that no decision would be required that day.

It was strange to have two scouts from two different clubs who knew each other quite intimately it seemed. They were representing the two Manchester Soccer Clubs; Manchester City and Manchester United.

Adrian felt honoured that they were interested in him as a player. Towards the end of the general conversation about the game that had just watched, out came some sheets of paper. Each man had a similar sheet. The idea was to obtain a signature.

Adrian had drawn the attention of scouts from two major league clubs. The signature they wanted was to give their club the exclusive honour of possible professional signings.

Adrian indicated that he was not ready to sign any papers. He spoke direct to his coach when stating that he was not leaning in the direction of becoming a professional soccer player. He was going to university and that was his main objective for the foreseeable future.

Both men appreciated what they heard from Adrian and stated quite emphatically that they had no intention of pushing him into signing something he was not sure about.

They thanked the coach and Adrian. Both of them handed a paper to him and said they would be pleased to hear from him anytime. As they left a comment was made about the way Adrian used his skills against a clever opposition.

Adrian asked the coach to stay.

"Did you know they were coming to see me today?"

"I knew they would be coming sometime. Actually this is not the first time. I have seen them at one of your games. I think we can expect more during the rest of this term from other clubs.'

"Why?"

"Because your reputation has spread around the country as a new soccer star".

"They can shoot that star down; I do not want to be a full time soccer player".

"I cannot stop the scouts from doing their job".

"Well if any more do come perhaps you can tell them I am too shy for interviews!"

"Oh and by the way, I feel greatly honoured that the two Manchester clubs are interested in me. If I was to make a choice between the two I think I would go for the City club".

"That's a good choice. But I do not want any scout putting you under pressure. You have a full load of studies to work on, and exams to pass with marks that will interest some grant givers. Rest assured, Adrian, I am on your side and will protect you from any unreasonable scouts that may appear on the scene".

They were on their way home in the car. His father had come to the game. Comments were made about taking longer to come from the changing rooms. Adrian told his father about the two scouts.

"What did they want from you?"

"They both had a piece of paper that they said required a signature".

"You didn't sign anything, did you?"

"Certainly not. I told them I was not interested in becoming a professional soccer player because I was fully focused on obtaining a university degree".

"What did your coach say?"

"He backed me up one hundred percent. And he will try to keep future scouts from getting to me. I told him to tell them I was too shy for interviews!"

His father had a good laugh at that one and could not wait to hear the guffaw from his mother.

CHAPTER 19

The Syston's were having an evening just reminiscing.

Adrian was in the middle of a pile of books doing some research for his next assignment, He was absorbed in his own thoughts so there was no hint of drawing him into the conversation.

They had been thinking about their baby girl and wondering what had happened to her. "I wonder if she will become a teacher or a nurse"?

"I do not want her to be an ordinary nurse, and I would hope she might consider teaching to be a bore', reply Dawn.

They decided that it would be the right thing not to inform Adrian about what they had been thinking; he certainly would not understand because he had been told his sister died in the hospital at birth.

Even so, they told themselves, it was only natural that they would be wondering what had happened to their baby girl who by now must be a lovely young lady.

The day had started with no projects in mind for that day for the Stapelford's. Betty had no plans. Clarence had been thinking, He made his way over to his daughter,

"How busy are you going to be for the rest of the day?" asked Clarence.

"Not too. Why do you ask, are you going to take me out on a date?" responded Mary.

"Yes, sweetheart, where shall we go – we mustn't let your mother know or she will want to follow us".

"You may not think it, but I am being serious".

"What? How about a date with your father?"

There were the usual chuckles when the flirting continued between father and daughter. Clarence and Betty had often commented about the wonderful relationship developing between father and daughter.

"My reason for wanting a serious chat is to find out more about your plans for university".

"Dad, that is not an immediate concern, but I would like to be looking ahead. At the moment I do not know what degree to go for".

"Then start with a general one and change as you go forward", suggested her mother.

"I have no leanings towards a profession; but that could change. A general arts course might be a good start then I could transfer to business studies or engineering later".

"I want no filthy overalls in my laundry; so forget engineering", chided her mother.

"They would be clean ones".

"Why?"

"Because my engineering must be in an air controlled office".

"The reason I broached the subject is because we must be looking for scholarships by the end of his next year" said Clarence.

"My form mistress has indicated that she has some ideas, but mentioned nothing specifically", responded Mary Elizabeth.

"I'd like to have your teacher's ideas, some time. That will give me more ideas as to what and whom to contact." said her father.

"I think I am going to start making a short cut in names", remarked Betty. "From now on I'll refer to my daughter as 'Mary E' and to your close friend down the street as 'Mary A'".

"You are very thoughtful darling. It would have taken me a lifetime to think of something so profound". Clarence was expecting a reaction from his wife. He got one. The cushion came flying at him.

"I like that abbreviation. I don't like using both names just to distinguish us. I'll be seeing her briefly later this evening and I'll inform her of our decision. I'm sure she'll go along with it with no difficulty", was Mary's response.

The two Mary's had been friends for a number of years. The friendship began when they were both included in a special team from their Youth Group at the Church. It was their first year in the senior youth group. During those years of building their friendship they found similarities in their desires and hopes. They became strong buddies; such was noted by the leadership and in fact by all the members of their Church.

They were both quite excited when they found that they both had the same commitment to the Lordship of Jesus. They were together at the special meeting regarding sex and marriage. It was the following day that they shared their thoughts about the items stressed the evening before. They both had committed themselves to remain virgins until marriage. That seemed to bond their friendship even deeper.

It was one afternoon both Mary's were having a shower after a sports session. Mary A's attention was drawn to the scar. She had seen it before and remembered the first time they had talked about it. Little information had been given except that Mary E had been told by her mother that it was due to surgery soon after she was born. When they were drying off Mary A mentioned that she noticed the scar again.

"Has your mother told you any more details as to why you had to have surgery soon after being born?"

"No. I have mentioned it a few times over the years and get the same answer. When I want to know more about it she says that it was traumatic and couldn't talk about it."

"It may become a problem for you especially if someone sees it and asks questions."

"I hope no one will see it, except you, of course".

"Have you ever tried to guess what the surgery was for?"

"Yes. But my guessing is awful! I'll need to depend upon my ingenuity if I get confronted by some inquisitor".

"So, in the meantime you have just got to live with it; and keep it covered up!"

They were active members of the Christian Union that met at their school. It was an important time meeting with other students and getting to know their faith allegiance. They encouraged each other in commitments and in their search for a closer walk with the Lord Jesus. Witnessing for Jesus among the other kids at school was a precious experience for the young believers.

Both Mary's had talked about future studies. Neither had any hard and fast desires relating to the subjects for study. They knew that they were destined for a university degree of some sort. They were excited about the prospects, but stated quite emphatically that any decision in that direction need not be made until towards the end of their time at the High School

Mary E. arrived at her friend's house and greeted her with, "Hi, Mary A".

"What's that all about?" she asked.

"My mother, earlier this evening wanted to make a distinction without have to say two names. She had decided for herself to use the abbreviation. I think I like it also".

"It sounds good. I think it will take a little getting used to. Please do not let it erode the use of our names though".

"Anne, I certainly will keep your name uttermost on my list even though I may call you A." said Elizabeth.

"In that case, Elizabeth, your name will top my list, though I am leaning towards the idea of using the E abbreviation" remarked Anne.

Both Mary's had agreed earlier that they would not be spending too much time together that evening not just because of a busy day to follow but neither of them had completed their homework assignments.

CHAPTER 20

During the last four years or so Adrian had built up a friendship that developed quite slowly. Neither Adrian nor Tristan seemed in a hurry to have a powerful unbreakable friendship. Other folk in their church wondered as to why they were becoming friends. They did not seem to have the same interest. Tristan was no soccer player and he was horrified to think of himself singing in a choir.

They were in the same group on a Sunday morning. Both were keen members of the Youth Group. They would sit together and be absorbed in each other's conversation topics. Sometime they would get together for an hour for a Bible study on their own.

As the friendship developed they both realized that there was a depth to their loyalty to each other. The Pastor noted it. He took them both out for coffee one evening just to be able to talk about their friendship.

"I have heard quite a few of our regular members commenting about your friendship", he said.

"Some of the people may wonder what he have in common", commented Adrian.

"They all know I cannot sing!" smiled Tristan. "also they are aware that I have two left feet so a soccer ball doesn`t always end up in the right place".

"Can I ask a personal question? But let me stress this, you can tell me to mind my own business".

"There is something attractive about Tristan, and it has been slowly developing into an acceptance. I think I want to say that he is becoming closer and closer and we are finding a deep sense of Christian commitment that is wonderfully attractive", commented Adrian.

"I would like to add that even though I am not able to join Adrian in many of his top pursuits I am deeply grateful for the way he has opened himself to me. I know there is a mutual love that is drawing us closer", added Tristan.

"That is what I wanted to hear. I have been observing you both and have recognized the spiritual growth in both of you. Friendships are important. They go through every kind of experience. There are new aspects that lead into precious elements of mutual likes or dislikes. Friendships are wonderful, when the Lord has His rightful place in each life; both are receiving the blessings and guidance of God. He is blessing you both, as individuals and as a couple. He does have a plan and purpose for you; it will not take you both along the same path, but will be part of his bountiful care for you both. He is in control, and wants to remain in control. It will be inevitable that your paths will divide, but the friendship won't".

That last statement from the Pastor was something they would never forget.

"There was something else that I wanted to pass by you both. We have received information relating to a special seminar at one of the larger churches in Manchester. I would like to see a goodly number of our young people go to it. It is for one evening, so wont clash with too much homework".

"Is it just for the fellows or is it open to all our youth?" asked Adrian.

"It's open to all".

"Why don't you ask them tomorrow night at our meeting?" asked Tristan.

"That is precisely what I intend, but I thought it advantageous to, pass it by you two first".

"So we could shoot it down?" retorted Adrian.

"Perhaps we should know what it's all about before we start thinking of pros and cons", remarked Tristan.

"It is for mature thinkers".

"That cuts out a whole lot of us", smiled Tristan.

"The person leading it is a Youth Pastor from a large church in Birmingham. He will be profound yet quite blunt; he will be sensitive but also explicit".

"That sounds sexy", smiled Adrian.

"I suppose that is how many of the youth will see it. It is sexy. His topic will be, 'What does God say about sex? 'Challenges of sexuality'".

"Is it going to be the usual 'don't do this or that'?"

"The best answer for me to make right now is, go and see".

"Then we will see what the reaction will be tomorrow night" remarked Adrian.

That night at the Youth Group the pastor raised the idea of the upcoming seminar. He had some leaflets ready to hand out to any who might be interested.

There were quite a number of questions. One girl wanted to know the qualifications of the speaker. The leaflet gave her the answer.

It became an interesting evening, both as a topic for open discussion and for the small group over a cup of coffee.

The general consent was in the direction of accepting the invitation. But it was obvious that not everyone would be going.

Adrian and Tristan were at a table with a couple of other fellows. The other two were not sure, they were afraid that it might be too embarrassing for them. Adrian and Tristan stated that they would be going because they may learn something more.

The Hall was crowded with young people. Tristan thought they were about eight or nine from their church. The others were together on the other side of the Hall.

The speaker was introduced. He was probably in his early thirties. So he was not old enough to be out of date with his material. He had a smile that was not artificial.

He opened with a couple of jokes that broke the ice. Then he warned everyone that they may be embarrassed but that was alright because it would not be exploited. He laid the challenge on the line.

"This will not be my application", he said, "It will be what God has revealed".

His talk was an exposition of selected passages of Scripture. He was very keen to point out the texts that included the words of Jesus. He was extremely frank but beautifully sensitive. The explicit facts were dealt with without trying to cause some to close their minds. It was obvious that he had taught these truths before to groups of fellow and girls.

"Jesus knows every little bit about each one of you", he said. "Jesus will not have one standard for some and different for others; nothing applicable to males that are not also applicable to females".

"You have been made male and female. God made the choice for each one of you from the moment of conception. You are what God made you, and now He wants you to know why He made you that way. Naturally it is for procreation. It is not for experimenting.

You are sexual beings, created for sexual purposes. He strongly urges, no rather commands, that you experience that when married. Sexual intercourse is for those who commit themselves to each other in the presence of God in marriage".

"There is to be no sexual expression outside of marriage. That is abundantly clear. God does not condone trial marriages. He does not condone 'doing it because it is something natural'".

"I understand that most of you in the Hall this evening have come from Church Youth Groups. I am presuming that many of you are born again Christians. But the challenge is for all and includes those who have not as yet committed themselves to the Lordship of Jesus Christ".

"My challenge to you right now is to promise the Lord you will remain virgins until you are married. You will then be walking daily with Jesus in a wholesome and holy way. The Holy Spirit has been given for you to help in facing challenges and temptations. The Holy Spirit will give wisdom when it comes to making serious decisions. So you will not be facing the future on your own, God is providing you with a wonderful Guide and Counselor".

It was a fairly long session, and it was followed by a serious time of questions and answers. "Whatever decision you make this evening rest assured that God knows why you made it, and He will give guidance in working out the details".

"There are counselors available at the front if any of you want to talk more about such a commitment and have prayer regarding it. But my last word to you all is 'Be what Jesus created you to be, and live accordingly. God will bless you and He will enable you to keep the promise you make".

Adrian and Tristan had been really inspired by this explicate presentation. Their comments were that of surprise at the details the speaker had been giving. Tristan was about to say something but Adrian jumped in first.

"I did it. I made the promise", he said. "I found the counselor very helpful in seeking to make a decision that would be in effect for a number of years probably".

"I fully intend remaining a virgin also, until the first night of my honey moon", added Tristan. "I too was helped by the counselor assigned to me".

About a week or so later Adrian met up with Tristan during a recess. "Are you busy this evening? I don't think I am going to be over-loaded with homework. Can you come to my place for a while?"

Tristan was always ready to give an affirming reply to anything that would mean time together at Adrian's house. So there was a great smile and nod of affirmation.

"Great, see you about seven o'clock".

The Grandfather clock was chiming the hour when Tristan arrived at the door. Adrian made some comment about him arriving just on time. They chuckled as they went up stairs to Adrian's room. Once inside Tristan asked, "Well, my friend, what is it all about this evening?"

"Just a moment." Adrian reached into a draw and pulled out a fairly large bunch of papers. "This is what's up tonight".

"What on earth is all that postage junk?'

"Some of it will prove to be junk, but right now it is part of some serious business." Tristan was about to ask a question but Adrian said, "This is about my future, probably our future".

Adrian scattered papers, brochures, schedules, and the odd curriculum, from various Universities onto his bed.

Tristan picked up some and scanned through a page or two then replaced them and did the same with some others. Neither of them spoke for quite some time. They were both engrossed in gleaning important ideas from the information scattered on the bed cover.

Tristan was tired of sitting, so he walked around the bed glancing at some papers he had not scanned. "I have made up my mind!" That was a tremendous explosive idea coming from Tristan. He didn't usual jump so quickly into an important decision.

"I am not sure how important this is at the moment. But this is where I stand right now." He pointed to one paper and said, "That's the course I really want to study" Then he points to a coloured brochure on the other side of the bed and said, and that is the University I want to attend".

"That's absolutely wonderful, Tristan. I still have a few questions though."

"One of the first things for me" said Tristan', "is to find out if that course is offered at that university".

"That's going to be my concern also," added Adrian. "I think I am certain as to the subjects I want to study, but does my university preference offer them?

"On the back of the brochure from Manchester University is a fabulous quote from one of the professors. Referring to Manchester University he writes, "It is a place where you can wander through knowledge," remarked Tristan. "I have a strange feeling that that is your first choice. Do you fancy wandering through some aspects of knowledge?"

"How did you guess my choice?"

"Well, for one thing I lost count as to how many times you picked up that brochure and replaced it in order to glance through another one."

"You are very observant", Adrian responded, "I have an inward bias towards that university. My concern now is to find out what courses they offer".

"I heard someone talking to my father the other day when they were chatting about schools and schooling. He mentioned, if I can remember clearly, that Manchester had a super Masters programme."

"Was that in connection with a Business course?"

"I think it might have been".

"I'll need to phone them or go on line. Because it is vital that I obtain that material before going any further with my search for the right subject at the right place".

The next day Adrian went on line and got the answer to some of his questions. He was delighted that they offer a B.A.(Hons) in Business. He had to tell Tristan so he ran round to his house to tell him. Tristan was still not sure where and what, but was pleased that his friend was going on in the right direction.

The soccer coach called his team together after one practice to give them information about up-coming matches. "The next one is quite new. There is a junior (but how junior I don't know) team at Manchester University that want to play against us".

""Will that be somewhat out of our league, sir".

"At the moment it may appear so. But I want to push you guys. You are a top team, and I would like to see you lick the uni guys".

"Have they mentioned a date, sir"?

"Yes. In a couple of weeks time".

"Have we time to prepare and perhaps be instructed in some new tactics?"

"We have time to prepare. You are ready. My encouragement will flow rapidly as we get closer to the date".

Both teams were walking out on to the pitch. Adrian commented that they look as young as themselves, so obviously first year students. The first twenty minutes were spent sizing each other up; at least it seemed that way to the spectators who were getting bored. The coach was either getting bored or else the feelings of the spectators were getting through to him.

The coach gave a hand signal which we knew to mean he wanted our captain to find his way over to his side.

"It's time to be your selves" he shouted.

The captain spent little time in urging his players into some sort of positive action. Within a few minutes the visiting team was taken by surprise when Adrian moved from mid-field up front and was allowed to slip past the defense. He didn't miss. The score was one nil at half time. The other team scored early in the second half. The rest of the game was a battle of the defenders.

As the teams were exiting from the field Tristan was close by and shouted to Adrian, "You may be doing that next year!" Other players didn't make any response, but the coach heard it. So while in the changing room the coach went up to Adrian. "What will you be doing next year, Adrian?"

"Oh. We'll have to wait and see!"

The coach wasn't satisfied with that answer he was sure there was more to it than that. He raised the question after a practice two weeks later. So Adrian mentioned that he may be going to Manchester University the following year; but nothing was completely certain, though he was planning on it coming into effect.

From time to time Tristan mentioned to Adrian that there was a girl in the youth group that appeared to be quite uninterested in him.

"How do you know? It's probably your imagination".

"No, not really. I do see Hilary frequently looking at you and trying hard to hear what you are saying".

"I'm not interested. I can't do with girls at this stage in my life!"

That raised quite a large guffaw

It was a strange situation. After the youth meeting and they broke up for refreshments, Tristan and Adrian could see only one table with a couple of vacant seats. They walked over and asked if it was okay to sit there. The girls gave a chuckle and a wave of the shoulders indicating they could join them. Tristan had a large grin on his faced, but he made sure no one else saw it; because one of the girls was Hilary.

The conversation was easy and general. Hilary mentioned that she had watched the game against the University team. Her comment, "you were excellent when you scored our goal". Then she blushed because she allowed her thoughts to race ahead.

Adrian replied, "I like the way you mentioned the scoring of *our* goal".

"Yes', she said, "I am a regular spectator at all our games". Her companion agreed that it was a great thrill for them to attend the soccer matches.

On the way home Tristan was dying to ask Adrian how he felt sitting at the table with Hilary. The chance didn't arise until just before going in the house.

"Hilary seemed interested in our soccer matches", stated Tristan.

"Yes, she seems like a great fan".

That was all. They said their 'good nights' and parted.

During the following few weeks Tristan noted that Adrian was almost looking around for a table with Hilary. There was once when the two fellows were first to a table and the girls came by and Adrian suggested they sit with them.

They left the Church rooms together and parted in the parking lot. The girls got into a car and the boys walked home.

It was a few days later, Adrian was waiting for a bus in the city centre. Just before the bus arrived, Hillary walked by, they started chatting. The conversation continued most of the way on the bus. Then the surprise. Adrian asked Hillary for a date. Her reply was a positive one with a gentle blush on her cheeks. He was shocked and surprised, but inwardly there was a spark of pleasure. This was not to be talked about with parents or others, he would not be telling Tristan.

Adrian had borrowed a car, He picked Hillary up and they drove off to see a show. Both became aware of how close together the seats were. There were no intimations of a desire to sit further apart. In fact it would have been impossible to be further apart; the seats were close together.

They enjoyed the show and walked back to the car

They were passing through an area designated for future development. Adrian was aware of Hillary doing something but he could not take his eyes off the road. He slowed down at a corner and Hillary suddenly threw back her dress. Adrian noticed but kept his attention on the driving. There was an entrance way just ahead so he pulled off the road and stopped the car.

Hillary wanted him to look.

"The colours do not suit you. Put your dress back".

She hustled quickly to do that.

"Why? Why did you do that?"

"Nearly all the girls tell me that that is what to do when on the first date with a boy that you like".

"Which girls? The ones from our youth group?"

"Some of them. They were trying to convince me that it was the only way".

"Did they know about us?"

"Oh No. It's just things they have said over many months."

"Why did you do it in front of me?"

"I don't know. I'm embarrassed at what I did, but it was the words of the girls ringing in my ears that prompted me to do it".

"Have you done the same with the other boys when on a date?"

"No. Certainly not".

"Then why with me?"

"I can't answer that".

Hillary started to cry. Amid her sobs she was muttering what a sinful person she must be. Would Jesus forgive her?

"Did you go to that special seminar a few weeks ago on sex and marriage?"

"Yes. I found it very challenging".

"And that had no effect of your planning for our date this evening?"

"It seems not. I am truly sorry. I won't be able to speak to you again without blushing. I won't be able to enjoy a talk and a cup of coffee. I'll be embarrassed even at the soccer matches".

"Well you shouldn't be. What happened has been forgiven. And when our God forgives He forgets. It is all in the past".

"I was at that seminar, that I made a promise to remain pure until marriage. Hillary I truly want you to make a similar promise".

He reached forward and pulled her to himself in an embrace that shocked him and melted Hillary. He placed his hands around her cheeks and pulled her close for a deep and lasting kiss.

For the rest of the drive home they were holding hands. There was a quick kiss as he dropped her off at her house, with the hope that no one was peeping to see what was happening.

A casual observer would have described Adrian as being on a cloud nine for the rest of his journey home.

Manchester University had been his choice, and he had received word back to say that he was accepted. Tristan had a similar correspondence from the University he had chosen.

Adrian's teachers had already indicated to him that they had information about grants and scholarships. Some had already been submitted. Adrian realized how fortunate he was to have teachers willing to do so much for him. The sports master knew that a scholarship would be coming for his soccer prowess.

It was an exciting time. Lots of hours were used in getting things all lined up for the big move to the University Halls of Residence.

CHAPTER 21

Mary E. picked up the cardboard box near her window and emptied the contents on to her bed. She was amazed as to how many pieces of literature she had collected over the past fourteen or fifteen days. She shuffled them around as she sorted the University brochures to one side of the bed and the course outlines from various colleges to the other side.

She stood back, and looked. She made sure she did not enter into an imaginative trance. With one massive shake of her head she smiled and decided to look at the colourful brochures from the various Universities she had been in contact with.

It felt as if she was arranging them in some sort of priority order. If so, it was not deliberate. It was due to the interest she had in those locations. She was not only thinking about the actual university, but the city as well. There were some cities she didn't really want to go to, but others fascinated her. Her thoughts then centred on not so much the studies as to the adventures of discovering new places.

She didn't want to go too far from home. So the Scottish ones were placed to one side, and so were those in the southern part of the country. That left the Midlands and North. She included Oxford and Cambridge in that group. Those cities didn't offer much attraction.

Birmingham might be alright and so might Leeds. Was she aware of skipping over one? Manchester was sitting by itself. She was not aware of placing it there. It must have shuffled itself! Or she could blame the friendly poltergeist!

She picked up the one from Manchester and went over to her chair. This was perhaps indicative of her up-coming bias towards that place. She liked the look of the campus and the variety of academic buildings. "Even the photos of the professors suggest that they are fairly normal", she thought. She wasn't timing herself in the reading but was keen to obtain as much information as would enable her to make sensible choices.

She went back to the bed and picked up the ones for Leeds, Birmingham, Nottingham and Sheffield. Not so much time was spent on these because her mind was being drawn more to Manchester. Leeds might be her second choice so far.

Her next trip back to her bed was to find the Study requirements and outlines. Again it was a careful search through to find what courses were being offered. And were they the ones that she wanted, or perhaps might want later. She was being careful. There was to be no quick decision that might not be the right one for her future academic work.

"Oh. If only that other University offered that course, it would be ideal!" It was thoughts like that that took up much of her time. She shook herself and told herself to be more disciplined and careful in assessing the multitudinous mound of information.

It must have been close on an hour later she pulled out two, the studies relating to Leeds and Manchester. This was going to be the big choice to make because she liked the look of both places.

She did not get launched on all the pros and cons because her Mother called to say that the meal was ready. "Come soon or it'll be cold. And it is not the sort you like cold!" Off she went and enjoyed her meal.

Her parents wanted to know how she had been getting on. They knew what she had been doing. They were interested in her two choices of Leeds and Manchester.

"Which is your first choice", asked her Father.

"I think it must be Manchester".

"Then Manchester it is", was the enthusiastic reply from her Father.

Then the conversation got around to finances. Her Father indicated that his savings would not last many terms, but he added that friends at work had given him organizations to contact. He was keen to make contact with the ones his friends had found helpful.

Mary E. mentioned that her teachers were working on ideas for her. There were at least two that offered valuable scholarships. "They seem very hopeful", she said.

Her Mother mentioned, "Perhaps we should make an appointment to see your teachers and share our information". "I am certain they would warm to that idea", replied Mary E. "I'll speak to them tomorrow and arrange a time for you, for us".

After that it was time to visit Mary A. to find out what they had missed or what they did not want to miss. In other words it was a special meeting planned for a specific purpose – it was to be a time together.

It proved to be quite absorbing as Mary E. shared some of her ideas for future college studies. Mary A. added that she would be doing the same next year, and would welcome the gleanings of her friend.

The next day Mary E. told her form teacher what had transpired the evening before. She asked if she would be willing to meet her parents, perhaps with any other teacher especially the guidance teacher. So a date was arranged for the following week.

It proved to be a very valuable evening. The parents were relieved that the school was likely to get such valuable scholarships for their daughter. They were also pleased that the guidance teacher was already involved in some of the paper-work.

On their way home Mary E. was quite excited. Her parents smiled with pleasure. Things were moving ahead for their daughter's further education. The conversation turned to what else they needed to do. What would she need if going into a dormitory? Would there be any advantage in looking for a room to rent, or shared accommodation with other students? Mary E. herself had not made up her mind as to what sort of place to look for, if she was honest her preference would be the dorm. Hence the need for more brochures, etc. Her parents were ready to joke about the fact that there was already such a massive pile of papers that they might need a large dump truck to get it all away from the house when Mary E left!

The papers had been completed for the Business Studies course, and posted to the University of Manchester. Her teachers were happy with her choice and indicated that they would soon hear back from them because her marks are above the minimum required.

It was a day of rejoicing when the post man delivered an official looking document. Mary E. had been accepted for the course requested giving her entrance to Manchester University that coming September. Parents, teachers, and friends were filled with pleasure. So thoughts were being fostered as to being a student and being trained for some interesting and exciting work in the future. What will that future be like for Mary E?

It must have been about three weeks after their visit to the teachers when Mary E. arrived home from school. The first thing that surprised her was the absence of food being cooked. She thought that might mean either a take-out or a bring-in. She threw off her jacket and shoes as usual and went into the lounge. She was surprised to see her father sitting in his usual chair. It was unusually early for him to be home. He didn't look very happy.

"How come you're home so early, Dad? Are you unwell?"

He didn't say anything except to invite her to come and sit with him.

"Dad, what's the matter. There is something wrong. What is it?"

He left his chair as she was saying this and went to the settee where they could sit together. He reached out and gave her a hug. She was fond of her Dad's hugs they were lovely and warm and comforting and overflowing with love.

"What is it, Daddy?"

"Your mother is upstairs resting. I'll go out a get something to eat a little later on".

"Why is she resting? That's unusual for her in an afternoon".

"She had a doctor's appointment early this afternoon".

"I didn't know she was ill".

"She, we, didn't tell you because we didn't want you to be worried".

"I am now".

He gave her a massive hug and whispered, "The doctor did not give any good news."

"What about?"

"She was expecting him to talk about possible minor surgery. Instead ..."

He couldn't continue as tears flowed down his cheeks. She cuddled up closer to him. And as he pulled her closer she started to cry.

"The news is not good. But whatever news comes to us we know that God is the One who is the great enabler. To use the doctor's words, 'it is inoperable'. Your mummy is very ill, darling".

"I want to go up and see her".

"Just a moment, sweetheart. I would like to go up with you. But we can't go with the evidence of tears on our cheeks".

They sat for a few moments of silence, just holding each other.

Her father spoke a short prayer for God to give them the strength needed at that time. They both felt a little more comfortable, so they got up and walked upstairs together.

"I'll just glance in to see if she is alright".

He held her hand and they entered the bedroom. Her mother was just beginning to sit up so they went to opposite sides of the bed and sat on the bed with her.

"I am so sorry, mummy, darling", whispered Mary E. reaching closer to her to give a hug and a kiss. The hug lasted a few minutes while no one spoke.

Much is said during a time of silence. The thoughts appear more powerful when not verbally expressed but communicated with a touch or a squeeze instead.

"It's nice to have you both sitting beside me on my bed. That hasn't happened for a long time. There isn't very much I can tell you other than what your Dad may already have told you. The doctor has promised that the pain can be controlled. But they cannot perform any surgery, because the tumors are too close to vital organs. I am not going to be bed-fast for some time, so I intend to be as active as usual".

"And I'll make sure you are not too active, my dear!" remarked her husband.

"What can I do, Mummy?"

"Perhaps help your father decide what we are going to eat. I'll be going down-stairs soon".

Mary E. and her father went down-stairs together. As they entered the lounge she asked her father, "How long?"

"We don't know yet. There are more tests and examinations to be performed. The doctor will tell us when he has more information to go on".

Mary A. was saddened when her friend arrived that evening for just a short visit. She couldn't understand why Mary E. had emphasized a 'short visit' until there was a tearful explanation. There were promises of special prayers from her friend and her parents.

Mary E. was in the midst of being depressed and anxious about what to do regarding her studies. She decided she would talk it over with her teachers.

Before she could say anything to her teacher the inevitable question arose first because there was a smile missing.

"What has happened? Where is your smile this morning?" asked the teacher.

Because she saw some tears in her eyes they went into another room. The teacher was given a full account of her present situation.

"I want to know whether I should forget about university", Mary E. said.

"That is not part of the discussion at the moment. We will continue as usual until we receive more details from the doctor. But I want you to know that I will do every possible to help you through this very difficult time. We will not announce it to the others in the class until you are ready to do so".

Tears were wiped away. They went into the class room together and the day began. But it was a confusing day for Mary E.; she wasn't able to concentrate on her lessons. The teacher noticed it and gave her a warm smile.

When she arrived home her mother gave her the usual kiss and hug. Mary E. smelled the meal cooking. It was a boost for her to feel that things were normal, or appeared to be so.

It was a couple of weeks when the doctor wanted to see Betty. Clarence decided that he would go with her.

There was some treatment the doctor recommended, but he told them that there would be an increase in the pain medicine to be taken as and when required.

Clarence asked the doctor, "Can you give us any timing yet?"

"It is only an estimate based on experiences with other patients. But it isn't imminent; it'll be three or may be four months, may even be a little longer".

"I will be as active as usual for most of the time" remarked Betty.

"I think you will also do as you are told sometimes!" joked Clarence.

"You will know how much you can do. But be ready for that time when your body says it cannot continue doing as usual" added the doctor.

Just before they left the doctor's office he reminded them that he will need to see Betty every two weeks.

Mary E. had gone home early that afternoon, so she was there when her parents returned from the doctor. Almost the very moment they entered the house she wanted to know what the doctor had said. Clarence told her all the advice and instructions regarding medications.

When they were sat down, Mary E. said, "but isn't there something else you know I want to hear?" Clarence was uneasy. Betty said that she would give the answer.

"The doctor could not be too specific. There would be some months …"

"Did he say how many?"

"He said that on experiences with other patients it could be three or may be four months, or even longer".

Mary E. just curled up into her chair and sobbed. Her parents choked up on their tears at seeing how upset their daughter was.

"It is going to take me a very long time to get used to the idea of you being so sick Mummy. I wish I could do something".

"You are right sweetheart", said Clarence, "We are so impotent, and we just can't do a thing to help, except to keep her happy and comfortable. And that is what we intend doing".

The weeks passed. Doctor's visits didn't reveal any new hopes. The other two members of the family were noticing that Betty was showing signs of slowing down. Even the slightest indication of being tired was viewed as a major setback, but they were being supported by the prayers of friends and fellow members of the church. Clarence would often cuddle up to Mary E. and remind her that God was giving them extra strength daily.

Mary E. had been thinking a lot about future studies. She didn't share much with her Dad or even with Mary A. But she did ask her teacher if she could talk to her and the guidance teacher. It was arranged for the next afternoon during a free period.

Mary E. was able to tell them something of her thinking. She had almost made up her mind not to go to University that coming September.

Her teacher asked her to explain a little more about that.

"It is obvious my Mother is getting weaker, and soon not able to do very much for herself. I cannot leave my Dad on his own to cope. I am needed to give him support even though I cannot do very much for my Mother".

"That is a very loving and generous thought, my dear:" said the guidance Teacher. "But we will be thinking ahead …"

"If you mean after she has died". There were tears forming in her eyes and it was a struggle to stop them flowing down her cheeks.

"We are concerned about your future", said her teacher. "We know it is going to be very hard for you. Mary, I want you to know that we are going to do everything possible to make sure you are supported during this sad time, and also to let you know that we are making tentative plans for your future".

That prompted a smile and a question mark on her face.

"It has been a pleasure for us to seek scholarships for you. Now I know that they are for this year. But I have had a quick chat with a secretary as to whether they can be transferred to the next year".

"We are convinced that you will not lose any of the scholarship grants that have been obtained for you", stated her teachers.

"Thank you for that good news", Mary said, "I was hoping that if I took one year off and then asked for entrance next year it would be forthcoming".

"There will be no difficulty. You are wanted by the University, it isn't just that you want to go there", remarked the guidance teacher.

"I am not sure just how much longer my Mother will have before she dies", mentioned Mary. "But my Father will need some help to adjust without her being around. And I thought that if I had a year that would be of great help to him. During that time he will be able to get new interests and friends. Do you think doing that for one year will be sufficient?"

Both teachers agreed at the same time.

They continued talking about other related issues for the following ten minutes. Then they ended their time together much to the thanks of Mary.

Later that evening when Betty was in bed Mary E. had a chance to talk to her Father for awhile. She shared a little about her talk with the teachers. He was exceptionally pleased to hear about Mary's time with them.

She decided that she would not go around to her friend's house that evening. "I can tell her all about it tomorrow evening", she thought.

The following evening was a full time bringing her friend up to date with her own thinking as well as the encouragement received from the two teachers at the school.

"I am saddened for what you are going through. But I must admit there has been a thought of pleasure to have you around here for another year. And more especially that I will be able to help you and support you at this time. And if your stay is just for one year then we will leave together for University at the same time".

There were occasional days when Mary E. didn't make it to school during the rest of that term; her Mother was very sick and needed attention. It was a term where Mary E. expressed to herself one morning that she was becoming more mature. Life had brought a great change and that she would boldly face those changes as they arose.

22
CHAPTER

The last few weeks at Manchester Boys High School were full of mixed feelings for Adrian. He was coming to terms with a major change. He was also noting how many friends will not be around the following year. It was not only at school but he was concerned about possible changes in friendship with the youth group at the Church.

His interest in Hillary was of no major concern, but he did like her. There was no evidence of his heart bursting at the thought of her not being around. He was sure that she hoped he would be home most weekends. A passing thought suggested that Tristan might help in that direction. Then the next thought, being the obvious one that he probably would not be home every weekend.

Most of the shopping for things he and his mother considered necessary, had been done. He went with his parents to view the dormitory accommodation he would be moving into. It was not a large room, in fact quite a bit smaller than his room at home. Yet there was ample space for a desk, bed, table and chair, a recliner chair, and a mat to slip on.

The Pastor had a special prayer on his last Sunday home. He called forward Adrian, Tristan and some others who were going to College or University the following week. It was a great sense of God's presence, and the assurance that the new adventure facing them was under the guidance and direction of the Holy Spirit.

After the service the people flocked around Adrian to wish him well. Hillary was one of them. After she had said her piece there was a slight hesitation. She bent forward either wanting to receive a kiss or deliver a kiss. It was a moment when the whole world stopped talking. Loud and clear where the thoughts about which one should or would kiss first. The people in the Church had become aware of the interest that they both had in each other, so Adrian decided he would make it a memorable farewell for them both as well as for the gaping members of the congregation. He just reached forward and drew her close to him for a loving hug and a meaningful kiss. That received applause especially from others in the youth group. And that of course brought a massive blush on the cheeks of Hillary. Adrian didn't think he was blushing! His parents thought they saw a slight change of colour in his cheeks.

When they arrived home Dawn informed Adrian and Howard that she had invited a few friends for a snack on Monday evening.

"Why?" was the comment from Adrian.

His Father helped with the answer by stating the obvious, "It's your last evening before leaving home".

"What a thought! Surely it doesn't mean that in effect I am being banished from home!" He knew better than that. His mother looked for special events in order to have a party. Not a large sit-down meal, but a substantial selection of savory and sweet.

Neither Adrian nor his father counted the number of guests. Someone had placed a table near the kitchen door upon which were various kinds of cookies and different savory tarts.

Food, or rather the consumption of foods seemed to be the main occupation of the crowd. No one could grumble because everything was so delicious.

Dawn broke into the general chatter and asked if she might say a few words. Whereupon Howard's loud whisper was heard by most people in the room when he stressed, "A few will not be too many!"

They were typical thoughts from a proud mother. She was pleased about the number who had come to send her son off to a new and large phase of his education. She knew that some of the mothers and fathers present had already gone through that stage as they had sent either a son or a daughter off to college or university. She took the opportunity of expressing a little of her faith that God had been in control of happenings in Adrian's life up until then; and she pressed home the point that there was absolutely no doubt God was going ahead of him.

We, I want all of you to prayer regularly for Adrian. Yes, I want him to progress well in his learning. I know he will enjoy his sports. But the social world in universities is full of people saying they have the best and everyone should do this and that because everyone else is doing it. Adrian is strong and has a solid faith, please pray that his faith will increase and not be shattered by friends or lectures. Thank you all for coming and sharing our evening together.

The people didn't leave quickly. Every person wanted to have a word with Adrian who was not always standing on his own. Arriving a little late due to late lectures Hillary stepped in and folk noticed the pink in her cheeks began to get brighter and was spreading. Adrian made sure the blush got worse because he went directly to her and gave a big hug and a kiss that brought a magic sparkle into her eyes. So as the folk passed they were saying their farewells to Adrian and smiled their good wishes to Hillary.

Adrian suggested to Hillary that because they had been standing most of the time they should find a comfortable cushion on the settee. "Make sure it's big enough for the two of us!"

Hillary became quite excited at Adrian wanting a big enough cushion for the two of them. She was certainly becoming more interested in Adrian than he was of her. Whether it has something to do with the feminine psyche will never be known. The tinge of pink in the blushes indicated that her thoughts must be racing ahead of the conversation taking place. She was enjoying talking with Adrian, but the thought of being close to him was making her heart beat a little quicker.

They had been sat quite a long time. It was Hillary that suggested that perhaps she should be going home as it was getting late. Adrian was almost ready to object because he himself was really enjoying being alone with Hillary. He did like her but he realized that his heart strings were not being stroked too vibrantly. There certainly was affection but he never gave a thought to it becoming love.

Hillary was dying to ask if they could write to each other. Adrian gave the answer that he was no great letter writer but he hoped they could manage a letter or two from time to time. Hillary got the message that she would not be receiving a letter every other day.

She asked if he would be coming home many times during the terms. He was uncommitted because as he said it depended very much on how much extra-curricula time would be taken up with sports, drama and choir.

Hillary wanted to know how serious he was about drama and choir.

"I like them, but I don't think they like me too much", he said with a chuckle.

"I'd very much like to come to some of your soccer games", she added.

"Most of them will be between other teams at the university, but I know there are some games with other colleges throughout the year. I could perhaps let you know where some of them might be. It would be wonderful to know at least one person in the crowd!" Her mind jumped ahead with the hope of going for a meal together after the game.

Adrian started to get up and Hillary jumped at the same time.

"It's getting late", Adrian said, "and I hear my mother and father are still up. They will want to say some 'goodbyes'".

At the door there was no long and involved hug with kisses, but it was a polite kiss and hug. He waited for her to enter her car and drive away before he closed the door and went inside to see his parents.

They both smiled. Their smiles were asking a question. He knew that his answer would not be quite the one they might be expecting. He smiled back.

They were sat around the table and he informed them that there was no long term commitment between himself and Hillary. He stressed that it was only a friendship with no commitment to take it further.

There were pleased because they did not want him to get involved to the extent of being a distraction from his studies. Also they were not sure that she was a good match for their son anyway.

After they had talked for quite awhile his father indicated that he wanted to pray, and as a family be assured of God's presence and guidance into the future. It was a great time of prayer. All three of them prayed and committed each other to the protection and direction of the Lord.

"This is going to be a strange night", commented Adrian, "I am heading upstairs to bed like I've done for years, but tonight it is different, because I'll will not be doing it tomorrow night."

"Yes", indicated his mother, "but the bed will always be there for you."

His father added, "Yes, because you are not leaving home, we are loaning you out for training and for the work the Lord requires of you".

Their 'goodnights' were accompanied with serious kisses and deep affectionate hugs.

Most of his things had been placed in the car the night before so it was only a last bag to be thrown in the back of the car. Adrian was pleased that both parents were coming with him because he knew that they would like to see what his room was like so they could picture him studying away from home.

The conversation centred about how frequently they might be taking him back to college. Adrian had told them the same as Hillary that his extra-curricula activities would be time consuming.

They had turned the corner which gave them the first sights of the University buildings. His mother wanted to know how difficult it was going to be finding the right building; "They all look so similar!"

Adrian had received a detailed map of the campus and his father was familiar with some of the buildings. They had no difficulty locating the residence. Actually there was a space for parking not too far away.

There were six hands on their way to the hall of residence every one of them busy carrying at least one package.

How pleased they were that elevators were handy to take them to the right floor. They navigated their way along the corridor to the right room.

Time for yet another 'farewell'. It started in his doorway then he decided he wanted to walk back to the car with them, He was very grateful for all their help getting him a room. He was also tremendously thankful for all that they had done for him over the years preparing him for this important move.

Just before they drove away his father informed him that from time to time they may even see them in the crowd at a soccer match. "Yes, Hillary also said that she might penetrate the crowd at a match sometime".

He waved as the car turned from the parking lot and commenced his walk back to the Hall of Residence. "I'm here!' he whispered to himself. Then reprimanded himself for talking to himself; the rest of the thoughts remained un-whispered. It seems as if he was trying to assess his excitement by finding different words and expressions. It wasn't long before he was back in his room unpacking and sorting out his bags, then to find a space to store the bags.

He had received his list of lectures and the lecture halls.

That was the big difference when it came to going for a lecture. The hall seated at least three hundred students. If sitting at the back the lecturer looked a long way off – fortunately the microphone allowed his voice to be heard clearly. He felt something of the impersonalness of lecturer and student. There did not appear to be many opportunities to ask questions, so he made sure that he would take advantage of tutorials.

It didn't take him long to get into his studies. He enjoyed learning. The subjects ahead of him were going to be important parts of training for his life's work. He patted himself on the back with an assuring whisper that he was being a good student.

He had not been in residence a week and already reps from drama and choir had visited him. Both said that Adrian was much needed for their up and coming presentations. He gave them both a positive response followed by a caution that he may have to curtail some of those activities as the studies became more demanding.

The soccer coach had made sure it was a convenient time to talk about the soccer team. The coach had already seen Adrian in action at the High School and knew that he would be an ideal player in his team. It didn't take long for the coach to get him involved because just before leaving he said, "Soccer practice tomorrow at three thirty".

Adrian looked forward to the following afternoon.

It commenced with general introductions of the new players. Some of the previous years were eager to mention which positions suited them best. Some of the new arrivals indicated that they were about to become new stars. The coach summed up, by saying that he had no clear positions for anyone of them at this early stage. He promised everyone a hard time because he would be very demanding, he expected the best at all times.

There was an announcement on the notice board about an Inter Varsity Fellowship meeting on Friday afternoon. Adrian made sure that he arranged nothing to clash with that. He was keen to join the meetings and he would be keen to work for the development and expansion of the witness of Christians in the University.

He was surprised to see quite a nice group of new students being introduced. It was wonderful to receive genuine friendship. A list of some upcoming speakers was announced. It appeared as if it was going to be an excellent term.

On his first Sunday he wasn't sure where to attend Church. He had spoken to a couple of fellows at the I.V.F. meeting. They mentioned a few places but they could give no certain place for fellowship and worship. He went to a local church service on Sunday morning. But he decided to go to the Albert Hall for the evening service. He was impressed by the message and the emphasis on the church's evangelistic outreach into the community. As he glanced around at the large congregation there were a few faces that he recognized from the I.V.F. meeting.

He decided that he would return to the Albert Hall on Sunday evenings, He felt comfortable, the worship and preaching pleased him. And no doubt he would be sitting with some of the others from the I.V.F.

The soccer coach announced details regarding their first match. It would be against a college in Chorlton. He knew the building. He had passed by many times.

The coach stated that it would not be an easy game. Then he gave a warning about one of their players. His reputation is anything but good. If he dislikes an opponent he lets it be felt. But also if there is a key player than he roams away from his position in order to give an illegal tackle. "Beware! I'll point him out during the warm up." "A couple of their players are from the teaching staff. One is the Prof. for the philosophy students. The other is a younger man, an assistant lecturer recently out of seminary training."

We were told to expect a challenging game; the result is not guaranteed for a win or lose.

There were a couple of weeks of lectures and practices. During a phone conversation he had mentioned the match to his parents. His father asked if he ought to inform Hillary also. The semi-verbal comment from Adrian indicated that it would be appreciated if his father did tell her.

The day arrived. It was a clean and clear day. It was just right for a great game of soccer. There was a college bus to take the players to Chorlton. There was a lot of bantering going on especially in regard to how the coach had allocated certain position to particular fellows. Adrian seemed happy with his position in the midfield as a half back or an extra forward. The coach had seen him play and realized that it would be right to try him in that same position.

During the warm up Adrian spotted his parents along the side line, the next time he looked in their direction there was a young lady standing near his father. He had a little flutter but told himself there was nothing serious at this stage and it must not be a distraction. Fortunately he had good control over his emotions. He was set to play the game and be the best he could be, not for the visitors only but for the sake of the team.

The coach had pointed out the dangerous opponent. Adrian took careful note about him.

The game was fairly evenly matched, going from one end to the other. Both teams were creating chances but there was no score at half time.

The coach gave a pep talk and ideas as to how to increase their effectiveness.

It seemed as though the coach of the other team had instructed them to be more serious. The second half was great soccer and thanks to excellent goal keeping it remained no score for the first twenty minutes of the second half.

The opponents scored a questionable off-side goal. The referee had turned his blind eye in the wrong direction. Adrian gave himself a reprimand because he felt that he had not done enough to hinder the movement towards goal. Five minutes later it was Adrian at his best. He had dropped back into defense, obtained the ball and dribbled well down field. He placed a perfect pass to the right wing and then he ran towards the left corner of the penalty area. The winger was an excellent dribbler and gave a wonderful forward pass directly to Adrian. He could do nothing else but score. The cheers from one section of the crowd were quite noticeable. But also the facial contortions of the 'beware' opponent sent an alarming message to the other players. He became a very aggressive tackler, most of the times resulted in the ref. whistle for a foul.

There had been a wonderful pass to Adrian in the penalty area when there was a rough tackle from behind. Adrian went down with a lot of pain. That brought his team members to gather around him for protection but there was a desire for revenge. But to the dismay of the team and certain spectators Adrian was helped off the field for the coach's magic spray. He was able to return to the field but everyone noticed that his speed was slower. One of his team got rough with the 'beware' guy, it took the opponent out of the game but also the referee showed a red card and sent the university player off. The game ended with a one draw. The spectators thought that to be a fair result.

Three people from the crowd came over to see Adrian. They were pleased to see him on his feet but wondered what damage might have been done to hinder his future in the team. The coach went up to Adrian's parents and eased their concern. "He'll be off for two or three weeks, he'll keep practicing; he'll be back in the team. We can't do without him!" To the surprise of his team mates they saw Hillary walk up to him and give him a massive hug. In fact two or three commenced cheering. That brought a mighty laugh from the whole team and others who were standing nearby.

The term continued with many challenging lectures and assignments. Adrian was responding quite positively and enjoying his time at university. It must have been a month or just a little more and he was back in the soccer team. They had missed him. Just from the first game the team had recognized him as being a key player for the university.

There was an end of term concert. Adrian enjoyed being in the choir. He had not taken part in the drama that term, and felt a little upset because he would have thoroughly enjoyed taking a part in the comedy that was part of the end of year celebration.

So, it was home for the holidays.

23
CHAPTER

The last month of school was a difficult time for Mary. She had adjusted to the change of direction in her life but was assured that it would not be permanent. She had quite a number of friends in her class that sympathized with her and endeavoured to encourage her by indicating that it was just a delay in her academic career.

But the 'unholy trio' had very different comments. They were the ones who boasted that the world was waiting for them to graduate from University so that they could begin the important task of putting the world right. These three girls were not liked just by the rest of their class but by most of the other girls in the school. They were boisterous and loud-mouthed. There was not one kind word to Mary, in fact it was quite the opposite. They ridiculed her for becoming a school drop-out; as one who could not cope with the pressures of an academic career.

The nasty remark on one occasion was that Mary was talking about her decision not to attend university this year was not just a hindrance to her studies, but something more permanent. They left her in no doubt they considered her incapable of coping with the pressures of higher education. You won't realize anything – we'll have the world at our knees, on their knees.

What arrogance! Those three are the epitome of self-righteousness and self aggrandizement. The world will be in a worse shape if they ever graduate and enter into a worthwhile term of meaningful employment.

Mary was very upset by the unhelpful and unsympathetic remarks. Her friends rallied around her with the truth about the "three unholy" girls. Some of her class had other more vivid and detrimental titles for them. Mary was encouraged by those who were asking genuine questions about her mother's health. They also pressed home the point that they were convinced it was a detour for one year in her studies.

Her teacher asked to see her during a break one afternoon. She had heard about the nasty things certain girls were saying about her. "They are not true. Those ideas are furthest from the truth. You are doing a noble and loving thing."

The teacher then went on to talk about how she was intending to help her during that upcoming painful year. She has been in touch with a professor at the University and explained why Mary would not be entering the college this year. The professor was sorry. As they conversed he gave assurance that the place was still available after the year. He also talked about how she could spend some of her time during that one year away from school.

"Which of the subjects would you like to do preparatory work on? Mary?" she asked

"I suppose Maths. is likely to be by major so some guidance in that direction could prove to be quite helpful".

"Well I have spoken to one of the professors and he agrees that we could spend this waiting year looking ahead. I will talk to him again and we will come up with some ideas. I want to help you. I will help you to the best of my ability. It will need to be a project that will bear in mind your valuable time caring for your mother and father".

"Thank you. You are so kind. I want to thank you also for being so understanding of my reason for the delay in going to university".

"We will make it a beneficial delay".

The graduation event was imminent. Mary E. had talked to her parents and her friend Mary A.. The opinion of her mother and father, especially her mother, was that she should attend the graduation. As Mary A. said, "It is your graduation. You have earned it. And also you are likely to receive at least one of the 'prizes'".

"But", added May E.. "All the others will be talking excitedly about where they will be going. I will feel left out of the enthusiasm".

"No you will not", said Mary A. "Your task for the coming year will be far more important than any of the other girls. It may appear to be a sacrifice. It may appear a hindrance to your academic progress. But rest assured that year will be precious to your mother and highly appreciated by your father, and you yourself will develop through the pain you will be sharing as well as finding out first hand just how God helps in challenging situations that you are going through".

Mary did go to the graduation. She realized how important it was for her. Her parents were delighted that she did not skip the graduation because she had studied hard. There was a surprise, it was announced that she had won the prize for the best encouraging personality in her year. Her friend, Mary A. was overly excited for her. They had a time which they would remember.

It had been so important for Mary to attend graduation. She looked back on it with some sort of satisfaction. The shadow of her reason for delaying leaving for University could not be avoided, but it did not overly distract from the pleasure of the celebration at the end of her High School years.

Betty was growing weaker as each week passed. Clarence was trying to cope with more work around the house, but Mary told him not to worry about it because that is why she would be around. It became a new chore for Mary. She had done some housework and cooking in the past but not 'full time'. She diligently compiled shopping lists only to find that on her return home there were some things not included on the list. Her main concern was to look for recipes that would be tasty for her mother.

It seemed to Mary that Betty was not eating so much. One day she made a comment about losing her appetite. Her mother had a wonderful smile and added "the aroma from the kitchen triggers a desire to find the taste meeting up to the promise from the aroma".

The first month after graduation was filled with learning experiences especially as her Mother gradually required more nursing care. Her mother helped her with some of the new challenges as they were being faced. She had spent some time nursing her aged mother, so was able to help her daughter from her personal experiences.

Mary was able to set some time to one side for study. Her friend Mary A. often came to visit her in an evening. Together they would look at some of the work the teacher was setting for Mary E. They both learned a lot!

"I do hope these studies will be good preparation for next year", Mary E said to her friend.

"They ought to be. Isn't the University Professor giving your teacher some guidance in this regard?"

"Yes. So I ought to be more content in mastering the work being given to me".

"You are doing just fine. And in actual fact I am doing quite fine also!"

It was soon after that Betty was showing more weakness, and she was asking for more pain pills. This triggered alarm bells both for Clarence and his daughter. They had been preparing themselves for this. They knew she must be entering a very critical stage – the tumours were winning the battle. Father and daughter spent more and more time hugging each other late at night when Betty had gone to sleep.

Betty was now spending more time in bed. It was too much effort to get out into the chair. This was causing more anxiety for her husband and daughter. They were spending time prayerfully asking God for more daily strength. They expressed their surprise that He was already giving them greater patience and wisdom.

The nurse was coming in more frequently. She indicated that the doctor would be visiting every other day. Mary commented to her father that the end may not be many days away. Clarence agreed. That brought tears to the eyes of both of them. In fact they had not realized that it would be their last week. Clarence didn't go to work. Mary shelved her studies. They lovingly spent a vigil over the wife and mother they loved dearly. When Betty was conscious she asked Clarence to say a little prayer. Mary would also add a prayer. There would be smiles all round and kisses and hugs.

"See you in the morning", commented Clarence to Betty, who gave a gentle nod indicating that she was looking forward to that.

"Jesus is here waiting for me", Betty said in a very weak voice. That drew Clarence and Mary close to her side.

"I love you both", she whispered, "night, night". Her eyes closed. Her laboured breathing stopped. The two grieving people did not need the doctor or the nurse to say, "She's gone". They both mentioned the importance of knowing where she had gone.

"There is no doubt. Jesus has taken her to heaven to the place he has prepared for her", said Clarence.

"Yes. I know she is with Jesus; she loved him very much", added Mary

The nurse reached out to cover her with a sheet.

Mary stopped her, saying, "I want to do that later, please". Her father nodded his approval.

The doctor indicated that he would give a prescription for them both to help with the pain of grief. Both shrugged their shoulders with a "thank you but we don't think we will need that".

The next couple of days were spent making arrangements for the 'celebration of life' service. They loved their pastor and trusted him to make the service relevant and meaningful as well as challenging to some of the unbelievers who would be there.

Many friends and members of the church visited them giving their condolences and prayerful support. The service was, as one person said, "a touch of heaven". Heaven's door had opened and Betty Stapelford had been welcomed home.

The house felt almost empty when Mary and her father arrived home after the funeral. There had been a pleasant time spent with refreshments and friends in the church basement. They sat together in silence for a few minutes. Then Mary reached over and gave her father a big hug and kisses and said, "I'll be here with you and for you. We'll comfort each other and together receive the peace and strength of our Lord. I want to say, we will continue to receive what he has been giving over the past few months."

"Thank you, sweetheart. You are so good to me and for me. We are being blessed daily, (no, in fact it is moment by moment,) by our Gracious Heavenly Father".

As the months passed Mary was becoming more efficient with her time. She was able to allocate valuable time to her studies. They were becoming more interesting and enjoyable as the weeks passed. Her teacher was very helpful; they met together once every two weeks. She was getting excited about the University adventure next year, or rather later that current year.

Her friend Mary A. commented so many times how much she was learning as Mary E shared some of her work. Clarence took quite a while to settle, he was often not looking forward to going home because of the empty chair. Yet he at the same time was looking forward to sharing time with his daughter who was caring for him exceptionally well.

Once a month Clarence took Mary out for a surprise evening, either a special meal or a show. They both looked forward being away from the house and spending time just being with each other.

Mary was pleased when her father started attending a couple of meetings for men at the church. He would often speak about one particular man who was becoming quit friendly. He asked Mary if he could invite his new friend for dinner. They agreed for the following Sunday. Mary was anxious to meet the man her father spoke so highly about.

The following Sunday was one of those special sunny days after a whole week of rain. That placed a better shine on the meal Mary had prepared. The friend arrived and was introduced to Mary, He had a wonderful smile and friendly disposition. As they progressed through the meal Mary was warming to him and thinking how fortunate her father was to find such a nice man.

Later that afternoon Mary was on her own in her room thinking about the future. She was happily telling herself how pleased she was that her father was having new interests and what appeared to be a great friend.

She was finding it much easier to anticipate her planned move to University after the summer. Her teacher expressed the pleasure she was finding in how Mary had coped with the bereavement. She was also impressed by how her widowed father was being helped to settle to the new phase in his life. "You've done a marvelous job, Mary", stated the teacher, "we are so proud of your decision and your ability to deal with the sadness and change of circumstances".

It was a day towards the end of August when Clarence took Mary for a drive in the car. He parked in a beautiful spot overlooking the dales. He had taken two director's chairs in the car so they found a nice place and relaxed.

"I want to say a big 'Thank You', sweetheart".

"What for?"

"For the extent of your love, for the encouragement you have been giving me, for the wonderful meals, for times of fellowship and devotions".

"Yes, Dad, I know. But I also want to say how impressed I have been with you as you dealt with the loss of Mother. It was a massive adjustment for you; and you are still in the process of watching God turning you into a wonderful new man".

"That was special. That was beautiful. That was so loving. I am lost for words, but suffice to say I thank God every day for you. You have been everything a daughter could have been over these past months, it would have been so lonely without you".

"I have become aware of the fact, Father, that it is one thing to be lonely even with a group of other people around, and that of being alone. It is the aloneness that lingers".

"In two weeks or so you will be packing your bags. "1 will have the privilege of driving my daughter to Manchester University. Leaving home and entering the world of academia becomes a whole new world".

CHAPTER 24

By the end of the first term Adrian had made a good many friends and also his reputation as an acceptable soccer player placed his name into numerous coffee-time conversations.

Adrian was quite impressed by the quality of the lectures, and his response was one of being quite eager to learn more. There were times he crept into the Library and curled up in a corner with the text book recommended by one of the Professors. There were so many excellent books recommended that he would have liked to have copies on his own shelves, but the expense was too immense.

The second term did not seem to have any special beginning, because the work immediately continued from where it left off before the break.

The leader of the I.V.F. announced in an early meeting that he would like a group of students to form a committee to look forward to special activities that would attract other students. Adrian rose to the occasion because he seemed to be bubbling over with some things he felt they should try out.

A time was set at the weekend. Four students had mentioned to him that they would like to help. Adrian's concern was that the time would be well used, so he made a point of stressing that in his prayers leading up to the time to meet.

It was an inspiring and challenging meeting. The leader had prepared well and was enthusiastic in regard to new expressions of their faith. One of the things he mentioned was his desire to bring in speakers who could speak about their work and their faith.

Adrian was happy that he joined the group. As he left the meeting his main thought was wondering just how the Lord will be using him during his time at the university. The thought of a speaker who is an expert in his field and to link that with his faith in God would be a great opening in inviting other students to the I.V.F. meetings.

The following Sunday evening he went to the Albert Hall for the service. During the announcement the Minister stood looking around the auditorium, then asked that the Students meet him in one of the small rooms after the service for some refreshments.

It was no great spread – a selection of soft drinks and cakes and biscuits. About seventeen or eighteen students were there, most of them from the university but there were a few from other Colleges in the city. Adrian's friendly approach soon attracted other students to meet and talk with him. The Minister's idea was to have a meeting like this once a month just to get the students together and with the hope of being able to do something special with them towards the end of the year.

Four or five of the students were from a Seminary and had been working with the minister the previous year in special evangelical outreach ventures. In conversation with them others became quite interested in the hope that something similar might be planned for them also.

On their way home to the residence the university students were expressing their joy, also their anticipation of what might be happening later in the year. As they travelled together they appreciated the fact that the meeting had been a good introduction for them to get to know each other. They were no longer strangers. No longer 'other' students. They were friends.

The next soccer match was with a college team from the Salford district. A rumour from some of the older students was that it was a weak team so the outcome ought not to be in doubt. If there was no victory that would mean that this year's team was inferior to previous years.

The coach directed a wonderful practice session. He was quite personal in some of his remarks because he stated that he wanted a personal relationship with each member of the team so that he could be direct with them. This was one of his ways of being a successful coach.

There was a bus to take the team to Salford. A few of the stalwart supporters were given a seat on the bus. When they got off the bus there was no wonderful entrance to a fancy stadium – just a gate with the name of the college above it. We were met near the entrance and taken round the back of the college building to the sports field. The whole team, expressed pleasure in it being a rich turf playing area. Any falling over under pressure from aggressive tackles would find an easier landing than on many sports fields.

It was good to see other university students in the small crowd. It wasn't long into the game when everybody for miles around knew where they were from and the team they were supporting. It was almost as if they had been trained by a professional in team support. That might have been one of the facts that caused the team to be relaxed. They had not been warned about any ferocious tackler among the opposing team.

At half time the university was winning two goals to nil. Adrian had received a great cheer part way though for saving a ball off the goal line. He had received a great slap on the back from the goal-keeper. The coach commended Adrian on his intelligent approach and awareness of any dangerous moves.

The second half saw Adrian closer to the forwards. The centre field players had gained confidence and that allowed him to venture forward occasionally; it also allowed him to kick a curving ball high into the net for their third goal.

There was no silence in the bus going home. It was a time of reminiscing the high-lights of a well matched game. The other team certainly was not an easy run over, they played very well. It was a good game.

The term ended with a slap-happy presentation. It would be an insult to call it a drama. The author was determined to remain anonymous. Some purists might have desired to hang and quarter him. The best report would have a simple one-liner. "Some of the audience laughed, occasionally!"

Adrian did not want to discuss it probably because at the last moment he was asked to take a part. Someone indicated that he was obviously inadequate to cope with such a part. Adrian was not entirely convinced within himself, but he accepted the part for the sake of the scared and scarred producer. It was a small part so Adrian realized that it was not going to demand a lot of memorizing. When he entered the stage he was welcomed with half the audience praising him and the other half ready to burn him at the stake. Obviously it was not a character that enhanced his jovial and presentable self. He performed an excellent bow to the applauding positive side of the audience. His bow was not as serious and professional for the other side.

To the surprise of all members of the cast when it came to the end they had to face a standing ovation. One silly woman shouted out for an encore! There was a fun party afterwards for the cast and production team.

Adrian had come to the end of his first year at University. There had been a few things that he anticipated. He had been thrilled with the quality of the lectures. The time spent with the I.V.F, group had been inspiring and encouraging. He was looking forward to what would develop during the next year,

He had been thinking about the long summer holiday. He secretly hoped that a part-time job would become available. He could always use extra 'pocket money'. His father had been making enquiries regarding summer work for him. The perfect idea would have been in a business office, but the firms he contacted were not in business for any part time student.

His minister at the Church called to see him. A youth camp has been planned and there was a need for some gifted leadership. But —there is always a 'but' when it comes to church volunteer work. "We cannot offer a decent salary, but your expenses will be covered and there is a guarantee that a little pocket money will become available." Adrian asked questions about what leadership roles would be involved. The more his minister explained the hopes for the Camp the more interested he became.

Adrian's summer was spent at the Camp. The leadership team was very open and friendly. He was surprised at the quality of the spiritual emphasis each week. It was wonderful to see answers to prayers as young people responded to the challenge of heading into a God-directed life.

One week he saw a girl he recognized. She recognized him and blushed. She was walking along with a boy. It was obvious that they were friends. It was the girl who came to a few of the soccer games but then stopped. Adrian was pleased that she had a boy friend, because one of the things he was not looking forward to have to show a friendly interest in her. He thought that might be expected by the folk at the Church. No one person mentioned her name to him. When her name came into any discussion it was always in connection with the 'new' friend she was walking out with.

The duties at the Camp were quite demanding but there was an absence of pressure to perform beyond ones means. He appreciated the relaxed atmosphere and decided that summer Camp might fit the bill for him another year. It was a pleasure and a privilege. He had used his time in service for Jesus, and Jesus had richly blessed him.

There had been adventures into the forest. Well, it was not a deep wooded jungle. There were some paths between the trees and they led to different clearings. In those clearings was the opportunity to let the imagination run wild. Various were the dangerous animals lurking behind nearby trees. It was spectacular to see the birds involved in chasing away some tree climbing creatures. More than one boy, and sometimes it was a girl that demanded on being appointed an aboriginal chief. At the end of the day it was impossible to count how many scalps had been 'won' during the escapades of that one day.

Adrian was developing leadership skills but alongside that his imaginations were expanding.

All the kids just longed for the cookouts; it was almost every evening that supper was enjoyed around the camp fire. And the leaders made sure that paper plates were being used. That would mean no hassles as to who would be delegated to do the washing up. The fire was the ideal place for the dirty dishes!

For those who could swim, there were set times for a team to go on the river in canoes. There was not one week when at least one canoe flipped over. Fortunately the water was not very deep, so it became quite easy to drag the saturated kids out of the river.

As a family they had set aside a couple of weeks for a family holiday. They went to a Holiday Home in North Wales. The ideal place to relax or if feeling energetic go on one of the mountain climbing trips. The weather was ideal and as a family they enjoyed each other's company and it became a time when love for each other grew and was evident to other holiday makers.

Adrian did manage to put his head into a couple of books. He classed it as preparation for the next term; He had no intention of calling it 'work' because he was very interested in the subjects chosen for summer reading.

The time came too quickly when it meant sorting and packing for his return to University. There was a farewell prayer of blessing from the Pastor on his last Sunday. He didn't count how many people came up and wished him well for his next year of studies. It was a good and caring Church.

It had been a good summer.

CHAPTER 25

Mary acknowledged how important it had been to stay home for a year to help her father adjust. By the end of the year she recognized that he was becoming more and more independent and that meant she could anticipate going to university in September. She had gone through some moments when she felt grieved about staying home. But those moments passed as she recognized that God had blessed her and helped her to mature as she passed through the period of bereavement herself and helped her father to find a new interest in a life without his dear wife.

The Church had been a great help. Mary appreciated every kind thought and deed. Such helped her along and was also an encouragement to her father.

Three or four times during the year her father asked pointed questions about her friends. He seemed at times over anxious that she should find a really nice young man. He was hoping for a wedding – but he made sure that he was totally understood, that it must be with a devout Christian young man.

Her reply was always the same. "Well, Dad, I have not found such a 'creature' in our Church, yet!"

His reply was always the same, "Then he will have to be an academic you bump into at University!" She would always chuckle at that because she envisioned a collision along one of the corridors with a professor whose mortarboard had slipped over his eyes.

At the end of Spring she noticed her father was often deep in thought. One day she tackled him. "Dad, what's the problem

"Oh, nothing!"

"Has the 'nothing' to do with me leaving home?"

There was a beautiful smile. She knew that he was not looking forward to being left on his own. That made her all the more determined to make those last few weeks precious and memorable for him. She insisted that they go on a holiday together, perhaps to the Isle of White. To her surprised he agreed and stated that he had been thinking along those lines also.

It did not take them long before a booking had been made and they were looking forward to their date.

The Isle of White is always more beautiful when the sun is shining. The day they arrived in Ventnor it was pouring with rain. Their spirits were not dampened though because the accommodation was excellent and they enjoyed the food; may be because they had not had to prepare it themselves. Her father was relaxed; in fact more so than anytime during the year. This pleased Mary; now she could anticipate being away from him knowing that he is adjusting well.

The sun came out the next day and 'promised' to stay out for the rest of the week. The island is not large it does not take very long to go from one end to the other; it doesn't take much longer to go all the way round it. But one of the wonderful things about the island is the abundance of sand and rocks. They enjoyed themselves. Neither had been so relaxed for a long time. They were feeling the benefits of a real vacation. They had lots of fun at the coloured sand beach. They had obtained a fancy bottle and were making major decisions as to which colour sand went in first and then the choice of colours to follow. They both admired their handy-work; "quite artistic", was the phrase her father used.

They enjoyed taking advantage of the afternoon 'special' teas being offered in the various restaurants in the small towns.

A new venture for them was to go to an evening concert. There was an element of comedy. They left laughing.

They had decided not to wear themselves out by travelling everywhere. So the days spent just sitting around talking and basking in the warm sunshine were times both of them would remember with great pleasure. Their holiday was enabling their relationship to deepen. There was no doubt about their genuine love for each other.

They both expressed sadness when they were packing their cases to leave for home. It had been a wonderful time away.

After the ferry had brought them to the mainland there was no long wait before the train arrived to take them north and home. On the train her father mentioned that he was looking forward to being in his own home and promised his daughter that he would be all right. She had helped him learn how to manage and so he was facing the loneliness of the future with confidence. He had some great friends at the Church and she knew that they would keep a gentle and loving eye on him.

There was not very much left of the summer. Mary had collected all the things she thought would be required. There were some items Clarence threw into a case with a humorous comment about them being "essential for a potential academic".

The Sunday before she was to leave for university the minister of the Church asked her to join him at the front of the congregation. He placed his hands on her head and asked God to bless and protect her, he asked for the Holy Spirit to guide her and keep her true to the teaching of the Bible. Mary heard her father respond with a loud "amen". Her "amen" was equally as loud.

All her things were packed into the car and they were ready to set off for Manchester. Clarence paused before leaving the house and held Mary quite close to himself and prayed for her protection and enjoyment at university, He asked the Lord to direct her paths regarding the subjects in which to major, and he prayed also for her spiritual growth and protection against heresies thrown at her by academics. He also asked the Lord to give him the support necessary, and he made a promise to God that he would regularly remember Mary at the Throne of Grace. There was a big 'amen' from both of them.

Conversation on the journey from Mansfield to Manchester centred round the prospects Mary would be facing. Clarence had incidents he remembered from his student days, many of them quite humorous.

There was a parking space fairly close to the entrance. Clarence commented that the Lord had moved a car out especially for them. He carried the cases while Mary bundled a lot of other stuff into her arms. Then there was a glance into the car followed by the remark that one of them was to make a return trip for the rest of the 'baggage'.

It didn't take them long to arrange the sparse furniture into some sort of shape. How many floor designs are necessary for a bed, an easy chair, a book case, a desk with a swivel chair to be allocated the right place in the room? Mary's comment was that they will most probably get moved around again and again.

The few things that were left in the car made one good arm bundle, so the need for a return trip was no longer valid. Mary said that she could cope.

It was the moment Clarence knew would come. It was farewell time. But how wonderful to know that it was not permanent but they'd be together again at the end of term. Actually there were tears trickling down the cheeks of both daughter and father.

"It's time sweetheart", said Clarence in more than a whisper. Mary wished she did not have her arms full but managed to free one while hanging on to the stuff with the other in order to hug her father, They were together – in fact neither one wanted to part – Clarence had to make the move.

"It's time", he said again. Her response was that his watch ought to stop running. With a final hug and kiss he slipped into the driving seat and started the engine.

She stood watching her father drive out of the parking lot and on to the road. Then, with a deliberate shaking of herself and pulling in her shoulders, she turned and made her way back into the residence.

As she got closer to her room another student stepped out of one of the rooms, they said "hello" to each other. The other one made a comment about being 'new students' to which Mary replied that it was the beginning of a new adventure. She mentioned that her room was a few doors further down the corridor. They walked together. Mary threw the things she was carrying on to the bed and invited the other student to stay awhile.

They exchanged their names and from where they had come. Mary was quietly asking the Lord if this was a student she could be friends with. There was something winsome about her. They exchanged a little information about the schools they attended.

"My name is Mary".

"My name is Betty".

"That will be easy to remember, my mother's name was Betty".

They entered Mary's room.

Betty was glancing around the room. On the desk she noticed a few books on top of which was a Bible. "Oh. Do you read that?" she pointed at the Bible.

"Yes, regularly", was Mary's reply.

"So do I!" she said with fervour.

"Isn't that just wonderful, we have only just met and now we know that we both enjoy reading God's Word" Mary commented. There was an obvious note of real pleasure in her voice.

Betty was very happy, she said more than a couple of times that this was an answer to her prayers and the prayers of her parents that she found another Christian student. Mary's reply was in a similar vein; many or her friends and relatives had been praying for this over a period of months.

Mary didn't get any unpacking done. They just sat and shared their experiences. It was Betty that broke the trends in the conversation by announcing that according to her watch it was time to go to the dining room. So they went off together for their first meal at University.

Much of the first week for these two new friends was spent finding the right lecture halls and making sure they had the right times for each lecture. The wonderful thing was that for a few of the lectures they would be together in the same lecture hall. Looking at the size of the lecture halls made them realize that they could so easily be lost amid the multitude of eager students.

The official notice board for the university was loaded with announcements. Many of them indicating that if they wanted a happy experience while at university they must join their group. "If so," Betty said, "We can forget most of the lecture, there will be no time to study!" There was one notice that attracted their attention; it was in connection with an Intervarsity Christian Fellowship that held regular meetings during each term.

"I was told to look out for the I.V.F. meetings", remarked Mary, "One of the members of my church back home had been an active member when at university and had indicated quite strongly the importance of such a fellowship. The main stable function kept him close to the Lord and enabled the Holy Spirit to guide against heresies being propounded on a regular basis".

"Then this is on the must list", confirmed Betty.

The next few weeks Mary was being exposed to studies at the higher level. The courses she had been given during the year after graduation from High School had helped. It was a great day when she met with the registrar and was told that she had been given two credits for the work done the previous year. That was two subjects she did not have to study so after making enquiries with the head of department she took on another subject that would normally have been included in the second year programme.

Mary and Betty made their way to the room where the I.V.F. was to be held. It was a steady stream of Students entering. From their appearance it would suggest that they were from various years and various disciplines. A fellow and girl got up and went to the front near a desk. The girl sat down and the fellow remained standing indicating he wanted to address the students present.

"My name", he said, "Is Adrian Syston. I am just commencing my second year. I have been elected to a leadership role this year, probably because I spoke too much last year! Newcomers please note there were no comments from the older students present. I did not insist that they keep quiet!

"Welcome to Inter Varsity Fellowship. It's good to see some new faces. If this is your first experience of I.V.F. then you are in for a treat. We read the Bible as God's Word to us. We trust the Holy Spirit to guide us into experiences of the truths we read. There is always a time of prayer towards the end, although sometimes we find it appropriate to spend time in prayer during a meeting.

"We have a small committee that does not pronounce large edicts but is basically the ones who give guidance and leadership in our programmes. This is certainly not going to be a typical meeting. Our desire is to let you know who we are and where we believe God want us to go during this year.

"We are giving an opportunity for everyone to introduce himself or herself. Where they are from and the course they are taking. And what your hopes are from such a group as this. I will ask the leaders to start and then without any particular order I'd like you all to share what information you would like with us.

"You may even think this to be a typical church meeting. Why? Because we will have some refreshments. That will give us a chance to mingle and get to know each other".

It was an interesting time listening to the various students and to know where they came from. Not all of them were from the U.K. There were three or four from Africa and China.

Mary and Betty were delighted with the meeting. They were in full chattering mode as they made their way back to the residence. They were both eager to indicate that they were going to not only enjoy that group but be able to participate in the fellowship.

CHAPTER

During the first month Mary and Betty had discussed possible churches in Manchester. They visited a different one each Sunday but after the service indicated that they did not want to return because it just did not feel right. Sometimes it was the singing, often it was the preaching.

One Saturday lunch time the topic came up again. Betty said, "A friend in my church worked in Manchester. She told me on one occasion that she attended a Church; I think she said it was on the east side of the city. It had a funny sounding name. She called it Beth Shan Church".

"That sounds like a Hebrew name, is it a Hebrew Church?" asked Mary.

"It doesn't sound like a typical English Church. There are 'Bethels' and 'Trinity', and lots of Saints", mentioned Betty.

"Is it any particular denomination?" asked Mary.

"I think it is a Pentecostal Church".

"The information I have received about them is that they are noisy, and way-out. Someone referred to them as 'Holy Rollers', added Mary, "But let's try it out tomorrow".

"Okay. I'll make some enquiries regarding service time and how to get there", promised Betty.

The next day they took the bus across the city and entered Beth Shan Church, not sure what to expect. They received a genuine friendly welcome from a couple of adult greeters. The church attracted a variety of nationalities. The singing was loud; but they expected that.

During one song there was an elderly man standing in front of them and he was not singing the words from the hymn book. He was loud and so was heard above the others sitting nearby. Mary poked Betty and said pointing in his direction with her thumb, "What?" Betty shrugged her shoulders, "Not sure".

During the sermon the young Pastor made reference to speaking in tongues. Mary whispered, "Was he singing in tongues?" Betty mouthed back, "It sounded like it!"

Both girls appreciated the careful preparation that the Pastor must have made. His careful explanation of some of the words in the text impressed them.

There were lots of comments on their way back to the residence. The man singing in tongues had impressed them. He sounded and looked genuine. There comments stressed the importance for them to find out more about what it meant. The hymns and songs they sang were familiar to them both. It was Mary that raised the point about the sermon. Betty agreed that the preacher had done some good preparation. Mary indicated that she had learned much about some words that were often used but never explained.

By the time they got off the bus they had agreed to go back again another Sunday. What had become the attraction? It was the enthusiasm of the singing and the helpfulness of the sermon.

Adrian had been quite impressed with the first meeting of the I.V.F. In conversation with the other leaders they praised the Lord for the potential for great times of fellowship. The girl who had gone up front with him was one of the committee. Her talents will be used in singing and in leading discussions.

The fellow that interested him in his first year had been sick and had missed much of his year. He was pleased to see him back and looking very fit. He had enjoyed having the cup of tea with Geoff after the meeting.

The following Sunday Adrian was setting off for the Church service and Geoff was coming out of the residence at the same time. They both indicated that they were going to a worship service. Adrian was ready to verbalize that they go together because he remembered seeing him in the Albert Hall on a couple of occasions the previous year. As they walked towards the bust stop Adrian mentioned where he was going. Geoff smiled and said he was going to the same place because he also had remembered seeing Adrian at the service previously.

They were both going to the morning service for the first time. They knew that the main service was in the evening, but wanted to check out a morning service. There were not so many in attendance but it was a time of blessing and encouragement.

On their way back after the service they compared morning and evening times for worship. They both agreed that the evening service was the main one to attend. It was also the one where there would be opportunities to meet with other Christian students attending other colleges in Manchester.

During the next few days Adrian found himself thinking about friends. He had made it a point of prayer that the Lord would guide in the development of friendships. He was convinced that God had brought Geoff into his life for a purpose. It was more than a coincidence that they bumped into each other at most meal times. Their friendship was to grow in mutual respect for each other and their willingness to seek the will of the Lord for their lives.

There were a couple of soccer games within a few days. The coach was concerned that his regular team may not be willing or ready to cope with two games close together. To his surprise most of his first team wanted to play the second game. It was a couple of the mid-field players who were involved in some other activity and were not able to play. The coach had a couple of fellows in mind. He received a willing response from both of them. They of course realized that they were second choice, yet both of them decided they would play their best to impress the coach but also to win the match.

The game went off well. Adrian noticed a few more supporters along the touch line. As he looked closer he recognized them as being from the I.V.F.

Two young ladies had obtained a couple of flags, not large ones, but a reasonable size, large enough to indicate which team they were supporting.

The flags, alongside the voices of their owners, almost became an explosion of 'well done'. This happened when Adrian scored an important go-ahead goal. There were but two minutes left before the final whistle. The game was a draw. Both sides had scored two goals. Adrian had one of his roving moments. He had helped in defense but had received the ball in mid-field. He was running forward with another player. They exchanged the ball twice and juggled their way between the defense. Adrian had continued his run to the edge of the six yard box; his colleague slipped a beautiful pass to him. He could do nothing else but score. If he had missed then he would have been mud especially among some of the supporters.

The two girls were so excited. It was the first soccer game they had attended but both agreed that it would not be the last. It was not a surprise when they concentrated their comments on one player. They knew him from varsity. They knew him as the leader of the I.V.F. They liked him. In fact on the bus, returning to their residence they were expressing something more than a mere liking. It was Mary that announced that such thoughts should be left until later in the university careers. Betty's response was a loud chuckle, which drew the attention of others on the bus. So, with a blush she made Mary aware that it was a beautiful feeling right now, then somewhat reluctantly agreed that such emotions are not quite right for the present time. There was a very interesting squeezing of their hands as they nodded approval of such a precaution.

At the next meeting of the IVF Adrian indicated that he had something important to share that evening. After the usual items of business, some were as trivial as usual, Adrian brushed his papers to one side and stood. The speakers didn't always stand. But the students present expected something different because Adrian did not normally stand to make announcements.

"At the last meeting of our committee we ventured into a new area for this branch of I.V.F". Adrian announced, "We are in the embryonic stage of plan making for a special event early next term. The theme will come under the umbrella of 'Missions'. We all want a presentation that will appeal to other than I.V.F supporters. At the moment we are anticipating that it will be just a one off evening. But my hope would be for a substantial follow up. Sufficient to announce, at this stage, that it will probably be towards the end of the first month of next term. I think that is good timing. That will give us the chance to decide what to do or what not to do regarding follow up.

"Whatever else we decide to night there must be a strong emphasis on prayer for the Holy Spirit to guide in every detail.

"Let's get praying!"

There was an interesting discussion to follow that announcement. But to the joy of the committee there were no negative attitudes. There were some interesting and helpful suggestions that the committee noted.

The time of prayer was inspiring; after which the anticipation was for a great meeting in January.

Mary and Betty were quite enthusiastic as the term went on. They were being absorbed in their studies, but they especially were grateful to God for the way in which their friendship was developing. They were noting the chances to specialize in various branches of their chosen subjects. Both agreed that if possible they would like to do an 'honours' degree. But this was not something to be decided at this stage; they would need to make such arrangements by the end of the year.

Adrian and Geoff were thanking God for their unity and future developments in their friendship. It had already become a recognized factor that the Lord had obviously been guiding in that regard. They both kept coming up with thoughts about the 'Missions' meeting coming up next term. Some were aired and allowed to float away, others were noted an placed on a list of things to be included, but only if God indicated quite clearly that such would be His will for such an occasion.

There was involvement in the choir. Last year, Adrian had taken part and enjoyed the practices and the special Christmas presentation. It was not long into the practices that the choir director had remembered Adrian giving a lead. Adrian wasn't really surprised when he was not asked but rather it was announced, that he had two special parts to sing, on his own.

Relatives and other friends were invited to the concert. It was a great time to celebrate the Saviour's birth but a wonderful way to close the term.

The I.V.F had a close of term party. There were lots of greetings and cards. Some clever student hung up a bunch of mistletoe. Committee members were not too happy but allowed it to go ahead. In actual fact it caused a lot of fun and joy. It was probably taken for granted that the kissing part was not to be taken seriously!

There were lots of farewells. Some commented that they could not wait for the next term to begin. Most of them were seriously looking forward to a time of rest and relaxation. They wanted to refresh their friendships and have fun with their families.

CHAPTER 27

The Christmas holidays were over. The students had a great time with their families and old friends. There were numerous parties each one giving the opportunity to get gorged. If any of the students lost weight over the break it was not the fault of the cook.

They had relaxed by doing things not done for a long time. Friends found it difficult to obtain a time for them to visit. The relaxing was actually being away from their books. That did not apply to the last week when they were reminded of the assignment required in the first week of term.

Adrian did not have any difficulty writing his assignment it flowed quite easily. It helped, of course, by being his favourite subject this year. Dates had never been a distraction for him; in any case there was no one eligible who might consider chasing him.

Mary had difficulty because she was finding it difficult to face yet another separation from her widowed father. He was excellent with her and gave her a wonderful Christmas. He also encouraged her with the assignment; it happened to be one in which he had excelled. What a tremendous boost for Mary. She was appreciating her father more and more. It seemed as if she was seeing him in a new vein since the bereavement.

There were lots of hugs as the students returned for the new term. Sometime a hug was accompanied with a kiss; there were times when the kiss was shunned; there were those who had their hopes dashed because no kiss came their way.

Christmas gifts were shown bringing expected positive comments. It was not long before Geoff arrived and went straight away to find Adrian. Something similar happened with Betty, she knew where to find Mary. The couples were on neighbouring tables, so there were a few 'cross table moments' of conversation. After the meal the couples left in different directions.

Geoff followed Adrian to his room. There was little or no unpacking/ sorting to be done, the little that was required could be done later. They both wanted to know what the other had been up to during the holiday. Christmas for each of them was a time of celebration. The Good News of the Incarnation was and is the basis of the Gospel. They compared party experiences. Geoff was alarmed by the attention given to him by a now grown up girl – there had been some flirtatious moments when they were in kindergarten. He found himself not being drawn into a relationship with her.

They spent a long time reminiscing. Geoff was anxious to change the subject. He asked quite pointedly if Adrian had any more plans for the Missionary meeting. Adrian was eager to share one new idea relating to a speaker.

"A pastor friend was telling me about one of his colleagues who went to Brazil as a missionary". "That would have been interesting", commented Geoff.

"It was more than interesting, I found it quite absorbing. He mentioned that his work had been along the banks of the Amazon River. He has not been working in towns but in small communities of indigenous people along the Amazon. He spoke of the language challenges. Then he mentioned about a 'new' tribe that had been seen near a large bend in the river. No one knew anything about them. This situation had become a major prayer concern".

"What a wonderful time you had with that pastor. Did he mention if the missionary was still in Brazil or is he likely to be on furlough?"

"That is the one major thing for us to pray about' said Adrian. "He is home on sick leave. That means he is not supposed to do any work".

"That's tough, on us!"

"Hold on. Don't jump too far ahead. He will be visiting relatives in the Manchester area towards the end of January.

"But if he can't work ..."

"Don't jump!"

"Okay I've got the message".

"I have already written a letter to him explaining who I am and what we are doing. There is the slightest hope, I hope, of having him talk to a bunch of university students that need not be classed as work".

"You must be joking!"

"Not entirely. But I don't think we should discuss this much more just now until we have received his letter of reply".

Betty had gone to Mary's room. There followed a bunch of girlie talk for about twenty minutes, before Mary wanted to talk more about their life and witness at university.

It was an interesting and informative time. They both learned much about each other. The chat naturally progressed to the I.V.F and how uplifting the times would be for them. They wondered about the special mission meeting that Adrian had presented before the end of the last term.

"I hope he does not want all of us to pack our bags and disappear in the African jungle", mentioned Betty, "I am not against overseas missions but somehow they have little priority in my thinking and planning".

"My mind is not quite that closed", added Mary. "I did say that I was willing to consider anywhere in order to serve the Lord. But my main area of interest would be in the UK and not in some remote bush environment".

A notice went onto the Board indicating a short meeting of IVF in connection with future programming. The date indicated was the following Wednesday at seven o'clock. That was a convenient time because no other activities had regular meetings at that time.

Adrian addressed the small group in attendance, "This is planned as a short meeting. I have no intention of it lasting until midnight. Later this month we are planning a special mission's emphasis meeting. I have the conformation of a speaker who is not to be overworked because he is on sick leave from Brazil. He has been working in remote villages up the Amazon River and has quite a story of learning a tribal unwritten language, amongst other things.

From my correspondence with him he knows how to present information to different levels of education. He is familiar with university groups as he is a graduate of London University.

There were a few questions none of which were negative. There was an enthusiasm for the 'something different' meeting.

One young lady came up to Adrian after the meeting had been dismissed and asked if she might ask a few questions about the up-coming meeting. They walked off together to the canteen and order a coffee each. They found a table not being used and sat there. Adrian asked for her name and why she was interested in the missions meeting.

"My name is Jasmyn", she said, "I have relatives in my family tree from Asia. I have grown up with Missionaries and mission themes".

"That's wonderful. How would you like to help in our preparations?"

"That's why I wanted to speak with you. One of my major's is 'Descriptive Art'", she said. "Can I be of help by doing a poster to advertise our special meeting?"

"I have been praying that our advertising will be honouring to the Lord and effective in attracting students other than the IVF people".

"My aim is that advertising should not only describe the event but will also add a touch of curiosity".

"You are a communicationist after my heart", said Adrian with enthusiasm.

They continued talking for quite some time. It was Adrian who broke the conversation by suggesting that spending all night would not achieve very much alertness for the lectures the next morning.

Later in the week Jasmyn found Adrian, she was carrying a large sheet of paper.

"Let's sit down for a moment, I've something for you to scrutinize", she said with a tremendously wide smile and twinkling eyes. She had roughed out a possible poster. Adrian's eyes popped out in joy and amazement.

Jasmyn had sketched a river with a small community built on one side and there was a boat with two brown men and one white man in it. Information about the meeting and the speaker was included. "This is not the final thing", she mentioned. "But I was wondering if something like this would meet our need?"

"I really do not have words to express an answer", he started, "But I am praising God for your beautiful talent and dedicated skill in making a powerful attraction for our meeting. Yes, please go ahead, my prayers are with you in order to complete what he Lord wants for that meeting".

They chatted and prayed and chatted again. The excitement was growing. Adrian had suggested that she not share the poster idea with too many friends because he wanted everyone to be affected by this presentation.

Fortunately there were no major assignments requiring to be written by the end of the month, so that left more time for the Christian leaders to meet for prayer.

It had been agreed, when the committee had met on the Sunday evening that the poster should be placed on the Notice Board the following morning.

It became an item of praise and discussion for the members of I.V.F, but they were so surprised at the comments they heard other students making about the poster. It was a week of answering some serious questions.

There were wonderful opportunities to invite people to the meeting the coming Friday evening. Adrian was so pleased that they had been able to book one of the larger meeting rooms that had slide and projector facilities.

The I.V.F supporters met together on the Thursday evening for prayer relating to the speaker, and for the students who would be interested in coming to the meeting.

On Friday afternoon a car brought Bob Brownlow to Manchester University. Adrian had been informed that he would be arriving around three o'clock. Two of his relatives were in the car with him. They all went up to Adrian's room and spent a valuable time getting to know one another. They prayed together about the meeting. Then they went off to the cafeteria where Geoff met up with them. They had a meal together.

They went to the meeting room about fifteen minutes before the scheduled start. There was an anti-room for the speaker. Adrian and Bob enjoyed being on their own for a few minutes in prayerful contact with the Lord.

Geoff headed towards the front and took a seat towards one end of the front row. The two men who arrived with the speaker found seats towards the back. Mary and Betty arrived early. They found seats on the front row at the opposite end to Geoff. They waved and greeted each other. Other members of I.V.F arrived. It had been decided that the IVF'ers would not sit together, but would scatter themselves in pairs across the room. It would be beneficial in the answering of any questions or comments from other students they thought. Other students started to arrive, some in pairs, mostly on their own, then a small group of four or five would enter and take over part of a row.

There was a sudden influx of about fifteen or sixteen men and women;

they decided they wanted to sit in a group so they took over the end seats of a couple of rows. Two men who were with them went to the front and sat near Geoff. He soon found out that they were professors from a Seminary in a different part of Manchester. They had received a notice about the meetings from the head of Religious Studies. He was the next person to enter and when he saw them up front he went along to be with them. They introduced him to Geoff; he indicated that they had met at different times around the campus. The local Professor told the other two that he had no idea that this meeting was being planned it was not something from his department. That intrigued the other two professors.

More students arrived and a couple of other Professors went and sat at the front with the others. Geoff was a little embarrassed at being surrounded by the big wigs.

The meeting was five minutes late starting, because a message had been sent to them that people were still arriving. Adrian and Bob came out of the ante room to centre stage. There had been placed a table and two chairs. There was also a podium if the speaker needed a place for his notes.

Adrian stood up and went to the microphone. "I am Adrian Syston, a second year student in Business Studies. I, together with a small group of students who meet as an I.V.F group had decided that a special meeting with a different geographic location, and an Anthropology element together with linguistics and sociology flavours should be explored. This is the result.

"I would like to introduce the Reverend Bob Brownlow as our speaker this evening. He has been a missionary in Brazil and worked in a variety of small camps along the banks of the Amazon River. He has had a variety of experiences, I am sure he has some interesting facts and stories to share with us this evening. Mr. Bob Brownlow, welcome to Manchester University."

There was applause of welcome as Bob moved up to the microphone.

"You have been told my name and that I've been working in Brazil. I'll not bore you with a lot of personal facts though I must admit that I am a graduate of London University". There were a few "boos". He raised a hand and added, "At the time I required my training Manchester did not offer the course, otherwise I might have ..." Cheers interrupted him. He told himself that he was off to a good start!

He then briefly filled in information about himself, family studies, call and destination for work.

"The first thing I was told when I arrived in Brazil was that I must learn a language I knew that to be an expectation. Then I was given tips as to how to stay healthy and fit; the comments that were added just stressed that such words to other people before me went unheeded sometimes.

"There was no language school to help me, because the language had not been reduced to writing. In fact part of my work would be to do just that.

Make it a written language. I spent the first week with senior missionaries in a large town. Giving me all the advice to either make me feel comfortable or to scare me into getting on the ship and return to a civilized country. I was helped also in the area of food. Nothing is purchasable in the place to which I was being sent. There you must learn to live as the natives, and eat the food they have. Additionally they informed me that I could buy a supply of canned foods of the stuff I liked or didn't like to take with me.

'It took me long time when shopping with the senior missionary lady. I was picking up two or three of each. She stopped me and put them back on the shelf. She placed the order, twelve of those, fifty of those, twenty-five of those; you might need a hundred of those. I stopped thinking! I had never done shopping like it any time in my life. My mother hadn't the money for such large quantities anyway.

"My helper learned over and explained that I would not be shopping again for many months. My immediate thought was I hope for a very large cupboard to house the stuff. She must have read my thought. She said that one of the things I would be making would be a cupboard.

"The day arrived. My cases and all the boxes of purchases were outside the door. It was only a matter of about fifty yards to the river. The boats were tied up, and servants began taking my belongings and storing them at one end of the boat; leaving room for me and a senior missionary and the boat owner.

"It took us over an hour to travel up the Amazon River. The owner pointed to a location just further up river. "That's the place, that is your place," he said. I was gradually getting into the frame of mind that this was going to be 'my place'.

"I'll skip the long story of building my so called house and furniture; of getting used to the climate and bush living conditions. The very first day I realized that was not going to be in a five star hotel with en suit bathroom, running water and electricity. What a dream!

"The language. That was indeed the first major requirement. My finger was forever pointing at things. I had a large pad and endeavoured to write down the sound of the words spoken for a chair, for a banana, for a boat, for the river, and so on. I was building up a list of sounds and I was learning them against the words indicated. This was going to be a tough assignment.

"One day a young man from a small community up river arrived. He was from one of a number of such communities that would be my field of service. He came right up to me with a large smile and said "sir". My first thought that it was a word for something I did not know. Then he pointed at me and said again 'sir'. My reply to him was 'thank you'. He tried to imitate my words 'thank you'. After quite some time I realized he was here to learn my language. I decided that he was going to be the person for me to learn his language. A friendship grew and we became partners. I was learning and so was he. When we went to his community I spoke a few words, then he spoke many more. This became a regular feature over the coming months. I was learning a language that had never been written down. All the communities along that stretch of the Amazon River had no written language and I was soon to find out that there were a number of different languages. My task was becoming almost insurmountable. But my friend became my companion, we went everywhere together. I was soon making short sentences, making sure I had the correct noun with the right verb attached.

"The months passed. I had been introduced to six of the communities along the river. It became know to them that I was a missionary, though they had no idea what that meant. As I progressed in my sentence structuring I began to insert some religious phrases. I had found one name that I thought would be the right one for my God. I was to learn what and how they worshipped their gods. I could then try to contrast their worship with mine."

For the following twenty minutes Bob described the life in a river-side village. He gave fascinating descriptions of a family at work and play;

types of food, their fishing experiences and animistic religious beliefs and practices.

Adrian just occasionally glanced out at the audience. They certainly were not bored. There had been one incident that caused him a little anxiety. Two students, their arms and neck covered with tattoos, stood up and commenced walking around. But they quite quickly made their way to the exit. Adrian breathed a sigh of relief; it could very easily turn into a negative demonstration. "Praise the Lord", he whispered; it was heard by the speaker who turned and acknowledge the remark with a nod of his head.

Bob had been describing the various communities he visited on a regular basis with his helper whom he called Mark. They worked well together. They both progressed well in the mastery of the language they were learning. Mark was proving to be invaluable, especially when faced with some questions in the remote villages they visited. They were accepted as a team and they took opportunities to testify about their experiences of Jesus Christ.

"I want to tell you one story", Bob said. "We were visiting the last of my villages one day. Someone informed us they had seen something strange happening at the top end of the river. There was a long stretch of river and then a sharp bend. No one had ever been up that far. A couple of men were out fishing one day and looked up the river. They saw two unfamiliar boats. The occupants were not known. After a few minutes the boats disappeared up a possible side stream. They said that they had seen these boats two or three times, each time they disappeared suddenly.

"We discussed this with the believers in that village. They indicated that they must be an unknown tribe. There was some enthusiastic discussion centering around the fact that they should be contacted with the Gospel.

"The next morning the two men who had told us the story, came up to me and Mark saying that they were willing to go up river and find out what was happening." Together Mark and I had been praying for the Lord's guidance about that situation. Together we asked, "Are we going up there today?" Their reply was in the form of indicating that the boat was loaded and ready.

"Within a matter of minutes we had checked that our supplies were going to be sufficient for a long day. The boat we were to use had an outboard motor. Few boats had such. Even the ones that had a motor only used them occasionally. They estimated it might take two hours against the run of the river which was quite strong at times. We were thankful for the motor. It was a tremendous help against the strong current.

"We were getting close to what they indicated was the top of the river. We could clearly see the beginning of a bend. The motor was switched off, and the oars were being used as we approached the bend cautiously. There were no signs of other boats; there were no signs of life. Mark pointed to a clearing. The owners rowed slowly and deliberately.

"It was a clearing and there was evidence that is was being used. There were no signs of people. We beached the boat and went ashore. There was a large area that was being used. The fire was still glowing, so the occupants had not been left very long. As we walked around we saw a stream among the trees. It was one that had been man-made. Two boats were moored alongside. Here was the evidence that people were living up this area.

"On our return the men who took us there stated quite emphatically that it was a tribe no one had heard about. For the rest of our journey there was much speculation about the people who lived on the bend. It was a quicker journey going home; the river flow was pushing us along without too much rowing.

"Almost the last words said to me by Amazon friends was, "We must send someone to the people on that bend with the Gospel.

I paused to take a well-earned drink of water.

I suppose there ought to be an application to every address or sermon. What is the application for us, today?"

There was silence. It became obvious that Bob was thinking and praying.

Bob shuffled his feet and moved around, then took up a fresh stand against the podium.

'It is perhaps decision time for some of you. Do you feel that the Lord may want you to work in a pioneer situation in some remote corner of the world?

"What sort of decision does the Holy Spirit want you to make? I suppose it could be a positive one like 'I will go anywhere', or may be an understandable negative one, 'I will not go to the overseas mission field'.

"Your decision has been made. For the positive response the Lord will guide in the preparation He knows what is required for the field to which He will send you. For the negative response the Lord will guide you also, your decision was to not go to the mission field and that is quite okay because if you all went overseas somewhere our country might quickly be empty! Your decision was a legitimate one, but you are required to prepare yourself for pleasing Him at home somewhere.

"There may be some who have not made a decision. That's understandable because it isn't every day you are faced with such major changes for your life. You have made no decision. That means that perhaps you have ignored the challenge because you are not ready for a major change. Sometimes the inability to make a decision is due to a lack of faith. It can be due to your present spiritual condition. The Apostle Paul wrote to the Christians in Rome, "Those who are dominated by the sinful nature think about sinful things, but those who are controlled by the Holy Spirit think about things that please God'. It is a fact that certain people are incapable of making a spiritual decision, because they have not received the Holy Spirit to guide them in such matters. They may lack faith because they have not yet been introduced to the One who willingly and lovingly gives faith.

"Let me just close in summarizing the fact that there are numberless people who have not yet heard the Gospel of Jesus. As St. Paul wrote, "How can they call on Him to save them unless they believe in Him? And how can they believe in Him if they have never heard about Him? And how can they hear about Him unless someone tells them? And how will anyone go and tell them without being sent?

"Thinking about the unreached people living on the bend up the Amazon River, how will they ever hear unless someone is sent to them? That someone will pioneer another tribe and learn another language. So that those people will hear in their mother tongue how much God loves them."

Bob paused for a moment; then turned to sit down. The strength of the applause was unexpected. Bob looked a little embarrassed. Our committee was on their feet with raised hands applauding. The visitors from the Seminary were doing likewise. Adrian glanced down to the front row; the professors seemed very genuine in their appreciation of the presentation. One of the professors beckoned for Bob to go down to him. He did so willingly. After a genuine handshake and introduction of himself and the other professors he expressed his gratitude for a very meaningful communication of the missionary message. He asked if he would be able to visit their seminary for a day of missions to talk about being a pioneer missionary, to mention the challenge of learning an unwritten language, of facing possible new ventures under the guidance of the Holy Spirit. By this time Adrian had joined them. As Bob agreed to find a date, Adrian asked if an invitation could come to the local I.V.F students. There was a very gracious positive reply.

Some of the students were in no great hurry to leave; they got into conversation with the I.V.F folk. It was evident that some of the students would like to meet with the speaker. Bob noticed this and asked if he could be excused to have a word with them.

The conversations lasted almost an hour. During that time Adrian had been approached by the local professors and was being congratulated on a well presented topic. One of them even mentioned that his opinion of Christians at the university was changing.

There was quite a large group that made its way to the cafeteria. It didn't take long before some of the tables were being pushed together. Bob was not being allowed to relax. He was being treated like a man on a mission.

Bob's two friends eventually came up to him and suggested that because he was supposed to be on sick leave that he ought to think about going home to bed. Reluctantly he agreed with them. He gave a few final greetings to the students around him, and a special message to Adrian and his group for organizing such a tremendous gathering. A very thankful group of students accompanied them to their car and waved them off.

Students talked about the Amazon River for many days. An indelible impression had been made

The I.V.F was never quite the same after that meeting. The IVF'ers had much to talk and pray about.

But studies got back to normal, and student life offered the usual routine.

CHAPTER 28

Mary and Betty had been in a conversation with a couple of students from the Seminary. They had not been talking many minutes before they realized that an interest was being shown in them by the two fellows. In one sense they were pleased that their personalities were being respected and that there was something attractive about them

They had no idea for how long they had sat in the meeting room. It was Betty that asked if they would like a coffee or something. Mary added, "The something will not include anything alcoholic!" both of them offered a large smile and indicated that was just right for them.

They went off to the cafeteria and continued talking about the missionary challenge from Brazil. Time was not being monitored. It was the two seminarians who apologized for having to break up their time together.

"Our front door will be locked. Fortunately we know the fire escape door will be left open for us" was the comment made by one of them.

The other expressed his appreciation for the time the two girls had given them. "I hope we can meet again sometime. Perhaps on some other subject and not just about Brazil".

His colleague added, "But we would like it to be biased towards missions".

Mary and Betty agreed separately that they would enjoy a future meeting. One of the fellows took a small diary out of his pocket, opened a few pages, and said, "How about in two weeks? It is a Saturday, no soccer game is planned, and I, we, will be just ready for a meal out and a good conversation with intelligent and lovely ladies".

"Thanks for the compliment", mentioned Mary.

"I am always ready for a good meal with interesting fellows" added Betty.

"Then that settles it, we are on for the afternoon and evening. We will pick you up here about three thirty, Is that okay?"

There was a positive nod and smile from both girls.

Term work had a priority for Mary and Betty, but they recognized the importance of a break from time to time. It was more than once that either one or the other had anticipatory remarks about the Saturday that was coming up.

"Did we find out their names?" asked Mary.

"I did", said Betty with a blush on her cheeks. "It was easy, Jack and Jim".

"The blond was Jim I'd imagine", quipped Mary.

Jim Waltham was indeed the blonde. Jack Barrington was the other.

The Saturday came. The pickup was on time. They had chosen a short trip ending at a particular restaurant. The time disappeared too quickly before they were back in the car heading for the university campus. With the car parked not one of the occupants wanted to move. They must have sat there for twenty minutes before one of them broke the spell by looking at his watch. There were some extremely pleasant 'Good nights'. And of course, "We must do it again sometime!"

As Betty got out of the car she asked if it was a good Christian question to request for phone numbers.

That brought a mighty chuckle and a bunch of phone numbers. There was a cute comment from one, "I hope I can remember the numbers in the right order!"

Two of the most faithful supporters of the university soccer team were Mary and Betty. They gave the impression that they were soccer supporters before arriving at university. There was most probably a few more observant supporters of the local team who just happened to notice the enthusiasm of these two girls increased tremendously when a certain mid-field man was on the ball. There was always a more vocalized exuberance when he scored a goal. Adrian Syston was thought to be their pin-up of the year. They always joined with the team and a few other supporters for the refreshment break after the game.

Mary and Betty were both good students, though Betty struggled with one of her subjects. They talked about that, wondering if it was a subject to be skipped or to accept the challenge that there must be more mental exercise exerted in mastering it.

Their friendship was being cemented by their regular times of prayer and Bible study. They both attended the meeting for the students, but they often commented that it was the time they spent just on their own that was influencing their spiritual development. I.V.F. was a notable factor in sustaining spiritual growth.

Graduation ceremonies at the end of the year would be affecting the I.V.F. considerably. Adrian, who had given such a dynamic lead, would be leaving. "Who will take over?" The latest comment about that was it would be decided at the beginning of the next year.

The friendships between Mary and Betty with the two seminarians were becoming more and more appreciated and enjoyable. After their evening meeting one Saturday it became obvious that cupid was beginning to play with some heart strings. It was noticeable that Betty made sure she was sitting next to Jim. They could not hide some of those moments when their hands met.

Mary had been concerned about something like this happening. It had been her prayer that the Lord would give her courage to raise the issue sometime. Was this the right time? 'Lord, guide my words, please'.

"May I please be serious for a moment? Something important has been floating around this head of mine. I am trusting that what I say will not destroy any of the wonderful friendship I've enjoyed and want to continue to enjoy". Betty made a noticeable move that indicated she wasn't sure where Mary was going.

"I had an electrifying moment some years ago when I was confronted by the Lord to make a serious promise. I promised the Lord that I would not desire or enter into a sexual relationship outside of marriage". She paused, wondering how to continue. But the other three were listening and did not appear to be embarrassed. During that pause Betty shuffled a little and it became obvious she was no longer holding hands with Jim.

"Jack", Mary said, "I think cupid has started over there". She pointed across the table to the other two. They laughed so loudly that those at other tables were looking across at them. "I'm sorry to be drawing some attention from other people".

She looked directly into Jack's face, "I love our friendship. I do not want it to change. We have much to share and enjoy together. What I have just said is not to have a detrimental influence on where we are at. . ."

"I …" Jack interrupted her; he had a genuine reaction showing on his face. He reached over and took her hand and said, "I love you for your openness and honesty. I admire you for your courage. I too had made the same promise to the Lord a few years ago. Yes. I too want our friendship to continue".

The other two smiled. Betty was about to say and so do I, but Joe was first in and explained that it was also true for him, but he went on to say "if a girl begins to shatter my heart strings then I will want to hold her hands so that she does not succeed in breaking any of them".

The conversation from then on that evening was comparing those special meetings that prompted such powerful promises.

They enjoyed being together; it became a dedicated item in their dairies, every second Saturday unless there was a soccer match.

Mary said "our next Saturday get-together has a problem. There will be a clash of interests. Our soccer team is playing away and we are ardent supporters not only for at home games but we travel in the coach when playing away. That Saturday is an away game. I want to be together with you but a priority on that day will be to shout support for our soccer team".

"That's alright." said Jack, "We are fanatic supporters of our soccer team, which, by the way, is the best in the district!"

"Now you should be very careful how you boast. When, or if you ever play us, we are guaranteed not to lose!" added Mary.

"That's okay with us because our team is playing that day so we will be required to shout for the best team in the district." said Jim.

Betty added, "Then we hope that one day you will be faced with an even better side".

A week later there was a phone call from Jim to Betty. There were a few giggles before Jim got around to the reason for phoning. "Next Saturday our soccer team is playing at home. Our opponents, we are told, are from Manchester University".

Betty responded, "Then if it is really our team you are in for a good match".

"Jack says the other team has one spectacular player, who, when he was in High School the two Manchester professional clubs went to see him play and wanted an interview with him. His coach tried hard to forestall them. We understand that he did not sign for either of them".

Betty said, "I think I know which man that was, so it seems that you are in for a big battle next week. We'll be there but not shouting this time for your team, we know where our allegiance lies".

Jim signed off by stating that he and Jack were looking forward to next week.

The following Saturday arrived; Mary and Betty made the usual arrangements to travel with the team as supporters. When the bus arrived at the college gates there was a reception committee waving the college flag and vigorously chanting their victory song. There was a little surprise for some in the group when two of their company went down to meet the visitors. They ignored the players; their eyes were on two of the visiting supporters.

Mary and Betty were looking out for Jack and Jim. There were the usual hugs and smiles. The girls immediately started waving the university team's colours. The two men brought out from the jackets their college flags.

The team went off to a changing room and the other visitors made their way around the back of the college building to the playing field.

It was going to be a strange afternoon, because two couples supporting each team were standing next to each other.

For 'safety' reason they found a spot near one corner. They were not entirely on their own. But they soon settled down to bantering and shouting for their favourite players.

The game started quite slowly as the teams were sizing up their opponents. This was the first time these two teams had played each other. It was an enjoyable first half with each team missing scoring opportunities.

The two fellows produced bottles of soda water for the half time break. During each sip the boasting continued; there was great anticipation for a challenging second half.

The seminarians took advantage of a defense mistake and scored. Adrian, who was the captain, mentioned to most of his team that they were now about to start playing.

Adrian was being monitored by two players, so he roamed around changing his position frequently. He had his chance when a loose ball came into midfield. He dribbled easily past three players. A full back approached with a sliding tackle. Adrian saw it coming; he flicked the ball to one side and quickly jumped over the sliding player then sliced his shot into the corner of the net. The goalkeeper didn't have a chance.

Ten minute later Adrian was helping in defense against a charging attack, He was able to win the ball, and then with some excellent passing worked his way down the field with his team mate. A wonderful cross ball came to him; he was in the ideal position. His left foot smashed hard and the ball rocketed into the corner of the net. The goalkeeper was nowhere near it.

The last two minutes were exciting. The play went from one end of the field to the other. There were chances at both ends. But no further score. The four supporters in the corner of the field were almost exhausted; it had been a noisy afternoon.

The supporters mingled with the players from both teams. Quite a few of the players went to congratulate Adrian and express their surprise at seeing him in a different role. They had been at the missionary meeting he had organized. Mary and Betty enjoyed introducing Adrian to the two friends.

Jack said, "I think we have a little surprise coming up. The visiting team is normally invited to stay for our evening meal. We persuaded our Proff to extend that invitation to two special visitors. He was somewhat reluctant until Jim's facial response indicated the importance of the girls staying.

They were not the only girls present in the dining room; a few of the seminarians had their friends or may be fiancées with them. It was an enjoyable meal and the table conversation centred on the activities of the afternoon.

The bus was at the college gate so the visitors made their way out of the college. Jack and Jim had their arms around the two girls as they walked towards the bus. There were some amusing comments and cat-calls from the players already inside, as the two girls said their farewells to the boys and found a spare seat.

The end of that term was the end of the girls first year. Both of them wanted their best results from the exams and assignments. They were hoping to be allowed entry into a 'major' programme. Mary wanted to finish with an honours degree in accountancy. This was when Mary appreciated the two courses her high school teachers arranged for her during her stay-at-home year. Betty had expressed a desire for an honours degree but had not decided which was going to be her best subject. But she stated that she would be content with a straight degree.

The Sunday trips to Beth Shan continued, though both girls stated they were not completely comfortable with the exuberance with some extreme expressions while worshipping. Also they still felt a little uncomfortable when someone spoke in tongues. They would comment to each other as to how anyone could give an accurate interpretation of sounds that sometimes did not sound like a genuine language.

Occasionally they joined some of the meetings for college and career groups. They even persuaded Jim and Jack to join them for one of the meetings. The girls did not know what they would do with the boys after that meeting. They constantly glanced at them to note their reactions because neither of them had been to a Pentecostal meeting before. It was an eye opener for them.

As they walked to the car and headed for a coffee place they were full of questions. Betty seemed to be the main giver of answers; though all three recognized that perhaps they were more speculations than real answers. The general assessment was that such a meeting was not on their list to be repeated. But it turned out to be a beneficial experience when in conversation with other students back at seminary.

Mary and Betty were invited to the seminary for a special meeting with a missionary emphasis. The seminary leaders had invited a leading African Minister from Nigeria to be the speaker. Locally he was referred to as a Bishop even though there had been no Episcopal ordination. But he had oversight covering a large area of over one hundred churches. It is possible that his involvement in negotiating the release of a group of girls that had been abducted from their village to become the play things for a troop of lusty soldiers, that had attracted the staff to offer an invitation to him.

It was a wonderful event for the girls. They were given a tour of the seminary rooms and facilities. Jim and Jack quite proudly showed them around. The girls wanted to know what kind of study rooms were available for each student. So the fellows decided not to show a bias to one or the other, they took them to see both of their study rooms. The girls were impressed to note how each student personalized his own room. Like their own rooms back at the university it was a matter of the best second hand furniture. But it was the pictures and posters that made the differences. It was not surprising to note that their bookcases contained similar books.

The meeting was to take place in one of the lecture halls as the Chapel would be too small for the number of guests expected. Nothing was mentioned about going early to make sure of a comfortable chair. Jim's sarcastic tongue-in-cheek comment was, "All of them are hard on the backside!"

Students and other friends were gathering quite quickly. But there were four seats on a row about the middle of the auditorium. Unless some over sized bodies placed themselves on the chairs just ahead they would have a great view of the platform. No big fellows arrived to obscure their view. Two car loads of IVF'ers found seats near the back of the room.

The speaker entered the platform with some of the professors. The head professor took the chair and introduced the speaker.

"We are fortunate to have Bishop Njoku with us. He has a large itinerary in the month he is over here. He is a leader among his people and is not afraid of controversy. He is reported as being a devout Bible expositor. But he has attracted the international press with his working with religious extremists. He will be recounting some of the challenges to the Nigerian Church at this time.

"We welcome you, sir, to our open missionary meeting".

There was an enthusiastic applause welcoming the Bishop. He very graciously raised his arms for the applause to slow down. He was not wearing a clerical outfit – he was in a tribal chieftain costume. It was a large free-flowing colourful robe, with a turban-type head dress of the same material.

"Thank you. Thank you. I am happy to be here in your country and to have this opportunity of sharing time with you this evening".

Most of the audience was surprised at the quality of the Bishop's command of the English language.

He described the district that he referred to as 'home'. His work area covered a large northern portion of the Igbo tribe. His address was centred on an incident that had been covered by the world's press – the abduction of approximately twenty young teenage girls from a school. The girls had not been found but the police were investigating an extremist organization that had infiltrated that part of Nigeria from the north.

"We have been very concerned for the safety of the girls. If they cooperate with the captors they'll be looked after. Some might be forced to marry a soldier. Most of them will be used sexually at any time.

"I have met the parents of the girls, to say the least they are extremely worried, and angry at the government for not protecting the school from such terrorists. The comment literally thrown at me by most if the parents was 'why did God allow this to happen?'

"Isn't that the question thrown at the Christian Church by the world whenever a major crisis occurs? No matter how tearful my answer – no matter how professional my analysis – no matter how sanctified a selection of words I used, they were not satisfied.

"I met one distraught teenager. He informed me that his girl friend was one of the captives. 'We had planned on getting married', he said, 'but now she may not be in good physical shape to become my wife. What am I to do?'

"Seminary students, here is an area of research for you. Find answers to unanswerable questions.

"While I was staying in the village there was a noisy disturbance one evening. I was visiting with the chief when a family with their neighbours came dancing and shouting. Their daughter had suddenly arrived from nowhere.

It seems the man she was with had enjoyed himself and then went to sleep. She looked around and could see no one. She quietly stepped away from him and as silently as possible she walked away from the village. She stated that she was not sure where to go but she kept walking. She made sure she was not seen by many people by going around a couple of villages. She did stop at one small place and someone asked what she was doing. She replied that she was hungry and thirsty. The woman was kind and gave her a drink and some roasted yam to eat. The woman did not ask many personal questions, she probably noticed the girl's nervousness. 'I do not know where you are going. Take this yam with you. God bless you'.

The next village she came to she recognized; her home village was just a few miles further. It was the middle of the afternoon when she saw her home. She stopped and wondered what to do. 'They will be very unhappy when they know how I have been treated' she told herself. 'I hope they will still love me even though I have been raped many times'. Some kids came running by, they stopped, and they recognized her. So they began shouting her name. Her father was at home with his wife and heard the shouting and rushed outside to see what was happening. Their daughter ran straight into their open arms weeping so loudly she could not say any words for a few minutes. They just collapsed on the ground. There was not one person without tears flowing down the cheeks. They were tears of happiness. Eventually the girl was able to say a few things to her parents and the siblings that had also gathered around. A neighbour mentioned that the chief had heard the noise and wanted to know what it was about, but nobody told him. The father said 'we will go and see him'.

"One very happy group, though still crying, arrived at the Chief's house. He made sure there was a chair for the girl to sit on and her family just gathered around her sitting on the ground. I was sat near to the chief. The girl was very self-conscious and found it difficult to look at us face to face. The chief was full of compassion and told her everything would be fine. She looked at me and I said God had helped her to escape and He was now helping her to readjust. I told her that she was not only to receive my sympathy but also my love.

"She slowly recited a little about her ordeal and her escape. The chief asked about the other girls. She started to cry. It took a few minutes for her to compose herself to give a disturbing hopeless answer. 'Most of them are pregnant. They have not killed anyone yet, but their threat remains for those who do not open themselves up for the men to do whatever they please and as often as they please. When the men are drunk they beat us as well as rape us. They provided good meals for us. At the beginning we continually asked them to send us back home. Their only reply was that we were now at our new home. There were no opportunities to go to Church. There was no sign of a building for worship anywhere. When some of us girls gathered under a tree one Sunday to pray they came and beat us then played sexual games with us. We had to make sure that if we were praying that they did not see us.

"She continued her story until the chief noticed that the girl was looking very tired. He told everyone to go home and for the parents to bring the girl back to him again tomorrow morning.

"I was present the next morning. One of the things the chief said was that the girl must try and remember all the details of her journey home. He wanted the senior officer of the local squad of soldiers to note the important details. The officer was present and heard more of the story. In his comments the officer said that he would be sending a small group of his men dressed as if they were terrorists wanting to join the group.

"I had to leave that afternoon, and I do not know what has happened to the soldiers the officer sent as terrorists. It could be they were not believed so would have been mercilessly murdered.

"Fortunately my work in Nigeria is not as emotionally demanding as that painful visit. We are experimenting with what you might call 'Theology by Extension'. I meet with the ministers and some of the elders from a group of maybe ten churches. I stay with them for three nights. We have two very long Bible school days. It is wonderful to see the effect of these teaching visits. Most of the members in the remote village areas are uneducated, yet they desperately want to know more of the Bible.

"The challenge I am delivering to the church leaders in this country is for more highly trained theologians to become missionaries. Their work would be primarily training leaders. The Church is growing numerically. Evangelistic outreaches are winning many converts. But they need good training in order to grow into effective witnesses. Jesus told the Apostles to go and make disciples, not just win converts.

"One of the most wonderful transformations taken place since I became a Christian is what has been called Africanisation. What that really means is that the white man is not the only leader, but that there is now a workable relationship between indigenous and expatriate workers.

"When God starts a revival he also challenges the church to provide adequate teachers. I am delighted to report there are signs of revival in my country, but the lack of suitable workers is very concerning."

Bishop Njoku continued giving illustrations from his work as overseer. His presentation was absorbing, informative and challenging. The applause as he sat down indicted that it was coming from an audience that had just been inspired. The professor gave his final word of appreciation and closed the meeting.

A few of the students came to the front with the hope of having a quick word with the Bishop. The mission's secretary asked for a signed photograph for the pictorial records. Jack and Jim had some things they would like to clarify but they decided that a coffee with the girls had priority. They certainly had much to share and discuss. It was time to take the girls back to their residence but it was mutually agreed they would continue the topic on their next time together.

Mary and Betty found much of their sharing time was spent comparing Brazil with Africa. From time to time they raised the thought as to how God would call them if He wanted them in Brazil or Africa. Both girls were quite adamant that no call was being heard as yet.

The end of the academic year was quickly approaching. The various groups and societies were planning their closing meetings. For those in the I.V.F. it was a time of sadness because there would be farewells to friends especially the ones who had been giving leadership to the group. The question of new leadership was raised but somehow it got deferred to the first meeting of the next year. Some names had been mentioned as possible leaders but they had all declined for various reasons. The girls made a point of staying until they had a word with Adrian in order to express their appreciation of his devoted leadership.

The last Saturday afternoon with Jack and Jim was also over-shadowed with sadness. Betty was the one to jump in and state quite emphatically that email addresses must be shared right then and there; and that would mean for certain that contact could be made between them during the long summer break. Mary would not be broken hearted if Jack failed to email. But Betty would be heart-broken if a week went by without some communication from Jim. Cupid had certainly been at work. It was a sad farewell which was softened by the sincere hugs of devout friendship. For Betty it was more than a hug she was hoping for, her hope was not dashed when Jim gave her a lingering kiss.

It was not just 'Goodnight'; it was farewell for the summer and a joyful anticipation for renewed friendships again next term. Betty voiced one of her hopes, namely, that they could receive each others' email addresses and that would mean "we can keep in contact". She had a blush commencing that was noticed by both boys. "I did not mean we could text five or six times every day. But it would be nice to hear a little about what was happening during the long vacation". Jim was eager to agree. So out came the diaries and note books and their email addresses were recorded by each one of the four. It appeared to be quite genuine that they really did want to keep in touch.

And they did keep in touch. Betty and Jim emailed each other quite frequently. While Jack and Mary only managed three or four emails, perhaps because they were active in other areas of interest.

CHAPTER 29

For Adrian and some of his IVF friends, university was the place to receive knowledge. Other so called extra-curricular happenings had to fit in to their academic time table. Lectures followed by assigned reading were also times when research assignments were allocated. Adrian did make time for his soccer, much to the pleasure of the coach. He did continue with the Choir but only those leading up to special presentations at Christmas and Easter, He was persuaded to take a small part in a couple of dramas. That summarizes the rest of his time at Manchester University.

His parents proudly attended the graduation ceremony. Other friends from home were also present. He remembered seeing one or two IVF'ers who had yet another year to go before it was their turn to be honoured.

Geoff had spent many an hour talking with Adrian about future prospects after graduation. Both knew they had to seek suitable employment. But they also realized that it most probably meant that they would not be close to each other for regular contact. Geoff announced one day that he had received an invitation to submit a resume to a business firm in Rochdale. He seemed quite happy about it.

Adrian's father had given him names of a few places in the Manchester area to contact. He mentioned one specifically – it just happened to be the place where he had worked for many years. From the things his father had told him and from the brochures they sent to him, he warmed to the idea of contacting them. A few days later he was called for an interview.

One of the first things the CEO mentioned was that he must not expect any special privilege just because his father was a senior member of the staff. Adrian made it quite clear in his response to that remark that as far as he was concerned at that time his father was not involved in his future. The interview went well. He was informed that he would receive a letter within a week.

After leaving the office Adrian wasn't sure that that office was where God wanted him to start. "Dear Lord, you have the right place – please let me know". That was a prayer repeated on a regular daily basis.

Among brochures he had received from different firms was one from a sister firm to the one where his father worked. It was not in Manchester city centre, it was in Chorlton where his parents still lived. He decided to check it out. He liked the look of the place. It was not surrounded by crowds of busy and not so busy people wandering along the streets. He took courage and went inside. The receptionist was helpful when he requested details regarding applying for work. The receptionist took out two sheets of paper from her desk and suggested that if he was really interested that he should have them back in the office before the weekend. Adrian had a question on his face "I can't tell you" she said, "but it could be urgent". Adrian thanked her and left with his two sheets of paper.

He called in to his parent's house. His mother had the kettle on, it was soon tea time. She was intrigued with what her son was saying. He curled up on a chair reading the pages given to him at the office. He was becoming very interested. He moved over to his father's desk and began filling out the answers to the variety of questions.

When his father arrived home the first comment was, "Are you moving in home?" Adrian replied, "I can't afford it!"

Howard noted the papers on his desk. Just a quick glance and he knew what they were, and where they were from. "That's interesting. It's very interesting". Dawn butted in, "What is so interesting today, my dear?"

Adrian had been watching his father, "Would you like to look over my answers?"

A valuable discussion followed. Adrian decided that he would personally take the application into the office the next morning. Howard expressed pleasure in his attitude and enthusiasm.

Adrian was determine not to appear over interested and so delayed his visit to the office until late morning. When he walked through the door the receptionist commented, "You are eager!" His smile and nod was his reply. He handed the envelope to the receptionist and she said she would make sure the boss received it sometime today.

"Why don't you take a seat over there", pointing to a rest area at one side of the quite spacious office. There were a couple of chairs and a rack of brochures about the services offered. "The boss is in this morning. I need to take in some mail so I will include your application. When I get back we might talk about times for an interview." She disappeared down the corridor.

Adrian had noted that it was a new building. The reception area was enormous. He found the leaflets informative.

The receptionist mentioned to the boss that the top letter was an application from a young man, "He's probably a grad from Manchester University"

She was about to leave but he said, "Wait a moment. I want to open this to see who it's from". "That's interesting", he said, "I have a feeling I know his father. Tell him I want to see him in a few minutes".

When the receptionist returned Adrian was absorbed in one of the leaflets. She actually came up to him to say that the boss may call you in, so hang around a little longer".

Sure to his word, the boss called his receptionist and asked her to send in the young man.

"He wants to see you", she said, "Down the corridor the last door on the right". It was quite a wide corridor. The offices appeared to be large because the doors where well spaced apart. He paused at the boss's door. He wasn't sure whether he was nervous or just apprehensive. He knocked. The voice invited him to enter. It was a large room with a spacious desk and file area. Out of the corner of his eye he spotted a lounging area to one side. There was a name plate sitting up on his desk with the name, ERSKIN BARROWBRIDGE.

"Come in Mr. Syston". He had obviously looked at my resume. "That is a familiar surname." "Oh No!" thought Adrian. "I knew, or rather I know a man who would probably be old enough to be your father". He noted Adrian's reaction. So he smiled and continued," It is no bad thing to know people with a name like Syston". Then there was a pause. Adrian wasn't sure whether that was a sign for him to say something or to remain silent. He plucked up courage, "I was hoping that my application would not be tainted by my family tree!"

There was a great chuckle from the boss. Adrian found himself chuckling also. It was a low key interview but the boss subtly poked in a challenge from time to time.

"What branch of business studies do you want to take with you into your career?"

"Business and Management, sir".

"Can you be a little more specific?"

"Strategy and how to be innovative, also looking at how entrepreneurship can be broken down into culpable segments in order to build up a workable attitude for progress and success".

"Are you planning on a dissertation on that subject?"

"At this time I am not anticipating a return to university for a graduate degree. I want to establish myself in all the protocol and energy required for businesses to be successful".

"Have you some ideal town or city where you would like to start work?"

"Not really, sir. I would like to be in a situation where I can be encouraged to learn the job. The location is not that urgent at this stage in my life."

"It has been good to meet you and hear a little of your hopes and aspirations. I will be writing to you within the next few days. Good morning, Mr. Syston."

"Good morning, Sir. And thank you for your time and interest."

At home his parents were waiting to hear how the interview went. His father's comment was that he could not go far wrong with that firm.

"I wondered whether the boss was favoured because of maybe some aristocracy in his family", said Adrian,

"Why do you think that?"

"Well his name sounded like it being a possibility".

"No his name did not bias his acceptance for the job, but his father's money might have!"

"It was an interesting interview. Very low key but he was subtle not devious. There would be a short question, almost missed, until I realized that he required an answer to it."

"You can go to many places and not find a better boss than Erskin. If you want someone to help you achieve your goals, than I would say he will be first class".

After they'd had lunch Howard asked his wife if they had anything special that afternoon. She gave a negative nod, inwardly wondering why the question.

"Have you any plans, Adrian?"

"Not necessarily for immediate attention. But one thing I would like is to visit a couple of other places on my list. Not necessarily to go inside unless just to pick up a brochure."

"Where are they located?"

"One in Salford the other in Eccles".

"Let's get the car ready; we can manage those two places this afternoon. We'll start in Salford and then return via Eccles".

Both were older looking buildings, but had attractive doorways and windows. In each place they parked the car and walked around for awhile to get a feel for the local environment. Adrian indicated that he would like to receive a brochure so went inside. The receptionists were kind and helpful.

On the way home Howard asked Adrian about his first feelings.

"I don't think I would like to work in either Salford or Eccles".

"Why?"

"I didn't like the feeling surrounding the locations. I'm interested enough to read these brochures and try to grasp a little about their business ethics".

The conversation continued on varied topics until they arrived home.

After they had eaten their evening meal, Dawn suggested that it might not be a bad idea just to relax for the rest of the evening. Adrian was quick with a response in favour of resting but added, "I would like just to glance at these two brochures, but not to fully digest them this evening".

It was the end of the next week before a letter arrived. It was from the Chorley branch. It was not a long letter, but very positive and complimentary. It was requesting that Adrian return to learn more about their business and to consider an offer.

Adrian was over the moon. He did not really expect such a positive answer from either place.

It was the next day he received a letter from where his father worked expressing regret that at that time they were unable to offer him a position.

He wasn't surprised. In actual fact he did not want to work in the same office as his father.

He talked over with his father about a possible date to return to the Chorley office. Howard made it clear that it ought to be soon because any delay may give a negative smear on his reliability.

"Well, it's Friday now; I'll phone and ask for a suitable time on Monday".

Adrian wanted to share his good news with someone, so he emailed Geoff. Geoff answered immediately expressing his pleasure and complimenting Adrian on finding some place he liked. He did indicate that he himself was settling in and was quite comfortable in that office.

The weekend dragged for Adrian. That was unusual for him because he was usually so active and involved in whatever was going on. As he analyzed his attitude, he very quickly condemned his impatience; his focus was on Monday morning.

Monday morning arrived. The sun was shining. He was happy and openly praising God for yet another new day. He also asked God for guidance during the interview later that morning. "I want nothing short of your purpose for me", he said to the Lord, "I'll keep my ears tuned to you for wisdom and direction".

His father was at work so there was no car to take him for the interview. It was a remarkably nice day, so he told his mother he would give himself plenty of time and walk. Walking also gave him time to reflect once again on the importance of the interview. His whole future will be depending upon the place where he is to commence work. He had a wonderful peace in his mind. He was assured that the Holy Spirit would be in control of his thoughts and decisions. He was also assured that Mr. Barrowbridge would be led by God in the discussion and decisions.

The receptionist gave him an extra large smile and pointed him to the seats in the lounge area. He was almost fifteen minutes early. That didn't bother him; it gave him the chance to scan another brochure.

"You can go through, Mr. Syston, he is expecting you".

Adrian walked the corridor and again paused before knocking to take in a deep breath and put on a confident smile.

"Good morning, Mr. Syston. May I call you Adrian, it sounds more human?"

Adrian gave a positive nod. Inwardly he thought that if I call him Erskin that might shatter the boss's image. So he kept the thought unexpressed.

"Your presence here this morning is indicative of a positive response to my letter, I presume. I want to introduce you to more of what we do here. It is important for you to know the ethics of our business. I will introduce you to other members of the office a little later. Every customer is honoured and respected. There will be no way any of us here will seek to criticize or demean the customer. But there will be the occasions when we will try to persuade them to look at the situation from a different angle"

The boss continued for some time. It was evident to Adrian that this was a regular feature before new staff was brought on board. Adrian was able to butt in with a question from time to time. That gave the boss a boost because it meant that the young man was eager to know more about the business.

"I am about to ask you a direct question, Adrian. Be prepared to take a moment if needed to think about the answer. I am expecting a serious and honest reply to my question. Do you seriously want me to accept your application for a position to work in this firm?"

Adrian did pause just long enough for a quick 'Please help me Lord'. "Yes sir. I have been considering it carefully and may I add, I have been praying for God to guide me. I will count it a privilege to work here. I am convinced that the guidance and encouragement you, and no doubt other employees, will share, will enable me to learn how to be a good steward and serve the firm with dignity and honour".

"That is an excellent starting-off attitude. Okay?"

There was a knock on the door. The boss said it was okay to enter. Janet, the receptionist, was carrying a tray with two cups of steaming coffee. I didn't ask you", she said to Adrian, "If you liked coffee. If not then I must make a note in my memory for any future occasion".

"Thank you, Janet", said the boss as she placed the tray on his desk.

The conversation was quite general during the sipping of the coffee.

"I'll take you around the office", said the boss, "You'll be able to meet some of the others who are working here".

It was an interesting trip down the corridor into the various offices. There was a basic similarity in each one; also there was a predominance of individuality and uniqueness. There was a smaller room at the end of the corridor. "That will be yours to start off with". Adrian noticed that it seemed bare but immediately he knew how to make it his own.

When they returned to the boss's office, he reached into one of his drawers and pulled out a sheet of paper and placed in front of him on his desk.

You will want to know about remuneration for services rendered" he said. "I have a basic list from which I work. I should say that not many of these amounts are sculptured into hard rock. The only one nonnegotiable is the first one. It is a starting salary because your first three months are trial months. At the end of that period we will sit down and openly discuss how the trial went and whether we both want a more permanent situation"

He told Adrian what his starting salary would be. "Have you any questions?" (He wasn't expecting any!) Adrian was not quite sure what his next comment should be, all he could think of was "Thank you, sir".

As he stood up to leave, the boss said just one moment young man. "Please sit. When do you want to start working?"

Adrian was embarrassed that he was about to leave without knowing when to come to work.

"May I suggest the beginning of next month?" That will give you extra time to holiday a little".

"That will be fine – just fine – thank you, sir".

Adrian had a number of chats with his father about what happens and how to cope with ones first day at the office. His father was able to joke a little about it, but in his serious moments Adrian found him very helpful. "It'll still be different though. I will need to make sure that I am being myself and not trying to be a seasoned worker".

It was a very important day. It was the beginning of his life's work. He made sure that in his morning prayers he asked God to establish that morning as a real beginning to his service for the Lord.

He was early, yet surprised that the boss was already in his office. The receptionist gave him a warm welcome. Adrian was half afraid that she was going to get up and come round to give a welcome kiss and hug. Another person entered the office and that forestalled anything Janet had hoped for.

He made his way down the corridor to his room. Some extra pieces of furniture had been added. He made a note of something he would like.

There was a note and a file on his desk from the boss. He wanted

Adrian to browse through the file and at coffee time he was to meet in his office.

The idea of browsing through the old file was to give Adrian an idea of the way information was collected and tabulated. It was a helpful meeting. The boss was well aware of first day nerves. Even though Adrian was unaware of being nervous the boss noted a little unease relating to everything being so new.

Adrian was told that for the first week he would be in the office of a colleague. The following morning there would be a new client. Sitting in gave Adrian an insight into going through the first stages of a contract and the kind of question to be asked in order to obtain personal information. It was a fascinating morning. Adrian was seeing how theory was actually worked out.

That first week was an eye opener into the intricate details of meeting a client and making the early steps to build up a profile.

The following Monday there was a note on Adrian's desk from the boss indicating that later that morning he would be receiving his first client; one of his colleagues would be present to be of help if needed. Adrian's confidence level was good; he just made sure that he was not over confident. It was an easy situation. He felt quite encouraged as the interview proceeded. An appointment was made for a follow-up meeting.

The colleague was impressed by the performance of the new man. The boss arrived; he had noticed the client leaving the building.

"So, how did it go?" Was that a professional question from the boss? The colleague responded by describing briefly what Adrian had done. "How did you feel?" he asked Adrian. "I was perhaps more nervous than I thought. I just changed my sitting position and determined to set the client at ease. It was a great experience. I felt good about myself while knowing that I have much to learn and some things are going to need changing. I am looking forward to the next session to see how the problem unfolds".

"Tomorrow I want you to work with another colleague in a totally different field. This will be the pattern for you this week. I want you to get the feel of the whole office, because as you know there are numerous specialties in Business Consultants. This afternoon spend time reflecting upon the morning and open a file on your client.

It was a fascinating week. As the clients varied so did the attitudes of the colleagues. There were numerous learning incidents, some of which would become instrumental in Adrian developing his own techniques. During that week Adrian was presented with multi personalities and individual's idiosyncrasies. He also realized that his clients were not from one specific branch of Business Consultants. He understood that this would be the feature for his trial period. The variety was an excellent exposure for him in those early days in his office.

Mary and Betty were very excited to get together again. They had kept each other informed about some items of news but that was not the same as being together. They had lots to catch up on as well as locating a couple of new lecture halls.

They were deep in thought one evening when they had been discussing the I.V.F. Both girls expressed concern in regard to the leadership. Mary stated quite emphatically that, "No one will measure up to Adrian. He is so gifted and the Lord used him to establish a meaningful fellowship".

Betty added, "Well we've only two more days before we have the first I.V.F. meeting. We'll find out something on that occasion. In any case they will have to appoint a leader because there is no way we can have an effective fellowship if we have no one in leadership."

Both girls agreed they could not sort out the details so just casually shrugged their shoulders and decided to wait for the upcoming meeting.

It was a joyful time. There was a buzz of people rehearsing incidents from their holidays. One young man stood. He was recognized by the old IVF'ers. In fact he was the only member of Adrian's committee. They knew his name, 'Jackson'; but knew nothing else about him. He stood up and called the meeting to order.

"I am not the leader for this year. We must ask the Lord to direct us this evening in seeking the leader that He wants to put into place for the coming year. I have no names to put forward. The old members will need to make suggestions. Some of the new members we welcome to our fellowship this evening. You may have something you would like to share, that's okay."

There were five names suggested. Three of them said they could not give the leadership that such a group required. To the surprise of Mary, but not to Betty, her name was mentioned by four or five people. Mary had turned to Betty indicating her surprise and also that she did not feel that she was capable of doing the job. Betty replied in quite strong terms that she was the only one capable of following Adrian. After a little discussion the other person stepped down by stating clearly and supportively that the choice of leader just had to be Mary.

Jackson looked directly at Mary and waited for her decision. She was praying for the Lord to say yes or no.

It was quite a few moments later when Mary got up and went to the front. There was an encouraging applause.

Jackson introduced her for the benefit of the new comers. "This is Mary Stapleford.. She was a regular at our meetings last year and was in charge of some of our discussions. She will do an excellent job".

"I am honoured", she said, "This is the last thing I expected to happen this term. I have some great shoes to follow because we all were amazed at how Adrian Syston led us over the past two years. All of us must be ardent in our prayers for our programmes to be under the direction of the Holy Spirit. We do not want just good meetings; we want the Lord's meetings. My aim is to step forward in the direction that the Holy Spirit prompts us. This must be my basis from which to lead, otherwise our times together will be mediocre. I am depending upon your prayer support, and together with you, look forward to how the Lord is going to bless our times together this year. Thank you for the privilege and honour of being your leader. God will be blessing each one of us,"

There was some applause that Mary tried to quell. Then Jackson stood up and indicated that this was time for prayer. It became an open time and a real blessing as many including some of the new members prayed. There was a pause and Jackson closed with a prayer of dedication on Mary and a prayer for guidance in all the activities of IVF during the coming academic year.

Mary and Betty had much to talk about on their way back to their rooms, and in Betty's room as well. Mary was still expressing surprise at her appointment. Betty stated that it was no surprise to her because that is what she expected in fact it was an answer to her prayers. "But what am I going to do? Just think of the things Adrian did, I cannot get close to organizing the things he did".

"You are not to try to do what he did Mary God is going to do things through you that he could not achieve through Adrian. So forget about the size of shoes he was wearing!" stated Betty. They talked more, and then decided it was time to pray and retire for the night.

The three trial months were up. There was a note from the boss sitting on Adrian's desk that morning indicating a time for them to meet together.

After dealing with some items of business and checking to ascertain the time of the next client. It wasn't until the middle of the afternoon.

He walked along to the boss's office at the appointed time. There was the usual greeting with the same request to sit. They had no major discussion on the weather and world news. The boss got straight down to business.

"Well, young man". That was always the opening. Adrian gave a positive nod of his head. "Adrian, your three months trial period is over. How do you feel? Has it been a successful learning period for you? Was it a meaningful experience? Do you think that you are ready for a permanent position?"

Adrian was not quite sure which of the questions he should answer first. He was just about to give and answer when the boss continued, "Our colleagues have given you a top mark. I have made my decision and I do not often have to change it".

"Sir, I have found it an honour to be part of this office for three months. I am feeling very much at ease – I am feeling at home. I am convinced that this is the work I want to pursue as a career".

"I am delighted to hear that. My decision is to offer you a permanent position here in this office. If your answer is an unqualified yes, then the job is yours".

"Thank you, sir. I appreciate the confidence you are placing in me. I promise to do my best and maintain the high business ethic already established in this firm. Thank you, sir".

"Then your permanent position commences at the beginning of next month. Welcome to the best firm in the North West of England".

The academic year went well for Mary and Betty. Progress towards final exams was gaining momentum as the final term approaches. They had found blessing and encouragement from the IVF meetings. Mary excelled in her leadership skills. There had been some discussion about an Open Meeting similar to last year's.

Mary had built up a small committee of five students; she shared with her hope for the Open Meeting.

"I feel strongly that the Lord is leading us into a 'Faith' topic" Mary said. The comments that followed helped to build up the importance of tackling such an extensive subject.

"How about, 'FAITH TO LIVE BY'".

The discussion that followed emphasized the enormity of such a challenge. Betty asked, "Yes, Great, But who do we get to lead it?"

"Betty that is a question you should not ask. Because at the moment I have absolutely no idea". Everyone had a good laugh. "One thing is certain though; we have time for some earnest prayer in that direction between now and our next committee get-together".

It was a couple of Saturdays later when the girls were with the seminarian fellows. During their meal together Mary asked if they would join in prayer for the next Open Meeting. As they talked about such a meeting as similar to the previous year, one of the follows asked if they had a working topic. Mary said, "Yes. 'Faith To Live By', is the challenge I would like to see addressed".

Then Betty added, "When and if we can locate the right person to be the speaker".

Jack responded quickly. "We have the right person for you."

Jim added, "Do you mean our divinity professor?"

"Who else?"

"So, who is this ideal person?"

"His name is Edwin Cambleford. He is a graduate of Manchester University. He holds the prestigious Doctor of Divinity degree. He is a wonderful communicator. He has an interesting approach to almost any subject".

"What is the best way to approach him?" asked Mary, "By personal contact or via letter or phone"?

Jim barged in. "Try both!"

"He might recognize me but it may not be to our advantage if it was a person to person conversation. I think it should be an official looking letter, carefully worded as to your needs and expectations. I would be more comfortable and confident writing a letter than talking on the phone".

Jack volunteered, "We could take the letter to him and explain that it is for a similar event as the one he attended last year".

"Thanks. I'll give some prayerful thought as to how I word the invitation".

"In whatever way you choose, it will be good and right", insisted Jack.

"But if I get the letter written I really do not want to wait two weeks until we see you next".

"When it is ready, get Betty to give me a call and I or we will pop over and get it. It will give us the opportunity to tell him what a wonderful effect I.V.F. is having again this year" said Jim.

"That's kind of you. I'll appreciate that help', was Mary's reply.

Doctor Cambleford did ask Jack and Jim some questions. He indicated that his first reaction was that the subject would be too large for one evening meeting. But when he re-read the title he was quite interested, especially in the application to be about personal faith as an academic belief and person experience. He had no hesitation in graciously accepting the invitation. A date was agreed over the phone. Mary booked the room immediately.

Mary made an appointment to meet the Head of Religious Studies. She asked Betty to go with her. He was easy to talk with and soon became quite interested in our subject for the Open Meeting. He expressed surprise that we were able to get such a high ranking speaker.

"It's good to have friends in high places', commented Mary. He smiled with a question mark on his face. Betty stepped right in with the importance of developing friendship with seminarians. He agreed to invite his faculty and students to the meeting.

The date came upon them very quickly. Mary had scribbled some notes for a poster. The student who did the poster last year volunteered to work on one for his year's Open Meeting; the one who did an excellent job. It was important to high-light the speaker as being a graduate of Manchester with perhaps the most prestigious Doctorate of Divinity in England, and may be the world.

On the evening of the meeting Mary had met Dr. Cambleford at reception and introduced him to the head of her department. The head of Religious Studies was also nearby. They were shown to the better seats on the front row.

It was almost time, so Mary asked the speaker to follow her into an anti room where they had special prayer for the speaker and for the listeners to hear the truth direct from God.

Mary became aware of some nerves beginning to speak to her. A very quick nod, 'help!" was sent up to God with an immediate reply. She called the meeting to order and explained a little about the purpose but spent her valuable few minutes on the subject and the speaker. She welcomed him back to his university and gave a suitable introduction.

Doctor Cambleford thanked those responsible for setting up this Open Meeting. He noted that it was open because he saw a number of his students from the Seminary. He was also aware of a goodly number of teaching staff from the university also.

"The subject before us is a challenging one. 'Faith To Live By', it strikes at the heart of religion. Religion is of no value unless it is expressed in the lives of the adherents. If faith is untenable to an academic then it is also inapplicable to the non-academic.

"Firstly we need to define faith. What is it? There is one passage in the New Testament that reads that directs us to believe that faith comes by hearing, and hearing by the word of God. That is an answer for Christians, it is also the challenge to those of others faiths or of no faith. Faith comes from believing something we hear. We cannot always remember how we have received some faith in the past. Because certain things are now taken for granted without going into theological discussions. There is another passage in the same New Testament that faith gives substance to what is not seen. Both of those passages bring a challenge to us no matter how far along the road of life we are at".

Mary had glanced round the audience and spotted her father sitting near the back. Towards the other side of the room she spotted a familiar face. He had crept in quietly and found an empty seat on the back row. He saw her looking at him and there was the beginning of a smile on her face. He placed his hand on his chin and waved one finger across his cheek. She was thrilled to see Adrian in the meeting; he left quickly right at the end of the address.

"Secondly we need to look at the different types of faith. These are just a few that I'll be addressing this evening. 'Saving faith', 'healing faith', 'mountain-removing faith' and how faith becomes the incentive when seeking guidance or direction.

He spent the bulk of his time on this section. He was provocative in places, he was emotional in places. As well as being informative in dissecting the meaning of certain Greek words, he was penetrative with the application of personal passages.

"Thirdly, I want to compare academic faith and personal faith".

His application was deeply personal. "Without some emotion academic faith can remain static and formal. Faith invites life; it boosts the quality of life. Faith is more than a rehearsing of words and phrases it involves the will in establishing the truths heard to become a living reality"

He closed by saying that some of his seminary students are with him they and he will be available to answer any questions later.

The applause, as he sat down, was immense.

The Head of Religious Studies had been asked by Mary to give the vote of thanks. He did a really good job and reiterated the need for question to be answered. Any student seeking an answer should take the opportunity of meeting with the team who are with us tonight.

People began to disperse but it was interesting how many wanted to talk. The speaker and his students with the IVF'ers were busy receiving comments of appreciation, and there were those who acknowledged being personally challenged.

The committee spent some valuable time with the speaker and his students over cups of coffee. It was agreed that the Lord had indeed spoken clearly. There was no one who could say they had never heard the Gospel.

In the middle of the week following a letter arrived from Adrian congratulating Mary on an excellent presentation.

The Open Meeting was indeed the highest point of the year for Mary and the IVF'ers. How pleased they were that new students were joining them for times of fellowship.

CHAPTER 30

The end of term was in sight. This was also the end of the year. This was the time graduating students were scouring the country and possibly the world for the ideal location to commence working.

Mary and Betty were in full discussion regarding possibilities for their future. Betty mentioned that she had been given two offices to contact, both of them located in Preston.

"Wednesday looks like being an easy day, why don't we go up to Preston to see those offices?" Mary suggested.

"Would you come up with me? You don't have to. But I sure would appreciate your company and support".

They agreed to go on Wednesday.

It was a pleasant ride on the bus, though Mary noticed that Betty seemed a little nervous or anxious. Mary found a topic of interest to take her mind off the ordeal ahead of her. They laughed and joked for the rest of the journey.

One of the offices on Betty's list was not far from the bus station, so they made their way there. Being near the town centre it was an older type building but pleasantly located. The receptionist was jovial and Betty soon lost her nervous bout. She received an excellent description of the office and the work being done. There were a few brochures handed to Betty; one of which was on how to submit an application for consideration relating to a position in the firm.

The other office was about twenty minutes walk. They didn't mind the exercise It was the ideal weather condition for a jog. They refrained from jogging, but enjoyed the walk.

The whole office building had been refurbished and redecorated. It had a welcoming reception area. The receptionist was friendly but seriously professional. Betty mentioned that she was a graduate student looking for a work situation. The receptionist turned to a bookcase behind her to pull out some brochures about the business. Just then a man came out from one of the doorways and made some sarcastic remark to the receptionist. She responded in a similar jocular manner. She made some comment to him and then turned her head towards Betty. He came round to stand near to her. "Call me Bill. I hang around here. I have to get up early and with an inadequate breakfast make sure I arrive here on time. Time is either boring or heavy, At five o'clock I make my way home to a meal and bed. Life is one bit of turmoil on top of another bit of turmoil". He paused and cast a piercing glance right through her. Betty thought that this was not a good advert for this business. She turned to face Mary who had found a seat and was eagerly listening to what was being said.

"Life here really is not that bad, unless you want it to be", said Bill. "By just one look at you it is obvious you are a recent grad and looking for your first job. Let me quite seriously express to you, my dear that you have come to the best place. You will not find a better anywhere up here in the North West. May I ask a personal question?" Betty gave an affirmative nod.

"What would you say is your real area of expertise or desire? I know, it is none of my business".

Mary thought that Betty had a strange change of attitude towards this man. She seemed to warm towards him, her face just opened up. "I don't mind you knowing what I hope to be proficient in. Human Resources and Management" she said quite positively and proudly.

Jim learned over to be closer to her and whispered, "I am not allowed to say things like this but if I was your father I would insist that you go right over to that table and write your application this minute. Good luck. I've got to go".

Betty stood a moment to recover from such an encounter; then made her way over to where Mary was sitting. Mary just looked at her and repeated what Jim had said, "If I was you father", and added, "I'd tell you the same".

Betty received an application form from the Receptionist. "But I do not have a resume or any references here with me".

"Just fill it in and if we want any references etc we will ask you for them".

"Mary", said Betty, "I hope you can help me with the right wording. I think I am a little overwhelmed at the moment".

"That's understandable", was Mary's remark, "Yes, of course I'll try to help".

Take your time, said the Receptionist, "there is no rush; we have the rest of the day ahead of us, just be as careful as possible with your answers and comments".

The receptionist gave an honest and sincere acknowledgement when receiving the completed form. "I am not sure when you will receive an answer but I assure you that an answer will certainly be sent to you".

Betty thanked the receptionist and with Mary they left the office and decided that the rest of the afternoon could so easily be spent window shopping. Later they caught the bus back to Manchester. Betty's comments centred on the fact that she had a wonderful peace about signing the application. "I think it will be a learning experience for me, but also I think I'll soon settle to the environment in Preston".

"Are you serious about looking for a summer job?" said Mary.

"I think it will be nice just to have something to do. I'm not sure how long I will have to wait to hear back from Preston", said Betty.

"I am not making any decision about a job yet. I have an appointment with our Department Head next week".

"Is that in connection with taking a fourth year?"

"Yes", said Mary, with a nod of her head. "At the moment I feel motivated so I would like the challenge of the 'honours' level".

"I am sure you will fly through it with honours". Betty paused wondering whether this was the right time to talk about I.V.F. "Does that mean, if you stay on for a fourth year that you will continue to lead the I.V.F.?"

"If they want me to".

"I don't see any doubt in that direction. You made an excellent follow-on from Adrian. In one sense I'm sorry that I will not be around to be blessed by you and to encourage you".

The day came for Mary to meet with the Head of Department. He gave her an enthusiastic welcome. "Well Mary, where do we start? Do I find you a job for this September or do I persuade you to stay on the academic road?"

With tongue in cheek Mary answered, "I am not sure where you will lead me!"

"I have on my desk two letters enquiring about you. From some where they have heard about your progress. But before opening them for you, the most important step right now is where do you want to be in September, in a job or in the academic arena?"

Mary was about to answer. "Excuse me," he said, "I think I know your reply. But let me be quite open with you. You have been the best student in the class, you have surpassed the hopes I had for you".

"I hear what you say. I have heard similar thoughts from time to time from your direction during this past year. Thank you for your assessment and conformation. To be honest I feel there is still an empty void needing to be filled. A fourth year honours course will have its challenges. Yes, sir, I would like to take the academic road!"

'Excellent. Your name is already on the list for next year. I took the liberty to recommend you for the fourth year. Good luck. I think I can promise a worthwhile position when you graduate".

"Thank you, sir. I look forward to sitting in on your lectures and taking part in tutorials with you".

Betty did not have to wait many days for the reply to her application. The official looking envelope arrived. Betty carried it, unopened, to be with Mary. A single sheet of paper. Two very short paragraphs. There were pleasant and encouraging words expressing their pleasure in accepting my application. "Please arrive ready for introduction to the staff and working conditions at nine o'clock on the first day of September."

"I've got it!" was the phrase that bubbled out of her lips. Mary was overjoyed for her and with her.

The last few days of the term were spent preparing for the coming year and making sure they had quality time for their friendship. The friendship would not end at the close of the academic year but would be something cherished for a long time after.

At the closing meeting of the term for the I.V.F. it was a time of reflection and thanksgiving. There was one item of business. Mary said it might wait until the beginning of the next term. It was Betty that informed the group that Mary was staying on for a fourth year. There was a little cheer and one fellow stood up and said, "I would like to propose that Mary

Stapleford be re-elected as our leader for next year." There was a unanimous vocal approval and everyone's hands were raised as a vote of 'yes'.

Mary attended the graduation ceremony and was delighted to see her friend Betty receive her degree. Inwardly she was anticipating a similar ceremony in twelve months time.

Then it was vacation time. Mary's father had booked a touring holiday in Scotland. She had never been up to Scotland so was looking forward to it. But also to have quality time away with her dad was something very precious.

They had a marvelous time visiting castles and lakes, watching the sheep roaming the hillsides and climbing some of them as well, museums and gift shops, tasting genuine Scottish food and attending a large Cathedral for Sunday morning worship. It was a great holiday filled with glorious unforgettable memories.

Adrian had settled in to the routine. As he received more clients of his own he often recounted experiences he had with other colleagues in those early days. It became obvious to him that Business was more than techniques and proficient use of time and resources. It was interesting and challenging to work with those who were about to start up in business and who were looking for more than just good advice. The joy he was getting was not just related to helping on a professional basis, but the learning experiences he was having were certainly being stored up for the future when he would be setting up his own office for Business clients.

One Saturday near to Christmas he had a surprise visit from Geoff. They had lots to share regarding their early experiences of the workaday world. They located a good eating place and spent quite a long time lingering over the food but just reminiscing. Adrian was able to update Geoff regarding the girls. He had a feeling that he was interested in one or even the two of them. He found out that there had been no correspondence shared between either of them.

They talked about their work. Adrian asked for Geoff to be specific if he was to place a sticker on his door or on his desk what would be his position in the firm. Geoff replied that he had pondered that for a time even before he started work. But during the experiences in the office he was probably leaning towards Economics. "My course was 'Economics and

Business Studies' – and I have a strong feeling about Ethics being brought into Business as well".

"How does your boss help you in your desires?"

"He is very considerate. He has often taken me aside and asked how I was fitting into the team. And recently the conversation has been centering on specialization. I think he sees 'Ethics and Economics' on my desk as fitting into the team he is building".

"I certainly see it as being essential towards any Business Assistance an office can offer.

Go with it Geoff, you'll make an excellent member of the team. Plus, I think, you yourself will get great satisfaction as you help people in that field".

Adrian had a favourite local restaurant so off they went for a meal before it was time for Geoff to head back to Rochdale.

"We must do this again", said Adrian.

"Yes, and you must come to be introduced to some Rochdale food" Geoff insisted.

The New Year opened for Mary as being the year to graduate and the entry into the work force .She spent little or no time thinking about life after the summer vacations. This term was leading to a climax in her studies. She was anticipating pleasure when the studies would be complete. But her pleasure was being fulfilled doing the study and research necessary for the assignments. Her Accounting professor was being a tremendous help and encouragement to her. It appeared as if she was his favourite student who gets all the privileges. He was anything but lenient regarding the assignments. He was always ready to demand more and better in the next one.

She was being blessed in her role as leader of the IVF. The Lord was helping her in the preparation for the meetings. It was also wonderful how she was led into contacting speakers for some special topics. She was often being congratulated on the meetings and speakers. She was giving some thought as to the possibility of an Open Meeting. If there was to be one then what would be the title and who would be the speaker.

She talked it over with her small group and prayed about it. One of the fellows said he had pondered a thought regarding the subject of how faith can be applied at work. The group considered that for quite some time.

The more they talked about it the more they could see great possibilities. But who could gave an adequate and challenging message on it. "We will need to find a Christian who knows how to communicate who is actively involved in the workaday world", was Mary's comment. One of the girls who had been in Adrian's group asked if she dare share a strange thought that was bobbing around in her head. With a smile, as was the case of all of them, Mary said they were wide open to even the most incredible of suggestions. She was not ready for the suggestion. It stunned her into silence. "Why can't we ask our previous leader?"

They were all silent. Nobody was aware of how long the silence lasted. Perhaps it could be stated that sometimes silence is golden.

"He certainly knows how to communicate", Mary stated. "Should we be looking for someone more mature? Someone who has been active in the world for more years than Adrian?"

"I don't think age means very much. He is experiencing work in a secular environment. He would know how to adapt a message relating to the task of witnessing not only by words but by ones very life", was voiced by another member of the group.

"We have a bunch of ideas on the table. Let us spend some quality time in prayer. If we are on the wrong road then the Lord will let it be known. After some considerable time praying Mary announced that it was time to go, but would the group be willing to meet again in one week to make a decision. "That will give each one of us ample time to seek the Lord on this. I want to be certain that whoever we choose is the right person for the job."

A week later the group met. Mary opened as usual with a prayer, and then asked each one to state what the Lord had revealed to them. It was interesting each one without any hesitation said they thought Adrian would be the ideal to lead their Open Meeting. Mary summed up by admitting she was surprised that there was a unanimous support for Adrian. "I think he will do an excellent job" she said.

It was agreed that Mary write Adrian and feel him out about the topic and for him to lead it.

It was over a week before Mary received a reply from Adrian. He admitted it was an honour to be approached for such a subject. He would love to tackle it. But he had a "but". He did not feel as if he had been in the workaday world long enough to have suitable illustrations for such a major subject. Mary's heart fell as she asked herself 'then who can we ask?' Her hopes picked up as she read the next paragraph. His thoughts went back to a teacher at Manchester Boys. He had been a policeman before going into education. He had graduated from Cambridge with a Bachelor of Divinity and had continued to get a Masters in Divinity majoring in Religious Studies. He was a wonderful teacher. He used lots of meaningful illustrations and had a marvelous sense of humour. He knew how to communicate. "I think he would be the lecturer you are looking for. I would feel free to contact him for you, if you so desire, and I would like to introduce him to the audience at your Open Meeting."

Mary was rejoicing. Everything seemed to be fitting into place and giving her peace that they were on the right road. She called her group together for a quickie after the evening meal. They were delighted and praised God for His guidance.

Later that week Mary received a phone call from Adrian. He had been in touch with the teacher at Manchester Boys; he was overjoyed to hear from me and warmly responded to the idea of speaking at the Open Meeting. "Have you a date?' If not, in conversation with him, he thought perhaps a Friday evening in November, but not near to fireworks night." Mary saw no difficulty but would need to check out a Friday on the Campus calendar. "I'll get back to you as soon as I can. It would be good to meet him with you to talk over our ideas."

Mary booked the date. Phoned Adrian. Then together they met with the teacher at one of Adrian's favourite cafes. Mary was soon drawn to J.J. Springfield. They had a profitable and productive meeting. They agreed that "My Faith and My Work" would bring a challenge to any student.

Mary left with praise in her heart because all that was left now were all the local arrangements with suitable advertising. One comment from a member of Mary's small group was, "Well he does not have a Doctorate but a BD and a Masters from Cambridge might attract some attention".

Mary asked for an interview with the Head of Religious Studies. She felt that it was imperative for that Department to know what was being planned. The Head gave her a warm welcome and was excited about the prospects of such a challenging Open Meeting. He would encourage his staff and students to take it in.

A poster was designed. There was a generous amount of vivid colour.

Words were chosen carefully. A poster does not require a large number of words, but a careful selection of a few can be attractive.

The I.V.F. meeting was held earlier in the week of the special meeting. Details of the expectation were presented by Mary. They had a time of specific prayer. God was to be in the preparations and the presentation.

Adrian arrived early and met with the I.V.F. group. They were overjoyed to see him again. He soon felt very much at home meeting with those who had been part of IVF in his day. Adrian had agreed to meet the speaker at the entrance to the building being used.

J.J. Springfield was welcomed by the I.V.F. group. His first comment was the attractiveness of the poster; he felt it was a wonderful introduction for the subject being tackled that evening.

The hall was slowly filling up. Some of the IVF'ers were feeling a little down because it appeared that a couple of other meetings were attracting students away from them. But their fears did not last long when three groups of up of to six people arrived almost simultaneously. It was quite noticeable that a good group had come from Religious Studies with three of their instructors. A small group also had come from the Seminary.

Mary led Adrian and J.J Springfield on to the platform. She stepped forward to welcome everyone. She introduced Adrian. He received quite a cheer from the students who remembered him. He briefly mentioned his time at University and how pleased he was to be part of England's glorious work force.

"I have been invited to introduce the speaker for this evening. He was one of my teachers at Manchester Boys. J. J. Springfield entered education from a few years in the Police force. His specialty while at Cambridge was subjects under the heading of 'Divinity'; that resulted in both his bachelors and masters degrees being in divinity.

"Welcome, Sir, to this Open Meeting. We are eager to hear about 'My Faith and My Work'".

Adrian waited for the speaker to arrive at the podium then turned and sat down next to Mary.

"Thank you for the invitation. It is a privilege and an honour to address you on this fascinating subject. It is intended that I be personal so forgive if most of my illustration are about me and the work in which I am involved.

"My Faith is very personal. In my younger years my faith was immature in fact I would class what little there was as being fickle. It was a word I heard about from time to time in the Church I attended with my parents. I think I must have been around twenty when I began to ask questions about 'faith'.

"I was quite serious in my searching for an understanding of what is faith all about. There was one occasion when a visiting preacher quoted a text from the Bible. "Faith comes by hearing, and hearing by the Word of God". His discourse was helpful. I think that was the time I realized that faith grows; it is meant to mature.

"I would read a passage of Scripture and a verse filled with promises would attract me. I read the truth. I believed the truth. I had learned the need to act upon the truth That was when faith came into the equation. Faith was the action required of turning a truth accepted in my mind into a truth being put into practice. On similar occasions that process was repeated and my faith changed. My personal aim throughout all these changing episodes was to have a more mature faith.

"My work as a teacher and prior to that as a policeman involved my time and my skills. It occupied many hours each week. It demanded my attention to details and the law, or the principles of education.

"As a policeman on active duty either on patrol or answering emergency calls, I was to attend not only in the capacity of a law enforcing officer but as a human with compassion. I was to always strive to understand why the people did what they did, even if it was something I could never do. On patrol one evening we picked up a drunk and disorderly man who was sleeping in a doorway. On the way to the station the senior officer driving the squad car said that the man would sober up overnight in one of the cells. I was disturbed by that comment and wondered why then I stated that I did not think the man was drunk because there was no smell of alcohol. I think we should phone for a doctor. His reply was certainly not for someone who was drunk. My gut feeling was that the man was ill, so I said that he could be a diabetic in a coma. His reaction was not too kind. But at the station when we could not get the man to walk we called the doctor. When he came and spoke to us he stated that he had called for the ambulance the 'suspect' was in a coma.

"On patrol one evening we noticed a group of kids – vandals we classed them as. I went out to talk with them. They certainly were not policeman friendly. But we entered into a conversation. I asked them about a youth drop in centre in the church just up the street.

"Most of them had been there from time to time. Did they think I would be allowed to go in and talk with them sometime? They doubted it. Why? Because I was a cop! I asked if they would walk up the street with me and they could go in and ask if a cop could come and talk with them. "They won't want a preacher!" I will not be preaching, was my reply. They went in and very soon the leader came out. He knew me. I informed him that all I wanted was a few minutes for a casual chat about safety. It was a wonderful opportunity for those kids to see me as a real human being with a genuine concern for their safety and wellbeing. I was able to briefly indicate that part of my concern for the youth of today was their need for a religious dimension; a faith dimension towards their problems. But first and foremost they saw me as someone who was truly interested in them as real people.

"I was called to an emergency one afternoon. A neighbour thought that the couple next door was having some trouble. When I arrived at the door they were surprised and wanted to know why I was on their door step. A neighbour phoned to say you were in trouble. Is there anything I can do to help? They invited me in. It appears that they were being criticized and blamed because their infant son had died in his crib. In the discussion I learned that the doctor was satisfied and there was no evidence of foul play. As the discussion continued I happened to mention that I knew what they were going through. "Oh, no you don't!" stated the father emphatically. I looked at the distraught mother and said quietly and kindly that I thought I did understand, because my wife and I had lost a fetus at eight months. The mother burst into tears."You are the only one who probably does know what we are going through." It probably is not widely known that a policeman can weep with those who weep. They wanted to know what had helped my wife and me. That gave me the opportunity to share briefly about our faith in God. God being someone who knows all about us and cares very much for each one of us whatever our circumstances might be. I believe quite strongly that that was, what might be called, a 'God-moment'.

"As a teacher relationships are important with the students and also with their parents. Teaching in the classroom is imparting knowledge but often the interpretation of that knowledge changes with parental input. What a joy it is to spot skills and talents that might even verge on exceptional. Contact with the parents is essential if a student with potential is going to progress because the parents are the encouragers.

"My faith is not exposed in verbal statements. More often than not it becomes the unspoken part of encouraging a student who is having difficulty with a subject or particular phrases. If it comes to disciplining then fairness is indispensable.

"In the religious knowledge class then I am able to make comparisons between different types of faith, different aspects of faith, and occasionally contrasting someone's faith with my own. I feel strongly that if Bible knowledge is being taught then there should be some aspect of belief involved. We read a passage of scripture and we either believe it or do not believe it. Then follows a discussion as to where faith becomes important in the understanding process.

"There was one time when a girl showed signs of a very high IQ. I must have placed her in the genius category. I had to come to terms with myself when my time was being shared more with her than with the rest of the class. Talking with her parents I offered myself to be available if they would like me to spend extra time with her.

"My faith in the class room had to be more obvious than talking about it. The students had to see it in my attitudes, also in my inter-personal relationships, and also in how I presented myself and prepared the academic material. I once read, "Unspoken acting is more powerful than unperformed speaking". Such wisdom was accredited to Anon – often a wise old man!

"The times I voiced my faith were in the staff room. The open discussions would become a challenge to reason and belief. Religion was a popular topic and always a divisive topic. There were occasions when in a serious sharing of ideas I was able to express my faith clearly and appropriately. Many were the occasions when I had to take my stand against some issues that were being proposed, because they fell short of my ideals and ethics.

"Finally, Faith is to be a dominant feature in our lives. A Biblical faith will prevail over the challenges of a secular world. A strong faith leads to a strong character, a strong character is essential if the Christian message is to have any effect upon the secular world surrounding us. "Faith is the substance of things not seen' – so we press forward in the certainty that God is in full control of our lives and will maintain his care and protection over us.

I remember there was a visiting lecturer speaking on the eleventh chapter of the Epistle to the Hebrews. He stated that, "faith exceeds humanism and avoids mere philosophical ideas". I hope I can quote him correctly when he said that the first verse in that chapter "is not a definition, but a description of how faith works. Faith is established conviction concerning things unseen and settled expectation of future rewards".

"My faith guides me in my decisions and desires. My faith is a precious part of my working life as well as my private life. It is not a Sunday outing it is a daily venture."

"Thank you for affording me this time with you. My prayer for each of you will be that you obtain a vital faith that is practical and workable. Jesus stated quite firmly on one occasion to his disciples, 'Have faith in God', and then continued, "I tell you that if anyone should say to this hill, get up and throw yourself into the sea, and without any doubt in his heart believe that what he says will happen, then it will happen!." It was quite interesting that Mark in his Gospel added the extra challenge to his disciples by pointing them to the fact that whatever they pray for they should believe that they received it and it will be theirs. "And whenever you stand praying, you must forgive anything you are holding against anyone else, and your Heavenly Father will forgive you your sins". What a mighty faith is ours!

God bless you all."

There was applause and expressions of appreciation as JJ Springfield sat down. Mary stood up to say something but was interrupted by the Head of Religious Studies. She invited him to the podium.

"I apologise for this intrusion. But it became more important as we listened to the speaker. I have something to share with you".

He turned to JJ and asked if he had received the letter. There was a positive nod.

"We will be seeing JJ more frequently in the future. I have written to him this week confirming the opportunity for him to do his Doctor of Divinity here at Manchester. A Manchester D.D is the most prestigious divinity degree in the U.K. Welcome, sir, we look forward to working together in the coming months."

There was an even louder applause.

Mary eventually thanked the speaker and others for attending the Open Meeting.

The final term was drawing to an end. That meant the last two weeks before final exams was cramming time. Mentally refreshing oneself from the copious notes she made from all the lectures. She reassessed some of the ideas thrown out by her professors. Also she refuted some obscure theories. Storing up facts ready for the multi-choice questions was important. Trying to guess what area the questions would likely cover was typical but senseless.

She told herself, "and then will come the day when all the hard work will prove successful". The day for exams arrived. Mary was quite comfortable with the questions. She really did not have to rely upon any last minute cramming because she had worked hard throughout the year. The large amount of the final was centred on the assignments. She enjoyed doing them. The Prof's were always generous in their assessment and comments.

After four terrific and rewarding years came the graduation ceremony. For Mary it was the graduation with honours. She was the pride of her father and friends. She had achieved her planned purpose.

Her Head of Department was true to his word. He arranged to meet Mary and had some papers on his table. "These are a few requests I selected from a bunch that came to my desk. I have pulled out three that I consider to be an ideal situation for you," Mary nodded her thanks. "I took the liberty to speak with the persons who wrote these letters. I informed them of the date for graduation. Each one asked if they could come and meet you. My reply was that I would speak to you and let them know your wishes and then give them a date suitable for you".

"I appreciate your help, and look forward to learning more about the situations you have mentioned. I want to know where they are located. If they are willing to come to me then that will save me having to make arrangements to travel separately to where they are located. Someone must have been talking to them about me if they are desperate enough to come see me!"

"They are within an easy reach of Manchester." One was in the city of

Manchester; another was in the city of Nottingham; the other was from Sheffield.

The date was chosen. A room was made available in the department. My Prof stated that he wanted to be present to meet them, but not during the interviews. The Prof had agreed times with them to make sure there was ample time between for a relaxing break. He had arranged for fifty minutes each throughout the morning. He told Mary that a lunch would be available after for us all.

Mary was somewhat apprehensive because interviews at that level had not happened for her before. They were official but genuinely friendly. There were personal questions about Mary; her home life, life-style and future ambitions. There were question as to which part of the country she would like to work. Each one was familiar with her academic studies, and specialties. They probed the area of accounting specifically. Each one brought leaflets about their individual offices. They boasted about their office as being the best in the district, and gave a brief list of the type of clients they were attracting.

The fifty minute slots went very quickly. Each one timed himself quite well without feeling too rushed to finish the interview with the space of time allotted. May's Prof thanked each one of them and invited them to lunch. He spoke with Mary on his way to the lunch room asking how she felt about the interviews. "They went well. I was anticipating most of their questions. They appeared very professional and eager to impress me with their work".

"I hope you don't mind having lunch with me and them, but I thought it would give us a more relaxed time for a visit".

It was an enjoyable lunch. The conversation was easy. Each one of the three departed with the assurance that they would be hearing positively from Mary within the next week.

CHAPTER 31

The first week at home for Mary was to be a 'take it easy' week. She had made three separate piles for the brochures received during the interview. She read them all and perused them again on the first day. There was a strong prayer for guidance. She realized that the decision would affect the whole of her future. She really did want to be at the place that would be God's choice.

Also she was introduced to a nice lady that her father was interested in. Sarah was in her middle forties; quite petite and blonde. She would come to the house and prepare evening meals for him. Sometime they would go to a show or to a church meeting. Mary noted that her father was really attracted to her.

The Manchester Office sounded wonderful. She liked the city. But when she started thinking about the office she was not so sure. She did not know for sure, but it would quite easily have been the same one where Adrian worked. That would be great to have a Christian colleague. But there was a negative bias that actually did disturb her, As she analysed it she was sure God was giving directions to her to look at the other brochures. The point was that she did not want Adrian to think that she was following him.

The Sheffield Office was in a brand new building. The office lay out was fabulous. All the latest modern gadgets were in place. Each office would give the impression of living in the lap of luxury. Is this something she would cherish? This would be quite a challenge.

She spent a long time re-reading the informative leaflets. "Lord, what do you say?" There was not an immediate verbal reply to her prayer.

Then the thought came to her – "it must have come from the Lord" she said to herself. If the location is within the large shopping mall then she knew that all shop owners had to open up every day. None of them were allowed to close on Sunday. The situation could be quite different for an office complex. But this bothered her for awhile. She placed the bundle of leaflets to one side. She had not definitely rejected it but somehow she had no peace because of a possibility of working Sundays. She had made it clear to herself that Sunday was not the day to go to the office and work. She wanted to preserve her Sundays for Church and worship, and opportunities for fellowship with other believers.

She came to the third pile; the leaflets regarding the Nottingham office. She liked Nottingham it was a warm and vibrant kind of city, It was nearer to Mansfield and home. The offices were much older yet the clients seemed to be more diverse than Sheffield. At the interview she was impressed at the emphasis on accounting. This was her specialty. That is probably why it became a point that was emphasized in the interview.

She re-read the leaflet that described the work of that specialty. With that leaflet in her hand she asked God for specific guidance. "Is this the office you want me to work in, Lord?"

Sarah, who had come early in order to meet with Mary, called her down, it was lunch time. She would listen for God's answer after lunch. Her father was home for lunch so she was able to share with them. Well, it was in response to a question from Sarah, "What have you been up to this morning?" So she shared her ideas about Manchester and Sheffield. Then said she was waiting for God's answer regarding Nottingham.

Her father was interested in her reasons for not wanting either Manchester or Sheffield. He thought that she would have been biased to one of those. For him Nottingham would have been third on the list!

"Do you think my Prof would talk with me on the phone about Nottingham? she asked her father. I don't see why not. He has been of great help so far, he is likely to have a word of wisdom for you" "Do you have a phone number for him during the vacation?" asked Sarah. The answer was negative but she wondered whether the department secretary would give it to her. That was unlikely.

Later in the afternoon she decided to phone the university and see if it was possible to get through to the Prof during the vacation. The immediate response was a clear, "no". She chatted further with the secretary who knew the closeness of the relationship between Mary and the Professor. "Let me contact him and ask", she said, "I'll call you back".

The afternoon dragged on as she waited for a phone call. She thought that God had answered her prayer during the lunch-time conversation. She looked at her watch numerous times. Then she heard herself state clearly that she was not to be anxious and that God is in full control. So she went off into the garden for a walk and then found a little comfort in one of the garden chairs. It was easy to relax on the verandah with the sun's warmth. She was dropping off into a slumber when Sarah called to say there was a call for her.

As she picked up the phone she said thanks to the secretary. Then a male voiced answered, "I am not the secretary today. I am out of office!" It was her Proff. "Yes", he said, "I am available for you even though I am on vacation as long as you make sure I do not miss my dinner engagement".

"Thanks for allowing me to intrude into your day of restful peace and quiet. It's just a quickie but very important. At the moment I am leaning towards the office in Nottingham. What can you tell me about it? Do you think that is where I should go?"

"Briefly, my opinion of the Nottingham office is quite positive. I am impressed with the leadership given by the CEO. He is a 'no nonsense man'. He makes it very clear where he stands in regard to expectations and achievements. Of the three who came for the interview I think I would warm towards him".

"Do you think my accounting skills will fit into his team? Can you see me being comfortable in his office?"

"You will fit in anywhere. I could see you also in the Sheffield office. But if Nottingham is your preference of the three then I would encourage you to go with it".

"That's what I needed to hear – but I wanted to hear it from you. How pleased I am that I disturbed you ease. Thanks a million, sir".

"You are very welcome. You will fit in fine. All the very best to you. There is a great future for you, which may not be in Nottingham all the time. I will be following your career with interest".

"Thank you".

Her father and his friend were eager to know his advice. "He was very positive. He had me down to go to Sheffield or Nottingham. To tell you the truth I think his preference would have been Sheffield, but he supports my going to Nottingham. He is convinced that I will fit in just fine.' Her father looked quite pleased; he must have been hoping for Nottingham.

That evening Mary went on-line to view the page of her choice. There were ten photos of the office building and some of the inside offices, together with a common room for tea breaks and snacks.

The other two were watching with her; interested in her movements and gestures. The comment from her father sounded so professional yet comprehensive. "The work space is adequate, you will not feel crowded. It looks like a proficiently organized layout of working space. It will lend itself to some serious and efficient work. I think it is a No Nonsense establishment".

"Dad", smiled Mary, "That is quite a statement. I am tempted to have you repeat it!"

"Don't bother, dear, your daughter heard it real good".

The next morning Mary was sat at her desk planning on the letter to be written to the CEO in Nottingham. She wanted to choose her words carefully. It was important, or so she thought, not to appear overly eager, but at least to express that she was convinced Nottingham is where she should go to start work.

That afternoon she walked on air, or so it seemed, as she directed her steps to the post box. Then with an audible whisper asked God to direct the response to the letter and confirm the choice of locations. The letter dropped into a space that was irretrievable from outside. That was not her desire anyway. "God Bless", she voiced as she turned to walk back home.

The reply would probably come in two or three days, she thought. But there was a tremendous surprise when the phone rang the very next afternoon. Sarah answered. "It's for you, Mary".

"Hello!"

'Mary, this is Armitage Broadbelt. I received your acceptance letter this morning. I am delighted that you will be joining my team. I have an office waiting for you"

"Thank you, sir. I am looking forward to working under your guidance".

"You most probably want to know when to start. Will it be possible for you to start on the first Monday of next month?"

"Yes, sir. I can manage that. I will need to decide whether to commute between Mansfield and Nottingham, or to look for some accommodation nearer to my work".

"My secretary will help you look for a place if you decide to live in Nottingham."

"That's very kind of you, sir".

"You are welcome. Good luck. See you. Bye".

There was just under a month to go before Mary was to start work. There was shopping to be done –"what would I wear on my first day at work?" For a girl like Mary that was a major decision. She had always been concerned about her clothes.

Sarah suggested that they go into Nottingham one day on "a mum and daughter" shopping spree. "Sorry I didn't mean to say 'mum'. I feel so embarrassed". "Don't feel embarrassed it is something new for me to enjoy as you become friendlier with my father. I don't mind at all, honestly".

They walked past the office in Nottingham where Mary would be working, but did not go inside. Both of them liked the office and Sarah expressly thought that Mary would be quite happy working there. It was a great day; they bought some stuff, had an excellent meal, and generally had fun together. It was a day of getting to know each other.

On their return home Clarence welcomed them with a meal ready to go onto the table. With tongue in cheek he stressed how long it took him to prepare it. Mary noticed a tell-tale bag on the kitchen counter and commented, "Dad that's so kind and wonderful of you, I class it as a beautiful kind gesture for us after our extremely busy day away from home". Sarah did not know how to react but she was obviously enjoying the loving sarcasm being expressed.

"Okay. That's enough of that. Please go wash your hands, plural or double plural, both of you; do not take time to have a bath or the food will have died".

It was an enjoyable time at the table Clarence wanted to know where they went and what they did. He was secretly admiring the lovely relationship that was developing between his daughter and his new friend.

Mary had a long heart to heart chat with her father about his new friend. "How serious is it?" she asked

"It is still a friendship in the developing stage".

"Are you hoping it will develop into something quite major?"

"I am still talking to the Lord about that, so I must not jump the gun and reveal too many of my deep secrets yet".

"Dad, Sarah seems a very nice lady. I enjoyed being with her for the day shopping. There were some wonderful vibes between us. I like her very much. I think I can say in advance that I love her".

"Take it steady sweetheart. Let me say quite honestly and sincerely that if anything does develop it is certain that she will not replace your mother".

"I know you well enough for that not to become an issue. I love you and I want you to be happy. I have from time to time asked God to bring a good friend into your life. So if this is the one as an answer to those prayers, then I will rejoice and praise the dear Lord for his goodness to you, to us".

A valuable time was spent sitting together on the settee. Their embrace was not short lived – it lingered, which allowed the hugs and kisses to go deep. It was a precious moment for both father and daughter.

The rest of the month went by very quickly. There were friends to visit and farewell get-togethers to attend. Each section of the church wanted to have their say. On Mary's last Sunday their pastor had a special part of the service as a farewell to Mary.

This is the day! "This is the day I start work!" "Or at least make the journey to Nottingham and get settled in my room with big commencement the next morning".

There was a normal start to the day with the usual breakfast. There were glances all around to make sure each box, or case, or bag, or package, was in place ready to be packed into the car. Clarence had taken time off from work and Sarah had arrived to help. It must have been a big job for the necessity for two adults to get her packed up and away.

The car was loaded. Mary went back into the house just to check, especially her room. In actual fact her room appeared tidier now that her things were out. Nothing caught her attention that had evaded the packing.

Into the car, and they were on their way. There was not too much conversation during the drive to Nottingham, Any comment made was either about the weather or the stupidity of 'that' driver.

Her father had booked a place for her to stay so they went directly to that address. It was within easy walking distance of her office.

Actually when they had the car unloaded and her things in suitable paces they all three went out for lunch. "Dad is paying!"

Mary asked her father if he was busy and needed to get back to work in the afternoon. He replied that the day was for his daughter. She asked if he would drive around the city to get acquainted with the buildings and streets. It was a pleasant drive as each one called attention to a building or some other familiar object.

When they got back to her room Sarah asked if she could help unpack some things. There was a suitable closet for hanging clothes and ample shelves and draws. Mary was surprised at how Sarah seemed to know just the right place for the things she carefully unpacked. Clarence busied himself by attaching an extra shelf or making sure a draw didn't stick every time it was opened.

The afternoon had gone. Clarence mentioned the possibility of them going home. But Sarah asked if they ought to have a bite to eat and a cuppa before. Mary shrugged her shoulders; her answer was a yes and a no. It seemed that Sarah won the day. They went out to find a cozy café a few streets away.

It became time for a farewell. Sarah was very genuine, and Mary responded with warmth and appreciation. Clarence took his time to get as much hug and kiss as he could. Clarence asked them to pause while he prayed for the room Mary would be using, and about the work she would be starting the next day, and for Mary herself to be kept safe and happy and experience the close presence of the Lord with her at all times. Mary added that they have a safe journey back home. And off they went.

Previous times when Mary had been left behind were when going to university. The first evening was spent exploring the campus. Here it was different, so she sorted the books on her shelf. She didn't have the determination to start reading any one of them. But she speculated the wisdom and challenge that was contained on the pages of some of them

She wondered how her father and friend were managing."They had a safe journey otherwise I would probably have heard".

In fact they had an interesting journey as they speculated the things that might be happening to Mary as she commenced work.

It wasn't late evening so Sarah decided she could stay awhile with Clarence. They sat and enjoyed a coffee. Somehow they both were sat on the couch. It wasn't long before they were holding hands as they talked. Clarence was very comfortable; Sarah moved a little closer to him. It was not just the warmth if each other's body but there were warm vibes flowing across from and to each other. The vibes flowed to an embrace which resulted in a lingering kiss. They were in love. The kisses and hugs became stronger.

"We must cool it", said Clarence as he moved away from her a little bit. "I agree", whispered Sarah, "but I don't want to!" But they did. It was Sarah who broke the spell by indicating it was time for her to go home.

It was next morning. Mary had set the alarm to make sure of being able to have her devotions before breakfast. She had estimated how long it would take her to walk to the office. She intended being there early and not to rush in at the last moment.

She was arriving at the same time as a couple of others, they welcomed her. The boss had informed the staff of a new person joining them that day. They appeared friendly, as did the others on their arrivals. The boss was never late and was always pleased to see his staff there ahead of him. He introduced Mary to the other workers, then took her into his office and had a long conversation with her about the business. He was keen for her to know the ethics and aims of his office. It was taken for granted that anyone working for him accepted such willingly and would give personal energy in living and working up to his standards.

He walked her down the corridor to the door that already had her name on. He led the way in and was about to sit at the desk then with as large grin on his face apologized. "That is your seat and I expect you to use it like a throne".

"Did he think there was a strike of royalty about me? No! It was his way of indicating the importance of the person occupying the seat".

"I have placed a couple of files on your desk. That's where you start. They are quite simple yet general, just right to get your feet wet. If you have any questions I am available, but you will find the way barred by a receptionist that knows all the answers anyway".

It was a learning morning. The challenge was not beyond her but at last she was working on a real file. She found a wave of inspiration that enabled her to settle. By lunch time she felt as if she belonged, even though there was a lot to learn.

There was a lunch time break but one member of staff stayed on duty while the others were out for lunch. Mary noticed that there was a staff lounge where it was convenient to bring your own sandwiches etc if you wanted. The Coffee pot was always ready. But for the first day Mary wanted to go with the others. It seemed there was a favourite small café about three minutes walk away. The owner was used to them coming. They sometimes joked with him about not letting any other customer's use their corner. It was a cozy family run café. Most of the food had been prepared on the spot. It was good healthy food and very reasonably priced.

It was a round table; Mary was one of five at that table. It was ideal for getting to know each other. It was obvious who would be friendlier than others. They were all professionals.

There was a lot of chattering on their walk back to the office and back to dealing with issues that were of paramount importance to the clients.

Towards the end of the afternoon the boss came into Mary's office. "I do not want you to tell me what is wrong. Because there is hardly a week that passes when some alert person confronts me with one of my weaknesses. I know everything is new and strange to you today. Your first day is important to you. How have you felt?

Mary was about to talk about one of the files. "No, he said, I want to hear you, because that will be expected of all your clients. Be quite personal with me about your first days' experience".

Mary was surprised at his approach. As she chatted with him she became very comfortable in sharing her experience.

"There will have been some negatives. There will be more days with some negatives. That is taken for granted in a business like ours. The negative is a gate through which you will go in order to become more proficient. I want you to know that I respect and appreciate the professionalism of each member of my team. But I do know that some personalities are easier to relate to than others".

"I am in a different world" said Mary. "It has been interesting to see how I was making the transition from the lecture hall to the business desk. I found that fascinating".

"Tomorrow will be different. The two clients file's you have been working on today will be here in person to meet you. One in the morning and the other in the afternoon. That does not mean you will have to take the whole of those sessions with the client. You are allocating that time to them and their business. Your personality must be in evidence from the beginning. The first impressions are always the most indelible, both for you and the client".

"Have a good evening, Mary. I am so pleased to have you on my staff". He turned and left the office.

It seemed just a matter of days before Mary felt that she was functioning in a professional situation and liking it. One day in the staff lounge she had taken a packed lunch for a change. She was not the only one. A girl from one of the other offices came in and soon they engaged in a friendly conversation. Mary mentioned about finding a good church, she had not come across one so far. There was a large smile spreading across the other girls face. Her name was Jenny. She said, "I have wondered about you ever since you were introduced to us. There is a spiritual aura around you – that means an attraction that comes from God at work in you".

"How wonderful to meet another believer", Mary remarked, "I have been praying for someone like you turning up".

"Why don't you come with me next Sunday? My church might be the one you are looking for".

"That's a great idea; I can't wait for Sunday morning!"

Jenny did not live too far away from where Mary was staying so she picked her up and together then went to Jenny's church. It wasn't a large Churchy looking building. It was a large multi-purpose hall.

"What brand of Christianity is this? Mary asked, with a strong twinkle in her eye.

"This is for real!" was Jenny's reply. "It is a Bible based Fellowship. Some people say that it was started as a following of the 'Toronto Blessing'. But some of the strange sounds that accompanied it have disappeared and everything now seems to be done decently and in order".

"I have heard a little about the 'Toronto Blessing' but that little information was not too uplifting".

"Then I can assure you we are not like 'that'".

Mary was comfortable with the worship singing at the beginning. She felt good singing some of the songs that IVF folk sang. The Pastor was about middle age and had an appealing presentation of a solid scripture exposition.

On their way out Jenny said, "Well?"

"It's okay", Mary smiled, "and I think I'll come again sometime!"

Their friendship grew and soon they were recognized as a church going couple by others in the offices.

CHAPTER 32

Adrian had settled in very well into the team. He enjoyed working with the others in the office, but he wanted more clients of his own. He welcomed the personal contact he had with them and he felt that he was able to help because he was getting to know more about them.

His boss was appreciative and fully intended to pass on more new clients to Adrian. He had great hopes for his future in the team. He had vision and easily grasped some of the dangers ahead for clients if they followed certain deviations. He was loyal to the firm.

He had been working for about three years when he received correspondence relating to a seminar for past I.V.F. leaders on, "Careers and Christian Growth", to be held in Bristol. He was quite interested in how to challenge young Christians to maintain spiritual growth when entering the work place. It was so important that Christians be able to bare a reasonable and effective witness among those with whom they worked.

As he was filling in the application form he wondered who else might be doing the same. He would look forward to meeting people he already knew but also many others.

The confirmation of his application had been accepted, and the dates confirmed. Enclosed was a brochure giving some of the details for the long weekend, Friday evening to Sunday afternoon. He noted the main speaker was Dr. J. J. Springfield, his old Religious Knowledge teacher at High School.. He was looking forward to meeting him again, and to find out something of the dissertation for his doctorate.

He was able to leave work a little early on the Friday. Travelling to Bristol on the "M" roads made the journey easier and quicker than any other routes. Booking in time was six thirty. for the evening meal. He arrived about six o'clock, it gave him good time to register and find his room. There were still about three minutes before dinner was served so he perused the attendance list. How delighted he was to note that Mary Stapleford was on the list, she followed Adrian as leader of the Manchester I.V.F. group. There were a couple of other names that he recognized from other universities near to Manchester.

He made his way to the Dining Room. Other attendees were arriving at the same time. There were jovial greetings being shared all round.

There was a head table at which sat the people organizing the Seminar as well as the speakers. His table was not far from the top table and he made eye contact with his old teacher, J.J. Springfield. Between his main meal and the desert his eyes wandered all round the room. He was obviously looking for a particular person. His head stopped moving, his beaming smile became quite extended, and his eyes twinkled. Then he said to himself, "Why am I reacting like this, anyone would think I had fallen over cupid or done something silly". His head nodded as she raised a hand and gave a return nod. Mary had been expecting to see Adrian at this seminar. They found their way to each other after the meal and walked together to the lecture hall for the first session. The speaker introduced the subject and then gave a brief idea as to what would be covered the next day. He did stress that this was not a holiday weekend; they would be working hard in each one of the sessions.

Adrian and Mary walked out of the lecture hall and found a lounge with some fairly comfortable chairs. They were so pleased to see each other and wanted to get caught up on what had been happening to them. There was much to chat about, and all too quickly it appeared as though everyone else was disappearing and heading for bed. They said their "Good nights" and walked to the elevator. They were on different levels; they both stated that they were looking forward to the sessions.

The three Saturday session were quite heavy, but very extensive in searching for the best ways to enable growth in spiritual things, and the breaking down of theories relating to how careers should be guided by the Holy Spirit.

There were open discussions at the end of each session which proved to be helpful and challenging. The little grey cells were whipped into working overtime. Most of the attendees thanked God that they were no longer full time students. There were others who would relish the opportunity to delve into some of the theories being exposed.

The discussions between Adrian and Mary centred on the fact that development of their work would be taking first priority, if there ever was some spare time.

The Sunday morning session was placed within the context of a worship service. The challenge of the message was for everyone to be completely handed over to the Lordship of Christ which also meant being filled with the Holy Spirit. There was a time of quiet prayer and meditation for individual's prayers to be answered. The climax was in partaking of the Holy Communion – Christ's redeeming love giving the enabling for whatever service Christ may be leading into..

There was some free time before lunch would be served. The meeting broke up into groups of four or five. Adrian and Mary were with three other fellows from universities near to Manchester.

After lunch Adrian asked Mary how she would be travelling back home. "I'll take a train up to Nottingham". "I don't think that will be necessary, there is at least one car with empty seats going north. The other three had travelled together in one car, so Mary did a mental juggle as to who or which car would mean not going to the train station. Adrian said, "Nottingham is not off my track. We have "M" roads most of the way and it is comparatively easy to go in to Nottingham for me. I would love to do it – I would be happy if you will give me the opportunity to drive you home"? "Okay that's settled", continued Adrian without waiting for a reply from Mary.

"Are you getting bossier in your later years?"

"Of course; especially where nice young ladies are concerned".

"So does that mean you have some young ladies hanging on to you?"

"Not really. I'm still a bachelor".

"So, boss, how about some lunch to give us the energy to tackle the British road system between Bristol and Nottingham".

They went off together with a big chuckle, just like a couple of teenagers.

It was a good healthy lunch. It was easy to pack the few items of baggage. Adrian remembered the roads through Bristol to the Motorway, They were soon travelling north. Their conversation was centred on the last session of the seminar. Adrian had made his comment once again about J.J.Springfield being his high school religious knowledge teacher. Mary commented how he had changed from when he had spoken at the I.V.F. meeting.

When they came to the turn off for Nottingham, Adrian asked where to go.

'If you go towards the city centre then I can direct you to where I am staying." It wasn't very difficult. Adrian knew the city centre.

She had guided him to the right street and then said, "There it is".

He pulled up in front of the house. He helped get Mary's things out of the car. He surprised himself by saying that he would help carry them to her room if she would like. It was a shy, extremely quiet whisper "I'd like that!" He enjoyed walking her up to her room and placed the things inside the door. He turned towards the door, but stopped and turned around to say how wonderful it had been seeing her again and thanked her for allowing him to drive her home. "I must away. God bless you. We'll see each other again sometime".

"Yes. Thank you for the lift home; it has been wonderful being with you again. Yes, we'll see each other again; not too far into the future I hope".

She walked with him down to the outside door and waved him off. She was elated at having been with Adrian for a whole weekend. She was sure if that happened too many times cupid would have fired all his arrows.

Adrian was reminiscing as he drove away from Nottingham. He too had felt the privilege of having the weekend with Mary.

245

33
CHAPTER

The friendship between Mary and Jenny developed quickly. That was due possibly because they both had been praying for a believing colleague. They found themselves doing many things together because their interests were quite similar. Mary actually adapted well to the new church, and with Jenny they became part of the young adult group.

When they said their farewells at the end of the day they decided whether they would have a packed lunch or go to the café. They didn't meet every evening only the ones for the church meetings or any other special event they wanted to take in.

Mary was in a recollecting mood one evening and she wondered why she had felt comfortable at work so soon. She was convinced it was due to the Lord leading her and Jenny together. So there was a quick prayer of thanks for the friendship developing with Jenny.

Mary was enjoying her work. Some of her clients were very interesting people. There was always time for some personal comments which meant that through personal comments they were building up a profile of each other. Mary liked that because she realized that if she really wanted to help her clients then she needed to know as much as possible about them. She had a good rapport with people she met, so it was easy for her to locate personality traits.

At the young adult meetings it wasn't long before two young men came to the same table Mary and Jenny were at and asked if they could join them. They of course were very cautious and said that it would be fine as there were plenty of chairs available. This move from the fellows became a regular feature at the meetings. Jenny remarked to Mary after one of those evening, "Those 'boys' seem to be getting more and more interested in us".

"It is becoming openly obvious. I don't mind as long as they do not want to be serious", commented Mary.

"I suppose we could get worse".

"But at the moment I am not interested in worse or better. I am not ready for a serious relationship".

"How will you know when you are ready?"

"When the Lord gives me the okay. That hasn't happened yet, so I don't know what it will be like when it does happen".

As the weeks passed it became more obvious that the two fellows were interested in seeing the girls more than just at the church meeting. The girls became more cautious.

They did agree to go out for a meal with them one Saturday. They brought their car and transported the girls safely to the restaurant. It was a pleasant meal.

As they were driving home there was a slight intimation that perhaps they should say goodnight with a kiss. The girls were happy about saying goodnight, but were hesitant regarding the kiss.

The boys got the message.

As they chatted together on their way home they were disappointed that they didn't get their hug and kiss. They thought that perhaps they should take it slowly in regard to meal dates.

Mary and Jenny also discussed their evening out. They wondered if they had been too ungrateful by not having a goodnight kiss. Marry said, "They got the message that we are not ready for such intimacy yet".

Jenny agreed, "I don't really think I want to enter into a kissing session with either of them".

"Then let's just stick to a coffee after the meeting", stated Mary.

The fellows got the message. Meal dates now seemed out of the question. The meeting at the same table for coffee seemed to be less. The girls noticed all this, but were quite happy about it.

It was just over a year later when Mary received a phone call from her father. He very rarely called. Mary had a momentary anxiety flash which soon disappeared when the voice was as friendly as usual but with an extra flash of pleasure. "I am so happy that you are available" said her father, "I was afraid that perhaps you were busy with a client or supping coffee with your friend".

"Yes, Dad. I am totally free at the moment!"

""I love you too, baby!"

"Okay Dad, what's worrying you, or what is about to explode".

"Do you like explosions?"

"Sometimes; why? What earth shattering news are you about to unload on me?"

"Sarah and I want to pick you up after work and go out for dinner".

"That is absolutely wonderful. I'm desperate for an expensive meal out. I'll be ready and waiting for you. By the way, I think there is more news than a dinner date!"

The car was waiting when Mary left her office. Two smiling faces welcomed her into the car.

"So, when do I receive the news now or during the soup course?"

"It might be sweeter if we left it until the desert course!" commented her father.

"In that case you could pick me up later!"

"Now that you are comfortably encased in the car we would not consider turning you out to be picked up again later", said Sarah with a beaming smile.

Mary had already jumped to a conclusion. Call it feminine intuition! She almost spoke out loud requesting a look at Sarah's left hand. But she maintained her discipline and silence.

They had just sat down at the table when Clarence coughed and began shyly to speak. At the same time he took hold of Sarah's left hand and placed it on the table. He was not half way through what he wanted to say when Mary interrupted and leaned over and gave Sarah a big kiss.

Clarence said, "What was that for? You have not heard the rest of my carefully prepared announcement!"

"Hold tight, Dad, I'll be over your way shortly for a big hug and kiss. I am so happy".

With all the hugs and kisses going on the waiter had to wait patiently before the decisions were made as to what to eat.

The conversation during most of the dinner was about the engagement and future wedding. But not until both Clarence and Sarah were totally convinced that Mary was comfortable and happy with her father and another women.

""One thing we want to stress", Clarence said, "Is that Sarah is not going to be a new mother, she will be my new wife".

"I've already accepted that, but that doesn't mean I will love her less. My happiness comes from your happiness; I think it is absolutely fantastic. God bless you both. I know he must have done already, but I want to emphasize that it is my prayer for you both that God will keep you close to each other and guide you into a wonderful and exciting future together. But, it is a big BUT, I promise you that I will from time to time invade the privacy of your romance and announce my presence as an exuberant observer and supporter".

"Thank you, darling" answered Sarah.

"I expected nothing different from you sweetheart", voiced her father.

"So, have you set a date yet?"

"Not definitely. We think an autumn wedding would be nice and appropriate. So we look forward to an Indian summer towards the end of September".

"Why appropriate?"

"Just looking at your father", said Sarah, "I think he will fit better into an autumn rather than summer". She then became quite personal with Mary, "Will you be my maid of honour, I cannot think of anyone more suitable. I'm sure your father would be pleased if you agree to be part of the wedding party". Mary had not expected that, but was most happy to accept such an honour.

Each time Mary was home more arrangements had been finalized for the wedding. It appears to be larger than at first visualized. Mary and Sarah spent a long time discussing various issues, but were quite happy that they agreed so easily on the plans being made. "I am not looking for a white dress", Sarah told Mary. "I want an ankle length, perhaps in a silver pale blue".

"That will match your eyes!" joked Mary.

"Then you should be in pale green, to match your eyes!" replied Sarah.

The idea for colours did eventually agree with the dress colours that were purchased for the special day.

The Special Day arrived. It was a glorious autumn morning, blue skies and sun shining its blessing upon the happenings of the day. It had been taken for granted that the bride would be beautiful, she was resplendent in her silver pale blue ankle length satin dress. The groom looked really posh in top and tails. The other attendants in their supplied autumn colours made it a memorable wedding. The service gave honour to the Lord. The two hymns were sung to the praise of Father God. The Minister's address was sound scriptural teaching regarding a bride and the husband; He was also amusing which was appreciated by all the guests. Photographs had to be taken according to the list presented to the photographers some days before the wedding.

It was a great day. Mary was so happy to see her father beaming with delight with his adorable bride. For Mary it was the beginning of a new relationship, but Dad was still Dad no matter who else was sharing him.

At Christmas time there was a letter from her old school in Mansfield. Someone had had a bright idea regarding a reunion of old sixth formers. The organizer wanted a quick feedback to see if there was a sufficient interest to go ahead with organizing such. Mary wasn't sure whether it was the ideal thing but wrote in the reply that she would be willing to join in such an event.

It seems that there was sufficient number of old students who were keen for such a reunion. It was planned to have it during the Easter break. There were facilities available for a Friday evening and overnight the weekend prior to Easter.

An official invitation arrived. There was to be a dinner in a local restaurant, and then it intimated that a pajamas stay over party was to be part of the enjoyment. That surprised Mary. They never had such parties in her day. They would move out the next morning; everyone would be responsible for their own breakfast.

It was a great gathering of 'old' faces; but also many others who were in earlier or later years than Mary's year. It was fun catching up on what had happened since leaving High School. Some of the stories were mediocre but others had quite interesting experiences. Some of the other rooms had been set aside as bedrooms, though not many of the attendees thought there would be much time for sleep. There was still a lot of catching up to be talked through. Mary was happy that some of her old class mates were there and it meant listening to more and more stories. She was very disturbed though when she saw some couples going off into individual rooms.

The group that Mary was with decided to have breakfast in a local café before heading for home. The general comment was that it was a great opportunity to catch up with old friends. Some, like Mary classed it as a one off; they would not attend any more reunions if planned.

She went home so that she could join the family for the Sunday morning service. Clarence and Sarah said that they were expecting Mary to come for the Easter weekend, She said it would be impossible to decline such an offer – in fact if she had not received an invitation she had already decided how she might invite herself to go home for the weekend.

The service was a great time of rejoicing and praise. Lots of 'Hallelujahs' were heard. The time at home was a joy. She was overwhelmed by the love of her father and Sarah. She still felt very much a part of the family.

When back at work, questions were asked about the reunion. So once again Mary retold some of the details but obvious left out some. She was back at work. There were clients to be served. Her mind was soon off the reunion and concerned with the details being presented from her clients. It was work she enjoyed because she was aware just how much help she was being to the ones in need of guidance.

34
CHAPTER

Adrian had been working for the firm for almost five years. He was not unhappy with his situation in fact he was extremely comfortable with his work situation. But a thought kept surfacing and was now demanding more attention. He was quickly realizing the importance of finding some quality time to deal with it.

That weekend was free from demanding events. So he decided that on Saturday morning after his devotions time he would get pen and paper and sit at his desk.

He had been conscious of a change needed regarding his work. At this precise moment he was in a debate with the Lord regarding a major change. He wanted to make sure that it was not some personal desire to reach but that it was even more than something he could ask God to bless; he must hear from God that it was His idea.

He lost a sense of time while in deep prayer about this. But the moment of enlightenment came when he knew it was what God wanted for him

He had been toying with the idea of setting up his own business, He knew that his father would be a tremendous help in that regard. He had not mentioned it yet to his father.

He was scribbling notes as to what and where. The place would be of paramount importance in order to attract business. It was a fabulous undertaking but he felt a strong determination to look carefully into establishing his own business. There were some on-line reports that gave important information he found to be of tremendous help.

Names were already floating around in his head as possible co-workers. He wanted it to be a Christian business and therefore he would endeavour to hire Christians.

He commenced writing names down on the paper. Against some he indicated the position they might hold in his business,

Geoff was the first name. He knew that Geoff would be interested in working with him.

Mary was the second name. He just hoped she would be interested in coming as his head of accounting.

There were a couple of fellows from other South Lancashire universities he had met at Bristol. He thought they might show an interest towards a Christian business.

He drew a line across that page with a note to say that more names would be added perhaps after talking with the first two on the list as well as discussing the whole affair with his father.

"What shall we call ourselves? That caused quite a bit of scribbling and crossing out. He was trying to find a term that would indicate that it had a Christian base. There was one he felt would be a good working title anyway. "KARISM BUSINESS CONSUTANTS SERVICES".

Was that too big? Were there too many words in it? There might be too many people who would have no idea what "Karism" was. "That's something else to talk to Geoff and Mary about".

The morning had passed and he felt like having some lunch. So he left his papers on the desk and went off to his kitchen for something to eat.

After his lunch he was convinced that he should share these ideas with Geoff; so he wrote him an email. He could also get his idea as to whether Mary would be someone to contact. The reply from Geoff was that he could meet Adrian for lunch the next day.

They had a great time together. Geoff became as excited as Adrian about the prospects of forming a Christian business. To Adrian's question about him joining the team it was a firm and definite affirmative.

"Do you think I have the nerve to write Mary and ask her what she thinks".

Geoff responded with a "Go with it. I'm sure she had a little attraction towards you!"

Later that evening he took a long time wording his email to Mary. Then after praying it on its way, he pressed 'send'.

She must have been sitting on her computer because there was an immediate reply. It startled Adrian at the suddenness of the reply. She also expressed her enthusiasm for him starting up a Christian business. She would like to talk to Adrian about his plans. In her enthusiasm she even suggested that he should come to Nottingham the next Saturday. And in brackets, "that is if you are not playing soccer!"

Immediately Adrian said to himself that he must make sure that there was no soccer next Saturday. In his quick reply he suggested a certain restaurant for lunch at midday. "Yes", became her reply.

He spent quite a few moments during the week in anticipation of being with Mary for lunch.

It was a good meal and a very pleasant time of conversation. She leaned quite favourably towards a Christian business. "Would you be willing to join me", asked Adrian. With a smile across her face she replied, "I thought you were never going to ask! Yes, I would love to be part of your Christian business".

He mentioned to her that Geoff had already agreed also. "But there will be other posts to fill so I hope you and Geoff may have some good ideas".

"I am friendly with a colleague; she would make an excellent Receptionist. Her name is Jenny. Put her name down and I'll talk with her son on Monday over lunch".

That's a very important position. Perhaps next time I'm through to Nottingham I can meet with you and her".

"Oh, yes, there is Betty. You remember her from I.V.F. I'll contact her and ask her for you if you like".

"Thanks. I think I had better start employing you right now as Liaison Officer!"

"Accepted!"

They had enjoyed their time together, in fact Adrian was feeling some difficulty in saying "thanks for the day and good bye until next time".

After all the excitement of the past week Adrian thought it time to talk to his father about his way-out plans. He decided to invite himself for dinner on Tuesday. "That'll give Mum time to find some decent food to serve her favourite son".

Tuesday just happened to be convenient to go home for a meal. One comment from Dawn was "What is he coming to tell us?"

"No, rather what does he want us to do for him?" retorted Howard.

Adrian arrived just in time for dinner, so after washing his hands, was told to sit down at the table. He sensed they were eager to hear why he had come home – "it must be for more than a mere meal" thought Dawn.

They were comfortable in the lounge after dinner. Both his mother and father looked directly at him. He did not wait for them to ask the question. "I've come home to tell you that I am likely to have a change in my work situation".

"Have you been promoted to the boss position", joked his father.

"Not quite. No one at work knows about this as yet. That is why I not only want you to know but I want some loving and serious feedback, I'm all ears!"

"I don't know why you are all ears, because we have nothing to talk about just yet".

"Right, Dad, here goes. I have felt lead to start my own business. I have prayed and think that God is leading me in that direction. I don't know where to locate it but I do know a few very talented Christians who are or might be willing to join me".

"Have you lost your mind, my son", stated his mother, "You have an excellent position in a very reputable firm. Why shake your boat into something that might even be a pipe-dream?"

"If it is a pipe-dream then I'll wake up quickly. Please wake me up for my sanity if nothing else".

"I'll sit with you for a long discussion but I will charge consultation fees; the going-rate for such is pretty high at the moment" commented his father.

"I've been on the internet to get a few ideas about starting a consultation business. The task is immense; but if God is behind it He'll make sure things move slowly in the right direction." "Oh, Yes, Please keep a careful record of the hours spent, perhaps you could also include mileage when you take me around to see various locations".

"I think that it is absolutely perfect that I have now retired. Why? Because my son has just given me a full time position in his new business".

His father was more in favour than he dared to expect. He could see the potential and he recognized the capability of his intelligent son.

He thanked them for the meal and for their willingness to listen to his pipe-dream.

At home his pen and paper came out once again, this time with ideas to incorporate in a letter to his friends and possible colleagues.

He decided to give a short questionnaire to get back some personal hopes and goals. He also wanted them to send a copy of the letter to any other Christians in the business field that might be interested.

"Name. Age. Qualifications. Year of graduation. Personal specialty. Willingness to develop and expand such specialties. Passion and drive for personal excellence. Committed to the business being built on biblical principles. He thought those questions could bring some interesting people into a Christian Business Consultation Services.

His first letter would be to Geoff and the second to Mary. Then he would ask Mary to forward a copy of the letter to Jenny and Betty. He wasn't sure whether Geoff had a Christian colleague or friend in the same field. He would then look up the addresses of the two friends he made at Bristol; he must also make sure he had their right names.

He didn't have to wait long. The first reply was from Mary. She was excited, she was willing to join the pioneer adventure, and she had shared the letter with Jenny who will be sending in her reply; she was over-joyed at the prospect.

A couple of days later Geoff's reply arrived. He was equally excited and wanted to know how he could help in the planning stages.

The two friends Adrian had met in Bristol were not as openly interested as he had hoped. But they wanted to be kept in touch with developments,. That was not too much of a setback for Adrian because he realized that he would not be able to employ too many people at the beginning.

The letter from Betty was encouraging and expressed her desire to learn more about the project. She indicated that it was already a point in her daily payers for God's guidance.

Adrian was offering praise and thanks to God for some positive feedback, He felt as if he was now already launched out on a mammoth journey.

The next two things required consideration. Where? And the need for all those interested to attend a day of consultation in some central location.

He would set a day, about a month ahead to give opportunity to change anything that might be in the way. He decided that a Saturday would be the most acceptable day for such a consultation. So he looked around for a suitable venue for a morning and afternoon session with a suitable lunch in between. He also hoped that he and his father might have visited various places with the hope of God saying this is where it should be located.

His father and mother were keen to find the right location. A day was set aside for a trip around some of the major urban areas that could be in need of a specialty consultation firm in their vicinity. His father had done a little research to find out some areas where there were few such firms. He felt that Sheffield could be one such area, and perhaps Stafford or even Derby as another Midlands area. They could not all be covered the same day.

Adrian was there bright and early on the morning of their venturing forth. His father had mentioned about some places but thought that they should go into the Midlands and cover cities like Stafford and Derby and others the Lord might direct towards while in that area.

During the conversation as they travelled, Adrian asked whether buying an already existing firm would offer more problems than starting from scratch. "At least", he said, "There would be a building with some office spaces as a basis".

"There is always a big but to doing something like that. For example there might be a clause in the contract to indicate that the present employees are to continue with the new owners. A new business in a new building will always be more attractive to new clients", were the wise words from his Father.

They travelled down the M6 motorway and took the exit that would take them to Stafford. It was an interesting city. The road into town took them through some attractive housing areas. Adrian did not feel too enamoured with the city centre. They drove around then parked in order to get the feel of walking through the streets of the city. They had noticed two Business Consultant firms. Both were in older type buildings but both with attractive fronts. If this was to be their location they would need to find a more modern area. There were two new mall-type areas, but Howard had a negative vibe to each of them. Adrian asked why he felt that way. All the businesses look healthy and smart but I just could not see a place where a Christian consultation firm would fit.

They had a snack lunch and then drove to Derby. Like Stafford, it was set in an industrial area. The industry did not dominate; it was all quite advanced. The town centre was more attractive even though there were many one way streets. They had driven through some of the suburbs and found a central place to park the car.

They found it easy to walk around past the shops and offices. Dawn expressed her pleasure with the feel of the city. While walking around they passed three Business offices that appeared successful.

Howard wanted to drive around just away from the city centre to see if there were any new malls that might attract a consultation business. Adrian was disappointed that they did not find the ideal location they were looking for, but he did like the city.

It was still afternoon so Howard suggested they could catch a glimpse of Leicester but it would be rush hour so they may have difficulty finding a place to park. "It's fairly close to Derby, so while we are in the area it would be good to have a look around".

It was another quite interesting city centre and great shopping areas on the way out to the suburbs.

Once again they did not find what they would consider to be a good location. The odd place could be made attractive in order to attract business. But Adrian had no positive vibe as being suitable for the business he wanted to develop.

Dawn suggested that they find a good place for an evening meal because it would save her having to make something later. All three of them were tired so they had a positive response to her suggestion.

The meal wasn't too fancy but quite tasty. They had the opportunity of making comparisons between the places they had visited. There were some natural positives in all three cities. But as Howard said, "There was not one place where I could see a new business drawing the clients necessary to build up a successful venture".

"The other day you said something about Sheffield" Dawn said to her husband. "Are there any other cities in that direction you would like us to look at?"

"I have already been thinking what day will be best to go over in that direction", he responded.

'I can't' take another day off from work, so it will have to be a Saturday, but not this week." said Adrian.

"Then let's make a date for the following week". All three were in agreement.

They were pleased to arrive home; it had been a very tiring day for them.

An email from Geoff was waiting for him. He wasn't too tired to read a letter from his friend. He wanted to meet for lunch on Sunday, but could he come to Rochdale. "I have a few ideas to share with you. I won't indicate them now so please let us get together on Sunday." Adrian wrote a quick reply indicating how intrigued he had become about some new ideas. And sure, he could make it to Rochdale, as long as he knew were to meet.

The next morning there was a reply from Geoff telling where to meet.

It was an easy to find place and Geoff was already at the door waiting for him. Fortunately it was a lovely sunny morning so he didn't mind waiting outside in the sun.

Geoff had chosen his favourite restaurant. There was always a special Sunday Dinner that would give pleasure to their pallets.

They had a lot to talk about as they caught up on the activities of the past month or so. Geoff was interested in their visits to the Midland cities and also their reactions.

"Well it is in regard to location that I wanted us to meet. Not many people are keen about the Industrial North West, or even the North itself".

"So, what or rather, where have you in mind?"

"I am sure you have already thought about Sheffield?" "Yes, my parents are bringing me over next week to see the city".

"Perhaps you have not thought of anywhere further north, like Leeds, or York, or Harrogate".

"No. I must admit my mind hasn't gone up that far".

"Well, I have my car parked around the corner; when we have eaten I want to take you for a ride".

"Just as long as you know that I have to return home this evening".

"That won't be a problem. So let's go".

"Where to first, we can't cover the three places you've mentioned?"

"I thought of Harrogate".

"That's the posh city!"

"Be that as it may, it came up in my imaginations the other night and

I went over to view the place and was duly impressed. Don't let the 'posh' put you off.

Geoff knew which roads to take that would be a great prep for arrival in the posh city. South Yorkshire is an industrial part of the country. It is not so black since the smokeless zones came into effect. It was a pleasant drive. Geoff was endeavouring to paint an interesting picture of the posh city. As they travelled along the road he was describing some of the buildings in the city centre. Because it seems that he is always hungry, mention was made of some of the eating places. He mentioned one that was famous for afternoon teas. Adrian's retort was that perhaps such should be sampled at tea-time.

Geoff drove around the city centre. They parked the car and walked around the centre streets. Adrian was getting a good vibe from the feel of Harrogate. They noticed some of the offices that would be a competitive challenge. But the general feeling was that there were possibilities to follow up.

He then drove through some of the roads leading to the suburbs. He had mentioned that there was one in particular that he wanted Adrian to see, because he thought it might fit some of Adrian's tastes. It did. He found it attractive and interesting. They parked the car and looked closer at the buildings in that area. Geoff observed that there was just one small business consultant office. Adrian's observation centred on possible venues for an office.

"How about a fancy tea?" asked Adrian. "Right. It will take us a few minutes to get there but I hope there will be a place to park".

There was a parking space just a few yards away from the entrance. The first impression from the outside was that it was different. The first impression from the inside was its poshness. A beautiful young lady with neat black dress and sparkling white apron greeted them and took them to a window seat. Adrian remarked to Geoff, "How much does that service cost?"

"Don't worry it's on me. You can pay next time".

It was a set menu. Thin cucumber sandwiches, selection of scones and fancy small cakes. There was clotted cream and strawberry jam for the scones. A silver tea service was brought to the table and the same waitress poured the first cups of tea; the best china cups were being used. (But on looking around all the tables each had the fine china.) She also had a genuine smile on her face when she wished us a very pleasant afternoon tea.

It was pleasant. It was delicious. It was definitely not for every day. It was the ideal place if a friend or client indicated that a cup of tea would be a good thing right then and there.

Their journey back to Rochdale was without incident. The conversation fluctuated from the fancy tea to the advantages of Harrogate.

Adrian felt a little lonely as he travelled home. But his mind was quite active as he considered the location for his business. He had some interesting details to pass on to his father in preparation for the visit to Sheffield. He was quite clear that they must visit Harrogate after Sheffield.

Soon after he arrived home he phoned his father to report on his day. Both of them were looking forward to the trip on Saturday.

It was a rainy morning when Howard and Dawn picked up Adrian and set off for Sheffield. Howard had lots of questions regarding Harrogate, His main concern being their reputation of the posh city. Dawn joined in by changing the subject. "There is one important aspect of a move or a location is the proximity of a good church," she said, "with an excellent pulpit ministry, warm genuine fellowship and the possibility of an appropriate support group".

"That's quite the challenge. All those benefits in one church", remarked Adrian.

"We'll be looking into that. I have made a mental note to phone some friend about that", was his father's reply.

When they arrived in Sheffield Howard decided the best thing would be to drive around the city centre and then move into the suburbs. They parked down town and walked along some of the streets looking not just at shops but more especially offices. Just a few caught Adrian's attention but when they stopped and looked more carefully he decided that they perhaps were not the best specimens. Some parts of the off-centre had plaza and strip malls but none appealed as the being the place to start a new business.

Howard then suggested that they go to the big mall on the outskirts of Sheffield just off the M1 motorway. They had to park and there was a lot of walking. Adrian was attracted to a couple of sites where there was office space to rent. They paused and chatted about each of them. There were some very definite positive vibes.

They went to the Mall Business Office to receive more details. They wanted to know, of course, the monthly rent, but Adrian was concerned about the opening hour's policy. One thing he said, "If we rented office space would we be required to open on Sundays?"

The reply was that all shop owners would be expected to open seven days a week. But the offices are not subject to that rule. It would be expected that the offices might have a skeleton staff for most of Saturday,

It was time for a rest – it was even time for something to eat, so they walked round to the Food Court and found some food items they liked. Dawn commented how nice it was to sit and relax for awhile. The table conversation was related to the mall as a site for the new business. Howard said that he had looked at the directory when they came in; there were two other Business Consultant type offices. "There was no indication as to whether or not they were Christian".

Adrian said, "But I am not sure I want competition from two sources in the same shopping space".

"I think you have a point that needs careful consideration", Dawn remarked.

"You've got a valid point", said his father, "I don't think I would want to start an office with that competition already established".

"Then lets head north and look at the posh city", was Adrian's suggestion.

Howard had looked at the map and recognized the journey would not be too difficult. So they set off north on the M1 motorway until coming to the exit Howard had said would be the one for Harrogate.

They did their usual trip around the city. Dawn felt quite comfortable with what she saw. They parked for their walk around. Adrian had the address of the place he had seen with Geoff. It wasn't too much of a strain for Howard to find, as he wound his way around the streets. They came to what was the beginning of a strip mall. There were a number of buildings already open. An office block had just been completed, so they had the chance of looking into some of the spaces for offices. Adrian was impressed by the spaciousness of some of them. He could visualize himself and team in them.

There was a business office. They went in for brochures and to ask questions about the future development. Adrian asked if there was a plan to have any individual offices among the new shops to be built. There was a surprise answer as the agent pulled out a blue print sheet of the next stage for building. He pointed to one spot on a corner and indicated that an office could perhaps be fitted in there. "Nothing has been decided yet".

"How soon will the final decision be made?" asked Adrian.

"In about six month's time".

"If I, we, were interested would it be possible to share some ideas for the layout of office space?"

"Yes, sir. It would be our privilege to personally design that space. But I suppose you would only be interested in the ground floor. There would be rooms upstairs for other offices. Are you interested?"

"Yes, sir." replied Adrian, "Please keep me posted regarding developments and costs".

There was a form for Adrian to complete. Before writing he looked directly at his father who was happy to affirm his action.

"We can do that with pleasure and if you are making a firm offer we will indicate the time for deposits, and outline the building process".

"Thank you!"

They had a meal in Harrogate then left for home. Naturally the conversation centred on the comparison between Sheffield and Harrogate. The more the differences were mentioned the more Adrian was being biased towards Harrogate. When there was a lull in the conversation Adrian was working on the letter he would be writing to Geoff and Mary,

After a long day they were tired so it was just a matter of dropping Adrian off, then Howard and Dawn headed directly for home.

Adrian relaxed physically for a few minutes but his mind would not stop work. So he sat at his computer and wrote an e-mail for Geoff and Mary. He expressed his and his parent's reactions to Sheffield, and then a more in depth account of their visit to Harrogate. He got more and more excited as the letter progressed. (The two friends on receiving the email would be left in no doubt as to where Adrian was leaning for the location of the new business,) As soon as he pressed the send button he was anxiously awaiting their replies.

Even though they were many miles apart both Mary and Geoff had the same thrill from Adrian's enthusiasm for Harrogate. Neither of them was in the habit of sitting at their computers late in the evening. But that evening as the reminder of a new message clicked they decided to open just in case it was an important message. It certainly was an important message because it would affect their futures. And no matter how late it was they did not leave their reply until the next day. Their enthusiasm bubbled over as they typed their response to his latter.

Adrian's reaction meant that he would be later going to bed. Their response was what he hoped for. The little grey cells started working almost ferociously as his thoughts were directed at a meeting for the potential members of the team.

Adrian had found a hotel not many miles from where he was living that had the right facilities for a lunch and afternoon meeting. He tentatively booked a date two weeks hence. Then he worked on the careful wording of his invitation. He knew Mary and Geoff would jump to the occasion but he wanted the two he had met in Bristol to come if possible. He wrote also to Jenny and Betty.

All six replied indicating their eagerness to learn more about the new venture.

It became a profitable time well spent. The two main topics were the formation of a business built on scriptural principals and to having right location. The discussions were frank and honest which helped to formulate further ideas to be considered. The two men from the northern centres were not willing to commit themselves to join the team but wanted to be kept up to date on the progress which would help them in their prayer support they had promised. Jenny was fully persuaded to join the team and Betty wanted a little more time to think about it, but was seriously interested.

He invited himself to a home-made meal and brought his parents up to date with the formation of a team. They were becoming as excited as their son.

Two weeks later Adrian arranged to have a meal with Mary and Jenny in Nottingham; he wrote to invite Geoff to join them.

They had a great time together. There was a wonderful time of prayer asking God to continue to give clear directions in regard to a business in which He would be honoured. Their prayers were very precise in regard to unity in the team. Before they parted Adrian announced that he considered that that was the beginning of Karism Business Consultations Service. The vision had been launched.

Now was the hard work of putting a multiplicity of details into a working model. He spent many phone calls with his father especially in regard to finance. "Where would be the right source for a mortgage?" he asked his father. The reply was that he would do some research. His father was indeed a valuable consultant. In fact Howard had placed himself as an unpaid member of the team.

CHAPTER 35

During the week leading up to the meeting with the six potential members of the team, Adrian invited himself to his parent's home for an evening meal. He hadn't really thought of a possibility that they would say "no". They had a positive response for Tuesday evening.

The meal was good. Dawn had lived up to her reputation of providing a tasty meal.

The conversation centred on Harrogate. All three felt right about the location. But they shared some of the problems they would be facing in regard to the layout of the office space, for Reception and individual offices. Dawn suggested that she would like to look around for impressive furnishings. The two men handed that responsibility gladly to her. As Adrian and his father became more deeply involved in the business side of the project, the need for professional help was obvious.

"Dad, I remember seeing a paper or rather an official looking document which I believe was the thesis for your Master's degree".

"Did you ever read it?"

"Not entirely, but I did some serious glancing through it".

"What was your subject?"

"Business Planning", replied Howard.

"Well. What more is there to say? May I look upon you as my very close consultant?"

"That depends where your finances are coming from".

"I might ask you for a loan to cover your expenses; could I?

Thanks, Dad. How about joining us on Saturday? I would like the others to meet you and for you to share some of your professional ideas; perhaps also for a future meeting for you to help us with Business Planning".

"Then I accept the office of Consultant".

"He took that for granted", said his mother.

Adrian had spent quite a long time praying for the meeting he was to have with the potential team. Looking at his watch he realized that it was time to set off for the meeting. It was to be an important day for him and for the others. Mary also had spent quite some time praying because she knew it was to be Adrian's big day and she wanted him to be encouraged and blessed by the outcome. Geoff too had made careful and prayerful preparation before leaving for the team meeting.

Adrian was pleased with the room that had been allocated to him for the day. He couldn't help but notice that there was a table set up for tea and coffee all ready to welcome the guests. He did a final bit of shuffling the chairs around; how thankful he was that they were not typical sit-up-and-beg chairs, but quite comfortable padded ones with arms, "They look too comfortable, someone might fall asleep".

No sooner had that thought past when Geoff arrived" he said to himself. "Good", was the first word out of Geoff's mouth, "I'm ready for a coffee. Oh. By the way; good morning Adrian, my friend, it's great to be with you again".

"It's good to see you my brother, but at least you could have poured a coffee for me also!"

They had just settled at the table when Mary arrived with Jenny. They were full of smiles. Without asking Mary if she wanted one, she made a straight line to the coffee table and filled two mugs. It was probably about fifteen minutes later when the other two fellows arrived. Betty made it a few seconds after the two men.

There was a time spent chattering and getting acquainted with each other. It was the first time many of them had met. Adrian became conscious of the time slipping away, so he interrupted the general conversation.

"I think we can start", he said. "You have got to know each other so there is no need for me to introduce you. I want you to know that my father will be joining us this afternoon. I have invited him because he has some words of wisdom he wants to share with us. I'll introduce him properly at the afternoon session. We must commence with a time of prayer".

During the prayer each one of the team became aware of God's presence and the assurance that He was going to be with them throughout the day.

"I would like each of us to share your thoughts and expectancies. You know that it is my desire to have a scriptural base to this project. God must be honoured in all our preparations and then eventually in all our business dealings. The title for our business is likely to be 'KARISM BUSINESS COUNSELLING SERVICE'. There is a location for our office that is being considered, though there is nothing written in stone as yet.

"Very few people will know what KARISM stands for. They might think it is the initials of team members! The word comes from the Greek language. It basically means, GRACE. In some churches Charismata is used for certain gifts of the Holy Spirit. It appealed to me even though it certainly is very different to the titles of other business offices.

"It is the working title I am using at the moment. We will need to have a decisive title by the end of the year when negotiations for the building space commence".

There were some interesting comments made during the discussion. Doubts were shared regarding the word KARISM. It was quite a surprise when Betty actually pushed her chair as if she was going to stand but changed her mind and remained seated. She strongly agreed with the title. She considered it to be appropriate for a Christian business. But her stress was that it would draw the attention of Christian businessmen, and importantly questions would be asked by other interested businesses. She stated that if she eventually joined the team she would be happy to work under such a title. Her comments gave pleasure to Mary as well as Adrian.

Then Adrian changed the topic of discussion.

"I would like Geoff to speak about this because he was the one who turned our attention towards Harrogate".

Geoff explained a little about the city and its emotional and political atmosphere. He gave an excellent summary of the situation that was attracting us. It was in a new area being developed and so there were no old buildings to be considered. He stressed that the building had not yet been completed in the second phase of the building scheme, but that if we were serious then our personal desires would be incorporated in the design of our offices. There will be rooms above us for rent as offices or perhaps even apartments. We will face the great challenge of starting a new business in a new area. But he assured everyone that I consider the location as the ideal one for such a venture".

There were voices of appreciation and also some personal questions that he dealt with admirably.

'I'd like to raise another point for discussion before we break for lunch", announced Adrian. "It is in connection with finance. From my research, I understand that I will require about forty thousand pounds at the beginning, but the amount would then be increased to one hundred thousand pounds for the first year. This means there will be some serious searches made for the best rates for those amounts. But I want to be completely upfront with you. There is no money at the moment. So I cannot offer any amounts for salaries. We may have to exist on less than we have been earning. Those of you who are committing yourselves to Karism I was hoping that you may be of help in this direction in the early stages. For example if you have any present clients who you yourself found and signed up, would it be possible for you to try and bring them with you? You couldn't do this with the ones your firm sent to you. Please be open and honest. I want all six of you to share in this discussion even though it may not apply to you, your ideas will be helpful".

There was quite an interesting discussion. It seems that most of them had already had this concern and had placed it as an immediate item for prayer.

The idea of a minimum wage was chewed-on for a considerable time. The concern raised was that rental accommodation would need to be addressed. Someone even suggested that perhaps a part-time job might be required in order to reach the level to cover their expenses."Perhaps I could go back home with my parents and commute", was one comment.

Betty asked, "You mentioned that there would be rooms above your office space. Would those rooms be included in the price you'll be paying each month? If so, then would that help towards some of the costs? But then, would members of the team like to rent space above their work? I seem to be full of questions" she smiled as usual.

Adrian commented, "That is certainly an idea to be considered. If so then we will require a very much larger amount than the hundred thousand I mentioned earlier. Even though some of the ideas being shared may seem at the moment to be way out, that's alright, it means that our thoughts are being progressive and anticipatory".

The discussion continued. It was a topic that could have taken the whole of the day, Adrian was pleased when he looked at his watch and was able to say, "It's time for lunch! Well it's time to get washed up and ready".

They had about ten minutes to walk around and see the place. Adrian's father arrived and joined the group that found their way to the dining room. Tables had been reserved for them, but the menu was open for personal choices. Adrian commented to his father that the food lived up to the standard given by a friend.

It was suggested that they walk around the grounds for a half an hour after lunch before resuming their discussions. There was a brisk breeze that helped to blow away any post-lunch drowsiness. They made their way to the room set aside for them. There was fresh coffee etc. on the side table.

Adrian started by introducing his father. He is not here because he's my father, but because of his expertise. He has worked for many years in this business and he knows all the pitfalls. If the truth be known he is part of the working team as a counselor and advisor. Just a little about him. For his post graduate master's thesis he presented a dissertation on 'Business Planning'. He has spent much of his working life helping clients make their business plans.

I have immense pleasure asking Howard Syston to inform us and stir us up.

"Thank you for that introduction. I have heard many in my time but I have a feeling that one was especially for his father. Thank you also for inviting me to be part of this special day as you explore the prospects and implications of setting up your own business.

"You need to have a Business Plan; which may include a mission statement, but not necessarily. You will be serving the comprehensive requirements of young and immature businesses as well as solving problems from existing service agencies. The team approach is the ideal because then you will be offering a balanced quality service. This will set you aside from some of your competitors.

"Each member of the team specializes in a particular discipline: including finance, marketing, management, human resources. Your business will provide help with making marketing plans, management development and advice relating to finance and human resources. Your presentation to the business world will be that you are experts available to serve and advise.

"Start-up firms will be your target because the new owners will not have your expertise with the practical range of knowledge required launching forward into the world saturated with a multiplicity of so called good ideas. These firms will be your largest market; they will not just be local but also from the surrounding area.

"There is a significant demand for this type of consulting service.

"Your services will be designed to help the effectiveness of those struggling to achieve the professional standard that the world is demanding. You will hope to convince your clients that your service will enable them to reduce their costs, and improve customer services.

"The start-up funds required, as you have discussed, will be of paramount importance because the most critical time for any new business is its first year. Much of your time will be spent advertising for customers. So it is essential that as soon as possible you do some serious study of advertising techniques, as well as deciding who is to be your prospective target. You may have to rely upon the talents of a reputable advertising agency.

"I think it is imperative that you work on an honest and attractive mission statement. KBCS aims to offer a Christian comprehensive consulting service. Your focus will be a professional and specialized service to meet the current needs of your clients.

"That, I think, is as far as I'll go today. You may want to have another meeting to look in greater depth at the issues raised this afternoon. Thank you".

There was applause; no one admitted to starting it! That presentation set the tone for the discussion that followed.

Adrian just sat back and absorbed the enthusiasm being expressed in the questions and comments. He was beginning to feel the need for a further presentation from his father, but that was something the team would decide later.

The allocated time for their meeting was running out. Adrian asked if anyone knew of a reputable loan company that he could contact. His father commented that he had some contacts, and that he would be in touch with them. They all agreed that the finances ought to be the priority at this stage alongside the publicity leaflets

As they were leaving Adrian asked Geoff and Mary if they could come for a meal during the coming week. They enthusiastically said they would like such a time together in order to share the concerns coming out of their day together. Howard said he would phone Adrian later that evening.

The main disappointment of the day was Adrian's conversations with the other two men. Both of them, separately, said they were not prepared to take the risk of joining his team. He thanked them for the contributions they made to the discussions. He was sad, but also somewhat relieved because he could not see how he could finance them during the early stages of developing KBCS. It only took a glance from Mary for him to know her reactions to the meeting. Geoff left with a firm handshake and a hearty slap on the back for a job well done.

Adrian was the last person to leave after he had settled the account. As he entered his car the thought plagued him – he had not had a warm hug from Mary before she left. During his journey home he had been thinking much, on and off, about Mary. Nearer home he stopped and grabbed a quick snack so that he did not have to prepare something for himself at home.

True to his word, the phone rang about eight thirty; it was his father. They talked for quite a long time about the meeting. Howard confirmed his interest in hoping to find resources to help with the start-up. After his father had hung up he opened his computer to look at emails. There were two that caught his eye. One from Geoff and one from Mary "I'll read Geoff's first, then I can spend more time thinking about Mary's", he thought.

Geoff was extremely complimentary about the meeting. One line intrigued him. 'I'm interested in an apartment above the KBCS office'. He was looking forward to their next time together.

Mary also expressed her pleasure and enthusiasm for the meeting. She was delighted at the thoughts shared by those present. There was one line that held his attention. "I'm very interested in the possibility of an apartment above our office'. She too was looking forward to the next meeting. He fantasized somewhat on some of her phrases; he sensed a flavour of affection creeping in.

One wonders why he dreamt of Mary that night!

The next day he wrote an email to Geoff and Mary in which he expressed the thought of not having a meal nearby, but that Mary comes up to meet Adrian, together they would go to Rochdale and pick up Geoff, then motor on to Harrogate. Let's make it for this coming Saturday. "We'll have a meal in Harrogate then go see the site for our office".

The email replies were positive. Geoff volunteered to choose a not too posh place for lunch in Harrogate. That pleased Adrian because he did not know of eating places in the posh city that were reasonably priced.

It happened to be a Saturday when he was not required for a soccer match.

Mary arrived about ten thirty, her opening words were, "So, obviously no soccer today! Oh. Hello Adrian my dear".

"I refuse to detect a note of sarcasm. Good morning, Mary my dear", was Adrian's reply. He actually placed his hand on her shoulder when he said that; there was no move to indicate that his hand ought not to be on that place.

He was ready to leave, so they got into his car and set off for Rochdale.

It was strange yet pleasant to have Mary sitting next to him in the car. Conversation was quite general going to pick up Geoff. As they stopped for Geoff to get in Mary started to move out to let him into the front seat; Adrian gestured for her to stay in the front. Obviously Geoff didn't mind the back seat which he found to be more comfortable than in his car.

All three were very relaxed and talked freely about the meeting but also about future prospects. They were a team. Adrian in his mind had finalized them as his executive committee. Mary was taking note of the places through which they were travelling as this was a part of the country that she did not know.

"This is the posh city" said Geoff as they were in the outskirts of Harrogate; he leaned forward to inform the occupants of the front seats. He was surprised that they were still quite separate with no signs of touching each other.

"So", said Adrian, "where do we go for a cheap lunch that serves good nourishing food?"

"I'll give you all the rights and lefts as we move ahead". He certainly was familiar with Harrogate. The place he had in mind was not in the city centre but on the road leading out of the city towards Leeds. From the outside it did not look very posh. Inside it was decorated tastefully and it had a cozy atmosphere. The menu surprised them; there was an excellent selection at quite reasonable prices. they enjoyed their meal and sat chatting for a while. It was Mary who indicated they ought to be on their way. She was the only one who had not seen the site and she was anxiously looking forward to see where it was located. On their way out Adrian noticed a table with free local newspapers. He picked one up and placed it into his briefcase.

It didn't take long for Geoff to direct the driver back into the city and then he knew the streets that would take them to their destination.

Adrian slowed down and said to Mary, "This is the site; I'll drive along to the location where our office will be erected". She seemed thrilled with what she saw. He parked the car and they walked around. Every step was important because they were assessing the future reality of a magnificent structure standing on this corner,

"If, repeat if", Adrian remarked, "this turns out to be our corner then there will be careful planning as to the outward façade. It can be an eye catching building, so we will be required to make it as attractive as possible".

They stood and then slowly walked around and around as they allowed their imaginations to give them unusual and positive emotions. They were lost in their future world and were unaware that the site manger had joined them. He recognized Adrian.

"Good afternoon Mr. Syston". Adrian turned quickly apologizing for not realizing he had come.

"Yes sir, I have brought my two future colleagues to speculate and fantasize about this corner.'

"Have you any questions that I can help you with?"

They were introduced.

"Yes!" They did have some questions which he answered very helpfully. Geoff asked about the other development that would be on this corner. "As I said to Mister Syston a few weeks ago, it will have two floors above which will be available for office space or apartments."

"If Adrian decides to have his office just here will he be required to purchase or rent the entire building?" asked Mary.

"That will be up to him. At the moment it is still available. He can then decide whether the upper floors will be offices or for accommodation".

The answer pleased Mary because she then enthusiastically told herself she would be nearer to Adrian, even though she had no idea where Adrian would be living, at least it would be close to where we would be working.

Adrian asked the site manager if the price had been decided yet. "We will know by the end of next week. I'll let you have a price list."

Geoff asked, "Are the plans written yet as to how this corner will look? If not I think a semi-circular front right in the middle would be very attractive". No one seemed to hear Mary's agreement to that idea.

"Would you like to join my team, sir?" the manager replied. "Perhaps you would like to add that there must be a large wooden entrance with bright brass hinges and handles?"

"I would readily endorse that", Geoff replied with a massive grin on his face.

After they had chattered further for four or five minutes the manager left the other three. Their faces were loaded with smiles. Adrian commented, "It looks as if we have already started to prepare to call this site ours". The other two expressed exactly the same view at the same time.

They returned to their car and sat for quite a long time looking and fantasizing. Mary said, "I can't wait to come here and start work". The other two laughed as they wanted to voice a similar hope.

As they journeyed towards Rochdale it was amazing how many ideas had been shared regarding the front and entrance to 'their' building.

As Geoff was leaving the car he asked about a future meeting. Adrian's comment was that he expected to call a meeting of his executive within a couple of weeks or so. "And who, pray, is the executive?" queried Mary.

"We, the royal we and us, will have some serious planning to do regarding advertising. I hope to locate an advertising agency this week that might help us".

"Keep me posted", said Geoff as they bade farewell.

Adrian and Mary were on their way home. There was no conversation for the first few miles. Adrian was trying hard to think of something to talk about. No real intelligent thoughts arose in his mind. It was a very brave move, he hardly knew what he was doing. He reached out his hand and placed it on her knee. He expected her to push it off, instead he became aware of a cool hand on top of his giving a little squeeze.

"Hope you don't mind", He said just a little embarrassed. She just squeezed and said, "I really don't mind in the least". There followed some small talk which was a sign of both being a little shy. Adrian broke the spell by stating quite loudly that it was a serious gesture. Her immediate response was to shuffle closer as far as the seat would allow.

That move was a signal for him to squeeze and say how much he liked her being close to him. She assured him, "It is something I like also; in fact I was hoping you would have shown such interest on our way up to Rochdale early today. Oh! forgive me. I ought not to have said that. That was my thinking taking control of my tongue".

"There is a rest area a couple of miles up the road I think we had better pull over for a few minutes". He even drove a little faster; he was eager to have a rest from driving. He took his hand off her knee to avoid any distraction.

He stopped the car at one end of the parking space. Mary shuffled in her seat as if they were about to get out of the car. "No, I think we can stay inside for a few moments." He leaned over and placed his arms across her shoulders. She pushed towards him.

"Mary, what are we trying to say?"

"Silence often says a lot!"

"The silence didn't faze me. The personal contact has been speaking loudly".

"Don't believe everything your inner ear tells you".

"Then please tell me something for my outer ear to believe".

"I do not think that this is the time or the place".

'Then when we get to my place please make that a good time for us to talk".

"Will do. But I have a feeling I'll be talking long before we get to your place".

"I'd like that," acknowledged Adrian.

"Because I will not be able to remain silent that long".

They did not remain silent. They spoke a little about their time in Harrogate, but mainly asking each other personal questions. They got to know quite a bit about each other.

He stopped the car in the driveway to his home. "I don't think I should take you home tonight, because as soon as we arrive at your place we will have to turn round and come back here for your car".

"I really wouldn't mind the extra journey it would be no inconvenience for me to return here to pick up my vehicle". There was a chuckle in her voice. They stayed in the car for a while then Adrian leaned over with his arms on her shoulder and said how pleased he was with the day and for her close company on the journey. "Good night. I'm looking forward to our next time together".

"Me too! Not too long to wait, I hope".

They got out of the car and gave each other a hug. Then she walked over to her car and waved farewell.

It was a pleasant evening of memories for Adrian. He could not think of anything other than Mary. He even told himself that cupid must have been in their car throughout the day.

The same was true for Mary also as she pondered Adrian's closeness and the hug. Actually she told herself she would not have objected if he wanted to kiss her. That thought encouraged some pleasant dreams for her that night.

It was the next morning when Adrian picked up his briefcase and opened it that he saw the newspaper. He threw it on to the table. "I'll look at you later", he said.

He had a very busy day at work and was quite tired when he got home in the evening. He had a shower and made himself a meal then grabbed the newspaper and settled into his recliner chair.

The front page of the paper told the stories of a Rotary dinner, a Parish women's gathering, a local teenager being successful in a swimming gala. He wasn't overly interested, so he scanned through the other pages. On the inside back page was a list of advertisements, a chimney sweep, a baby-sitting service, an odd job gardener. The page opposite had some block adverts; a carpenter, a tax service, at least five garages and car dealers, locally made ice cream. He really was not interested until he spotted one near the bottom of the page. 'ADVERTISING' – a new office in the city that had transferred from Leeds had just been opened. They invited interested customers to contact them for information regarding any advertising needs they had.

"I'll give them a call in the morning", he promised himself. There was nothing to indicate that it was what he required but there could be no harm in enquiring.

When he made the call a girl answered mentioning a little about the services offered. Adrian asked to speak to the boss or someone in charge. She very politely pressed an extension button on her phone and a man answered. He mentioned his name. So Adrian introduced himself. Then Adrian asked if they might be able to help him. The boss wanted to know more details. He mentioned that he was expecting to open an office in Harrogate as a Business Consulting Service. "I want some initial advertising; leaflets as well as for Professional magazines".

"We can help you in those areas. One of my team specializes in that field and he has much success in recent years. I have a couple of leaflets that explain a little of what we can do, would you like me to send copies to you?"

"Yes, Please".

"It would be our pleasure in serving you. When you've read the leaflets, please feel free to contact me at any time".

"I'd love that. Then I could make an appointment to see you next time I am up in Harrogate".

"Good morning, Mr. Syston, I look forward to meeting your needs".

"Thank you for your offer. I'll be in touch".

That evening Adrian phoned Geoff informing him of the advertising advertisement. He was thrilled and he knew the area where the office was located. After they had talked for a time they agreed to go together to meet the advertising people.

Adrian thought that this would be a good excuse to phone Mary. When she answered the phone her voice gained a flowery tone. She too was pleased about the possible advertising help. But she heard more than advertising, during the time Adrian was on the phone.

Adrian arrived to pick up Geoff. He was ready and insisted that he take his car this time for a change. He knew Harrogate quite well so he had no difficulty finding the Advertising Agency. It was a smart looking building and attractive reception area.

They stated why they had come. Adrian gave the receptionist his name.

She pressed a button on the intercom and the boss came out to meet them. "Good to see you, Mr. Syston. Please come into my office and we can chat about your needs."

It was a quite spacious office, attractively decorated and some comfortable chairs near a mahogany highly polished table. As they sat down the boss indicated that this was not his usual work surface. The conversation proved to be very informative. Geoff nudged Adrian and with a nod indicated his pleasure.

Another worker came in with a few files, which he laid on the table. He was introduced as the person spoken about during the phone call. "If you ask us to do work for you, this is the person you will be dealing with. He has brought some of his work to show you what he's capable of achieving".

That was a fascinating session as files were opened and discussed. Adrian became more convinced that this was the right Agency to use. Geoff was very impressed also.

Adrian opened his briefcase and took out a few sheets of paper on which there were some rough ideas as to what he thought he wanted. The expert didn't take long to grasp what was wanted. He said that he would like to spend some time thinking it over and then turn to be creative.

So Adrian left his sketches of a poster; his idea of a leaflet, a rough sketch of their business name for over the entrance to their offices. Geoff said that he thought a business card would be ideal at this stage especially to include in any correspondence.

The boss said that he would send copies of ideas as soon as they were ready. Adrian asked if copies could be sent also to Geoff, and gave him his address.

They left the agency office elated. "I was so pleased at what they showed us", said Adrian. "I was quite impressed with their attitude towards your sketches", Geoff said.

It was an interesting drive back to Rochdale. For Adrian it was a lonely ride after leaving Rochdale. How he longed for Mary to have been in the car with him. His thoughts were a jumble of Adverts with Mary for the whole of his journey.

After having something to eat he phoned Mary. She was waiting for his call and was thrilled that Adrian had found a competent advertising agency. He was so pleased when she started talking about something other than advertising. "I wish you had been with me in the car, especially coming home." After he had said it he thought it was perhaps a little unwise.

"Then next time make sure you take me with you, and then you will not be lonely." Under her breath she added, "I'll make sure of that!"

"I'll keep you posted in regard to procedures relating to the advertising".

They exchanged some words of endearment and hung up. Both of them wrapped up in thoughts of each other.

It must have been about ten days after his visit to Harrogate that a package arrived by post. When he saw who it was from he opened quickly. He spread the sheets out on his table and was amazed. "What a fabulous job", he thought. He had no sooner dropped that thought when the phone rang. It was Geoff. He was bubbling over with pleasure at the specimen advertising pieces.

"I feel quite certain that they will do the job well and professional", he told Geoff.

Geoff's reply was. "I cannot think of anything better".

"So what is the next main task?" asked Geoff.

"Finance", replied Adrian, "But I am hoping my father will have some ideas when I see him at the weekend".

"I'll be praying that what he has to share will be as great as the advertising package we've just received".

"Thanks, my friend". And they hung up

The weekend was taking a long to arrive. Adrian had already 'booked in' for two meals on Saturday. It happened once again that there was no soccer.

His father surprised him with the amount of research he had done. There were four firms to choose from. Each one appeared very reputable.

Adrian took a few minutes to browse through them. Then he asked his father, "Is one more workable for me than the others?"

His father had a good laugh at that one. "My son", he said affectionately. "This is the world of real business we are treading on; we cannot afford to be hasty on this part of the venture. This will either make or break you. It is dangerously serious when we are talking of thousands of pounds, or rather hundreds of thousands of pounds."

"So, what I want to know right now before we progress to any one of these offers, is, are you buying just the ground floor or are you venturing into the two floors?"

"Dad, I don't know whether I am crazy, but at the moment I feel biased towards the whole building, not just the ground floor office space".

"Have you a reason for that bias?"

"I think it is to do with apartment space. All of my workers will be looking for accommodation of some kind".

"This has nothing to do with wanting your lady friend living on the spot, does it?"

"I could so easy say a blushing and resounding 'no'; but that would not be entirely correct. Yes, Dad, perhaps it does have Mary in mind".

"Has the developer given you a price yet".

"No. But I think there must be some idea by the end of this month".

"Then wisdom must prevail. We make no clear decision until we know what amounts we'll be looking for. If it is just for the one hundred thousand, then I think there is one of these that I would go with".

He had a long talk with his father; and his mother added her comments to the discussion. It was a challenging time. Adrian was wondering if his knees were already knocking. Then his mother put her hand on Adrian's shoulder and said, "My dear, you can be fearful of this project, but if this is what the Lord wants for you then everything will work according to His will for you".

"Thank you, Mum. I sure needed that. I trust the Lord that this venture will be His, right from the begining. I do not what to attempt anything that is outside of His will".

CHAPTER 36

Adrian had never felt impatient before, but his waiting to hear from the developers was trying his patience. He could do nothing about it, so he decided to think more about Mary. She was more exciting than waiting to find out how much the office or office block would cost.

Actually both areas of thought were regarding the future. Both had the prospects of being expensive. He considered Mary as less expensive in the early stages but if it developed into matrimony then the expenses would certainly increase. Whereas if it was with the development then the future prospects, hopefully, would mean decreasing costs. But! It was the 'but' causing him some anxiety. But the monthly repayments would be an on-going challenge in the early months until the business built up.

Mary was the most comforting project to think about. It was a past-time he was truly enjoying. She was very attractive physically and also spiritually. She was intelligent and conscientious. She was committed to his vision of a business venture. But at that precise moment he was interested in his personality getting involved with her personality. Not in a sexual sense but in a close friendship. Cupid's bug had bitten deeply.

He was soon lost in thought.

It must have been about half an hour later that the phone rang. Inwardly he felt slightly annoyed. He was enjoying his thoughts. His "yes'" down the phone may not have been his usual bright self.

"What's wrong sweetheart?"

"Oh! I'm fine".

"It didn't sound like it".

"Well to tell you the truth the phone bell disturbed an important and fascinating time with my thoughts".

"Oh, yes. Was it another woman?"

"No. Thank you. Why did you think it was a woman?"

"Well isn't that what most men think about when they have nothing to do?"

"I've got plenty to do".

"That's not answering my concerns".

"Oh, by the way, why have you phoned me?"

"At the moment that's my business".

"Will you dare to make it my business?"

"Only if you tell me your thoughts".

"My darling ..." That was the first time of using that mode of adoration. "I was actually lost in thought; I was thinking about you".

"Then you must have got lost!"

"Why?"

"Because that is why I was phoning you. I got to the end of thinking, I wanted to start talking".

"Well done, darling. I am extremely pleased you disturbed me. Because I wanted to feel you closer to me".

"Well, there is probably another reason for me phoning".

"It sounds very intriguing; another reason?"

"I too want to be much closer to you, talking isn't totally satisfying. I want you to come down for the weekend and take me out on a date this coming Saturday".

"That is not a good reason that is an outright demand. Yes, of course. You mentioned weekend, so I'll need to find a bed and not travel home for the nigh".

"It's already arranged," Mary paused, then continued "Jenny says you can stay at their house, as long as you are a good boy!"

"That settles it. I'll see you in time for lunch. I'll come directly to your place soon after eleven. I promise to be on my best behavior for Jenny's benefit".

Friday afternoon Adrian received a phone message from the developers.

It was the long awaited news. The costs had been finalized, and both options were still open for Adrian. A decision must be finalized in two weeks. He was given the two amounts. Both sounded quite high. But now he had to make a choice. He wanted God's choice. Either option was larger than he had hoped. He promised to get back to them within the two weeks.

He wondered whether he should share this news with Mary, but decided to leave and talk to her about it the next day.

He phoned his father and mentioned to him the amounts. His father wanted him to go round to their house to save a long phone call. "I'll come round as I am. Can I come immediately? Please keep a little food on the table for me. See you soon".

His mother had saved some food. In fact he suspected that she might have done a quick shuffle and added extra.

His father had copies of suggestions already laid out on another table.

They had two sheets with the costs labeled.

They looked at the first option of just the lower floor. Howard chose the offer he liked and placed it on the first sheet.

Another offer also had the right potential for the lower floor. That one was added also.

It came to the whole building. Howard was fearful and anxious. Hear is one offer but it costs the earth in monthly mortgage payments. There is a second one that might be negotiable. But just look at the amount required.

"Adrian says it stands to reason that with no personal money available the decision is whether or not enough work to cover that much larger sum can be anticipated".

"If the two floors above are set up as apartments then that would bring in some income each month. It would certainly not cover much but would be a big step towards it"

"Do you think you'll get tenants for them?'

"Mary has said that she would really be interested, because she'll be looking for accommodation anyway".

"What about Geoff?"

"I think he'll probably commute in the early stages".

"What about you yourself?"

"That has still to be decided. It is certain that I will be looking for some accommodation."

"Would you take one of the apartments?"

"At the moment I'm not sure, Dad".

"Then would you consider hiring a rental agency to deal with the apartments?"

"This is where I am totally undecided".

"If both you and Mary take an apartment each, then an agency is obsolete. It becomes a book keeping item for monthly rentals to be paid into the capital account. Repairs will be minimum for the first couple of years I'd imagine".

They juggled offers around. They had pros and cons going for each of the offers.

"Dad, what would you do? Would you consider taking a monthly loan to cover some of the mortgage? Or do you anticipate the first mortgage will be sufficient to carry us over until we start seeing some meaningful income.

"My answer", said Howard "would entirely depend upon how much faith I had in attracting suitable work".

Dawn asked Howard to come into the other room. She was anxious and even nervous in making her suggestion. "How much can we help him?'

"Do as much as he would really need".

"I know it depends which offer he takes, but I was hoping we might offer to help for the first two or three months?"

"I had been thinking something similar. You know, even if he takes the larger offer, I think we could cover at least two months".

"If this is our mutual decision then when do we tell him, now or another time?

"It will need to be soon because he must finalize his offer next week sometime".

"Then let's leave it until after the weekend".

When they returned to the other room Adrian was juggling offers with each sheet.

"Dad", he said, "I hope it will not be too unwise, but I favour the whole block. I have enough savings to pay for the first few months apartment rent. I would anticipate that Mary would be the same, I'll find out tomorrow from her. When is the deadline for accepting these offers?"

"I am sure we have at least another month or even more".

They sat and chatted about other things over another cup of tea.

Adrian thanked his parents for their love and wisdom and concern, also for the food. "See you one day next week. Love you both. Good night".

He was tired so was soon on his way to bed. He decided he would email Geoff the next morning with the suggested costs for the offices indicating also that he would be away in Nottingham over the weekend.

Adrian awoke. He was wide awake. He felt bright and was indeed cheerful. That, he thought was a good start to what he hoped would be a pleasant and important time away in Nottingham

He had not forgotten to email Geoff with the latest news. It was only a moment after he pressed the 'send' button that he noticed an incoming message. It was from the advertising agency. That was important so he delayed setting off until the email was complete. He then spent some time reading and thinking about the contents. After a few minutes he decided to print it and talk it over with Mary sometime during the weekend.

As he was driving through the town towards the Nottingham road his attraction was captured by some flowers for sale. "I can't remember whether I have ever given flowers to a girl friend, but I suppose there is always the first time" So he pulled over and bought a bunch of various colours and with a pleasing fragrance.

It was a new experience for him to be knocking on a door ready to hand a bunch of flowers to the lady that opened. When the door opened it was another female, it was Mary's step mother.

"Oh, my dear, how thoughtful of you to think of me with flowers".

"Well …"

"I didn't really think you loved me that much!"

The voice from inside the house said, "Don't hog him all morning on the door step; you will have all the neighbours spreading rumours".

As he walked into the room his hand was behind his back. Sarah could not contain a large grin emerging on her face. Mary noticed the grin.

"What's wrong, Sarah?"

"It's not a wrong grin it is a right grin – or something like it".

She chose to ignore her and looked directly at Adrian. He stepped forward and with his free hand he hugged her close to him. She began to gasp for breath. So he loosened the tight grip and brought his hand forward and pushed the flowers towards her nose. She gasped with surprise and with pleasure. They stood holding on to each other.

Sarah broke the spell by telling him to take off his jacket and stay awhile. She added, "I'm in Nottingham to visit a friend in hospital, so

I took the opportunity to call in and see Mary. I had no intention of upstaging you, in fact I did not know until just a few minutes before you arrived that she was expecting an important visitor".

"I'll stay and have a coffee with you and a short visit then I'll be off", said Sarah.

It was an hour later when Sarah mentioned it was time for her to head in the direction of the hospital.

"What about lunch?" asked Mary.

"I'll pick up something at the hospital and then I can visit my friend early".

With that she said her farewells and good wishes for them both for the rest of the day.

Mary had the eating place all organized and an afternoon shopping and possible sightseeing. Adrian had never been to the small restaurant along a few back streets. The outside didn't look to elegant but Mary assured him the food would be great.

True to her word the food was wonderful. It tasted just like home cooked food. Adrian commented a couple of times during the meal that he hopes to remember how to get there because he intended returning to try other dishes on the menu. They lingered over a second cup of coffee. They were seated in a quiet corner so there was no rush to leave.

"I thought we could spend a leisurely walk around the Victoria Centre. I am not desperate to do any shopping but there might be the odd surprise!" Mary said.

"I am not sure whether I am in the mood for surprises", volunteered Adrian.

"Don't spoil the vague possibilities".

"I would never dare do such a thing!"

"Then let's go find a suitable place to park and venture forth on foot to pass some shops".

They bantered in small talk for quite a while before going off arm in arm full of smiles. Both were excited about the love vibes streaming from one to the other.

It was a very pleasant afternoon. Inside some shops the odd thing was inspected but not purchased. As they passed through the food court

Adrian decided that walking round the shops was thirsty work. Mary dragged him to one side to what appeared to be her favourite watering spot.

Conversation was at a standstill. Adrian was wondering what topic to raise. When Mary announced, "We do not have to worry about an evening meal".

"Now what have you cooked up?"

"It wasn't me. Jenny told me yesterday that she is preparing an evening meal for us at her place. She set no time but suggested that we arrive early rather than late".

"That means I can drop off my suitcase before we eat".

"I have a feeling she may have organized something else. She didn't say anything, but I'm suspicious".

"It seems as if I am the pawn that needs to fit into whatever surprise pops up next!"

Jenny lived on the outskirts of the city. Mary directed the car along some of the quieter roads, and into the residential area. They crossed over the Trent River and along the Melton Road.

They turned into one crescent and Mary noted the house number. It was a nice looking building. There was a pleasant landscaped garden in front and an attractive arch over the doorway.

"I presume Jenny is still living at home with her parents" said Adrian.

"Yes. And that is why they have a spare room for you".

They parked and walked up to the front door to ring the bell. It wasn't many seconds before the door opened. It was Jenny's father who welcomed them to step inside.

They deposited coats etc in the hallway and then entered the lounge. Jenny and her mother were seated on the settee. They stood up to welcome the visitors. It was a joyful introduction. Friendship developed instantaneously. They were all at ease.

Jenny's mother slipped out and returned a few minutes later with a tray of drinks and nuts. "This is safe to drink", she said with a grin, "My daughter gave me strict instructions as to what to put in the punch, or rather what not to put in".

It was a great time for the parents to get to know other people their daughter would be working with. Jenny was missing for a number of minutes. Soon after she retuned her parents informed the visitors that they had a meeting to attend so would be out most of the evening.

Jenny disappeared again. Adrian and Mary had a chance to pass the time sitting close to each other. They enjoyed it so much that they were afraid they made the wrong response when Jenny announced that dinner was ready. She didn't hide her smiles at surprising them.

It was a marvelous dinner. Her mother had helped her prepare some of the vegetables. But it was evident that she had had a busy afternoon in the kitchen. She had chosen some of her parents' best dishes and glasses. There were three candles in the centre of the table, so the lights were turned down low and they enjoyed their meal in candle-light. There were various positive comments as the meal proceeded.

Jenny kept her eye on the clock, so she started to clear the table. Mary helped her, and soon the washing up was complete.

Adrian took the opportunity to read the email from the advertising agency. He was intrigued by how far they had developed ideas. There was one he intended talking to Mary about, if the conversation took a lull he would introduce it while Jenny was with them.

When the girls came back into the room they commented how wonderful it was to find the man awake and alert.

"Sarcasm! I will not lower my dignity to challenge it. Good to see you two gorgeous lasses. What have you cooked up for the rest of the evening?"

"I have no idea", was Mary's response.

"Well, I've given it some serious thought", added Jenny.

"Such as?" queried Mary.

"I knew that you two would be uncomfortable sitting close to each other for the whole evening. It would verge on boredom. So my little grey cells became quite active."

"So what have you …?" interrupted Mary.

"We are going out. I was allowed three tickets so I bought all three".

"For what?" asked Adrian.

"Now that depends. It depends on how serious you are. It depends on what interests you".

"What sort of interest do I require, Madam?" asked Adrian.

"There is a musical event at my church. There is a visiting ensemble that's been before. They are excellent. There will be refreshments at the end. And it isn't far to go. In fact you probably passed the Church on your way here".

"What time does it start?" asked Mary.

"Seven o'clock. But they are not always prompt".

"If I do get bored, not with the company, but with the music will I be allowed to kick my shoes off and relax?"

"Adrian, you can't do things like that in a church meeting", chuckled Mary.

"Come on. Get your clothes on, it's time to go".

"So, we have no choice, Mary, It seems that just because I am staying the weekend that we are under orders. Time to start marching!"

Off they went - an obviously happy trio.

The concert was wonderful. Adrian commented that he could not have planned a better evening even if he tried! It was a professional and well organized concert which also acknowledged the sovereignty of God and encouraged the audience to offer praise to His wonderful Name. There were unusual tit bits to eat afterwards. The people were friendly. Those who knew Jenny came over and asked to be introduced to her friends.

On the way back from the concert, conversation automatically centred on the concert and the friendly folk at the reception afterwards. Then there was an unnatural lull. No words, just silence.

Mary broke the silence with a word to Adrian. "When you arrived at lunch time you mentioned receiving an email from the advertising agency. Is there any of it you want to share with us?"

"Yes. There is one point that I think is of paramount importance to this whole venture. Perhaps we should leave it until we get back to Jenny's".

They were not many minutes before pulling into the driveway. Jenny's parent's car was not there yet.

When they got inside Jenny asked if anyone would like a drink and something to chew. The response was a sound that might have been expelled from a bloated vagabond.

"I take that as an expression of no interest. So let's sit down and hear what Adrian has to share from the advertising agency".

"I am very impressed at the professionalism of the boss. He has a wonderful talented team working for him. I am informed that the web page is almost ready for us to view. They have a series of short ads for news papers and magazines. But the one item I want us to discuss is in regard to our name. I think the boss must be a Christian because he is raising the name 'KARISM'. His concern is that it will not communicate easily. He states that the full name ought to be used, 'KARISMA'. He thinks that Christian business people will respond more positively to that. So how do you feel?"

"I like the sound with the 'A', said Jenny.

"Being a charismatic I fancy it with an 'A', agreed Mary.

"No scratching eyes out – not any shy sarcastic disagreements. Guess what? That is the response I expected from you two".

"What about you? It's your project. You came up with the name originally. Do you like their suggestion?" remarked Mary.

"Actually I am beginning to feel very comfortable with the new name. I'll email Geoff on Monday and tell him of the change".

"If they have other suggestions and an assortment of adverts, when will we get the chance to see them?" asked Jenny.

"In my reply to them I will ask the same question. Because I want us all to view them. I value all your ideas".

"When I receive an assortment of their suggestions then I want all three of you to view them with me. Can you two girls come to my place? It'd be easy for Geoff. I think I could persuade my patents to prepare a meal for us. I know my father will want to see them and he'll have some valuable comments to help us".

"When would Geoff be available?" asked Mary. "Knowing him I am sure he will be able at any time unless he has found some new attraction! Perhaps next Saturday?"

""If you are that keen, then make it ten o'clock at my place. Final. I will inform Geoff of your decision and fully expect his approval".

Mary said, "That's excellent. So, what about going to Church tomorrow morning? Where do we go? All three of us go to the same place or go to separate places?"

"That's a major problem. How about calling a committee meeting to consider the choices?"

"In that case", Adrian, "I'll vote for the three of us because I wouldn't trust you alone with Mary. And I would like to go to Mary's Church".

"In that case the committee has adjourned and the decision made. What time do we meet my dear", Adrian said to Mary.

'The service starts at ten thirty, so if you and Jenny can pick me up at ten, then we'll be on time".

As Mary was leaving, Jenny's parents were arriving back home. A few minutes were spent in saying their 'good nights'.

The four of them chatted for a time, and then Adrian excused himself, and went off to bed.

"Have a good night", Jenny's mother said, "I'll call you for breakfast soon after eight thirty".

Adrian and Jenny were ready to leave for Church about nine forty-five.

Mary was waiting for them. They arrived at the church quite early. They had the choice of all of the comfortable pews. Neither of the two visitors had been there before so Mary took them around to show off their facilities.

It was a blessing to worship together. The whole service was an encouragement to all three of them.

They found what looked like an attractive little café. The food was not as attractive as the building. As they were driving back to Jenny's place and passing over Trent Bridge Adrian slowed down and said because it was a lovely afternoon he thought a venture down the river would be the ideal way to enjoy an afternoon.

Jenny said, "I think you should take me home first and then you both will bask in each other's sunlight as you skip along the footpath hand in hand".

It was a romantic afternoon. There were a few fishermen hoping to catch something for their tea. Various small boats bounced up and down. A couple of small sailing boats were catching enough wind to keep them moving.

There was a bench on a bend in the river which caught their attention. They were soon sitting close to each other and finding plenty to talk about.

The afternoon passed too quickly.

Mary mentioned a suitable place for a meal. And Adrian noted that he ought to head towards home perhaps immediately after they had eaten.

That was the end of a perfect weekend. Adrian hoped they would be able to do it again, and yet again. Mary implied that she certainly would be working on such a possibility.

Adrian drove Mary home and said his farewell. Mary was disappointed and demanded a more gentlemanly 'farewell'.

That resulted in a long lingering hug and kiss. Both out of breath, they whispered a 'good bye'.

Adrian's drive home was filled with mixed memories. He was now convinced that the love bug had bitten both of them. There was much to pray about.

When he got home he made himself a cup of tea and sat at his desk to write an email to Geoff. It became a longer one than usual. He knew that he must bring Geoff right up to date on business and personal matters.

It didn't take long for Geoff to give his reply which was a "positive on all fronts".

He didn't think it too late to phone his parents. They were eager to know about his weekend, and excited about the news from the advertising agency.

There was no hesitation about them hosting the meeting for the following Saturday.

All three arrived at Adrian's place around ten o'clock. He didn't give them time to take their coats off. "My parents are expecting us. It could be a long session, so let's be on our way".

Dawn had cleared the large table ready for them. So Adrian unloaded his brief case with the specimens from the advertising agency. There were placed mats at each seat because the coffee was ready. It was going to be ever-ready during the morning with a fresh supply after lunch.

Adrian suggested that he would like to deal with the name of the firm first. "We want to know who we are talking about".

That didn't take long. Each person said their piece. Everyone was in agreement with the new name, KARISMA.

The agency had presumed the acceptance of the new name. The specimens produced used it.

Adrian commented, "My first impression was a good one. The art work is attractive but not gaudy. Shades of the two colours they chose draw attention to the name and also to the content. The logo and colours are repeated on all the pieces. I understand the video makes the same links.

Each one at the table wanted to talk about what they said was their favourite. Adrian stepped in and expressed his pleasure and appreciation at their openness to share their reactions. "But, I think we should deal with just one item at a time. Some of the comments will automatically be carried over when thinking about other pieces".

The morning disappeared so quickly. They had a valuable time assessing the various specimens.

Dawn had sensed that their discussion was less serious so she poked her head into the room and announced that lunch was ready. "Go, and polish your noses or whatever, and come in here".

She had the table laid. She did indicate that there were no place names, so it was a free for all as to where they sat.

Conversation changed. Dawn butted in, "I would like to hear a little about what went on earlier". Howard assured her that he would fill her in, but did mention the decision relating to the change of name. She thought that very appropriate.

They didn't go back to their seats immediately after lunch. Howard insisted they should walk around the garden two or three times to fill their lungs with some fresh air. It was a pleasant break and there were numerous comments about the flower beds and flowering shrubs.

Back to business. Adrian shared some of his thoughts and wondered about the number required of the various items. "We do not choose all of them. The ones that appeal to us should be the ones required for our first printing. Some of the business cards could be used immediately with our present contacts and potential clients".

Adrian's father stressed the importance of good advertising. "But it has to be appropriate and timely. The agency has left a suitable gap on most of their suggestions for a photo of your building. Has there been any recent suggestion as to an estimated date when the building will be ready?"

"Not yet", replied Adrian, "I'm hoping for news before too long. I think I'll drive up next week. I can also call in at the advertising agency". That brought a loud comment from every person around the table, "Can I come!"

"Any volunteers to drive the bus?" asked Adrian.

Their meeting broke up late afternoon. When in the car Geoff asked if there were any plans for a meal before heading to the various homes.

Mary mentioned a place they had been to on a previous visit. Without any more comments Adrian made sure the car knew which turn to take for the desired eating place.

Adrian then drove home and the others entered their vehicles and headed for home. Mary shuffled close to Adrian, she wanted a farewell kiss. At the same time she whispered if there was a possibility for her to accompany him up to Harrogate. An extra squeeze and lingering kiss gave her the positive answer she was expecting.

Adrian was by himself. It was an opportunity to reflect on the discussions earlier in the day. He soon acknowledged the success of their time together. He began making plans for the visit to Harrogate. His father had also asked him if he could go to Harrogate as well. He planned phoning the advertising agency on Monday morning – he would ask if they would be open on Saturday.

Saturday morning arrived and he had hardly finished his breakfast when the door bell rang. He went to the door but before he opened he shouted, "If that is you, next time you see me ask for a key".

As he opened, her wiggling hand was stretched out to him. He took it and shook hands bidding her welcome. "If getting a key means missing out on a hug and kiss, then forget the key" she said.

His father had offered to drive because his mother also wanted to be with them. Adrian drove over with Mary to his parents' home, they were ready.

Soon they were on their way to Harrogate.

The conversation in the car was quite orientated. Males in the front and females in the back. They drove directly to the site. They were all eager to see what was developing.

The builders had started on their building. The outside walls were up to roof level. There was evidence of some work being done on the inside also. They got out of the car and walked around. The site manager had noticed their arrival so came over to speak with them. He was able to give them an estimated date for completion. It was a little later than Adrian had hoped for, but nevertheless it was a date they could work around. The manager promised to keep Adrian posted as development progressed.

They stood looking at what had already being erected. Their

imaginations' worked overtime. Each one of them silently wishing their time away because they longed to see the finished building.

It was Dawn who broke the spell. "You won't get much lunch day dreaming!" she said, with a broad grin on her face. With that she started to walk towards the car.

It was a major decision whether to go to the advertising agency first or have lunch first. Howard volunteered a tummy satisfying answer. "Food first. Then we'll have no distracting thoughts when at the agency".

So after their meal they made their way to the advertising agency.

The designer had prepared well for their visit. He had some new suggestions to talk about. Again they were very impressed.

"We will ask the builder to let you know when everything is finished. You'll then be able to do the things you want to do. And, of course, take the necessary picture for publicity".

"I will take more than one picture. Because when it comes to the brochure we'll need different ones. But the inside ones will have to wait until the office furniture is installed".

"Can we finalize details of these leaflets? But I do want to make a firm request for about five hundred (or whatever number you might suggest) Business Cards while I'm here today. We can be using the cards in our day-to-day contacts as soon as possible."

"No problem sir, you'll receive them in the post during the week".

"You mentioned the details over the doorway. Do you have any ideas for the format, and font style?

I'll make sure you have some samples in the same package as the cards".

"Is it possible for you to put that together in a permanent mould and erect it in its suitable position?"

"We can do that with pleasure. We would send you a photo of it for approval before making it permanent".

"As far as advertising is concerned", said Mary, "I've seen, sometime in the past, a booklet called "The Shepherds' Guide". Does such exist in this area?"

"Yes, Ma'am. It is on our list of possible contacts. Actually we have one man we like to think is our expert. He has a shelf full of Magazines and booklets that are the source for us to explore when considering the extent of our advertising in the community and areas bordering ours".

There was a general chat about the various specimen ads. The consensus was full approval and impatience in waiting for the finished products.

There was much to talk about in the car going home and much thought for a number of days.

The cards arrived as promised. They looked great. Adrian's parents were pleased. It was his mother that asked, "Wouldn't they look more professional if there was a logo on it; and on all the advertising as well as at the entrance to the building".

"That's a tall order, but I will be on the phone with them", said Adrian, "I think it is of paramount importance for them to come up with something soon like that".

There was contentment amongst the team. The advertising was in good hands and the specimens were encouraging.

CHAPTER 37

Mary was on the phone to Adrian one evening and the conversation got around to office furniture. They agreed that it was time to start looking around at possibilities.

"We want it to match everything throughout the building. So we need to choose something exquisite for the reception area and then the same style into the four or five office rooms'.

"I'll make some enquires as to manufacturers of modern office designs", volunteered Mary "and may I dare to suggest, that our next meeting should have a clear objective; namely, office furniture".

"Yes, my dear, you may dare. Do we invade Nottingham or are we going to look around up here?"

"Leave it with me for a few days so that I can find suitable outlets, and we'll take it from there".

"You are quite a darling. Would you like to be my private secretary?"

"You will never be able to pay my minimum salary!"

It was Friday evening when Mary phoned next. "Make sure you bring a cheque book because you are, I presume, coming down tomorrow. There are two outlets to visit; one here in Nottingham, the other in Derby".

"Are they both open during the afternoon as well?"

"I thought we could do the Nottingham one, and then have some lunch before heading over to Derby".

Two or three of the designs attracted them in Nottingham. They obtained brochures for them. They were more impressed with the outlet in Derby. They appeared to have a larger selection but the new designs looked as if they would fit into their new office building. Again they had a selection of brochures to look through.

They were pleased that the makers' addresses were on the brochures. It would necessitate another day out when they had chosen the right designs.

"Your Saturday's are being taken up with business, what's happening to your soccer?"

"I manage a few practices but I am really missing the games. My sacrifice is worthwhile, especially when you take up my time!"

"The next Saturday is already booked. I am coming your way because one of the outlets is just north of Manchester in Oldham".

"Why don't you bring a case and stay for the weekend, my parents will be delighted to have you".

"Have you asked their permission?"

"Not really, but I think they spoil me by fulfilling my dreams"..

Adrian emailed Geoff telling him of the visit to the office furniture factory in Oldham. He gave the address and indicated that they would be there around ten thirty. It was going to be great if he could join them as well.

Mary drove straight to Adrian's parents' home on the Saturday morning. They welcomed her and Howard took her case and placed it in the room she would be using. Dawn asked if it might even be possible for them to travel up to Oldham and see the furniture. "I don't see why not. I'll phone Adrian and tell him I have arrived".

'Did you ask Adrian if we can come?"

"No. It can be a surprise for him when he gets here".

"He always enjoyed surprises".

"He still does!"

Howard entered the house from the garden to announce his son's arrival".

There was a bleep on the horn. Mary said, "He's letting me know he is ready for me. Let him come in first, and then we can inform him of the change in plans".

When he came into the house there were kisses for everybody.

"Well I think we should be on our way, sweetheart".

"There has been a change of plans" replied Mary.

"So, what's now?"

Howard came to the rescue. "Dawn wants to make it a foursome instead of you two going on your own".

"Oh. Is that so. Then who may I ask is driving?"

"We'll drive. But I want you to know that we are paying for lunch".

"In that case let's get ourselves ready and be off".

The outlet was easy to locate. It was on the edge of town on the south east side. It was quite an extensive factory building with a show room at one end.

As they entered the reception area Adrian spotted Geoff already there. He came alongside his mother and said, "Mum, there'll be an extra mouth to feed at lunch time."

Geoff was welcomed with great pleasure. Adrian filled him in quickly with the present situation.

They were in no great hurry so they stepped around many items they had seen in the brochure. Then they came to a separate section of new and developing models. There were a few pieces that attracted them amongst the new items.

Out of the five visitors three of them had different favourites. So it meant trying them for comfort, but also how they showed off the personality of each person sitting on them.

Howard announced that he would be the judge of the other three. There was a reluctant appreciation of his offer. But Howard asserted that there was no alternative!

There was no first choice when it came to comfort. But each of them was surprised at the styles bringing out attitudes and personalities. The salesman had numerous comments to make about their personalities changing depending on which chair they sat on.

Interest was narrowing to one model. It was very attractive in modern wood and brass fittings. The salesman knew that they were shopping for the whole office building, not just reception and offices, but waiting room also.

He went to his computer and came back with copies of every piece of furniture they required. Howard and Dawn were amazed at the quality and executive appearance. Dawn was the one to ask about prices.

""What is your price for the reception and waiting area together with five offices?"

"Why five offices, mother?"

"You staff will want to expand when they see what they will be sitting on!"

"This is the latest model. I have not been given prices as yet. Give me a few minutes while I go see the manager. He may want to come back with me with such a possible large order.

It must have been ten minutes later he returned with the manager who was genuinely interested and courteous.

"If you make a firm offer on the actual amount you require I will give you a pre-sale price. But I would want pictures for advertising and the opportunity to let future buyers see these items in use".

Adrian commented, "That will not prove difficult. And if you get lots of orders perhaps there might even be a Christmas gift under the office tree for us!"

Mary apologized for interrupting, "But are you likely to have apartment furniture in a similar style?"

"We have not planed that", the boss replied, ""But it might be possible".

"I only ask because there will be two apartments on the floors above the offices; and if they are being offered fully furnished, I'd like …"

Adrian interrupted "Now be careful what you say, after all you are a biased possible customer!"

"I'll consult the design team", said the boss, "And I'll get back to you if you are interested in furnishing the apartments also".

They all took seats while Adrian and the boss negotiated payment details.

The boss was pleased that the finished product was not required immediately. He wanted a minimum of one months notice. Adrian agreed to such reasonable terms.

Adrian approached Geoff and Mary separately for their candid opinion; after all they would be using the furniture. There was not a slight hesitation from either of them. They considered the quality as being very superior and would give a very generous impression to clients.

Dawn was true to her word, they did pay for lunch.

Geoff thanked them for lunch and made towards his car.

In the car on their way home Adrian and his father were talking finance.

"When do I start borrowing, and how much – the full expected amount, or reasonable installments?"

"That depends on the lending company. We must meet with them soon and map out some details to help us in the next stage of planning.

The following week Adrian and his father met with the lending company. It was a worthwhile meeting and generous plans were agreed to in regard to the money required for the building and office furniture. Howard mentioned to his son that it was a great deal for them. They left the office with a promise to contact them a few days ahead of when the money would be required.

It was two weeks after their visit to the furniture factory that Adrian received in the mail suggested sketches of the furniture for the apartments, As he was looking and fantasizing he had the thought about how to finance the requirements for the apartments. He wondered if the two people who would be living in them would be willing to pay for the furniture and other equipments,

He gave it some serious thought. He gave himself a rough estimate and began to look at his savings. He thought that he could carry it. Then he made the decision that if the occupants did pay for the furnishings of their apartments, then they would have no monthly payments for rent until the amount had been credited. He hoped that Mary would go along with the same idea. For one thing it would save a large amount of loan repayments,

He decided to phone Mary. It was a long phone call. She eventually agreed to the idea but was not sure whether she had enough savings to cover the cost. She would ask her father if he could help. So the call was made longer as they fantasized living next door to each other.

She wondered when she might get a chance to see the sketches. Adrian volunteered to take her out for lunch the next Saturday in Nottingham.

Over lunch they both expressed their delight in the prospects of having both apartments matching.

They decided that before anything was finalized that they would pay another visit to the factory and see more details.

It was about ten days later that Adrian received an email stating that more details were available to the sketches for the apartment furniture.

A couple of weeks later they had a free Saturday so they planned a day out in Oldham. The new designs were wonderful. Both apartments would have matching furniture, it will be very smart.

Mary commented, "They are the same, they look just like us, we match them completely!" They could not wait to move in, and begin using them.

There was a phone call from the site manager in Harrogate asking if Adrian could go up and see the building. It was almost finished and it was important to make some definite decisions for the decorating …

A few days later he was able to finish work early, so he set off for Harrogate straight from his office.

The building was looking fabulous. He loved the arched entrance way.

He was surprised at the space in each office. The Reception area was top rate with a suitable waiting area off to one side. The site boss had various suggestions to share with Adrian. They spent a very happy hour going over colours and designs.

The end was in sight.

Now the money is needed,

Now the furniture should be ordered.

The advertising people should be applying their products. That would include the initial ads for professional magazines and the Shepherds Guide.

On his way home his thoughts concentrated on when to open the business.

I think it's time for another get-together of the team. I'll ask Dad if we can have it at their house and for Mum to prepare lunch for us. It certainly is not as expensive as going to a café somewhere. And with my father being a member of the organizing team he'll be on the spot for answers from his long experience of the business, I'll invite myself over for diner tomorrow evening.

He had no need of his persuasive words, his mother welcomed him home. They had a great informative and explorative time. Howard felt it important to get the whole team together as soon as possible.

Adrian emailed Geoff and Mary, he asked her to bring Jenny, for them to meet the coming Saturday at his parent's place. He suggested they arrive around ten o'clock. He warned them of what the discussion would be about. "It's important business", he wrote.

The three others were well on time. Dawn had coffee ready for them as they arrived. Adrian asked them to sit comfortably while he updated them.

He stressed the point that things were reaching a climax. That advertising is on the ball. That office furniture has been ordered. That the decorators are putting final touches to the building. That he himself is excited and anxious to start work.

"One of the things to do today is to set an opening date".

He had the furniture plans laid out on the table. He had photos of the building process to help them visualize moving in. He was open to ideas about early financing until a list of clients was formed. What about the apartments?

"Is there any way in which we can bring some clients with us? Most of our present clients are tied to the firm we work for. But if there are any that we ourselves have signed up then perhaps they can come with us. What do you think?"

The consensus was that most of our present ones were tied to the firm they work for.

'This is an embarrassing question, but I want to make it. Do not give any answer that will be an embarrassment to you. Usually in a new business the first workers are not asked to help finance the beginning struggles. But there can be benefits down the line, I hope!"

One suggestion was that perhaps the workers could donate their first three months without pay.

Mary wanted to speak to the apartment case. "I am probably going to be one applying for one of the apartments. I have looked through my savings and I think I'll have enough to purchase the furniture and equipment required for one apartment".

"If so", said Adrian, "that would mean you would live rent free until that initial amount was covered".

"That would not be too difficult", said Howard, "it will be a simple matter of book keeping".

Geoff wondered if it would help if he worked part time for the first half year or so.

Jenny thought she may be able to take on a part-time job for a similar period.

"We are looking at the unknown", said Adrian, "because we have no idea how soon we'll be getting fee paying clients. There will be an enormous need for faith directed praying. The Lord can bring clients in soon after we open. He knows our desires and he knows our needs, Thank you Lord, this is your business".

There had been valuable comments shared amongst all those present. The morning was going fine.

Adrian glanced at his watch. "I think it would be a good idea if we moved away from the table and spent the next half an hour in prayer; I've already mentioned that He knows our needs. Now I believe He is waiting to hear from each one of us. We accept ahead of time that He really does answer prayer. And He will be answering the prayers we bring to the Throne of Grace right now".

Dawn heard what she thought might be the last 'Amen', so she announced that lunch was about to be served. "You have five minutes to do what you have to do", she said.

Adrian's comment was quite favourable in so far that there were two tables; one for working at, the other for eating at.

They were all ready for food and drink.

They enjoyed the meal and then they enjoyed a walk around the garden to get some fresh air before their afternoon session.

"So," said Adrian with an anticipatory pause, "When do we open to offer our services?"

Geoff asked, "Have we any dates fixed for when the building will be ready for our occupation".

"There is nothing final at this stage. But we have been assured that it will not be later than the end of the year."

Jenny suggested, "A new year – a new building – a new business!"

"Very well stated", added Mary. "If we open in the New Year, when can I move into the apartment?"

Howard asked, "If you are looking at an opening date. Ask the big question, what is left for us to do before we can commence doing business?"

That took up the discussion for the next hour. The task seemed insurmountable. But as Jenny remarked, "God works wonders when He is in charge." "Right, now I have a clean sheet of paper in front of me", stated Howard, "Tell me the things to be done in order of priority".

"Are you exercising your management skills, my dear", asked Dawn. "You had better take the centre chair!"

Geoff volunteered, "How much of this can we do; I mean the other three of us?"

That was an excellent suggestion because each one began to offer their interest or expertise for some of the jobs to be done. By the time items had been accepted by one or the other there was just a workable handful left for Adrian. And his father said he would help with them also.

They were all ready for a time of prayer. So much had been achieved and so much was left to be done. God had proved His involvement in the whole project, so they approached Him with confidence with their requests. It was a great way to complete their day together.

Dawn was thanked for her hospitality. One bright spark muttered, "can we come again next week?"

Dawn's reply was definite, "No! You've got other things to get on with".

They all went home happy, but tired. God had enabled them to achieve much during the morning and afternoon.

A few days later Mary phoned Adrian. She just wanted a chat, she said. After a few chatty comments Adrian asked, "Now, what is your main reason for calling? Just to tell me you love me?"

"Yes and no".

"That is an extremely pleasant and positive reassurance or whatever".

"The love is reassurance. The other is a possible venture for us. So which would you like first?"

"I'll take the love all the time, which in itself is a real venture or adventure".

"Well, here is the venture part of my reason for calling. If the apartments are going to be fully furnished, then we have some shopping ahead of us.

The builder will be doing all the required fixtures but we have the appliances to choose.

"The builder might have a firm to recommend".

"Anyway, we must make some choices ready for them to be installed".

"If there is no soccer for your priority on Saturday, can I be the second choice for your time and presence?"

"I never thought you would ever get around to your real reason!"

"I'll fill up with petrol tomorrow so that I am ready for an early start on Saturday".

Mary started making enquiries ahead of Adrian's visit. There were two or three places of interest and she noted their addresses.

They looked around the places Mary indicated but nothing took their fancy. In one place the assistant was helpful, he came back to them with some brochures. "We have none of these in stock as yet, they are quite new".

Just a quick glance indicated that there might be something to think about; they said 'thank you' and left to find a place for lunch.

It was a slow lunch, they had plenty of time. The brochure contained some challenging designs. They needed a fridge-freezer, a stove, and a dishwasher. Perhaps we should look at the possibility of a washer/dryer also. When they had made their choices they found that they were manufactured in Holland. But there was an agent in Leeds.

"I'll email the builder with this information. He may be able to obtain them with a discount for us".

"That's a reminder. How soon do we need to find the funds to pay for the inside of the apartments?"

"Certainly before the end of the year".

"Will they require the whole sum or some easy monthly payments?"

"My guess would be both. A fairly substantial amount will be required up front and the balance perhaps over six months or so".

"Then I must start saving rapidly!"

"I'll contact the furniture people on Monday. I know we ordered the office furniture, But I don't think we made a firm offer on the apartment furniture.

It could all be delivered at the same time. With the building almost complete the delivery could be direct to our site. That means the delivery people would help to place the pieces in the right rooms, and also in the apartments upstairs".

"Oh yes, I must confirm with the builders regarding the fixtures in the apartments. We will need TV outlets in the lounges and master bedrooms. We'll need phone outlets in at least two places in the lounges, in each bedroom, in the kitchens, and in whatever space we will use as a study.

"I want an intercom from the reception office to my apartment; that can be part of the intercom to all the offices.

Perhaps we could have a TV outlet in the waiting room area near Reception.

"It's going to be important to get all these ideas taken care of before the final decoration is done.

Oh Yes, The room behind the desk in reception will be used, one half as a store for files, the opposite side for office supplies. Both areas will need suitable shelving and cupboards.

"There is another reminder that to the left of the reception desk there is a small anti-room for refreshments, a table for a coffee maker, shelves for mugs, a sink and a small fridge.

"Most of these things ought to have been thought about seriously long before now."

Glancing back on that list Adrian decided it would be ideal for him to go over to Harrogate and talk to the builder. The sooner the better, the earliest possibility would be Monday after leaving work early in the afternoon.

On Monday morning Adrian phoned the builder to make sure he would be available later that afternoon. Everything was okay with the builder.

It really was imperative for Adrian to talk to the site manager. Some of his suggestions meant altering what was already completed. Though the site manager assured him that the new ideas could be incorporated easily; some of the fixtures like shelves and cupboards might have to wait until after 'opening'.

Adrian drove home almost breathless with joy as he contemplated the new items being part of the new building.

He realized that decision time was quickly coming up. When does he leave his present job? When does he commence to live in Harrogate? Will he live there alone for the first two months or so?

Along the road his joy was mixed with anticipation of moving. He arrived home safely and tired. He was not long having a quick snack, a shower and heading for bed.

Mary phoned later that week so was able to hear the latest from Adrian regarding the trip to Harrogate and the new items to be incorporated in the building. She was thrilled with the update.

He shared with her his decision making dilemma, when?

She wasn't very helpful because she wanted to make the same decision.

Adrian asked a question regarding the wisdom of when to move, and should it just be one person in the first stage.

Mary's comment was that her hopes were a decision for one; for one couple who were madly in love.

"My heart is thinking something like yours, but I'm afraid at the moment the big issue is related to finance and when we can look to a near future for such close proximity to each other".

"I'll to have some deep serious prayer on this. I want us both to be together; but I also want God to direct the stages leading up to our anticipated union."

"Have you any date in mind for your departure to the North?"

"No. But I think it will be early in the New Year".

"What about the other members of the team?"

"I would want them as soon as possible. What I want to do in those early weeks is to make as many contacts as possible with the business world. I hope for interviews and openings for articles on our venture. Perhaps to travel around the major cities and look for possible future clients. I will. require some expert guidance along those lines."

"I have a very strong feeling that I could give expert encouragement along some of those lines!"

"The ideal response is for us to sleep on it!"

"Lovely talking with you sweetheart, let me know developments. I will phone you again in a few days if for nothing more than to hear you voice".

"Good-night, darling. I'll make sure you are kept up to date, and in good voice!"

Once again it was imperative that Adrian had a chat with his dad. So a quick phone calls. His mother answered. "Can I come this evening to see dad, but it'll be nice to have something to eat before!"

"I'll set the table now. You'll have to cope with left-over's tonight".

"They'll taste real good!"

'Howard opened the conversation while still eating. "So what is imperative tonight?"

"I've been considering when to go Harrogate. I'd like to go up before the others are ready. Is it feasible for me to anticipating working part-time? For example work here Monday to Wednesday, and then up there Thursday to Saturday?"

"Have you talked to your boss about this yet?"

"No. This is the preliminary to that".

"It will be unusual, but your boss will understand the situation, I'm sure".

"Being up there for a few days will give me opportunities to meet with the business world and check out the churches. Do you think there might be a Christian Business Men's meeting?"

"More than likely. So find out what day they meet before you ask about days for part time".

"Have you any contact that will help?"

"Give me a couple of minutes and I'll phone the local secretary, he will know or at least be able to find out".

"That answer came quickly. The Christian workers' meeting is on the second Thursday for lunch. They call it 'workers' because there are some business women who join in. I'd like to come with you to one of those meetings to bring greetings from the branch down here".

"If I can find a client or two while up there it would help with expenses. That is a priority for specific prayer".

The evening went well. Howard was able to encourage Adrian about starting off part time. Adrian went home all primed to take his boss for lunch the next day.

His boss was very interested in Adrian's new venture and agreed to a part time experiment for a few months, if nothing serious developed then he could return to full time. The boss insisted on being kept abreast of developments.

Over the next few weeks Adrian, in his spare time, mused about the various aspects of the business that could be advertised and also looking for qualified personnel to fill specialist offices.

He talked with Mary at length during one phone call about the various items that would come under Accounts and Accountancy.

Adrian raised the point regarding Auditing.

It had been covered slightly during Mary's studies, but she insisted that she could not class herself as a specialist. But she remembered that Betty wanted to specialize in that field. But having lost touch recently was not sure what post graduate work she had done towards specializing in Auditing.

Adrian was interested in Betty. "Perhaps we should keep in touch with her because we may need to encourage her to join our team".

The third week in the month Adrian had planned two days off to attend to some details in Harrogate. His father said that he would like to join him.

They set off early in order to be on time for the lunch. They booked into a hotel near to the business site. There was time for them to look around their office building. They had much to discuss at what they saw.

And then drove off for the meeting. Howard had obtained the address. It was not difficult to find. There were about twenty cars parked already so Howard commented that such would indicate an excellent turn out for the meeting.

They were welcomed and when the leader heard where they were from he wanted to know why they were attending this meeting. The person knew the friend of Howard. At the beginning of the meeting there was an official welcome to the visitors. Adrian was drawing the attention of some of the local business men. There was quite a challenging discussion while they were eating. And there were genuine hopes to meet up again at future meetings.

Father and son spent most of that evening talking about some of the people they had met. There were two or three likely future clients. It was well worth coming to have such wonderful contacts even before business started.

Adrian mentioned that he intended attending as many of those meetings as possible while working part time.

The next day they spent with the site boss confirming the list of extras that Adrian had sent to him.

They went upstairs to the apartments. Most of the items on Adrian's list had been dealt with.

Howard was thrilled with the furnished apartments. "Next time we come up we can stay here and not in the hotel." Adrian agreed if for no other reason than it would be cheaper.

"As long as the electricity, heating and water are all connected; we can manage without the phones," was Howard's observation.

Just after three o'clock Adrian announced that all the items on his list had been dealt with. Howard immediate pulled out his cell phone and called Dawn announcing their arrival for dinner later that afternoon.

During their journey home they both praised the Lord for His help and guidance. They were looking ahead to a great adventure.

The next day Adrian had quite long phone calls with Mary and also with Geoff. He was excited as he filled them in with the progress being made. They both wanted to go up to Harrogate and see for themselves. Mary admitted that it was not convenient for her during the next few weeks. Geoff mentioned that he might drive over one day and see things for himself. Both of them said they could not wait to get started.

Adrian spoke to them about his plans to work part time for a few months. This meant he would be up there at weekends. One of his ventures was to locate a 'good' church.

The builder informed Adrian of the closing date for payment. Adrian then phoned his father and asked help in contacting the company who had agreed to give a mortgage.

They obtained the necessary cheques. Howard agreed to travel up to Harrogate with Adrian. They spent the morning with paper work and moving-in plans.

Howard made the suggestion that when the others start coming up to Harrogate that Jenny could stay in Mary's guest room and Geoff stay in Adrian's guest room. Even though that was looking ahead sometime it was an important aspect to keep in mind. For one thing it would save on expenses in those early weeks.

Their journey back home was one of excitement and accomplishment. Adrian mentioned a date when he would start part-time. His first weekend would set the pace for his future. His new life was about to begin.

The following two weeks were spent buying supplies for his kitchen and bathroom. Mary told him she was jealous of him going up there alone. He teased her by saying he might let her accompany him sometime; as long as she brought supplies for her kitchen etc.

His boss organized a sending off party for Adrian even though it was only for half time each week. It was an encouragement to hear the staff wish him well. The day chosen for the party was the afternoon before he was to leave the following morning. Adrian was thrilled at the comments received and began to feel the challenge of going out on his own.

His original plan was to go up to Harrogate after work on the Wednesday. But this first time he didn't leave until the Thursday morning.

He arrived at the site and drove slowly to the office building. He was full of positive and challenging thoughts; his emotions were mixed. As he unlocked the office door and walked towards the reception area he paused and offered a prayer of thanks and asked for guidance in maintaining his promise to establish a Christian business that would start each morning with a word of Scripture and a prayer.

That reminded him to find a bible for office purposes.

He decided to make his office at the reception desk for some of those early part-time visits, and gradually get his own office in working order. So he would act as his own receptionist. That first day he located the appointment schedule and placed it in a prominent position near the desk.

"I wonder when I'll insert the first appointment" he said to himself.

After he had carried the kitchen and bedroom things up stairs he decided to go out for lunch. He'd buy some extra food for his meals and commence with his first evening meal on the new stove.

He made a mental note that no phone calls were received on his first day. During the evening the phone did ring. It was Mary wanting to know what he had been up to all day! She also wanted to know when she might be allowed to visit him! She'd bring her own food!

The next day he spent some considerable time looking though brochures and leaflets of other agencies in the area. He followed up some on the internet.

The following morning he went through the Shepherds Guide. His advert was quite prominent. He noted some possible contacts with the hope of future business.

The next weekend he concentrated on items for wall posters regarding the services being offered.

One was a general one regarding the whole business of Karisma Business Consultancies and Services.

-A separate one with the Mission Statement in attractive fonts.

-Reliability in right management of resources.

-Consultancy; Seminars, Mission Statements, Five year assessments.

Those assessments would include Goal setting; goals achieved; goals still in progress; goals changed; goals abandoned and why?"

Accounts.

Costs and fees; business accounts; deposit accounts; Pay Roll.

Income Tax.

Corporate and personal tax returns. Tax preparations.

Auditing – a future development.

As he thought about the items under accounts he found himself longing for Mary to join him.

There were two churches he wanted to visit on the Sunday. They had been mentioned when he was at the Business Worker's meetings. They were not hard to locate and as it happened one of them had their main service in the evening. The worship and pulpit ministry of both were quite satisfactory.

.A few people welcomed him and asked about him and his work.

He drove back home after the evening service He was tired when he arrived home but felt the need to fill-in his father about his first weekend in his own business. It was an informative and interesting conversation.

A few weeks later Howard phoned Adrian asking about his next visit north. He mentioned that it was the third week, and the business men's lunch would be on the Thursday. Adrian confirmed. Howard wondered if he might drive up with Adrian for the meeting and then also added that he would like to stay up for the weekend and help with any of the details requiring attention. That idea sat well with Adrian. If for no other reason than it would be excellent company. They'd have fun together. His father would no doubt have some ideas for leisure times. Though none such were planned, there was always a space or two for innovations.

Instead of Adrian driving up on Wednesday evening, he left it until Thursday morning. They arrived in time to push their bags into the reception area and then move off for the Meeting.

The others at their lunch table wanted to know all about the new venture. The Lord must have placed them there, because they had some wonderful ideas for Adrian to follow up on. Howard was able to place some valuable phone calls the next day to some of the suggested people and firms. One of which needed further information. They even wanted to meet with Adrian and seek advice regarding how they could be helped. Howard was on the ball and asked when they would like such a meeting.

They appeared quite urgent and indicated that they were working the next day, being Saturday. Howard said he would call back within a few minutes.

He was bubbling over with excitement when telling Adrian of his contact. Howard mentioned that if they could go tomorrow then he would be able to go and give support. Adrian agreed.

Howard phoned back. They were delighted with such a quick response. He obtained the address and agreed a time to meet.

This was a big boost to both father and son. Frequently during that afternoon they wondered what help was needed. Howard indicated that whether it was small or large, it was the beginning. The new firm was in business!

That evening Adrian phoned Mary and Geoff asking for their prayers for the next day. Howard also asked Dawn to do the same.

The address Howard had been given was in York. It was a city north of Harrogate. They had no difficulty finding he place.

The person who owned the new work being established was so pleased that Adrian was free to come at such short notice. A couple of his staff was there with him.

Adrian made a mental note of the comfort established early for the meeting. There was a confidence and expectancy, a willingness to assess the possibilities, and openness for present and future help. Howard encouraged Adrian to accept the challenge even though his two colleagues had not yet joined the firm in Harrogate. Adrian assured them that he was willing to help them.

He was impressed by the eagerness of the boss to receive help. He raised the question of whether they would welcome a one day seminar to help them assess where they wanted to go with their business. There was a positive response to this idea. So Adrian planned on leading a seminar for them at some future date. He stressed that the date should not be too far into the future because he recognized the urgency for them to get started, yet to start with the right goal.

The boss wondered if Adrian could be available in a month's time.

Adrian's response was that would give him time to plan the sessions for the day.

The boss raised the point of costs. Adrian promised to have a figure for them before the seminar.

He knew he'd have to give some serious thought in regard to charges for his services; he would talk to his father about that later.

The boss took them all to a restaurant in York for lunch. He expressed his great pleasure in meeting them and entering into a working relationship with Adrian.

It was a very excited couple in the car driving back from Harrogate. That evening the same three people received phone calls.

The following two weekends Adrian was in Harrogate were encouraging. Various letters and brochures arrived in the post as well as responses to the ad in Shepherds' Guide.

One of the phone calls was from the "Business World" editor, asking for an interview with photos. It was his desire to give a good report about the new business starting up.

Adrian thought about this interview; his concern was that a photo shoot at that moment would be quite bland. Then he thought that Mary and Jenny could come one weekend then he could arrange for some photographs to be taken. Perhaps the interview could be at the same time.

The editor was ready to wait for Adrian's word as to the best time for both and he indicated that Saturday's were a possibility.

He was spending some valuable time outlining his one day seminar. The morning would concentrate on Mission Statement and Business Policy and Philosophy. The afternoon session gave more time to accounts, etc. He definitely wanted Mary up for that weekend so she could lead the afternoon session.

He phoned her right then. She answered quickly and was surprised to hear Adrian's voice. "It's not like you to phone during a busy day. What's urgent?"

"You are my sweetheart. You are definitely urgent".

"Okay. What do you want?"

"I want you – isn't that enough?"

"No. Because I am not available, due to my work load".

"Tough. I have a job for you".

"I'm not in the business as yet".

"Well this is premature testing of what I hope will be a fertile field".

She wanted to know all about the visit and was keen regarding the one day seminar. She whole heartedly agreed to the date. She would come up on the Friday night to try out her apartment.

"I hope you will be able to give sometime to a breakdown of what we can cover during the afternoon session. Her reply was that she was already working on it. She appeared to be very keen about this first business day for them both.

"Oh, I need to have a cost amount for them. They would like some idea of the costs about a week ahead of time".

"That will be difficult – a trial and error situation, because we have no idea of our costs that need to be covered. But I'll give it some prayerful thought. The best thing is for us to present our present costs for such an event as a basis for our future development."

"That's an excellent idea. Thanks sweetheart".

"There is another development. An editor of a business magazine is asking for an interview and photos. I would like you and Jenny to be in on that, and perhaps Geoff could come up that day also".

"Sounds good. Sounds feasible. In which case, I agree to it!"

The rest of that weekend Adrian was flying high. Things were moving far better than he anticipated. He had to tell himself that this was only a beginning. A full time work load for the whole team was something much more.

Mary arrived on the Friday evening, Adrian had driven up the day before..

They had talked on the phone comparing notes and ideas. They were both geared up for an interesting day.

Adrian started by expressing the need for an intelligent and comprehensive Mission Statement. He stressed the importance of them taking part, sharing their ideas. They all had a writing pad. Adrian from time to time made a question for them to deal with. He gave them time to write down their ideas.

The idea was that their ideas would be shared later on in the day, as they built up a base for the business profile and philosophy.

At the end of the day both speakers and the local team were delighted with the progress made. There was mention of costs. Adrian, with a smile on his face, said, "That's why I brought my Finance specialist with me!"

Mary chatted with him and gave him the estimate."It includes travel as well, of course". The boss was pleased with the amount, he felt that it was very reasonable.

Mary stayed over in what would be her own apartment which was on the floor above Adrian's apartment. She had brought a load of things with her, so she was able to cope. They went to one of the churches on the Sunday morning. She left to go home after they had been out for lunch. Adrian wasn't much later before he set off for home. It had been an interesting weekend. The one day seminar had been a glorious success. All the way home he was contemplating similar one day events for various locations.

A Saturday morning was decided by the editor of the magazine and the team members, Geoff would find it easy going. Mary would bring Jenny and probably stay over-night. In fact they would go up to Harrogate after work on Friday.

It was a happy bunch that met in their new premises that morning. Each one found his or hers own office and made sure the seat was comfortable. Their minds shot ahead to when they would be there in full business attire and attitude.

It was late morning when the editor arrived with his photographer. It didn't take them long to decide on the locations for the shots. Adrian asked his team to make sure they were showing the right action for their positions..

The editor had some quite searching questions for Adrian. He searched for the real motives behind his starting up a new business. He learned a lot about the Mission Statement and the spiritual application to business ethics.

He managed a couple of questions to the other members of the team to make his article a little more expansive.

The photographer knew what he wanted, and took some excellent shots both inside and outside.

The editor had some positive and encouraging remarks for the whole team. He anticipated the development of a successful business. His closing comment was, "I am looking forward to doing another interview with you in four or five years from now".

After they had eaten lunch Adrian asked if they could stay a little while because he wanted to share some ideas as to when they should open up shop. Geoff stated quite emphatically that he would work part time for the rest of the year. Jenny indicated that according to her friends she would have no difficulty getting a part time job for those early months. Mary noted that she would be able to carry some of her present work to help her finances.

Adrian expressed his desire for the business to start before Easter. There will be adverts out regarding Income Tax returns both corporate and personal. "This will give us a little income during the first month or so".

They all agreed that Easter would be the ideal time, and they could start planning accordingly. Each one at one stage or the other expressed their personal prayers would be in that direction.

Much of the planning had been accomplished. Now the patience and wisdom would be required in dealing with the promotion of Karisma Business Consultants and Service.

CHAPTER 38

Adrian was finding the winter weekend trips quite demanding. He longed for Spring and that would mean getting close to opening. He was making some good contacts and the response from the article in the Business Magazine was encouraging. He was able to follow up on some of the contacts and they were delighted that the new business was taking shape.

Adrian was contemplating handing in his resignation in order to live in Harrogate full time. He decided to make it closer to Easter. He was actually receiving orders, which helped him feel more confident in making his major decision.

Mary was having similar concerns. She felt happy about the prospects of continuing with some of her clients. Such would be a help to her as well as the business.

Jenny was ready to move and was delighted when Mary said she could share her apartment for a few months.

Adrian planned a retreat day on the Tuesday following Easter. That would give them a spiritual boost for the new adventure. A notice was ready to hang on the door, 'OPEN FOR BUSINESS'; it would be in place for the Wednesday morning. It seemed that all the team had planned to be in their respective office for the whole of that first week.

Some personal enquires came in when the office lights were on. That gave Adrian impetus to start offering booking dates to prospective clients. He said to himself frequently how he hoped Jenny would be on site soon. There were some individuals as well as a few businesses asking about Tax Returns. Adrian was enthusiastic in his replies that his staff would be available for bookings after Easter.

His next phone call to Mary was one of excitement in the growing interest in the new business, and also his emotional interest ought to come quickly so they could share in the early stages of their working together. He decided that Mary ought to start giving some thought to charges. He had scribbled a few notes so he told Mary to expect them in an email someday soon.

Mary kept the conversation going longer because she was eager to share her developing feelings about the work and about their relationship. They were both sorry when it became time to throw some kisses over the phone and express God's blessing for a good night's sleep.

The next time Adrian was in Harrogate he set priority on an email with suggested charges, to Mary. He began to write his email and then inserted his suggestions.

MONTHLY OFFICE EXPENSES
MORTGAGE
TAXES
INSURANCES
BUILDING AND CONTENTS
PERSONNEL
THIRD PARTY
SECURITY
CLEANING SERVICE
HEATING,
LIGHTING
PHONE WITH INTERCOM AND INTERNET
VIDEO AND TV OUTLET
RECEPTION
OFFICE SUPPLIES
TOILET SUPPLIES
COFFEE SUPPLIES
MAINTENACE SUPPLIES
WINTER
ICE PELLETS
SNOW PLOUGHING
WINTER SUPPPLIES

"During this next month I will keep a tag on the expenses occurred, that monthly sum will give you a little help. In fact I could back date it a little so that you can have that information to work with."

After sending the email he looked through the receipts of the past few months. He took an average of the heating and lighting, all he had for the phone was the monthly charge and a few calls. He had a copy of the Comprehensive Insurance for the year. He had a brochure on his desk about Security. During the winter he only had one bag of ice salt.

He decided that he might just as well send another email with this information and it would be one less thing to cause some concern.

Mary replied to both emails by scolding her lover for giving her so much extra work to do. She stated that the average over the past few months was a help. She indicated that the averages were a firm basis on which to start guessing. "I might have some ideas for you by the end of the month, so in the meantime do not get any expensive ideas."

Mary was able to compare her present office expenses alongside the ones mentioned by Adrian. The more she analyzed the details the more prayer was her concern. Where would all the money come from without a major monthly income? But the anticipated costs were proving helpful for the early months. She expected a steady income from doing Tax Returns. That would not only give them work to do but was of help in regard to the time involved in doing certain jobs. She knew right at the beginning that adjustments would be necessary after a few months in order for the business to succeed.

Mary and Jenny were busy planning their move. They were excited but also apprehensive. Their prayer life became the stabilizing factor for them The Holy Spirit was giving wisdom and guidance they hardly dreamed possible. There were regular comments about "this is just a beginning; this is how the Lord is going to bless us when the business is up and running". Both of the girls realized the wealth of their experience would be a blessing in the struggle of those early days.

Geoff phoned Adrian and they planned a Saturday together in Harrogate. Geoff had been doing some deep thinking about his role in the business and he was eager to share his ideas. They had a valuable time together. Adrian appreciated the thought Geoff had given to his partnership in the new work.

Geoff was convinced that he must give half time for perhaps the first year. Adrian suggested that perhaps he could share the apartment for the days when he was in Harrogate. That certainly would be of help.

Adrian invited himself to his parents for an evening meal fairly frequently. His father's experience was proving invaluable. He was helpful when it came to Adrian quitting work and heading north full time. It was a surprise when his father stated that he wanted to go with Adrian for a few days to help him settle. They had a good laugh about that. His mother's comment was related to the 'good' idea of her husband being away for those few days..

When the time came to pack everything Dawn had packed a large box of food for them. There was another box of extra things she knew would be required in setting up the kitchen. Adrian had accumulated some nice things over the years of being on his own.

With having the new furniture in the apartment there was the need to sell the things from his old place. His father recommended a firm that would deal with everything for him.

Two weeks before Easter Adrian was given a farewell party by his boss. He did not expect some of the gifts presented to him. Some items were the latest gadgets for office use. It was a wonderful send off.

Howard had hired a trailer for his car. Dawn was amazed that so much space had been used up with things. She prayed God's blessing upon them. They were off.

They were so pleased that the weather was kind to them. The journey had no mishaps. The unpacking into the office and the apartment went very well. In fact when the vehicle was empty Howard made the comment that his stomach thought his mouth was on strike. So off they went for lunch.

The afternoon was spent putting things in rightful places and then standing back and commenting that it all looked good in the apartment. They had a few things for the office so they went downstairs and got them unpacked. Howard looked at the Appointment Calendar on the office wall. He was impressed by the number of appointments already listed. Adrian switched on the answering machine. There were three messages. Two from companies wanting to transfer their tax accounts to Adrian. The third was for a possible one day seminar on goal setting for a firm in Barnsley .

Howard said, "It is evident that business has already started.. How encouraging to receive those three messages, on the very first full day of your permanent stay here in Harrogate."

He phoned his wife later in the evening telling her of the ease in unpacking and the three messages regarding future work. She was so pleased and decided that such was information to share with her friends.

The next morning at breakfast they were talking about the possibilities ahead of them. Adrian asked his father if he would like a trip to Barnsley to find out just what that firm would like on a one day seminar. Howard agreed readily. It would be a nice trip out, and would be able to compare it with the one earlier in York.

The first thing Adrian did when going down to the office was phone the number in Barnsley. There was a pleasant voice answering the phone. When Adrian introduced himself the receptionist said that the boss is in and transferred through to him. There was an exchange of names etc and then Adrian asked if they would welcome a visit as a preliminary to an actual seminar. The suggestion was welcomed whole heartedly. They agreed for early afternoon that day.

It was a good drive. They did not have a detailed street map of Barnsley so they stopped a few times to ask direction. There was a café just a couple of blocks away from the office to which they were going.

They were able to relax over lunch as no set time had been agreed upon. The receptionist welcomed them and directed them to a large conference type room. There was a large mahogany table with comfortable plush chairs; she mentioned that the boss would be in shortly, he was on the phone with a business client..

It was only a couple of minutes before the boss arrived and introduced himself. Adrian mentioned that his father had driven him over and that he was classed as "a consultant to his son".

The boss had obviously spent some valuable time thinking about what he was planning. Adrian was quite impressed. Howard had a few questions that helped to fill in the full picture of the needs. Costs had been mentioned and Adrian's response was that his finance colleague was working on costing and it would depend upon how many staff members would be involved. They chatted for about an hour; and the boss was delighted with the prospects Adrian outlined for a one day seminar on goal setting.

A communication bell had been pressed and the receptionist arrived with a tray of teas and cakes. Adrian commented, "I can now see your need to find out more about goal setting, though you seem to have things moving in the right direction. Inner refreshments place clients and others at ease.- that's an excellent goal already in place!"

After they had chuckled their way through the cakes and tea it was time for the visitors to take their leave. The boss thanked them for coming and the date had already been set on the calendar.

On their return journey Howard was thrilled with the day. He was excited about the early developments of the consultancy side of the new business. Adrian commented that he thought the one day seminars might be a major part of their early work load.

I have a wonderful feeling that God is already blessing your venture", Howard said, "It is a great encouragement to see requests for your services coming in".

Howard had decided to return home on Good Friday. There was a morning service at one of the local churches they attended. Howard took Adrian for lunch and then returned home.

Adrian had a spell of loneliness. The spell didn't last long. The phone rang, "Where have you been?" Was the question before he even said hello. "If I burp that will tell you where I have been", was Adrian's retort. Then followed the endearments, and the loneliness had been shattered. "Why are you not right here by my side?"

"Because you have not invited me!"

"Then take this as a permanent request. Your place is by my side!"

"This is a word to let you know that 'loneliness' will not be required in your vocab. very much longer. Jenny and I will be arriving early afternoon on Monday. Make sure the kettle is on, both of us like tea as long as it is in china cups".

"I'll switch on the heating pads so your beds are not too cold", he replied sarcastically.

It was a long phone call. Both Mary and Adrian wanted to talk. They also were forward looking as they anticipated a growing closeness to their friendship.

Adrian shared with Mary the trip to Barnsley with his father and the growing prospects regard the day seminar. She just bubbled over with excitement."So business has started."

""Yes, and there are a couple of people asking about corporate income tax returns. So there is something waiting for you,"

"I'm ready for anything!"

"Okay Then may I say that Monday cannot come too soon. Goodnight sweetheart:".

Adrian relaxed on Saturday. He even went to a local soccer game and shouted for the Harrogate Team. A person standing near to him wanted to know more about this new man on the block with such enthusiasm for soccer. After the game this man asked Adrian to go for a meal with him. In their conversation it soon became evident that Adrian's enthusiasm was being explored. The man he was with was one of the coaching staff and jumped when Adrian told of his past soccer experiences. "When can you start playing for us?"

"Not until my girl friend gives me permission!"

"Would you be really interested in playing?"

"Yes", answered Adrian, "Soccer has been part of my life, I enjoy it and there are some trophies to prove that I have been on the winning side sometimes."

"It sounds as if you'll be a good member for our team."

"Well, this afternoon I had itching feet. That mid-field needs a lot to be desired."

"We have never had a great player in that position. My team members do not like playing in that position".

"I can understand why"

"Why? What position do you play?"

"Mid-field!

"Then give me your phone number and I will invite you to one of our practices."

"I would like that. But it must be known that I am just starting up a new business here in Harrogate so my free time might be limited".

"Nevertheless you need to have a little time for exercise."

"And I feel the need for some regular work-outs"

"Great meeting you, Adrian, I will certainly be in touch."

"Thanks. I'm looking forward to the possibility of playing again"

"That was an interesting contact", he told himself as he drove home. Having watched the team playing, he could see himself in his favourite position helping the team to more success. "That's something to persuade Mary about. I'll approach it by informing her of my desire to take her out for good entertainment when she settles in".

There was a large crowd for the Easter morning service. The choir director spoke to Adrian during the refreshments following the service. The conversation became quite involved so the choir director suggested that Adrian join in his family for lunch, "I'll tell my wife to put more water in the soup!"

It was a pleasant time getting to know the family as they celebrated the resurrection of Jesus. He felt comfortable with them. The wife said that he could stay for the afternoon and then go to the evening service together. During the afternoon he was aware of their senior daughter eyeing him. It had been obvious at the lunch table. Her mother must have noticed it and thought it might be an embarrassment to Adrian.

As they talked about the new business the mother asked how many people would be working there. Adrian was able to fill her in with the details and tried not to stress to prominently about Mary and a possible engagement not very far into the future. The daughter's face dropped and she made some excuse to go to her room.

Adrian enjoyed meeting another family. He was building up a good list of friends. He went hope happy and expectant. Just another few hours and his co-workers would be arriving. But one especially was more than a mere co-worker. She was causing quite a lot of deep thought. There was some serious thinking about their future. Some quite drastic decisions were required. Certainly God had to give clear guidance regarded the big step he was contemplating.

He had a restless night because he was overly excited about Mary arriving the next day.

The first thing he did when he entered the office was to go on line to find out what shops would be open on Easter Monday. Not many! But more than he expected, and there was one he was pleased about, though not open all day.

Geoff arrived about eleven thirty. About half an hour later the two girls arrived. So it was a matter of unloading the cars and getting them settled.

Adrian caught Mary, she was on her own, and asked if they could leave the other two to the unpacking. "Why?" she asked. ""Let's say, 'we'll see'"

Adrian called to Geoff and Jenny telling them they were on their own for a little while, that Mary and he would be back shortly.

"So, what's all this about?" asked Mary.

"There's something I want to show you. It couldn't really wait until tomorrow as we will be occupied with the 'opening'.

There was a parking space just outside the door of the Jeweler's shop. Before opening and getting out Adrian leaned over to Mary and asked, "Do you love me darling?"

"You know very well that I do. Why do you need to be reminded?"

"Will you marry me?"

"Will I what? I have been desperate to say 'yes' to that question. When?"

"Not today! Let's go inside they will be closed shortly."

"They browsed for a few minutes. Adrian asked a young man to show them the rings on a certain sheet. They were all sparkling and beautiful. Adrian picked out some and tried them on. She liked them all. There was one with three diamonds he liked very much. He got hold of her finger and tried it on. It was a perfect fit.

"What do you think, sweetheart?"

"It's glorious. Yes, sweetheart, I'll marry you"

"But not before I've paid for it!"

So she slipped it off and handed it to the young man who had a face full of smiles. He filled out the sales slip and Adrian paid for it on his visa card. It was placed into a neat little box, which Adrian placed in his pocket.

On the way back in the car they discussed when to announce their engagement. Adrian said, "Our Minister is coming in the morning to lead our devotions. We'll ask him to announce it before he starts. So I'll slip it on your finger just before we gather for the special devotional time, or at least just before the Minister gets up to start.

Mary agreed, she didn't want either of the other two to know about it. "Tomorrow will be a wonderful surprise to them, or maybe they have been expecting it. When we get back we'll phone our parents, or it might be safer to email them so that the others will not be tempted to eavesdrop. We ought to ask them to send their greeting via the minister, so we must include his email address. He can read them out after he has made the announcement."

"We'll call in the take-out café for some food for this evening." said Adrian. "In that way they'll know why we went shopping!"

When they arrived back the kettle was boiling and a pile of sandwiches were on the table. Before any question could be asked Mary placed the package of food on the kitchen table and at the same time mentioned that is was their meal for that evening.

The afternoon went well. All four enjoyed moving things around until everything looked to be in the right place. There was little to move around in the apartments. But each one personalized his or her own office space. Jenny had some wonderful creative ideas for the reception area, she asked the fellows to help her. When she was happy with it, she asked that all three of them go outside and then come in and describe the welcome feeling. It was amazing. Jenny had brought with her a shield she purchased at a craft sale a couple of weeks earlier. It had been placed in a prominent place and gave the ideal welcome to those who approached her desk. The initial feeling was one of warmth and professionalism. Jenny was praised for her genius. Leaning against the wall was the poster to place in the widow tomorrow: "OPEN FOR BUSINESS".

The evening was spent just thinking about the possibilities in their future together.

Tuesday morning arrived. All four were up early. The girls had decided to prepare breakfast and invite the men to join them. There was no hurry to break up from breakfast as the minister was not due until a little before eleven o'clock. They would have their meeting in the conference room but prior to that they would test the comfort of the chairs in the reception area..

Their minister arrived about fifteen minutes early. So it was a matter of introducing the ones he had not met. They talked about the devotional. The minister expressed his pleasure in being invited to perform this important dedication service. They were getting ready to move into the conference room and the door bell rang.

"Who can that be? We are not open for business as yet. They had to ring the bell because he door automatically locked."

Adrian went and opened the door. To his surprise he recognized the people standing there. He called back to Mary and asked her if they should be allowed in. It was their parents. On the phone the minister had talked about the important opening dedication and decided that both sets of parents might like to be present. They had travelled independent of each other and arrived almost the same time at the front door of the office. They were pleased to meet the others and the minister. Adrian managed a quick moment to inform the parents of the secret and not to mention it..

There were enough chairs for all of them around the conference table. It was an oval table and the minister was placed at one end. He stood up behind his chair.

"To say the least this is an important day and an even more important event as we dedicate the place and the workers to the Lord. May I say how much I count this a great privilege. Now before I start there is an announcement that I must make. (Adrian had already found a secret moment to put the ring on Mary's finger). I am sure the angels in heaven are rejoicing this morning, because I am. Adrian and Mary are now engaged to be married."

There was applause from Geoff and the others responded likewise. They were all out of their chairs and wanted to see the ring. The parents now could voice their pleasure and give the couple a mighty hug,

It was at least ten minutes later when the minister mentioned that perhaps they should start their devotional meeting. He had chosen three verses from the scriptures and after reading them gave a short prayer. He then applied the scriptures to the business that was being dedicated. He spoke highly of the responsibility the four people had accepted under God. Then offered a prayer of dedication on the premises, and a special prayer for wisdom and courage for those who would work in this Christian venture. There were some loud and praiseworthy 'Amen's'.

It was the ministers' suggestion, to go upstairs and dedicate the two apartments. Mary and Adrian at the very same moment said "Yes. Please". So upstairs they all went. It was Adrian that asked if the apartment rooms were tidy. It was Sarah who stated that if they were tidy that would not be a good sign. "It must appear as if they are being lived in."

There was quite a detailed and inclusive prayer for each apartment.

Then the visitors were given permission to inspect the rooms. Later there were some wonderful comments about the exquisite appearance of the apartments.

Downstairs the visitors wanted to see the layout of the business facilities. It met with great approval. When they had all returned to the reception area Mary announced that it was time for lunch. The place had been reserved for us. "I have just phoned and there are four extra places available"

Adrian suggested that they double up into three vehicles..

It was a wonderful time eating and fellowshipping together. The parents were speculating as to how long they must wait before getting dressed up for the big day. No hints were given to them. Jenny moved up close to Mary and whispered, "Can you give me a hint?" There was a negative shrug from Mary with a smile cracking both sides of her mouth.

The rest of the afternoon was spent either in the reception area or upstairs in one of the apartments. The fact of a few cars being parked outside the office building did not go unnoticed by most of the workers on the site.

It must have been just after five o'clock when Mary's father announced the intention of having a celebration dinner at one of the hotels. "Both sets of parents will pay the bill, but that does not give freedom to order the most expensive food on the menu. But please come and order your favourite, and allow us the pleasure of giving you this special treat". Adrian's father indicated that he knew the ideal hotel.

They were shown to a corner table. Howard went aside with the waiter to ask a question. He seemed to be happy with the answer. They were comfortable and the waiter came to the table and expressed his congratulation to the engaged couple. He placed a couple of bottles of wine on the table. Adrian mentioned that such was not required..The waiter's reply was that it was non-alcoholic wine that had been specially ordered by a member of the party. He opened one of the bottles and poured out a glass for each person. They had a fabulous dinner.

Dawn mentioned that it would be quite late by the time they arrived home and wondered if there might be vacancies at the hotel for overnight. The waiter overheard that suggestion and was soon at their table with a reply that rooms are available for them.

They lingered after the meal as there was no hurry to leave. They had moved from their table into the lounge area. It was not a very busy evening for the hotel workers. There was almost some reluctance to move when one of the party thought it time to say some 'goodbyes'.

The four went back to the apartments, and the parents hung around a bit longer before they retired for the night.

Early the next morning Adrian went down to the office he wanted to put up the 'open' sign. He was too late. Jenny had beaten him to it. She had it in a prominent place that no one passing could miss it. Mary phoned down to the reception and stated that breakfast was ready and that it was not going to become a habit but the men could join them because it was opening day.

They met for Adrian to lead devotions. Then on the stroke of nine he proudly stepped forward and opened the door. Karisma was now open.

It was lunch time when two men came in and asked at reception for information regarding income tax. Jenny told them that it was possible to make appointments. She also said that costs would be compatible with other places offering the same service. They both made a booking right there and then..

When they left she opened the intercom with the other offices and informed them that business had started. The responses were exuberant. Jenny informed Geoff and Mary that they both had an appointment, "so please see the appointment calendar!"

The Staff meetings became more challenging and more demanding; they were also longer when they discussed the day seminar coming up. Adrian wanted both Geoff and Mary to be part of the day seminar. Jenny would be left in charge of the office. In fact he was expecting them to take valuable parts in all future seminars also. Adrian hoped that the phone would keep her busy that day.

The phone requests were mainly for Tax Returns. Mary hoped that eventually she might get into something more demanding. The next three weeks went by quite quickly and pleasingly.

The evening before they were to go up to Barnsley for the Day Seminar, Adrian's father phoned and asked if he could sit in on the seminar, there was a nod of approval from the team.

Adrian's father was up quite early and arrived in Harrogate in time to share breakfast with the team. Howard and the larger car so all five could travel together to Barnsley. They were anticipating an interesting day but recognized the challenge that faced them. This was a beginning for the team. They hoped for many such days in the future. This whole day together was a great beginning to the work of Karisma Business Consultants and Service.

The day went very well. Each speaker was professional and extensive in presenting their parts of the Seminar'. The response was wonderful and very much appreciated. In the question session they asked quite intelligent and penetrating questions. The team was required to put on their thinking and remembering caps.

Howard had great praise for the team and their presentation. It was his topic of conversation for most of the journey back to Harrogate.

Jenny wanted a full report as soon as they arrived back in the office. The men left it up to Mary to bring Jenny up to date. She was delighted with the response from the audience and also from the team.

Howard decided to stay overnight before travelling back to his home. He joined the team for breakfast before setting off.

Geoff also left to return home. He said that he was looking forward to his end of the week time with the team.

Business gradually built up. It was encouraging for them that more interest was being shown in other than Tax Returns. Mary was being challenged in the future seminars regarding Financial Planning. She spent a lot of time discussing future possibilities with Adrian. Adrian praised the Lord after one session with Mary for giving such an expert to be their finance specialist.

Her side of the business was developing very well. It was surprising how many questioners came asking if she was available to help solve problems and give advice regarding financial planning. She mentioned to Adrian one day her surprise at where the requests were coming from. It was from a much wider area than they thought possible at first. But as one customer was satisfied his or her friends were informed about the professionalism, and so Mary was building up an excellent reputation.

Adrian found himself being asked to attend team meetings in various towns and cities. He was being involved to give advice, so he recognized that the Consulting side of Karisma was also developing. His father phoned every second week wanting an update on how things were growing.

Jenny was in her element. She had been given freedom to develop her own techniques and she was pleasing herself on a regular basis. The other members of the team were being impressed with her efficient approach to the questions and problems that were being presented to her by possible future clients on the phone. Her remarkable tact was paying dividends because she had the ability to get the enquirers to book an appointment to see one of the team.

When Geoff came for this half-week he was not allowed to sit and play computer games very often. Jenny had booked something for him. After six months he chatted with Adrian and asked if he could become full time. He had been looking around Harrogate for an apartment.

As it became close to their first anniversary, in a team meeting, Adrian made the comment that he thought one of the empty offices ought to have someone working in it. They talked for some time about what expertise the new team member should have. Geoff was fitting in well because he seemed to be specializing in 'economics and ethics'. Mary thought that perhaps someone else should help in the finance department. Adrian asked if she had anyone in mind. "I'd like to contact Betty. She indicated that she might be interested sometime. Am I clear to make contact with her and see how her plans are working out?" The general answer was affirmative.

It was about a month later Mary mentioned to the others that Betty would like to come over and see us. It would need to be a Saturday because she would not want to take time off and cause a stir. It was agreed that the team would like her to come over the following Saturday.

Betty was early in fact it didn't take her as long to travel to Harrogate as she thought. The team had just finished breakfast. Betty's comment was that she hoped they had left a drop of coffee for her. It was a joyful comment as they were recalling happy days in University. Jenny was happy with the coffee machine because they were refilling their cups during the period of reminiscing.

Adrian suggested that Betty be taken around and shown where the work was being done. She had been impressed with the building from the outside now she was pleasantly surprised at the quality inside..Betty was curious as to what each person was specializing in. That gave each of the team the chance to fill her in with what had developed over the first year or so.

Betty asked, "If I joined your team, what area would you want me to work in?"

Adrian replied. "What have you been concentrating on in your office?"

"I suppose you could say that I did a lot of trouble shooting with the finance division. But I am interested in, and I think my specialty would be, 'Human Resources"

"Mary'", said Adrian, "Do you ever have troubles that require shooting here in your office? Or are we too efficient?"

"I am sure I could create a few problems that would require an expert sharp shooter!" commented Mary with a chuckle.

Adrian had phoned and booked a table in a restaurant for lunch. They needed two cars so Betty volunteered to use hers. They had a good meal followed by a lazy coffee time. Betty was sat between Mary and Adrian at the table. There were lots of questions for them to answer. As the meal drew to a close Betty was more convinced about her future.

Betty asked about accommodation in Harrogate. Mary mentioned that Jenny had shared her apartment for a short time until she found a suitable place. Jenny said there were a couple of vacancies in her apartment building; and the rates were quite reasonable..

Betty asked Adrian if they could go some place on their own to talk for a few minutes. There was a lounge adjacent to where they ate, so they went in there. Betty shared her feelings and thoughts quite clearly. Adrian was a good listener and made the right comment to lead her into sharing more. They must have talked for about twenty minutes, Then Adrian said, "May I ask you quite frankly, Betty. do you want to come and work here with us?"

There was a pause. Obviously Betty was saying a quick prayer. And so was Adrian. "Yes. I would like that, and I feel very strongly that God wants me to say 'Yes'". They both stood up and Adrian came forward and gave her a great embrace.

At that precise moment the others entered the lounge. It was Jenny's voice that sounded the note of surprise. "That's what you get up to, is it?"

Betty was embarrassed. Mary came to the rescue and went directly to Adrian and embraced him with a mighty kiss. "I love you", to which he responded with the same phrase.

"I have something to share with you", said Adrian. "You caught us;

there was nothing more to it than offering Praise to the Lord. Betty wants to join our team. I told her it would be, it would make us very happy".

All the team members crowded around Betty, they all wanted a hug.

Jenny wondered if Betty had time just to pop around and see the apartment. "It will give you an idea to think about". Mary wanted Betty to know that she could share the apartment for a short time while finding the right place.

"I'm required to give one month notice. So as it is almost the month end I could resign at the end of next month." Geoff volunteered to help her move. The others were also willing to help as much as possible.

Betty asked Jenny, "would it be convenient to see the apartment right now before we go back to the office?" They agreed. The others went back to the office.

Mary asked Adrian what position Betty was to fit into. "She mentioned 'human resources'. That is certainly an area we need some work on. This means we'll have to wait for a help-mate with the finances." Mary's comment was. "I'll start looking again for the right person for the Income Tax portfolio!"

As the Income Tax return season drew to its usual close there was a lull in business. Mary was making contact with some of her previous customers, but making sure they were the ones she initiated. She had many positive comments from her investigating letters. The typical reaction was they would love to transfer their work but the distance to the office was persuading them otherwise.

There was one that promised to keep her as their 'special agent'. Mary opened up a file for them. She was pleased and excited because it was quite a large firm with some excellent opportunities for expanding her services for them.

Betty had indicated that she would work part time for the first three months or so, until more business came in. She found a good and satisfying part time job in Harrogate.

Geoff was busying himself doing research on 'Time Planning'. It was proving beneficial to himself but it was certainly building up his arsenal of material for the Seminars.

Adrian was often away meeting leaders of other businesses. He always had on hand a selection of booklets regarding the work of KARISMA.

He was pleased with the response for one day Seminars. He decided to be careful as to how many he booked. He tried to keep them to one each month, though he found the interest from some people to be more urgent so he slipped in a couple for some of the earlier months.

At the end of the first year Adrian closed the office for one day in order to spend some time with the team assessing where they had come from, and prayerfully looking ahead to the coming year. One of the things that brought pleasure to the team was the response from the articles and adverts in the trade magazines. The One Day Seminars had proved quite effective and the positive feedback from them was encouraging. There were many excellent comments which the advertising agency used in further publicity.

Mary reported on the financial situation. "Though pathetic at the very beginning it has become more healthy". She leaned forward and looked directly at her fiancé and suggested that perhaps a motion would be in order for a slight increase in salaries. That brought a mass of amusing comments.

Then Adrian spoke quite seriously in favour of them pursuing the prospects of more meaningful and realistic salaries. "Because God has obviously been blessing us in this past year I want to look forward with faith as we make decisions relating to the future of Karisma".

Both Geoff and Betty were looking forward to working full-time. There was a pleasant shout of approval from the rest of the team.

They spent about quarter of an hour in prayer,

Adrian asked Mary if she could recommend a suitable percentage for the increase. After doodling for a few moments she came up with her suggestion. Adrian nodded approval and the whole team seemed satisfied with that idea.

Adrian held up the calendar for the coming year and already there were some very encouraging signs of progress and development of Karisma.

Adrian said to Mary one day, "I think we should make an appointment to see our Pastor".

"Why? Do you think we should become members of his church?"

"That's perhaps something we ought to think about. But I did not have that in mind".

"Then why ought we to make an appointment with him? We can see him anytime at one of the meetings".

"If we want to speak to him about something specific then I think we should make a specific appointment".

"Now, what's up your sleeve?"

"Well it is related to that ring on your finger. We must make a definite date for the wedding, and start making plans for the service".

"Well, why didn't you tell me that at the beginning?"

"I was just being formal".

"How soon do we arrange to meet with him? Let's look at the calendar and choose a date for the wedding".

They spent quite a long time choosing the date. They thought about which would be the nicest season. They realized also that the date must be suitable for the parents and the guests. They chose a date three months hence.

Adrian picked up the phone and dialed for the Pastor. After a few seconds of general comments Adrian mentioned the reason for the phone call. "We want to make an appointment to see you. There is a marriage coming up so we want to make some decisions about such an event". The pastor was free on Friday evening. The time was agreed.

"You'll have to plan your attire and bridesmaids etc. etc.

How many guests do we want? Perhaps that is a matter to discuss with parents".

"This is starting to be an exciting time. It'll get even more exciting the more plans are finalized and the closer we get to the important date".

Most evenings after that something or other would come up about the wedding. It was going to be a big occasion.

CHAPTER 34

This was the day when Adrian and Mary had an interview with their minister. The original intention was to talk about the wedding. He spent most of the time talking about marriage. They already knew most of what he mentioned but the happy couple enjoyed being reminded. The minister did eventually get around to the wedding day. It seems that most of what the engaged couple wanted was already part of his marriage service.

The evening with the Pastor proved interesting and enlightening. They appreciated his input to their plans. The dates were suitable for him and the Church.

"One thing I feel is important for you both. You are apparently very healthy. But it is always a good thing to have a full medical before getting married. That will give proof that you are fit for each other!"

"Is that absolutely necessary?" asked Mary.

""No, it is not a legal requirement. But I consider it good for you to know that everything is okay. You have plenty of time, it is not immediately necessary. It is just one other item to place on your list of things to do".

They left the Pastor's office with a lot of things to think about and plan for.

They decided to make an appointment with their doctor.

They didn't have to wait a long time for an appointment; the doctor was free the following afternoon. So they took time off from work and went for the medical. The doctor was friendly and genuinely interested in their future hopes. At the end of his examining he said they were to go for a blood test. They raised eye brows at that; he told them it was always a good thing as part of a full medical.

They found that the blood clinic was open on Saturday mornings. That meant Adrian was free for his soccer match later that afternoon. Mary expressed pleasure that the needle was not blunt. Adrian whispered quite loudly that he was not very fond of vampires. Blood was taken and they were informed that the results would be sent direct to their doctor.

The report from the Blood Lab was a surprise for the Doctor. He phoned the Lab Director and asked if they would retest the blood samples. The Director told him, "We have done so, because when I saw the report I felt that something was wrong. We did the retest in separate rooms, and under close supervision. The results were the same". "Thank you," said the doctor, "You obviously know why I am concerned. I appreciate your professionalism".

It was the following Tuesday that both Mary and Adrian received a phone message from the doctor. He wanted them to come in and see him as a follow up from the medical exam. They took that as being the norm. An appointment was set for Friday evening. He requested Adrian and Mary be at his office at ten minutes past seven o'clock.

They were there on time and the doctor was waiting for them. He reiterated some of the things he mentioned during the examination. He did not comment too much about the blood results. There was one thing he wanted to follow up. During his examination he saw that both of them had a scar on their buttock.

"I want to ask a personal question, the same question for each of you. You know that you have a scar".

They said "Yes" together; they looked astonished at each other.

"Does that look mean you were unaware of the other one having a scar? "Yes".

'How did you get that scar?"

"I was told that there was an operation when I was a small baby", said Mary.

"I was told the same, word for word." added Adrian

"Am I to believe that you have not seen each other naked?"

"That is true; that pleasure is awaiting us on our honeymoon", said Adrian.

"That's hard to believe in these days of promiscuity. Oh, I wasn't implying anything sinful".

"We are Christians and have been saving ourselves for the marriage bed", said Mary.

The doctor didn't know how to answer that one. "That's noble of you!" was all he could think of saying.

There was a pause. The doctor was deep in thought. Then he said he didn't want to shock them. They looked at each and then looked at him.

"I want to ask you something quite personal. I am not trying to be sensational. I am not deliberately trying to embarrass you. But as you are soon to be married I think this of major importance that you see your partner. I want you both to discreetly uncover the area of your scar".

Both of them were shaking their heads negatively.

"My friends I really do think it is necessary for both of you right now that you know about each other. Please go into the anti-rooms over there and come back with that part only showing".

There were two anti-rooms. They both gingerly came out holding up some pieces of clothing.

The doctor asked Mary to look at Adrian. She hesitated then plucked up courage and looked. She let out a loud "Wow!" as she saw the extent of his scar. "Now just turn round, Adrian you look at Mary". He also was a little hesitant but did with a big blush in his cheeks. "Wow!" also escaped from his lips as he kept gazing. "This is impossible; isn't it, doctor?"

"Many of my colleagues would say that it was impossible. But here is absolute evidence that it is very real. Enough seen, please make yourself look as neat and nice as when you came into my office. I really did not do this to embarrass you but I did think it necessary".

They sat and talked for a few minutes.

The doctor then came with another surprise. "In the room next door some people are arriving. And we'll be going in to be with them in a few minutes time. In that room you will see your parents and your minister and a retired doctor. I have called them together to help me find answers to some major questions that I am struggling with".

"Why are they all in there", thought Adrian. Mary had the same thought.

"At some stage of the discussion I will be asking you to do the same as you did for me; expose your scars".

"We can't do that in public", was their objection in harmony.

"There is perhaps only one person in there that has not seen a scar like that, namely your minister. But because he asked you to have a medical I

341

invited him to this meeting. My motive is far from seeking to embarrass you and others in there. But it is required in order for me to find an answer to a question no one has answered for me as yet. The answer lies in there. The answer is of paramount importance to you both. Please bear with me. Sorry, that was not supposed to be a pun!"

They looked at each other. They gave each other a loving hug and whispered in each other's ear; "I think we will have to do it. We did it for the doctor; we can do it for our parents".

"Okay. Please follow me. Just inside there are three chairs for us. I'll introduce you, but that shouldn't be necessary".

They went into the adjacent room. The minister had a knowing grin on his face and he gave them an encouraging nod.

"Thank you all for coming. You are wondering why I have called you together. It is mainly because I have one very big question that no one so far has been able to answer. Having performed a full medical examination as suggested by the minister of Adrian and Mary, and reading the results of the blood tests I am hoping that you can help me. I am having trouble understanding the birth dates. Mr. and Mrs. Syston can you confirm the birth date of Adrian".

They mentioned the same date as on the forms.

"Mr. Stapleford and I are sorry you lost your first wife, can you please confirm the birth date of Mary?"

He gave the one that was on her papers.

"Are you really sure about that?"

There was a long silence.

"The hospital has no record of a baby girl being born that day and later given up for adoption".

There was another long period of silence.

"Well it has been the one we have been celebrating ever since Mary was ours".

"But?" said the doctor.

"Well … in actual fact that was the day she was born to us, the day we received her from the hospital. It was a few years ago I found a copy of her birth certificate and noticed the date of birth. My late wife had reported the date on which the baby was given to us". He apologized if there had been any trouble. His new wife hugged him and gave him magnificent support.

Adrian's mother and father had tears streaming down their cheeks; they now knew why they were there.

"I have invited my friend, a retired doctor, to meet with us. He was the attending physician for Mrs. Syston during her pregnancy. Can you please tell us about that pregnancy?"

"It was one of those interesting cases that a doctor will never forget. For the first few months the pregnancy was quite normal. Then I noticed some changes which I monitored carefully. One day I suggested that a scan should be done. With results of the scan I called Mrs. Syston to my office.

"She came with her husband. I laid the scan on the table and informed her that she was about to have twins. That was not just a surprise but a mighty shock. Her husband's comment was from that moment on he would think in doubles.

"My patient was getting bigger. One day I mentioned to her that we might have to bring the birth day forward because she would not be able to deliver the twins except by c-section.

"The day was set for the procedure. Everything went according to plan; then the surprise. The nurses were told to quickly prepare a larger incubator. I saw twins who were joined together. I carefully lifted them on to the table and after cleaning them we laid them in the special incubator.

"It took a long time for the mother and father to get over the complicated delivery. We settled on a time when the twins would be separated. But a question that has not been answered is why a boy and girl were joined. They were not joined with an organ or any vital part.

"The surgery was a success and the parents were glad to see two lovely babies, in the same bed. They thrived".

He was thanked for his report. Then the doctor turned to Adrian and Mary and asked them please to prepare themselves. They went into the previous room and did the required re-arranging of some of their clothes, then returned.

There were sounds of surprise from most of the folk in the room. The doctor quickly said that this was nothing sensational but this was necessary to find the answer to his question.

"Adrian. Mary. Will you please turn round and show your scars".

There were loud gasps of shock and surprise right across the room. The minister seemed more embarrassed than anyone else.

"Doctor, can you tell us about these scars?"

"I can assure you that they are my scars. Or rather scars that I made. These two people are the joined twins that I separated in our local hospital".

There were more gasps.

Adrian's mother could not contain herself any longer and shouted out, "that's Adriana".

Mary asked the surgeon that if he separated them could he please come and put them back together again for a few moments. "I mean scar to scar".

He was very willing to oblige. Mary was heard to say "we were joined and now we are together again". Adrian added, "Yes. We are one".

"Adrian and Mary, you are not mere siblings you are twins and not normal twins but separated Siamese twins. This was the question I could not answer when your DNA's were the same"

The minister then made his comment that there would be no wedding after all. Adrian was quick with a comment, "Do not cancel everything. There might be a celebration of a different nature instead of a wedding", then he added, "and presents will still be expected!"

The meeting was over. There were lots of hugs and kisses between the two families. Mary was getting to know her birth mother. There was much rejoicing among both sets of parents. Though inwardly Adrian and Mary were devastated to be informed they were not allowed to marry each other. Actually they were putting on a brave face because their hearts were shedding massive tears.

In frequent intervals one or the other would say "brother" or "sister". After all they were not just siblings, they were separated twins.

That evening they spent a long time getting used to the disappointment and the excitement. They sat hugging each other on the settee. For many minutes they did not speak. The fact of no marriage was mortifying them on the inside.

Being a twin was bursting their joy strings. How could two lovely people be going through such extreme turmoil?

Mary moved to face Adrian and said, "Nothing has changed. Everything has changed. Nothing has changed I am still very much in love with you. My love that has been growing over many months has not changed now that you are my brother. I must admit that I was hoping for you to me by husband".

Adrian reached over and held her left hand. "I am still madly in love with you, darling. This ring is a symbol of our love; it states that we have committed ourselves to be faithful. The love we had for each other yesterday has not changed today. Instead of looking forward to you being my wife, the earth shattering regulations regarding a wedding have not changed my feelings for you now that you are my sister".

"Yesterday our growing love for each other was anticipating the joys of sexual intimacies", expressed Mary.

"Today our tremendous love for one another will be swallowed up in the sanctity of family relationships", answer Adrian.

They said their 'good nights' as they had done for a long time.

The next morning they made their way to the property agent. They had made a deposit on a new house and they wanted to see it again. This time their fantasizing was different.

It was strange, but they both started going up the stairs. At the top they paused. Mary said, "Until yesterday we would have turned left and gone into our bedroom. Now what?"

Adrian said, "This is the house for us. God must have known what was going to happen yesterday. It's wonderful that we have two identical bedrooms with private bathrooms".

"That will give us a major headache though. Who will go to the left and who goes to the right? That is if we decide to keep this house".

"Well right now we will go right to the one we have not looked at very much".

"Does that mean we intend staying here or are we building ourselves up to cancel the purchase?" was Mary's query.

"Sweetheart, our love for each other has not changed one little bit".

"I know you are not suggesting we intend to live together".

"Mary, darling, the love that we have has not changed. I can't live without you. It sounds as if I am advocating us shacking up together. Well I am!"

"You are what?"

It was a very deep, thought provoking pause.

"There is no law which states that a brother and sister cannot live in the same house. We would be under the same roof but have our separate bedrooms. We would not be shacking up in the same bedroom".

"It will be difficult coming to live here because we were expecting to come as husband and wife. Though we first of all should decide whether we are strong enough to live in the same house; the one planned for after our wedding. Can we face the challenge, successfully?"

"Our love cannot change darling. If you still want to live here. I want to also. It will be our joint home", assured Mary.

"If we are about to be that revolutionary then we must quickly check it out with our parents," said Adrian.

"My parents are staying up for the weekend. My understanding is they intend going to church with your folk in the morning".

"Do we talk to them separately?"

"I thought going out for lunch together might help us to relax".

"You are not just a pretty face you are loaded with wisdom! If we go to church with them, then we can sound out the minister also".

"That's settled. Thank you Lord".

"What are we to do with ourselves this afternoon? Presumably we're going somewhere for lunch".

"Yes, and afterwards it might be good to go to the Mall and just look around."

"Are you serious?" asked Mary.

"Very serious because we might see something we have forgotten"

It was a busy afternoon, and of course there were a few items that appealed to them.

They found it easy to relax for the evening. So much of the conversation centred on their new found status. They just had to sit on the settee together, and that meant being close and cuddly.

"There is nothing evil about siblings hugging each other," said Mary.

"The wedding may be off, but your ring stays on" said Adrian with a strong feeling. "It is the symbol of our commitment to one another. You may have to wear it on a different finger instead of the marriage finger."

"If you place your signet ring on the right hand finger then I can do the same with mine; we'll match and be balanced".

They said their 'goodnights' and went their separate ways until the next morning when they would meet and head for church.

The time spent with the minister and their parents proved satisfactory. They were pleased, and considered that their children could face the challenge of living in the same house. The couple thought they would like to still have a service in the church with the emphasis on Christian relationships and followed by a house warming.

They decided to keep the meal arrangements for the invited guests. But they still had time to re-adjust the planning to fit the new emphasis.

Monday morning at work, Adrian as usual called the team together for a prayer. But his opening statement was, "I have a very important announcement to make. I ... would like, he paused, "to introduce you ... to ... my ... twin sister." That took a lot of explaining to the other members of the team. The excitement of such news had disrupted their composure. The comments openly and unreservedly expressed were varied and revolutionary. Fortunately there were no early morning clients.

They had the service in the church on the day they had chosen. The minister did an excellent job in his message on relationships. He mentioned about the new house and had a special prayer of blessing upon Adrian and Mary as they faced an unexpected future.

A big happy party followed and anyone interested could go along to see the house. About half of the guests wanted to see where they would be living. The minister wanted them to know that there would be a special house blessing.

They had received numerous presents; mainly ones that had been purchased as wedding gifts but were just as necessary as house warming gifts. It was a happy day.

When the guests and families had all left, the house felt empty and quiet. They sat and reminisced with no concept of time.

It felt like time for bed. Adrian took hold of Mary's hand and they walked upstairs side by side. At the top of the stairs was a designed small lounge area. They paused then went in and sat on the settee.

"Before we part I am convinced that we can start a protocol of how our 'goodnights' should be performed!" said Adrian.

"Just as long as they remain personal and affectionate, for after all we are twins."

"Yes, twins who are madly in love"

"And who now have to curb some of their emotions," added Mary.

"Just look at what happened because we were willing to expose our unbelievable scars", was Adrian's comment.

"And the thrill of being put back together for a few moments", added Mary.

"It's still hard to grasp that we have matching scars; that in itself is so incredible; but is no longer unbelievable, it is a glorious fact that is real evidence of the time we were inseparable".

"We were one", said Mary affectionately, "and we had planned to be one as husband and wife, but now as brother and sister with matching scars we have the evidence of having been one."

"I am sure either one of us will from time to time ask for the scars evidence to be seen", answered Adrian. "So let's feel the thrill of being together as we were at the Doctor's office".

It was a brief moment; they both showed their scars and placed them together.

Adrian said, "And now we know that we are twins and not wife and husband".

"We can praise God for bringing us together and is now allowing us to share this beautiful house! We have committed ourselves to him and he will surely direct our emotions and our future paths for his glory".

POST SCRIPT

The doctor who separated the twins soon after they were born still does not know what caused them to be joined together.

Printed in the United States
By Bookmasters